Someone's arms were around her. Her head seemed to be pillowed against a muscular arm. With a certain amount of dread, she opened her eyes to find them caught in two black pools that stared at her intently.

'And where will you go now?' asked Hassan.

'I have nowhere to go. André is . . . was all I had in the world.'

'I'm sure. But since you didn't love him, I had thought perhaps that you had something in mind.'

Yasmin marshaled all the strength she had, and wrenched herself from Hassan's grasp. *'Didn't love him? Of course I loved him.'*

'Loved his money is more likely, I suspect.'

'Money! How can you talk about money at a time like this! You are horrible. Absolutely horrible.'

'And I suppose that you think André loved you, too, eh?'

'Yes, I do,' Yasmin said, whirling to face him.

'He didn't love you.' The eyes that held hers were black with cruelty. 'He was fifty-one years old, and what are you, eighteen? Seventeen? Don't you know what happens as a man gets older? He didn't love you, he loved your age, your beauty, your smooth clear skin. You know nothing about men and how they think.'

DIANA SYDNEY

Pleasures

GRAFTON BOOKS

A Division of the Collins Publishing Group

LONDON GLASGOW
TORONTO SYDNEY AUCKLAND

Grafton Books
A Division of the Collins Publishing Group
8 Grafton Street, London W1X 3LA

A Grafton UK Paperback Original 1987
Reprinted 1988 (twice)

Copyright © Diana Sydney 1986

ISBN 0-586-07305-1

Printed and bound in Great Britain by
Cox & Wyman Ltd, Reading

Set in Times

For Habiba, whom I will always remember

PART ONE
Tangier, 1972

1

The hills behind the city were slowly changing color as the sun slipped into the sea, and the temperature was dropping noticeably. Without seeming to hurry, Abdul Khadir made his way along Rue Sidi Bouarrakia and out of the Casbah. As he walked, it occurred to him that the doorway to a ridiculously high profit was on the verge of opening. After all, the girl was a virgin and quite pretty. With wealthy Europeans like this French baron, the possibilities were limitless. Ahead of him a string of Berbers on small, swaying donkeys were leaving the bazaar, on their way up to the mountains. The luminous light caught and then danced on the coins and bracelets, which seemed to drip from the womens layers of veils and robes.

The palm trees lining the road swayed fitfully as their fronds caught the early evening breezes off the Mediterranean. The palms were old and bent from years of wind. Khadir, annoyed at being behind the slow-moving Berbers, quickened his pace and passed the little donkeys. Their measured steps were no match for his. He continued walking at a rapid pace until he started climbing Old Mountain Road, then slowed a bit.

Below him the lights of the city twinkled and danced like marshlights on a midnight-blue pond. Khadir could hear the wailing call to evening prayer drifting up from the mosques in the old town. The foothils of the Rif were covered with spotty green scrub, and years of wind off the sea had bent the cypresses alongside the road too. But he wasn't interested in looking around him. He'd seen it all before. It didn't have the same attraction for him that it had for the tourists who came in droves to the exotic, mysterious city.

Even though the evening was balmy, Khadir pulled the blue-gray djellaba close to his short, heavyset body. In another culture he might have been sensitive about his height, but in his own culture height was a meaningless distinction. Only maleness counted, and Khadir was most definitely male.

The wind was beginning to pick up, and a fresh, crisp smell replaced the dry dust of the day. The sea air cleansed his nostrils of the smells of the Medina – incense, fresh meat, donkey dung, coffee, and mint tea all mixed together in a strange perfume. But, again, none of this made an impression as he pulled at the coarse fabric of the djellaba. He was working out precisely how much he would charge the baron, and by a complex process only he could understand, had arrived at one hundred thousand dirhams. Lost in appreciation of his own mental bargaining, he paid no attention to the car that almost sideswiped him on its way down to the throbbing city below.

Abruptly he turned onto a road lined with windowless white walls that stretched into the night. This was the area where the wealthy Europeans had their luxurious villas. Without looking up, Khadir walked until he arrived at a high, grilled gate. He was admitted by a turbaned figure cloaked in a gray djellaba and told to wait. Tapping his foot impatiently as he stood in the marbled foyer, Khadir glanced around at the heavy gold-framed paintings. A small, satisfied smile appeared on his face at the sight of such wealth, and then disappeared just as quickly.

'You will excuse me, won't you?'

As his servant Zayd left the room, Baron André de Saint-Clair pulled himself out of the comfortable armchair. For a moment he stared into the ornately carved marble fireplace without speaking. An expression of profound irritation flickered across his handsome face, then he shrugged. 'Amazing. I can't imagine what this man wants, but I'm sure it won't take more than a few minutes.'

Nicholas Chambers shrugged and took another sip of his brandy. 'Don't give it a thought, old man. I'm perfectly comfortable here. With you or without you.'

André followed Zayd out into the hall. The tall, spare Moroccan had been with André for four years now, since he had bought the villa. Zayd's ink-black eyes rarely smiled and seldom betrayed his thoughts. The sharp hooked nose set under heavy brows gave him a severe and sometimes threatening look. But Zayd was a model butler, even if he was lacking in humor. If he had been wearing a cutaway and striped trousers, instead of the heavy blue djellaba with the white kaffiyeh held onto his head with a thick black cord, he would have done justice to any British butler, perhaps more so, since Zayd never spoke of his personal life, or his feelings about his employer.

In the main hallway André stopped in front of Abdul Khadir, who nodded briefly in greeting, as Zayd silently disappeared.

'You will please forgive this intrusion, but the matter I wish to discuss is best dealt with privately . . . in person.' Khadir raised his eyebrows suggestively as he spoke, then slid his eyes quickly around the room. There was no one else in evidence, so he continued. 'Do you still wish to purchase Yasmin?'

André's mouth dropped open for a split second, then snapped shut again. 'You mean you've decided to start her working?' he asked, trying to hide his dismay.

'It's time,' answered Khadir. 'Don't you think? But of course, if you've changed your mind, you can still always purchase her for the first night. Perhaps that would be enough, eh?' Even though his voice sounded nonchalant, Khadir's eyes never left Baron de Saint-Clair's face. As he spoke, he saw the haunted look flash across the baron's eyes, and decided to press his advantage. The Europeans who came to his brothel always enjoyed themselves. But Khadir knew that at other times most of them expressed open distaste for what went on behind the walls of his compound. In their own homes they claimed to be disgusted over the buying and selling of human beings, but didn't seem to show much compunction about using those very same pretty human beings whenever they felt like it. A complex hypocrisy, he thought.

Khadir didn't know why the baron wanted Yasmin, and he didn't particularly care. Whatever his reasons, Khadir intended to drive a hard bargain. Yasmin was from the Rif, and although he had to pay more than usual for the beautiful girl, Khadir had been able to get her for a very good price. The girl's poor simpleton of a grandfather didn't know how much she was worth. Khadir mused for a while on the millions of little ways that humanity had of acting stupidly. As a dealer in human flesh, he didn't see things in quite the same way other people did. He judged differently.

He considered Yasmin Karim a perfect example of human stupidity. Her grandfather didn't want her around because she was a half-breed, and her mother had been in the wrong place at the wrong time – she'd had the misfortune to be raped by an American soldier. Such things occurred with regularity after the Tangier International Zone had been abolished and France and Spain had recognized Morocco's independence. That was in 1956, and there had been tremendous unrest as all the different elements in the teeming city had tried to find a new niche for themselves.

When Yasmin's mother could no longer hide her pregnancy, she lost her position as a servant. She went home

12

in disgrace to her family, where she gave birth to a girl. Though ostracized, she managed to protect Yasmin from her angry family by sending her out with the goats, off to find sticks, anything to shield her from resentment because she was not Moroccan, and even worse, because she was female. But then the mother died of tuberculosis, and there was no one left to protect Yasmin. Her grandfather thought she was worthless and unmarriageable and couldn't wait to get the exotic yet troublesome beauty off his hands. But Khadir knew her worth. Of course, his criteria were different. The grandfather's loss was his gain.

'She is worth one hundred thousand dirhams,' Khadir said blandly. 'She will make at least that in the first year.'

André blanched. '*Mon Dieu!* But that's almost seventy-five thousand francs!'

'Consider it a bride price,' said Khadir. He smiled briefly, showing a mouth full of strong even teeth stained light brown. He wondered whether the baron was planning to bargain. Khadir watched him carefully, trying to assess how badly he wanted Yasmin.

'*Sacrebleu!*' muttered André grimly, staring sightlessly at the tops of his shoes. He ran a hand through his thick, black hair. The coarser gray hairs that were beginning to spring at the temples resisted the gesture, and a light film of sweat appeared on his forehead. The thought of Yasmin working in Khadir's brothel, or worse, later being sold into one of the numerous filthy cribs in the Casbah, made him almost ill. It drove every rational thought from his brain – as Khadir had known it would. 'All right, then. One hundred thousand dirhams.'

'In Krugerrands, if you don't mind,' said Khadir, a broad smile creasing his face. 'Even though I am a businessman, the master of a brothel doesn't usually have a checking account.' Khadir chuckled at his own joke, and the fact that the baron didn't even try to bargain. 'By the way, I have heard that gold is also going to be a very profitable investment this year. The price will start climbing very fast and very soon. You might consider purchasing some yourself.'

With a wave of his hand André dismissed the financial advice. It was incongruous. The mere fact that he was having this conversation with this man was appalling enough. Having it reduced to the level of chitchat about investments was horrifying. 'When?' he asked.

'Tomorrow night?'

'Yes.' André began to turn away distractedly. Then he paused, not wishing to insult Abdul Khadir with a show of bad manners. 'Until tomorrow night, then.'

'*Ila al-laqaa,*' said Abdul Khadir, nodding as he opened the heavily carved wooden door. 'There will be no need to call your man. I will close the gate behind me.'

André slowly returned to the drawing room. With the setting of the sun, the night air had grown chill. He saw that Nick had put a few more logs on the fire. The flames were now leaping in the fireplace, casting long shadows, which skittered across the thick Oriental rugs covering the black marble floors. The shadows danced up the walls, alternately obscuring and then illuminating the gold-framed portraits and tapestries.

'Problems?' asked Nick as he looked up at André's troubled expression.

'Not really,' André answered shortly, dropping into the deep wing chair he had so recently vacated. 'It was Abdul Khadir.'

'That whoremaster from the Zoco Chico?' said his guest, looking suddenly more interested. Nick leaned forward in his chair. 'Sounds interesting, old chap. Anything you'd care to share with a friend?'

'No, no,' André said bleakly. 'It's nothing like that. He came to see me because I'm going to buy Yasmin.'

'Yasmin? Good God, man, what for?' Nick said,

14

shocked. 'Can't you just pay her little visits in the Casbah?'

'No,' said André, a note of misery creeping into his voice. 'I couldn't stand the thought of what her life would be like.'

'Why is this little whore so different from the rest?' Nick asked, looking at André sharply. Curiosity overcame his planned witty remark. 'She hasn't started working yet, so how can you know she's worth it?'

'She's so intelligent,' answered André. 'Her eyes are always sparkling. I get the feeling she has great potential. Do you know what I mean? Besides, I just can't bear the thought of seeing that sparkle disappear . . . and of knowing what's going to happen to her.'

Nick's baritone laugh filled the room. 'Potential!' he said sarcastically. 'I'll second the fact that she's got potential all right, but I wasn't thinking of her mental equipment.'

'Don't be an ass!' André snapped. 'You know what I meant.'

'Of course. You said something about sparkle, I believe. And I suppose you think you're the man to keep that intelligent sparkle in her eyes, eh?' laughed Nick. 'What pompous self-aggrandizement!'

André scowled, his tone low, dangerous. 'And what's it to you? Were you waiting for her too?'

'Now *you're* being an ass,' said Nick, shrugging lightly. 'But do you have to buy the girl? Why, it's almost as if you were getting married, you bloody fool. Unless of course you're just buying her because you feel the need of a permanent laundress, or a kitchen maid.'

'I fail to see the humor,' said André curtly.

'I can see that. But I think it's time you tried. After all, when was the last time you bought a human . . . or anyone you know bought a human?'

'I still say this is not a situation which demands humor.

15

Even though you know for a fact that I deplore the slave trade that continues to go on in this part of the world, it's not what you think. Perhaps this is my way of setting her free.'

'Setting her free? That's liberal drivel if I ever heard it. Besides, what good would that do her?' Nick asked. 'Her freedom is no good to her in this place. What's she going to do with it, I ask you? Get a job as a salesgirl in the Suk? You and I both know that's impossible. The only thing she can do with her freedom is go back to Khadir, or someone just like him, and get a job as a whore. No self-respecting Arab would marry her anyway, so that's out of the question.'

'I suppose you're right,' said André, twisting his hands as they gripped the arms of the chair.

Nicholas Chambers had been in Tangier for three years, doing the preliminary engineering work for a huge hydroelectric dam. Both men knew that the rapidly modernizing country still held onto outdated and sometimes cruel social rules.

André had been introduced to Nick by his banker, Henri LaMarquette. As often happens in foreign cities with small European populations, business acquaintances soon became personal and social friends.

It was an unexpected relationship. Nick was a boisterous, jocular, and outwardly typical product of the English public school system. André was more subtle, more elegant, and a shining example of the expatriate French nobility. Although the two would appear to the outside observer as worlds apart, temperamentally they complemented each other, and they always enjoyed each other's company.

When André had bought the villa on Old Mountain Road, he had immediately been drawn into the tightly knit social world of the other jet-set expatriates who owned villas and mansions on the picturesque and exclusive stretch that ran along the coast. But it was an insular group. André often felt as if he were part of one huge ingrown social class. Even so, he loved the city of Tangier with a passion that almost bordered on a mania – which was why he had decided to spend most of his year there instead of at his vineyard in France.

He'd done an excellent job of setting up his estate in Auxerre so it would run smoothly without his direct management. After discovering that the year-round social scene was vastly different from the vacation mentality he had lived in when just visiting, he finally relaxed into the life of Tangier. His estate manager was one of the finest wine makers in France, his lawyers in Paris were fully able to handle the real estate owned by the Saint-Clairs, and he was able to stay in constant touch with both areas plus add to the wealth he already had by investing in Morocco's burgeoning economy. His Paris bank had a branch in Tangier, and investments in iron ore, asbestos, cobalt, and copper were excellent ways of using his powerful business acumen while he lived what might be viewed by an outsider as a life of indolence.

It was a life that he had felt drawn to the first time he'd set foot in the country, before Moroccan Independence had been declared in 1956. At that time he was thirty years old, unmarried, and at loose ends. He was also rapidly becoming a playboy. His father was in full control of the vineyard, which produced a creditable high-priced Chablis. Even though André was supposed to be learning, he was still not his own man.

His own life was prearranged, set, ordered, and fully known to him. He would learn everything about making wines, and then on his father's death, would inherit everything and make wine. He would marry and produce sons, and they would grow up and make wine. Not that there was anything wrong with that. It was a comfortable existence, and one full of tradition. But André's soul demanded spicier food. Tangier, with its heavy influx of writers, painters, con artists, spies, and stateless wanderers, provided it.

Suddenly remembering they'd been talking about buying a woman, André snapped out of his reverie. Abruptly, he got up and poured himself another drink. 'More?'

'Yes, if you please,' said Nick, holding out his glass. 'So I suppose you'd better face it, man. If you buy her, she's yours. In sickness and in health, etcetera. To do with as you wish.'

'*Merde*,' André muttered. But his expression altered. This was the first time he had actually considered having Yasmin here in the house – to do with as he wished, as Nick had so crudely pointed out. Up until this moment it had all been an intellectual exercise, but the enormity of the situation was beginning to strike home.

'By the way, how much does a person go for these days?' Nick asked, glancing at André out of the corner of his eye.

'Too much.'

'Would you consider being a bit more specific? Or are the details embarrassing you?'

'Seventy-five thousand francs.'

'*Merde* is right! That's a lot of goats, old man. I'd be embarrassed too. But then again, you will have her to do with as you wish,' repeated Nick, softly. 'God, what a delightful thought. I envy you. I could think of a few things to do with that little minx myself, given the opportunity.'

'I'm sure,' André muttered, but he wasn't paying much attention to Nick. He downed the contents of his glass and turned a glazed expression on his guest. 'Didn't you say you had to stop and see Sir Nigel at the club this evening?'

'Yes, I did. How shortsighted of me to forget,' said Nick, pulling himself out of the chair. 'There was so much excitement here, I couldn't tear myself away. That man is such a bloody bore.'

'You'll give him my regards, won't you?'

'But of course,' said Nick, leering as André accompanied him to the door. 'I suppose since you'll be busy, we won't be seeing you at the club for a while?'

'*Nomme de Dieu!* Would you get out of here?' snapped André. But a little smile began to turn up the corners of his mouth. He handed Nick his raincoat, giving him a gentle shove in the direction of the door. 'I'll have Zayd throw you out if you don't hurry.'

With a feeling of relief he watched the tall, broad-shouldered man walk to the car. He listened until the sound of the engine disappeared down the mountain road. Now, at last, he could be alone with his thoughts.

Yasmin. Her name conjured the delicate perfumes mixed with the heavy, cloying scent of hashish that filled Khadir's compound. The brothel was actually a very pleasant place to spend the evening. Tucked in the center of the Medina, it was hidden behind a high, blank wall. The partially roofed, colonnaded inner courtyard was hung with a profusion of bird cages. Around the edges of the court were long, low divans heaped with pillows. That was where the customers waited.

Looking up, one could see the landings with their beautiful wrought-iron balustrades. A long staircase curved along the wall, and behind the closed doors was any diversion you wanted. Bathed in sensuality, all the surfaces were soft, yielding, enveloping. The girls, each different and each carefully chosen, were clean, and instructed in the art of pleasure. Abdul Khadir ran his business well, and trained his girls with care.

Buying them as young as he could get them from poor families in the Rif or the Atlas Mountains, Khadir brought them into Tangier for a period of apprenticeship in his house. He didn't break them in right away, while they were green and frightened. First he used them as servants or maids to the working girls. When they could comprehend without fear what was expected of them, he put them to work. Now, André thought, it was time for Yasmin to begin work.

Although he'd only seen her the few times when she brought coffee or a pipeful of hashish for him to enjoy before going up the spiral staircase, André had been immediately taken with her. She was small and delicately boned. Her large, gray eyes glittered with mischief. Inside the compound she didn't wear a veil. He had been able to enjoy all the delights of her sweet, pouting mouth and the delicate blush of her fair skin. She always wore long, loose caftans made of fine silk covered with delicate scrolls of embroidery. The fabric clung and moved with her as she walked. His mind gave him a replay of her slow, studied walk, how she carried herself with an air of grace befitting a princess. The delights of the small, recently developed body underneath her garments, were only subtly hinted at, but intriguing none the less.

They'd both seen her, of course. And he and Nicholas weren't the only ones, just as Khadir's wasn't the only brothel in Tangier. Far from it. There were hundreds, all part of the tourist trade. But Khadir's was clean and relaxed – a kind of second club to many of the men they were acquainted with. For all André knew, anyone could have asked to buy Yasmin. After all, they all watched the new girls with interest – some more than others. But there was something about Yasmin that had captured his attention.

Trust Nick to remind him that it wasn't just her mind he was interested in, though that was, if not the first, the second thing that made him look at her with a more proprietary glance. They all knew when a new girl came,

20

and they all knew they'd have to wait for her, since that was Khadir's way. It heightened the tension, so to speak. But this was one girl André couldn't bear the thought of sharing.

It was a completely new sensation for him. He hadn't been able to help asking questions about her. Khadir had told him everything he knew, without reservation. Business sense would be one way of describing it. Or would horse sense be more appropriate? André shuddered. He was feeling more and more like a horse trader every minute. He didn't like the feeling at all, but at that moment it wasn't the only sensation he felt.

As he thought of that slender body, he could almost feel what it would be like to strip away those layers of transparent material and touch what was undoubtedly sweet, deliciously scented, silken skin. He got up and poured himself another brandy. This was going to be a long and difficult night. Perhaps the alcohol would dull his senses and take the edge off his desire.

One hundred thousand dirhams! *Mon Dieu!* But she would be worth it, every bit of it, he thought, unable to clear his mind of erotic images. Abdul Khadir was playing him for a fool, he thought, but he didn't care. It was only money. He had wanted Yasmin from the first time he'd seen her – and all for himself. That was the complicated part. It was why he'd asked Khadir if he could buy her. Clever Khadir had been slow to respond, saying he would have to think about it. But André was sure he had waited in order to drive up her price. Khadir had said he would decide whether she was for sale before he put her to work. That way André could enjoy taking her for the first time, and the price had gone up and up as André's desire for her became less and less controllable. Khadir was nothing if not a good businessman.

Thoughts of money should have cooled André's ardor, but his fantasies drove out all other considerations. He took a bottle from the liquor cabinet, and leaving the drawing room, crossed the wide marble entrance hall and climbed the staircase to his bedroom. The wind off the Mediterranean was becoming strong. He could hear the branches of the eucalyptus scratching against the windows in the hallway, and wondered if another storm was on the way.

Opening the heavy door to his bedroom, André crossed the thick Persian rugs and threw himself fully clothed on the pale gray satin cover of his bed. He poured himself another drink, even though his head was beginning to whirl from the alcohol. But this time he was thankful for the dizzying sensation. It usually heralded a leaden, dreamless sleep.

This night, however, his sleep was not peaceful. He lost consciousness, but then the demons – some in strangely cut business suits, some in djellabas – chased him relentlessly through a labyrinth of alleyways. All the while, Yasmin danced just out of reach.

He did not awaken until noon. His head felt as thick as a melon. After gulping down two cups of strong, Turkish coffee, he dressed quickly. It was late, the credit offices closed at four, and he had some complicated and delicate business to transact. How in hell was he going to explain the Krugerrands? he wondered.

André carefully maneuvered his restored pre-war Hispano Suiza through the throngs of tourists and Arabs that clustered along the road. On Boulevard Pasteur the cafés were full. Colorful striped awnings protected the drinkers from the glaring afternoon sun. André considered stopping, but decided against it. Who knew how long the transfers would take? Things in Tangier had a way of taking much longer than expected. He took a deep breath and climbed the marble steps of Credit Française, pushing open the massive carved grille doors.

'*Bonjour*, Monsieur le Baron,' murmured the red-uniformed guard. The gold braid on his jacket winked as he bowed slightly. André nodded, and continued to the back, where the offices were situated. Taking another deep breath, he entered one. Baron André de Saint-Clair did not have to bother with knocking.

It had been just two o'clock when he went into the office, and it was not until late that afternoon that he again climbed into the car to make his way back up the coast road. The streets were cooler now, and he passed veiled women carrying balls of fresh dough to the *farran* – the public ovens. Men driving small donkeys loaded down under dirty bundles shouted, '*Balek! Balek!* Make Way!' As he drove up the mountain, his first thought was of a cool, very strong drink. His second thought was of Yasmin.

At exactly eight o'clock by the chimes from the tall, ornately inlaid clock in the corner, Zayd opened the door of the library. He ushered in Abdul Khadir. Behind him was a small figure muffled in a white wool haik. The hood was pulled down, obscuring even the eyes, the only part of her body left uncovered. After Zayd closed the door, and only then, did Khadir speak.

'*In-shallah*, my friend,' he said, nodding briefly. 'Shall we do business?'

André rose from the chair somewhat unsteadily. He had been drinking without a break since his return from the Credit Française office. But when he saw the bundle of robes and veils behind his guest, his head suddenly cleared. Walking to the Regency desk near the window, André opened a small drawer and pulled out a hand-tooled red leather pouch.

'Here. Count them,' he said, handing it to Khadir.

'*Shoukran*,' murmured Khadir. He carried the pouch over to the divan and emptied the contents onto the low table. The tabletop was a beaten silver tray, and the

23

coins made a loud ringing noise as they hit the metal then skittered to the edges. Khadir counted as André watched Yasmin. She had not moved since coming in the door, and clutching a bundle tightly to her chest, she still kept her head lowered.

Slowly approaching her, he could almost feel her tension. She looked ready to jump and run at any moment. André gently lifted the hood of her cloak, but she kept her eyes modestly downcast. It occurred to him that this might be proper demeanor for a girl in her situation.

He shifted his attention back to Khadir. 'Is everything correct?'

'It's all here as, of course, I knew it would be,' said Khadir, scooping the last handful of coins into the pouch with a satisfied smile. He knotted the string and slid the pouch under his djellaba. Removing a small packet from inside the folds of wool, he held it out to André.

'Hashish,' he said, grinning. 'Compliments of the house, you might say.'

André took the packet, and brushing past Yasmin, accompanied Khadir through the main foyer.

'Please let me know if there is a problem,' Khadir said as he stepped out into the garden, 'although I doubt there will be any. She's obedient. *Ila al-laqaa.*'

André raised his hand in parting, and closed the door behind him. When he entered the library, Yasmin was still standing exactly where he had left her. Her sleek black head, the hair smoothed tight across her skull, was still bent. The determined little mouth, shaped perfectly for kissing or for pouting, quivered slightly.

'Why don't you take off your haik?' he asked her. 'You'll get too warm if you leave it on.'

Opening the cloaklike covering, she let it drop to the floor without a word, her eyes firmly fixed on the carpet as André let himself look at her carefully.

Her caftan was made of transparent lavender silk. Tiny

24

embroidered buttons went from the hem to the neckline
and up each sleeve to the elbow. Delicate leaf patterns
were stitched in gold thread on the material. An underdress of sheer rose-colored silk was visible underneath,
falling to the tops of the hand-embroidered leather slippers. They were *babouches*, the pointed, multicolored
slippers all Arab women wore. Her hair had been pulled
back from her face and braided in many strands, in the
Berber style. Each braid was mixed with satin ribbons
and gold rings. A delicate chain, from which dripped a
profusion of silver coins, hung across her high forehead.
At her wrists were beaten silver bracelets, and around
each ankle was another delicate silver band. Her soft
gray eyes were lined with kohl, but André could see the
fear and uncertainty lurking in their depths. The picture
of a small animal looking down the barrel of a gun flashed
through his mind. He quickly dismissed it.

Taking a step toward her, André tried to make her feel
more at ease. 'Why don't you sit down,' he said.

Yasmin slowly began to sink to the floor, right where
she was standing, but André caught her elbow. He led
her over to the divan. She sat abruptly, then shrank back
into the cushions. Her fear was palpable.

It was probably well founded, André thought. What a
pity the government allowed this kind of flagrant abuse
of the antislavery laws. After all, he could do anything he
wanted with her and there would be no one to complain.
Least of all Yasmin. And she probably expected the
worst. Suddenly guilty, André thought about how he was
merely enjoying the fruits of this laxity. He owned
Yasmin, as far as any Arab in Morocco was concerned,
and at the thought, his guilt was replaced by an almost
uncontrollable wave of lust.

Quickly rising to get himself another drink, André
remembered the hashish Abdul Khadir had left. Thinking
perhaps it would make things easier, he prepared a

pipeful. As he carried it to the low table, he wondered how much Yasmin had been taught before coming to him. The thought excited him. His eyes roamed over her body, tracing the curve of the small, apple-shaped breasts outlined by her dress. It was so sheer, he could see the faint shadow of her nipples through the fabric. He became aware of a certain discomfort inside the tight strictures of his pants, and cursed Western clothing.

Sitting down, he inhaled a small mouthful of the pungent smoke, then handed the pipe to her. She raised the stem to her lips, sucking in deeply. Suddenly her eyes flew open and her hand flashed up to her throat. Without warning, she was seized by a violent fit of coughing. He tried slapping her on the back, but that didn't help. Not knowing what else to do, André quickly handed her the glass of brandy on the table, and she sipped at it slowly as the coughing subsided.

'Are you all right?' he asked. She nodded, but didn't say a word. This is ridiculous, he thought. She's absolutely speechless with fright.

Thinking it might relax her, he decided to question her about herself. 'Where are you from?' he asked, when she was more in control of her breathing.

'The Rif,' she answered shortly. 'Near Chechaouene.' She raised her eyes to meet his. He was momentarily caught up in the deep gray pools, noticing for the first time that they were flecked with yellow.

'How did you come to be in Abdul Khadir's compound?' he asked, collecting himself.

'My grandfather sold me after my mother died. He said no one would marry me because I had no father, and besides, he needed the money to buy wives for my cousins.' Her voice was flatly contemptuous as she raised the brandy glass to her lips, taking a long sip.

'Did you mind?' asked André, curious.

26

'Mind? What was there to mind?' said Yasmin. 'It is not so different from getting married, you know.'

'But certainly it's a little different!'

'How? When my friend Hadija got married, her father sold her to a tribesman from the Atlas Mountains. She had never seen him before. Off she went on the donkey, inside a cloaking of rugs so no one would see her before her husband.' Yasmin sniffed in amusement. The brandy was loosening her tongue, and she seemed more comfortable. 'He was probably some dirty old man who slept with his goats.'

André laughed, and Yasmin smiled up at him as she continued to talk. This was more like the Yasmin he remembered.

'And, of course, she could easily have smothered before she got there. No air could have gotten inside that heap. And the donkey swayed so! Hadija probably got sick all over him on their wedding night!'

Yasmin leaned back against the pillows and went off into peels of laughter. She put her hand to her chest as her laughter subsided, and the gesture clearly outlined her breasts against the thin material. André was having a hard enough time controlling the raging sensations that flooded over him. Now he leaned forward abruptly, pushing her back into the couch cushions. Before she could move, he covered her lips with his. Her soft little mouth tasted faintly of licorice tea as he forced his tongue between her teeth. Unable to resist, he explored the inside of that little cavern, thrusting his tongue against hers. One hand firmly imprisoned her head so she couldn't pull away. That left the other free to drag her dress roughly up over her knees.

Vaguely aware of a trembling in her rib cage, he ignored it as he searched for the warm crevice between her legs. Yasmin moaned softly, and though he knew

27

dimly that he was moving too quickly, he couldn't stop himself.

He kissed her mouth again, more softly this time. Then he raised himself up on one elbow and tried to unbutton the rows of little buttons. But it seemed that the loops were smaller than the little knobs of thread, and he couldn't for the life of him get them undone. Yasmin's eyes stayed tightly shut. The corners of her mouth trembled slightly, but she lay still. Exasperated by the buttons and beyond patience, André pulled hard. The wispy fabric shredded away in his hands. At last she was naked before him, wearing nothing but her bracelets, anklets, and slippers.

Her loveliness was startling. It was more than he had considered possible. He remained still, stunned at the sight. Then, sliding his hand down from the line of her delicate collarbone, across her small peaked breasts to the jut of her hip, he felt her muscles ripple under his hands. He stroked her gently. Her warm skin was smooth as satin. He traced the curve of her breast with his fingers. Her pointed nipples were pale pink against the light brown of her skin. Dipping his head to her breast he ran his tongue around one dainty nipple. It hardened against his lips, as his teeth gently grazed it. Inhaling sharply, he pressed the hardness between his legs against her thigh, rhythmically.

Doucement. Go slowly so you don't frighten her, he thought with difficulty. But his mind was clouded by urgency.

Her legs were pressed tightly together, but he forced a hand between her violently trembling knees. Drawn by the dark patch at the juncture of her thighs, he forgot any attempt at gentleness. With animal strength he parted them roughly, opening her up to his gaze. With a groan he slid his fingers along the inside of one thigh, grazing

28

his thumb over the little mound. The delicate shell-pink lips were visible through the silken hairs.

It was more than he could stand. Still holding her legs apart, he stood and quickly pulled off his trousers. Tossing them carelessly over a chair, he began unbuttoning his shirt. But the sight of her lying across the divan like a broken doll made him forget his shirt. Yasmin was trying to shrink away from him, pulling back into the cushions as far as she could. He caught her shoulder with his hand, pinning her down. Without looking up at her face, he knelt between her legs and pushed. But the obstruction he met was a strong one, and as he pushed again, her eyes flew open and she cried out in pain.

Looking up, André saw her eyes – the startled whites, like those of a small, hunted creature. Then he realized that tears were streaming down her cheeks, and her shoulders shook with silent sobs. At first he was unable to comprehend it, because of his aching need. But then, caught by the terror in her eyes, he suddenly realized what he was doing. He was forcing himself on a fifteen-year-old child. She was outraged, and absolutely mortified.

Pulling away from her abruptly, he turned his back and dragged on his clothes.

Mon Dieu, I am worse than the lowest of animals, he thought, even though at the same time his body was screaming for release. The muscles in his jaw clenched tightly as he pulled on his pants and strode to the bar. Gripping a bottle, he stormed out of the room, took the stairs two at a time, and fled into his bedroom, slamming the door behind him. Then he threw himself, cursing, onto the bed.

2

The light beaming in through his windows was so intense, that the first thing André was aware of was a brilliant red haze on the inside of his eyelids. Damn Zayd! The shutters had never been closed last night.

The second thing he was aware of was Zayd's voice piercing his strangely sensitive eardrums.

'What should I do with the girl who is in the library?'

André opened his eyes briefly, but shut them again at the intense pain that pierced his head. It felt as if a spike were being driven into his temple.

Girl? What girl? he thought. And then it hit him. Yasmin! Yasmin was still downstairs where he'd left her. *Nomme de Dieu!* How could that have happened? And then it all flooded back.

'Is she to be returned someplace, or just put outside the gate?' Zayd asked blandly, his words an insistent reminder of André's ghastly error. For a moment, André thought he saw a rare flash of amusement cross Zayd's face, but then it was gone.

'No, no,' André mumbled as he slowly pulled himself out of bed. 'She stays here. I'll be right down. Do nothing.'

Zayd turned and stalked out of the room, and André made a rapid examination in the mirror of the ravages of his night of drinking. He groaned, and quickly pulled on his clothes. He'd have to shave later, he thought, hoping the sight of his bristled face wouldn't terrify the girl even more.

Quietly he went down the stairs and entered the library.

At the sight that met his eyes, he was consumed with guilt.

Yasmin was sitting huddled on the floor, her haik wrapped around her shoulders and her face streaked with tears. The kohl on her eyes had been washed down her cheeks, and her tears had made rivulets through the dirt. She looked like a dejected beggar child.

At the sound of his footsteps she looked up, a mixture of misery and fear written in her swollen eyes.

'Will you send me back to Khadir?' she whispered, her voice barely audible as a fresh torrent of tears cascaded down her face. She rocked her body back and forth, sobbing. Faced with such a picture of misery, André was moved to wonder which she considered worse – being returned to Khadir or being violated by him. It occurred to him that there might be a great deal of shame involved in being returned. Maybe she thought she would be considered defective merchandise. He knelt at her side, trying to calm her and make her stop crying.

'What did I do wrong?' she choked out between shuddering sobs.

'*Rien, ma petite,*' said André soothingly. He put his arms around her and tried to lift her to her feet. 'You did nothing wrong. It was I who did wrong, not you.'

Yasmin flashed him a curious look, a blend of disbelief and surprise as her weeping began to subside.

'But I . . . I mean you . . . I was supposed to . . .' she stammered, trying to express as delicately as possible that she understood what should have taken place last night. He realized that she also understood she had driven him off, and that, she knew, was unforgivable.

'Ah, *pauvre petite*. Don't worry about last night. I can only apologize to you for pushing you so,' he said, turning away. Just holding her in his arms for that brief moment reminded him of how much he wanted her. What he would give to be able to take her this very moment. But

31

he couldn't do it. No matter what she was supposed to be, no matter where she had come from, she was obviously still a child.

That was a very real problem he realized now. What in heaven's name was he to do with a child? This wasn't what he'd planned on at all. *Dieu me garde,* he thought, suddenly horribly depressed. He didn't know the first thing about children – or young girls for that matter. He couldn't just keep her around the house. He had to do something with her. But what? He couldn't trust himself to do the right thing, and yet he couldn't bear the guilt of doing the wrong thing, either. Scylla and Charybdis, he thought glumly – 'caught between a rock and a hard place,' as the Americans put it.

André glanced at Yasmin. He'd just have to worry about it later, he thought. At least for the moment what had to be done was simple enough. She needed a bath and some sleep. He would just take the whole business one step at a time. Perhaps the answer would miraculously present itself – but he didn't feel like betting any large amounts on that supposition.

It was already improbable that she was here in his villa at all, and so very accessible; it was the validation of all his fantasies. Yet he couldn't touch her, couldn't lay a finger on her. Holding his feelings in tight control, his only thought was to make her comfortable and then get out of the house.

André led her upstairs. Yasmin hung back ever so slightly, as she gazed in wonder at the row of idyllic nineteenth-century landscape paintings that hung along the curved wall of the staircase. He seemed to remember from somewhere that the Koran forbade realistic depictions of the world. Decoration was always stylized.

On the landing André stopped at the door next to his. Turning the sculpted brass doorknob, the heavily carved door swung open, revealing a room filled with elegant pieces of furniture. There was a large ebony wardrobe inlaid with tortoiseshell and scrolled floral patterns. The imposing four-poster bed was flanked on either side by two fragile bedside tables of mahogany, with brass and silver pulls. Cream-colored satin drapes hung at the tall windows which overlooked the garden, and glowing Persian rugs were scattered on the black marble floors.

Yasmin gasped when she saw the room, and pulled back. 'But this is not for me,' she said.

'You don't like it?' asked André, surprised. 'Well, no matter. You may change it any way you like, *ma chérie*. It's yours. I can certainly understand your dislike of European furniture. It's nowhere near as comfortable as Moroccan furniture.'

'No . . . I didn't mean that,' Yasmin whispered, pulling the haik close around her body. 'It is too beautiful. A room like this is not for me. It would be better for a princess . . . not for me.'

'Ah . . . *je comprends,*' laughed André. 'Now I understand what you mean. But it is definitely for you. I want you to be happy with me. Don't you see that?'

Yasmin nodded, but a look of sadness crept across her face.

'Merde!' exclaimed André, breaking the stifling silence. 'You must be starving. I will call Salima and have her bring you something.' He strode across the room to pull the brocaded satin bell rope hanging near the door.

Again, an awkward silence descended until there was a light knock on the door. André opened it to admit Salima, quickly explaining that Yasmin needed a tray of breakfast. He added, 'And if you should want a bath, Salima will draw it for you. The bathroom is over there.' He gestured toward the door to the right of the white satin-covered bed.

At thirty-five, Salima was already old. Her nut-brown face was heavily lined, and the years of hard physical work showed. Her large, doelike almond eyes were soft and brown and usually filled with motherly warmth. Not that Salima was weak. Short, and with broad shoulders, her arms were surprisingly strong. So were her broad and callused hands. But she didn't want to work hard for the rest of her life, and she was a widow who also didn't want to try and find another husband – or worse, go live with her sister's family. No. This was a good job, an easy one by normal standards, and Salima intended to keep it, taking great pains to take care of her 'foreigner.' But sometimes she couldn't help wondering about these strange people with their funny clothes and even funnier ideas.

Now, Salima decided to keep her thoughts about Yasmin to herself, and avoided looking André in the eye. Wiping her hands on the front of her dress, she looked carefully at the girl with the dirty face, standing in the middle of the main guest bedroom of the villa, one of Salima's favorite rooms.

The first thing Salima noticed was the magnificent quality of the girl's haik and underdress, so much more elaborate than her own simple haik and cotton under-dress. It was obvious to Salima that the girl was not intended to be a serving girl in the kitchen.

As André watched the play of expressions across Salima's face, he could see that Zayd had told her something about the girl in the library. But Zayd didn't know much, so Salima probably knew even less. But on the other hand, he realized, sometimes the Moroccans had access to more information about what the crazy foreigners did than they let on. Both Zayd and Salima probably knew everything. They probably even knew how much Yasmin had cost him. He was appalled, but there was nothing he could do about it.

He had an inkling that what he suspected was true when he saw the look of combined pity and disdain

Salima cast at Yasmin. The young girl shrank visibly under her all-encompassing glance. But Salima turned quickly and walked across the room. Yasmin lowered her head and followed, almost running into her as Salima abruptly stopped in front of a door. Tentatively, Yasmin gave the door a light push, and it swung open easily.

She gasped with delight, clapping her hands together. The bathroom was white marble, the tub huge and partially sunk into the floor. The spigots were molded of polished brass in the shape of swans, and one entire wall was glass. Outside, the thick leaves of a eucalyptus tree made the room look like a greenhouse. Two doves were sitting on a branch. They craned their necks, looking in through the window curiously.

'Oh yes, please,' she smiled. 'I would love a bath in this room.'

'Good,' said André. 'Then it's settled. You will eat and bathe and rest. I have to take care of some business this morning, so I will leave you.'

A look of dismay crept over Yasmin's face. 'You will come back tonight?'

'Of course!' he answered reassuringly. 'I will come back tonight.'

André hurried from the room. It wasn't until he was in his own rooms with the door closed that he could breathe normally. Dismissing a shudder, he took a shower and shaved with care. He knew he had to get away. Being alone with Yasmin was an incredibly subtle form of torture, and he couldn't bear the pain. And he had thought it would be so easy! Now he had to find ways of avoiding her, or he could not be held responsible for his actions. That much was clear.

Driving up the coast road that wound along the sheer cliffs, he wished for a moment that he'd chosen a life-style that required his presence in some office all day, every day. That at least would give him an excuse for staying away from Yasmin. But he had no such job. There wasn't even a minor stockholders' meeting scheduled for today, though under ordinary circumstances he never attended them; Henri LaMarquette notified him of whatever he needed to know.

Today he would have given his right arm for a stockholders' meeting – even a tour of the mines! Business was the only explanation he could think of to excuse his absence from the house.

But why did he need an excuse? he wondered. The girl had already wrought radical and terrible changes in his life. She made his life seem both empty and far too full at the same time. He wondered what Nick would think of the whole business, and decided he'd probably laugh.

Abruptly, André decided to spend the day at the club; a few sets of tennis would help.

The day was beautiful, but hot. As he drove, the roar of waves crashing against the base of the cliffs was muffled but ever present. Across the Straits he could see the rocky mound of Gibraltar rising out of the water. Beyond that, Spain and Algeciras were only nineteen miles away, yet so distant in manners and customs. Here in Tangier, he thought, just an hour from Europe on the hydrofoil, and a person was lifted out of the twentieth century and unceremoniously deposited in the Middle Ages.

André pulled onto a curved road bordered on one side by a wall of cypresses. A long expanse of white wall bordered the other. The wall stretched as far as the eye could see. Much farther along there was a huge, ornate wrought-iron gate. He pulled the car in front of the gate, and an aged Moroccan wearing a pale blue turban swung it open to admit him.

Nodding his thanks, André drove into the gravelled parking area at the side of a gracious white building. Slamming the car door behind him, he made his way past the marble fountains and up the wide front steps. The water in the fountains splashed unevenly, and the air was filled with a heavy, floral scent. Ahead, in the dim, cool interior, he could hear the light buzz of conversation, and beyond that, the distinctive popping sounds of tennis games in progress wafted up from the courts.

As he made his way into the large room filled with deep easy chairs covered in hand-tooled Moroccan leather, he heard his name called by a deep and familiar voice. 'Baron! Join me, won't you?' Nick Chambers said. Then, laced with sarcasm, 'You must tell me all about your latest acquisition!'

André cursed under his breath as he glanced around the room. Thank God it was practically empty. Only a pair of middle-aged matrons, obviously English, were seated on a sofa against the far wall. He dropped into the chair next to Nick's.

'Too much for you, eh?' said Nick, a wicked, impish smile spreading across his face. In a gesture that was more theatrics than habit, his hand drifted up to stroke the handlebar mustache that adorned his top lip. The perfect bloody, ruddy Englishman, thought André, watching him out of the corner of his eye.

'Yes and no,' answered André, hedging.

At that moment a large Arab materialized at his elbow, and stood there silently.

'I'll have another gin and tonic,' said Nick, not bothering to look up.

'Make that two,' said André, a brief smile on his face as he went back to contemplating the palms of his hands.

'Well, how was she?' Nick insisted as he leaned forward with more than his usual interest. There was a predatory gleam in his eye. He looked like a bloodhound that had just caught the scent. 'Was she as good as you thought she would be?'

'Actually, I never got around to it,' André said bleakly, staring at the ceiling, trying to look unconcerned.

'Ah, so she gave you a little trouble, did she?'

André was silent for a moment, wondering how much he should confess. He didn't know if he would be able to continue this charade of masculine prerogative. He decided it was simpler to just describe what had happened, and the hell with Nick's opinion.

'No,' he said slowly. 'She didn't give me any trouble. I was the one who couldn't manage it.'

'Ah, well. No matter.' Nick coughed discreetly into his closed fist. 'At our age it's to be expected now and then. Take heart, old chum. By tonight you'll be back in rare form.'

'No. Unfortunately, it wasn't that. I couldn't bring myself to do it. At the last minute she cried, and I just couldn't.'

'Hah! Women,' Nick snapped gruffly. 'They act like they don't know what's going on, and then they use their tears to manipulate you all over the bloody place.'

'I'm afraid they were genuine.'

'Genuine, my ass! Don't say I didn't warn you. Virgins are always trouble. I have managed to avoid them for most of my life. And I'm positive that my life has been better for it. Let some other poor clod deal with all the wailing and the keening. I only want them when they know they're in for a good time.'

'She's too young, Nick. At her age, she should be going to school wearing one of those ghastly blue pleated uniforms, carrying her books, and giggling with her silly friends. She shouldn't be catering to an old man's sexual whims.'

'Don't be an idiot. You're not that old. Forty-eight is the absolute prime of your life. She should be thankful to have a man who is in such decent shape.'

'Well, perhaps she is, on some level. But I still have to deal with my own upbringing. I don't know what to do about it, and it makes me feel like *une bête* – an animal.'

'Christ! People and their bloody psychological problems!' laughed Nick. 'And furthermore, fifteen isn't that young in this country. The girls mature early.'

'Some do, perhaps. But it's more likely no one cares if they're mature or not.'

'Well, you know there is something to be said for young flesh. Veal is more tender than beef, old boy. Lamb is sweeter than mutton.'

'That's a repulsive metaphor, Nick. I'm surprised at you.'

'Then you've even more psychological problems than I thought. And you look perfectly ghastly too. Let's have a game of tennis . . . sweat out all the liquor you've been swilling. Your eyes look like eggs fried in blood, for Christ's sake.'

Once on the court, André felt the tension in his neck and shoulders begin to drain out of his body. As he smashed the ball back after one of Nick's adroit serves, he forgot about Yasmin and concentrated on his game. But Nick was in top form that afternoon, and despite all his efforts, André lost five-love.

'Find some other poor bastard,' André said, declining another game. '*Merde.* You're too much for me today.'

'That's because I haven't been wasting my vital essences on drink and debauchery.'

'Just on drink.'

'Not at the same rate you have!'

Later, in the showers, André soaped himself vigorously. He was beginning to feel clean once again. He allowed the sharp jets of water to pummel his back and neck, then turned it briskly to cold. Slapping himself, he stepped out of the stall and wrapped a heavy cotton towel around his waist. It was true that he was in good shape. The lean muscles of his thighs and belly were knotted just enough to give him a balanced form. There was no fat on him anywhere, and the smooth planes of his face were tanned by the Moroccan sun. The only thing that began to show his age was the graying hair at his temples.

He slid back into his trousers, leaving his pin-striped broadcloth shirt open at the neck. He was feeling a good deal better. Nick was sometimes right, though not often, he thought. An affectionate smile crossed his face at the thought of the tall, rangy Englishman he'd befriended. Nick's dry, acid wit had been a big help to him on lots of occasions. This one was no exception. However, André mused, perhaps he still needed one more thing before he returned to the villa to face Yasmin.

There was always Claire. Cool, collected, sensuous Claire. She was never out of sorts, and always available, it seemed, for a quiet interlude in the afternoon. The thought of relaxing with someone familiar lifted his spirits. He glanced ruefully down at the half tumescence that refused to go away. Apparently, he was still suffering from his almost unnerving need for Yasmin. Yes, Claire was just what he needed.

When he returned to the main salon, Nick was settled in his chair with the air of someone who plans to remain indefinitely.

'You'll have to excuse me, *mon ami,*' André said, his face expressionless, 'but there are some things I have to take care of today.'

Accepting André's excuse for what it was, Nick took a long pull on his drink.

'Glad to see you're feeling better, chum.'

'No thanks to your vicious game of tennis,' laughed André. 'But I must get going.'

'By the way, chum, there's a polo game this weekend – if you can make it! And remember: *Illegitimii non carborundum!*'

At André's blank gaze, Nick burst out laughing. 'That's Latin, you illiterate. It means. "Don't let the bastards get you down."'

Mon dieu, André thought as he made his way to the row of telephones on the desk. Schoolboy jokes, and from a man past fifty. He dialed the familiar number.

Claire was home, and as André drove down through the modern section of the city, he marveled at her delightful combination of availability and lack of possessiveness. It had been three years since the beginning of their civilized little affair, and he'd always wondered at her ability to keep him at arm's length; although, after thinking about it, he decided it might have been his ability to keep her at arm's length. Who knows? He only knew in retrospect that he had never actually worked at it.

Claire was tall, slender, and elegant, always beautifully coiffed, and never ill at ease. Her low, well-modulated voice sometimes took off in peals of laughter. But that was rare, and always controlled.

Claire Beranger had a husband, but apparently he lived permanently in Brussels. As far as André could figure out, she lived permanently in the delightful, spacious flat off Rue de Belgique. She never mentioned money, never mentioned problems of any kind for that matter. And she was always charming. The perfect mistress, André thought to himself as he stepped into the *ascenseur.* The little elevator was one of the several delights of paying Claire a visit. It was open on all sides, the glass enclosed by wrought iron and filigree, with a little bench covered in slightly worn red velvet at the rear. From inside, the passenger could look at each floor that passed, as well as up to the roof through the clear dome-shaped top of the elevator.

There was only one apartment on each floor. When André opened the door of the *ascenseur,* he was in an intimate foyer filled with potted plants. He turned the bell key, the mahogany door opened, and Claire caught his hands in hers, ushering him inside.

'Darling,' she smiled, 'how delightful that you called. It feels as though I haven't seen you in ages – though, of course, I saw you just last week at the Pendleton Rolfes' garden party, didn't I?'

André kissed her warmly on the cheek, then raised her slender fingers to his lips.

'What a hopeless romantic you are.' Claire sighed, her mouth twisting into a humorous smile. She pulled her hand away and led him out onto the terrace. 'I must say, you're looking marvelous. Would you like something to eat or drink?'

'Thank you, no. I was just at the club when I had this uncontrollable urge to see you. I'm sorry if I disturbed your afternoon. Were you sunning yourself?'

'Not really. I was reading that ghastly new book everyone recommended. It's one of those novels with thinly disguised movie stars . . . but anyone with half a brain can figure out who they all are. I'm afraid I couldn't put it down. Isn't that terrible?'

'Come, sit down next to me,' said André, patting the cushioned chaise. Claire picked up the book she'd left lying at the foot, carefully placed a leather bookmark in the pages, and put it down on the floor.

'So tell me everything you've been up to, André,' she said, smiling languorously. The heat of the day was wearing off, but it still wasn't conducive to quick movements. Claire seemed to be feeling the effects of the heat as well. She lifted the heavy blond hair off the nape of her neck with one hand. The loose, white linen shirt she wore fell away from her body, revealing her breasts. They were the same even tan as the rest of her skin. No swimsuit lines marred their perfection. The movement caused her breasts to sway slightly, and she smiled as she saw André run his tongue across his lower lip, watching.

'Not too much to report, *ma chérie*,' he said, casting his eyes over the patchwork of brown and orange rooftops of the city below. From Claire's terrace it was possible to see the rabbit warren of buildings in the Petit Soco. In the distance occasional minarets and towers reached up to scratch lightly at the sky. 'And you?'

'Same old whirl, I'm afraid.' She laughed softly. 'Fairly dull, actually. Did you hear that silly Austrian woman talking the other night? One would think Tangier was the hub of the European social season, listening to her. And that uncouth Belgian! Wasn't he awful? Tangier is overrun with a whole new breed of dreadful bores. I think it might be time for me to take a little trip to the continent, or perhaps England.'

'A taste of the real world, eh?' André smiled, looking at her again. 'And what about me? What am I supposed to do here without your delightful charms to chase away the doldrums?'

'You're sweet, my love,' murmured Claire, running her pale pink fingernail up the inside of his thigh. 'But I'm sure you'll think of something to do with yourself.'

André shot her a glance. Did she know about Yasmin? No, of course not, he thought. News travels fast in this place, but not that fast. Then he wondered if he should tell her himself. She was bound to hear about it sooner or later. But how could he tell Claire – witty, civilized Claire – about Yasmin? It was unthinkable. He could just imagine what she would say: Bought a young girl out of a brothel? How very old-fashioned of you . . . how sexy . . . how uncivilized. There's more to you than meets the eye, isn't there?

No, he couldn't tell her, André thought. Not right now . . . perhaps later. Perhaps tomorrow, when he'd figured out what he was going to do with Yasmin. Perhaps he could just tell Claire that he'd bought her to help Salima, to save her from a life of sexual slavery. Maybe Claire would believe him, though probably not.

At the thought of Yasmin, he remembered why he was

there, reached out and slowly began to unbutton her linen blouse. He pulled it slightly away from her, and looked at her naked body.

'I can see that you're prepared for my visit,' he said, a grin drifting lazily across his lips. 'You've neglected to put anything on underneath.'

Claire laughed. 'I always sunbathe in the nude. But I think we'd best go inside. Nude sunbathing on the terrace is one thing, lovemaking is quite another.'

'I suppose you have a pack of goggle-eyed admirers out there,' André said, gesturing to the other terraced buildings he could see. They looked to him like large white faces with many gaping black eyes, all focused on this terrace.

'I certainly hope so,' she said with a smile, as she walked slowly into the apartment. Stepping through the paned French windows that led from the terrace, she shed the long shirt onto the floor. 'Come in out of the sun and join me.'

André followed her undulating back as she led him into the bedroom. He undressed carefully, folding his clothes neatly and placing them over the back of a delicate gold and white chair. Claire lay back on the bed watching him.

'What a beautiful man you are,' she purred as she lay there, stroking herself. Her eyes dilated slightly as they drifted below his waist. She held out her arms to him. 'You'd better come here, and let Claire take care of that.'

It was well after sunset, and well after dinner, when André rode down in the glass-enclosed elevator. Relaxed and sure of himself, he felt invincible as he stepped out into the scented night. Climbing into the car, he turned it around and followed the streets thronged with tourists looking for nightclubs and thrills. He relaxed, knowing that after Claire, he would be cool and detached with Yasmin.

Whistling tonelessly, André drove through the night. He had missed dinner, and for all he knew, Yasmin might even have fallen asleep. Good. That would put the problem off until tomorrow. But as he let himself into the house, he saw that the library doors were open and all the lights ablaze. When he strode into the room, he was greeted with a sight that was surprising and pleasing at the same time. Yasmin was seated in a pile of books. Open all around her, they created a small hill with her in the center.

She looked different, and it took André a moment to realize why. Her hair. No longer tied back in the rows of braids, it hung free, falling in a sleek, straight drop down her back. The glistening black shower reached almost to her hips. The glowing blue-black was set off brilliantly by her dress. André wondered where she'd gotten it. After all, he'd torn the other one to shreds. But then he remembered the bundle she'd been clutching the night before – it must have been her clothes.

A diaphanous white caftan embroidered with pearly flowers covered a pale yellow underdress. Her skin seemed to glow through the sheer material, and André felt unaccountably depressed at the sight of her delicate beauty. He was unable to move or breathe for several seconds, realizing how hard it was going to be to have her in the house.

He might have stood there all night, he thought, if Yasmin hadn't noticed him. Startled by the sound of his footsteps, she looked up and smiled sweetly.

'What wonderful things these books are,' she said slowly in French, her voice filled with awe.

'You read?' asked André, surprised.

'Only a very little,' she replied. 'I went to the school in my village for a while. When my mother died, I had to

45

stay home and take care of my grandfather and my uncles. They didn't want me to go to the school anymore. My grandfather said it was a waste. No . . . I was looking at the pictures. They are so interesting. But with most of them, I can't figure out what they are about.'

'Would you like to learn how to read?' André asked. 'I mean, really well?'

'Oh, yes, I would love that. Then I could spend all my time in here, reading these books. There is so much to know, so many places I've never heard of, so many things to find out about.' Yasmin's eyes were glowing. 'What does this say? I do not understand what is happening in this picture.'

She held the book up to André, who took it from her hands. It was one he'd had since childhood. He began to read aloud from the facing page, and as he read, she leaned against his thigh, her eyes fixed on the print. It was almost as if she thought she could somehow absorb the meaning of the little black marks by listening and looking at the same time. Amused by her hunger for information, André kept reading.

But as he read, he became more and more aware of the pressure of her arm on his thigh, the warmth of her hip as it leaned against his. The delicious calm that he'd managed to snatch in Claire's apartment was rapidly vanishing. And yet Yasmin, in her innocence, was unaware of the effect she was having on him. He forced himself to focus his eyes on the pages in front of him. The sweet smell of her hair seemed to be acting as an irresistible aphrodisiac. Once in its hold, he knew he wouldn't be able to free himself.

'I have to stretch for a moment, *ma petite,*' he said, rising with difficulty. In a flash she was standing beside him, pointing to the page that was open. Unconsciously, she leaned the length of her body along his side. Her hard little breasts pressed against his arm.

'Just one more!' she begged.

With a moan, he let the book drop to the floor. He turned and caught her hair in his hand. Yanking her head back, he held her tightly against the aching hardness in his groin. Then he slid his hand down her back, grinding her against him even harder as he crushed his mouth against her throat. The uneven fluttering of her pulse was like the heartbeat of a trapped bird. Both her hands came up to his shoulders, pushing him away. The tension in her body arched her into a taut bow. André tore his mouth away from her throat, and as his eyes met hers, she suddenly relaxed in his grasp. Her eyelids fluttered down, as if trying to hide her thoughts from his gaze, and she stopped trying to get away from him.

But her limp resignation said more than any amount of struggle. André again bent his head and captured her licorice-scented mouth with his, enjoying the pleasure of her taste. He slowly and gently caressed her lips. Then, surrounding them completely, he snaked his tongue between them, trying to open her up to him. Her lips were like the delicate petals of a flower. Beneath, her teeth were like smooth pearls. He could feel her back quiver against his hand.

Perhaps he was holding her too hard? He relaxed his grip, but she was still limp, still unresponsive. Releasing his hold, he pushed her a little away from him. As he raised his head, her hands came up abruptly, pressing against his chest. He tried to see her expression, but she kept her eyelids down as she caught her breath.

Merde! This is no good, he thought. She is going to let me do this, but not because she wants to – she will because she thinks she *has* to. That's not good enough. God, what an impossible situation!

Letting his arms drop to his sides, André backed away. He watched as her eyes flew open, wide and startled.

'I'm really very tired, *ma petite,*' he said, tearing away

from her, strangling on the words. 'Perhaps we will read more tomorrow.'

Yasmin started to say something, but stopped herself.

He sensed that she was afraid he meant for her to accompany him, and said, 'Stay down here in the library as long as you like.' Although he wanted her more than anything else in the world at this moment, he couldn't ask it of her. It was painfully obvious that she was not ready. 'I am going upstairs to bed.'

With that he turned on his heel and left the library. He climbed the stairs to his room slowly, wondering how long it would take for her to relax in his presence. Or worse, how long it would take before he took her by force regardless of her wishes.

As he entered his room, it occurred to him that he should somehow try and arrange schooling for her. A tutor, perhaps? Was there a school somewhere that would accept her at this age, with very few skills? A tutor would probably be best, but then again, that did not solve the real problem he faced. He felt torn completely in half. On the one side was his civilized exterior with its nicely formed notions of propriety and human dignity; on the other, an animal that wanted nothing less than total possession of her – regardless of her feelings, and regardless of what was right.

The best thing, he thought, was to get her as far away from him as possible, until she was a little older. But where could she go? This was the only place she could go, and it wasn't a very good place for her at all. He would have to think of something, and quickly too.

André wondered idly what other Europeans in Tangier did with their children. He had never thought about children, but he dimly realized that he hardly ever saw them. They must go off to boarding school in Europe, he thought. But how did someone go about finding out things like that?

Shaking his head in wonder, he decided that sometimes life was full of the most incredible surprises. The unintentional consequences of a few trips to a whorehouse had landed him in the most uncomfortable position of having bought a woman, who then turned out to be a child. Now he was a sort of father, and totally unprepared for it. He was also far too embarrassed to ask any of the family types he knew what he should do. One question would lead to another, and God only knew what they'd think.

Maybe Nick would be able to do the research, he thought glumly. But he would take his pound of flesh for it in stupid jokes. At least Nick knew some funny jokes. Eventually, he'd let it drop.

André let out a sigh and crawled into bed.

PART TWO
Lausanne, 1975

3

The room was strewn with clothes, as if a violent wind had struck. All the closets were empty, the contents in heaps over every available surface. The place was in chaos. The drawers were all open, and under the open suitcases and travel bags, two narrow beds were barely visible. Three large steamer trunks stood open on the floor, and what little floor space was left was covered with odd collections of shoes, handbags, books, and papers.

'Free at last!' whooped Hilary Branford, throwing a handful of underwear over her head. 'Oh, Lordy, free at last!'

A lacy pair of panties fluttered down past Yasmin's head, coming to rest on her shoulder.

'For heaven's sake, Hilary. Stop! It's hard enough finding things in this mess without you throwing panties in the air!'

'I can't help it, Yasmin. This is an absolutely glorious day, don't you realize?' She rushed to the window, gazed out, then started to sing, 'No more pencils, no more books, no more Hawkeye's dirty looks!'

'STOP IT!' giggled Yasmin. 'Someone'll hear you! And besides, you shouldn't call her that.'

'Who cares,' laughed Hillary. 'What are they going to do? Throw me out of school? They can't touch me. Once you've graduated, you're safe!'

'Just pull yourself together and help me find my black shoes, will you?' said Yasmin. She was trying to sound annoyed, but couldn't escape Hillary's contagious merriment. 'They'll be here any minute! For someone who

53

really wants to get out of here, you certainly aren't getting ready very quickly.'

'Oh, Yasmin,' said Hillary, flinging herself on the slender girl, giving her a hug. 'It's so wonderful to be leaving, but I'm going to miss you.'

'I know. I'll miss you too. But we'll see each other again, I promise.' Yasmin gazed fondly at her roommate of the last three years.

'Out from under the watchful eye of the Hawk too. Ooh, we'll have such fun, won't we?' Hillary smiled a secretive smile as she started throwing books and papers into the trunk near her bed.

Yasmin nodded in agreement, but in the privacy of her own thoughts she realized how much she would miss Madame Duchamp. Even though all the girls referred to her as the Hawk because she was totally impossible to get around or fool, Yasmin had always liked her very much. She looked around the room, remembering how it had been when she first came to Lautremont. She had been so terrified, and Madame Duchamp had helped her glide around all the obstacles that faced her.

On that first day, as she sat in Madame's office next to André, she had barely been able to concentrate on anything at all. Madame Duchamp and André discussed her as if she weren't there. But Yasmin couldn't listen – couldn't focus on more than three words at a time. Her mind was so ablaze with all the new experiences she'd just had, she was convinced that if one more new thing happened, she'd crumble and disappear altogether.

'Of course, she might be lonely for the first few weeks,' Madame had said, her voice filtering through Yasmin's over-loaded consciousness. A tall graceful woman of uncertain age, Madame's hair was pulled back in a severe bun at the nape of her neck. The dark high-necked dress and single strand of pearls she wore were the epitome of classic elegance.

Madame Duchamp crossed her arms slowly and deliberately. She glanced at Monsieur le Baron over the tops of her glasses. 'As you can see, none of the other girls are here yet. I thought it would be a good deal better if Yasmin and I spent some time together, alone. After all, she can barely read, and her French is appalling. The language is no problem, really, because we have girls here from all over the world. They learn as they go along. However, I will have to tutor her intensively in reading and writing. The tests indicate that she is extraordinarily bright, so I do not anticipate any problem – however, she must also learn some of the etiquette of the school. She must be prepared for her first weeks here in the company of the other girls.'

The thought of being surrounded by a hundred other girls was only a little bit worse than being so far from Tangier, so far from anything that was familiar to her at all. Yasmin stared fixedly out the paned casement window. The walls of the building were at least a foot thick, made of perfectly hewn blocks of stone. The interior of Madame Duchamp's office was paneled in dark brown squares of wood. The narrow casement windows were hung with royal blue velvet curtains pulled back to let in what little sun managed to get through the forest of ivy and vines that climbed the outer wall. The furniture was large, cumbersome, and dark.

Outside, beyond the circle of crisply manicured lawn in front of the school – once an indifferently designed château – there was a long drive lined with stately trees. Beyond them an exquisite wall of snowcapped mountains rose in the distance. Not much different from the Atlas Mountains at home, Yasmin thought, yet so very, very far away.

'And I will see that her uniforms are ordered,' continued Madame Duchamp, 'but she won't need them for

55

now. Her regular street clothes will do very well until the term begins.'

Yasmin's mind wandered again at the mention of clothes. She was thinking of how many changes she had been through since that night Khadir had brought her to the villa. The strange way the baron had acted in her presence after those first two nights in his house had persisted. She had been left alone most of the time. Zayd and Salima had only spoken to her when it was absolutely necessary for them to do so. She had tried more than once to engage each of them in conversation, but they hadn't responded to her attempts.

And then suddenly André had announced that he was sending her to school. She had been delighted at first, but when it had become clear to her that he was sending her away – far away – her delight had been replaced by a nagging anxiety. But it was impossible to deflect André from his plan. Phone calls were made, arrangements completed, and André and Yasmin boarded a plane for Paris.

The whole time, Yasmin knew she was not doing what was expected of her – what Khadir had explained, and Turkana had crudely demonstrated. But the baron hadn't even touched her again, and Yasmin hadn't been able to bring herself to do whatever it was that she was supposed to do to make it happen. She was a hopeless failure.

Unable to comprehend at first the enormity of the change he had in mind for her, Yasmin had tagged along behind André, docile and miserable. It was only after they disembarked at Orly Airport that she fully grasped what was happening. But then such a whirlwind of bustle and activity had assaulted her, she had been unable to dwell on it for long.

As soon as they checked into the Nova-Park Elysées – before Yasmin even had a chance to assimilate all the sights and sounds and smells they had encountered in the taxi – André had knocked on her door. His room was next to hers. It also had two double beds, which left Yasmin wondering which to sleep on.

'Come, Yasmin,' he'd said, glancing away from her nervously. 'We'll get something to eat and see the city.'

He led her down the hall and they stood silently waiting for the elevator. Yasmin had been mildly horrified when they'd first gotten into the elevator on the way up to their rooms. As the doors whooshed open in front of them, André quickly glanced at her as she hesitated before going into the little box. He smiled at her look of resolute determination, then thought of all the wonderful things he could show her. Paris was the best place of all to introduce her to modern Western ways because it was such a wondrous blend of old and new.

It was Yasmin's first time in an elevator, and she wasn't expecting the whoosh of the doors as they shut. Even more upsetting was the sensation of speed coupled with rising. It was like the airplane, only in a building. But André had put his hand on her shoulder, and that steadied her somewhat.

'It's been two years since I was back in Paris,' he said as they rode down, 'and several years since I've lived here. This is going to be as much fun for me as it is for you. I'll take you to all my favorite places, I'll show you everything wonderful that there is to see in this city.'

The excitement in his voice was infectious, and Yasmin began to relax. The tension that had held her from the moment he'd announced his intention to send her away began to dissipate.

I have so much to learn, she'd thought to herself. *I hope it doesn't take too long. I must remember everything . . .* everything I see and hear. That way, perhaps I'll be able to go home soon. The thought of home brought her mixed feelings, however. She wondered about her

57

grandfather and what he would think if he could see her now, or what her cousins and uncles would think.

She wondered, too, about her father – who he'd been, where he was, and what he was doing. She knew he was an American, but maybe he was here in Paris. There were so many Westerners here. So many tourists. Maybe he was one of them.

Of course, Yasmin didn't know who he was anymore than her mother had. She didn't even know his name. Sometimes she'd tried to imagine what the man must have looked like. Was his hair dark? Was he tall or short? But always she came up against a blank wall, an empty space inside her head. All she could imagine was a uniform.

Once, some American soldiers had come into Khadir's brothel in Tangier. She'd looked hard at them, looking for any sign or indication that one of these men might be the man who'd ignited the spark that was her existence. But, of course, there was nothing. And, of course, they were all too young to have been her father. The soldiers had gone upstairs, one by one. She hadn't seen them leave.

But none of that mattered now. Soon she would know how to read, and she would be able to go home. All she had to do was get through whatever was going to happen next. How hard could it be? The tension began to build again, and as the elevator doors opened, Yasmin tried not to think about all the changes that were happening to her so fast.

As they walked through the lobby, elegant women cast inquiring glances at her. Their eyes swept from the *babouches* on her feet, up to the veil on her face. Then they turned to whisper to each other, adding to her discomfort. André hadn't noticed a thing, but when they stepped out onto the busy sidewalk, she pulled back.

'What is it, *chérie*?' he'd asked. But then he, too,

noticed the curious stares of the people on the street. 'But, of course! Your clothes. Would you like to stop first and get something more Parisian?'

'Oh, yes. But I wouldn't know how to decide what to get. Everyone is wearing something different.'

'Would you like some blue jeans?' he'd asked, an amused look on his face. He was watching her as she stared at two girls who'd just walked by. Their bottoms were encased in skin-tight pants that looked as if they'd been spray painted on.

There is certainly nothing left to the imagination, thought Yasmin, looking slightly pained.

'Well, not to wear right away,' said André, laughing. 'First we will get you some nice dresses.'

'And shoes and stockings,' added Yasmin, trying to sound as if she knew what she was doing.

'What will it be first? Clothes or food?' asked André.

Even though her stomach ached with hunger, as Yasmin saw how people stared, slowing down as they passed, she said firmly, 'Clothes.'

André had glanced up and down the street in this most elegant of avenues in Paris's eighth arrondissement. There were expensive shops, sophisticated restaurants, and couturier salons as far as the eye could see. But it was not what he had in mind for the moment. It was obvious that Yasmin needed everything, head to foot, and he knew just where to go for that. He had put her in a waiting taxi, and they'd driven to a wide boulevard where tall glass and marble buildings soared high above the street.

'I think we'll find everything we need right here,' he said as he paid the driver, then stepped out. 'Would you like to see Au Printemps? It's a department store.'

'A department store?' she'd asked, as they walked through a set of swinging glass doors. But then she'd been faced by a room so vast, and so filled with beautiful things, that she could only stare. André quickly marched her past all the different counters. They were, in fact, not that different from the stalls in the Suk, she thought, as they'd gotten into an elevator.

Once they stood in front of the crisp saleswoman who wore a long tape measure draped around her neck, the serious buying began. As André explained to the woman's frowning, prissy mouth that Yasmin needed to be outfitted completely, the saleswoman's small eyes lit up. Yasmin was quickly led back into a tiny room as André, seated on a small, uncomfortable-looking chair, waited.

Two hours later, faint from hunger and exhausted by what felt like a hundred zippers and a thousand snaps, Yasmin had stepped out of the dressing room looking very much the young Parisian. She had chosen to wear a light summer cotton dress. The skirt belled out prettily, falling just to her knees. The bodice was high, and cap sleeves left her arms feeling bare and chill. She hadn't been able to stand the feeling of the brassieres the woman had selected for her. Instead she chose to go bare-chested under the dress. The saleswoman had not batted an eye, merely saying, 'C'est bien. You don't need one of those, anyway. Your bosom is naturally very high. You needn't bother with it at all.'

On her feet were a pair of sandals with low heels. Delicate leather thongs encased her toes and slender straps encircled her ankles. The saleswoman had packed her old clothes in boxes, along with the rest of her purchases.

'Please have them sent to the Nova-Park Elysées,' said André, paying the bill. 'We have other errands to run.'

Then he turned his attention to Yasmin. 'Now you look quite lovely,' he said. 'But you looked lovely before too.'

Yasmin felt awkward under his scrutiny. She wished he would talk to her more, but he seemed so stiff and distant. Ever since she'd first come to live in his house, he'd avoided her, not talked to her. No one talked to her. She was lonely and hungry for companionship.

There was an inscrutable smile on his lips. 'How does it feel to be wearing your new finery?' he asked. 'Strange?'

'Very strange. There is so much showing,' she'd answered, feeling silly. She wanted to describe it, tell him how naked, yet how modern she felt. But he made her feel stilted and graceless. It was hard to forget that he'd bought her, and now he was sending her away. He didn't like her. That much was clear.

'I wanted the shoes with the very high heels, but when I tried them on, I couldn't walk. How do the women learn to get around in those?' she asked. Yasmin tried using the lighthearted but carefully distant tone he seemed to prefer since he had told her she was to call herself Yasmin de Saint-Clair and that she would be going away.

'I've often wondered that myself,' said André, chuckling. 'They practice, I guess. But it's just as well, because we're going to do a lot of walking today. Even if you knew how to wear them, your feet would feel terrible by tonight.'

Yasmin had nodded, pleased that she'd behaved correctly, and they'd left the store.

'We must eat,' said André, 'but before that, we must find a taxi.'

They'd strolled along the street until they came to a taxi stand. In a matter of moments, one pulled up to the curb.

'Rue de Miromesnil,' André commanded as they settled back in the seats. Then he turned to Yasmin. 'I know a very nice restaurant that I think will amuse you. You can see into the kitchen and watch the chefs at work.'

The taxi sped through a maze of streets, and moments later he had handed her through a thickly padded door into a lovely plant-filled room with a tiny garden in the center. Wisteria, ivy, and roses climbed a green trellis against the wall, and Yasmin could see into the glassed-in kitchen on the other side of the room.

'*C'est pas de la nouvelle cuisine*,' he noted as he examined the menu, 'but that is just as well.'

Without asking Yasmin, he ordered *jambon d'agneau fumé* – a smoked leg of lamb that was surprisingly sweet, and not too far from what Yasmin was accustomed to. She had not particularly liked the *pleurotes* – a mushroom too exotic for her tastes, but she had adored the *petits fours*. Thoughtfully, André asked the proprietor to wrap a few in a napkin for them to take along.

Feeling a good deal better, he had taken her to the Louvre. There, Yasmin fell completely under the spell of the paintings. They strolled through gallery after gallery. It was only when the closing bell had rung, that André was able to convince her to leave. He'd chuckled. 'They'll lock us in here for the night, and they turn the lights out, so you wouldn't be able to stay up all night looking at pictures, either. We have to go, Yasmin.'

That night after dinner in the hotel, Yasmin was so exhausted she had fallen into a practically drugged slumber. And the following days had been much the same. As they went from place to place, all the different layers of visual stimulation threatened to completely overwhelm her.

He showed her Paris and everything in it from the Trocadero to the Jardin du Luxembourg – from the Sacré-Coeur to the Bastille. He showed her the Luxor Obelisk in the middle of the Place de la Concorde, the Eiffel Tower, the Arc de Triomphe, and the Observatoire on Montparnasse. They explored Notre-Dame and took rides on the metro. They went to the Opéra that was built on an artificial lake used by the fire brigade. They went to the Musée Grévin – the waxworks.

And every night Yasmin fell exhausted into her bed.

She had wanted to get her hair cut short like the French

girls she saw in the street. She wore it in a thick, twisted knot at the back of her neck, and she thought it looked old-fashioned. But André was adamant, horrified at the suggestion.

'Never! Never cut your hair. It is glorious like that, and I would never forgive you.'

His face clouded over with that curious mixture of anger and sadness that she sometimes saw when he looked at her. The look was so intense, so black with meaning, that it always caused her to turn away. It reminded her of that first night in the white villa. He had looked at her that way then too. But never again had he kissed her or touched her the way he did those first two nights. For that, she had been grateful. The memory of those nights filled her with a mixture of dread and longing that she was unable to define.

The sound of Madame Duchamp's voice pulled her out of her reverie and back to the view out the window.

'If there is any problem, or if I feel that she cannot handle the work, I will contact you at once, of course,' Madame was saying in a voice that sounded reassuring.

'I am sure that she will be very tractable.'

'Yes, I'm sure. But we don't want her to be *too* tractable, do we?' Madame Duchamp gazed at him shrewdly. 'After all, she has to learn to be independent. We must make her into a modern woman. She has much to overcome, this adopted child of yours. Moroccans are not known for training their young women to be outgoing free thinkers, are they?'

Yasmin looked out the window as André and Madame Duchamp went over her course of study and what Madame intended to teach her in the three weeks before school officially began. She could see a little church with a pointed tower off in the distance, and she was reminded of Notre-Dame. 'The house of God,' André had said.

63

How funny these people were, thinking that they could induce their God to live in a house. No matter how beautiful it was, Allah would never live in a house, she thought. He would feel far too confined. Allah wanted the desert, the sky, and the stars.

And how funny to make such big buildings to live in. Anyone could tell you that when the goats moved, you had to follow them. And then what do you do with your beautiful buildings? You can't take them with you, can you? So then you become trapped by your buildings, and that finishes your freedom, forever.

Then, suddenly, Yasmin and Madame were standing, shaking hands, and André walked to the door. He beckoned Yasmin to follow him, and there in the dark paneled entrance hall he took both her hands in his and looked searchingly into her eyes. They burned with painful intensity, and for a moment Yasmin thought she would be totally consumed by the fires in them. But just as quickly, he lowered his head and kissed her lightly on the cheek.

'Remember what I told you, *chérie*. Never speak of Abdul Khadir, or anything that happened before you came here. I fear your little classmates would not understand.'

Yasmin had nodded, unable to speak. But her heart was thudding with fear. A wave of unspeakable loneliness washed over her at the thought of being left in this forbidding building.

Then he continued in a louder voice, 'And I expect you to write me a letter every week. I will also write to you. That way, you will practice writing as well as reading, and tell me everything that is happening to you.'

He had kissed her once more, this time on the forehead, and then he was gone.

* * *

64

'I just wish you were coming to Radcliffe with me,' said Hillary, her voice filtering through the mists of Yasmin's memories. A few more crashes came from the depths of the trunk, as Hillary heaved more books into its cavernous maw. But before Yasmin could reply, Hillary was off on another tangent.

'And of course you'll have to come to visit us in Southampton. Ask your father, I'm sure he won't mind. And we'll have such fun, we can ride all day if you like. We have a stable full of simply divine horses, and you would love that. And we'll go to parties. They have hundreds of parties all summer. Everyone will be absolutely crazy about you. After all, you practically qualify as a baroness, and a French one too. They're simply nuts over royalty in the States. My parents never care where I am or what I do, so we could have sexy adventures with anyone we want – or better yet, everyone who asks! Wouldn't that be terrific after this nunnery?'

The last of the books went careening into the trunk, and then Hillary shoved a pile of tangled clothes, sweaters, socks, and underwear into her suitcase, and sat on the lid. The suitcase didn't want to close.

'So try and get him to let you come this summer!' she said, bouncing on the suitcase. 'Damn! This stupid thing won't close. Yasmin, would you help me with this?'

Yasmin stepped over a stack of books and leaned down on the lid while Hillary forced the snaps shut. She glanced at her fondly, wondering how she ever would have managed without Hillary's constant and torrential flood of featherbrained observations.

At first it had been very irritating. Yasmin wanted to be alone with her memories and her thoughts. She wanted to hug the awful loneliness to herself. She was too far from everything she'd ever known, and only her books were not threatening. The vistas they opened made her finally forget how very odd it was for her to be in this school in the first place. And all during this lonely time, Hillary never let up. Eventually, without appearing to, she gave Yasmin massive amounts of information. Hillary dragged her out of her self-imposed shell and into the life of the school. Clever Madame Duchamp must have known that Hillary was just what Yasmin needed. And Yasmin was thankful to both of them.

'Oh shit!' yelped Hillary, pulling her cotton shirt over her head as she stood near the window. 'They're here! Quick, help me find my skirt. God, I bet I packed it, and now I'll never find it.'

'No, here it is,' said Yasmin, handing her a pale pink linen skirt.

'I have to hurry. Now, promise me you'll write every day, and make sure you visit me this summer!' Hillary said. Then she snatched up her suitcase with a groan, and jammed a floppy denim hat on her head. Grabbing a huge leather purse stuffed with a morass of papers, ripped-up paperback books, and makeup that threatened to cascade out all over the floor, she kissed Yasmin affectionately. 'Write!' The door slammed behind her as she dashed out.

Yasmin looked out the window and watched as Hillary climbed into the Rolls Corniche waiting for her in the circular drive. A pale arm thrust out the window and waved as the car slowly drove off. Yasmin waved back, even though she knew Hillary probably couldn't see her. That is, if she was even looking. By this time, Yasmin thought, she had probably begun her characteristic barrage of disjointed, but funny, anecdotes to keep her parents amused on the drive.

Yasmin returned to her packing. Her trunks were still in the room awaiting shipment, but it was quiet and still now that Hillary was gone. She suddenly thought about André. Soon he'd come to pick her up. How handsome he had looked yesterday as he watched the commencement –

lean and tall, with brilliant blue eyes that gleamed out of his tan, strangely young-looking face. His hair had more gray in it than she remembered, salt and pepper now. She wondered if André noticed any changes in her. But he'd said nothing to her if he had.

'*Tres distingué*,' Hillary had crooned up at him liltingly after they'd been introduced. 'How come you didn't bring him around more often?' she'd whispered in Yasmin's ear, staring hungrily at André. He was wearing a beautifully tailored navy blue suit, his white silk shirt open at the neck. 'He may be *your* father, but he's not mine,' she'd hissed as Yasmin stared at her in pretended horror. And Yasmin had wondered why, indeed, he hadn't come around more often. She had wanted him to, but André always had some business to conduct, some trip he had to make, some problem that needed resolving, and so he'd never come to visit her.

During every one of the term vacations he had given her excuses. He'd never sent for her, never brought her home, and she'd stayed at school with a scattered few others. During the summers he'd arranged for her to take special student tours.

The mid-year vacations weren't so bad. After all, there were always papers to write and stacks of books to read, and it was so peaceful being able to work without any noise. But the summers had been hard. Oh, the trips had been interesting, there was no denying that. There was a tour through the castles of the Rhine, and a special Art History study session at the Sorbonne, and then finally a whole summer of the antiquities of ancient Greece and Rome. And always under the watchful eye of the tour guide who was usually a middle-aged, blue-haired, matronly professor who thought of the girls as her innocent flock of lambs.

In a way, of course, they were. The predators, the wolves were everywhere, devouring them with hooded eyes. But what a flock of lambs to have to tend! Everywhere the troop of laughing girls went, wolves were lurking in doorways, sitting in cafés, leaning against lampposts. But that had been kind of exciting. There were never any boys on the tours, only tittering, whispering girls. At each hotel, a collection of intense, hot-eyed men would hang around in the street in hopes that one of them would manage to slip out of the fold. When the girls all left together, they hissed incomprehensible, guttural things in their tender ears. Regardless of the language, however, the meaning was always clear.

Some of the girls managed to slip away at night. They usually came back near dawn, tousled and sleepy. The next morning, when it was time to get up, they always had circles under their eyes that looked like bruises. The blue-haired keeper would always send them to bed with hot broth to drink, afraid that they were getting sick.

But Yasmin had never dared to broach the comforting safety provided by the guides. Those intense stares and the whispered invitations of those sleek, predatory men made her strangely uncomfortable. The hot, swollen sensation she always felt made her think of André. That strange sinking, melting sensation returned now as she thought about him coming to collect her today.

There was a light knocking on the door, and Yasmin went to open it.

'Well, my dear, I see that you're actually making a dent in the rubbish in this room,' said Madame Duchamp, as she looked around. There was an amused expression on her face. 'I would have thought that after all these years, I'd manage to get used to the clutter you girls seem to thrive on. But I must admit, it still makes me shudder just a bit. Did Hillary get off without injury?'

'As far as I can tell,' Yasmin answered, collecting a shoe from under the bed. 'I'm going to miss her. She always makes me laugh, even when I don't want to.'

'I know. She was a delightful child, and now she's a delightful woman,' answered Madame. 'You two made a very good pair. You managed to have a sobering influence on her, and she brought more vitality to you. Every now and then, my judgment on these things is correct.'

'Your judgment is always correct, Madame.'

'You are very sweet to say so, Yasmin. And I shall miss you too. You really provided me with a very interesting challenge. What an adventure, to take a little, uneducated Moorish girl, and turn her into a sophisticated lady of breeding. Rather like my own version of Pygmalion. It makes me feel just like George Bernard Shaw.'

Yasmin laughed at the thought. 'Fortunately for you, you don't look the slightest bit like George Bernard Shaw.'

'Or act like him, either,' said Madame, a smile on her lips. 'Did you know, I once heard a funny story about Mr Shaw. He was visiting Vassar College when one of the more brilliant students came up to him and said, "Mr Shaw, I know you are considered one of the world's great wits, but I, too, am considered a great wit. I assure you that if we were to have a conversation, I could easily give you tit for tat." And Mr Shaw answered, "Tat." The girl, it is said, fled in embarrassment.'

'That must have been a long time ago,' Yasmin said giggling. 'Nobody in *this* school would have been embarrassed by such a thing.'

'Far from it. One of our girls would probably have driven Shaw from the room in embarrassment, judging from some of the conversations I've overheard lately.'

Yasmin lowered her head, a light flush coloring her cheeks.

'But certainly not from you, my dear. You are a trifle odd in that respect, I think. The rest of my charges seem to be suffering from advanced cases of terminal hot pants.'

Yasmin gasped, both shocked and delighted to hear Madame speak this way. Her hand shot up to cover her mouth. 'You know, if anyone ever heard you talk like that, Madame, I'm sure they would have an entirely different opinion of you.'

'No doubt you're correct. But if they did, there would be no controlling them at all. Am I right?'

'I'm afraid so,' smiled Yasmin.

'I don't mean to make it sound as if you're all so awful. However, even so, I always feel just the way you girls do at the end of the term. Free at last. Free to be a normal human being, and not the game warden I have to be during the year.'

'Now that I'm leaving, I feel that I've missed someone rather special all these years,' said Yasmin, looking at Madame with new understanding.

'Not necessarily, my dear,' she answered, wisely solemn. 'But I want you to know that if you ever need anything, or anyone to talk to, you must always look on me as a friend. You're more than welcome to visit me, or stay with me, should you happen to be in Geneva. I would be delighted to see you, so you must not hesitate for a moment. Is that a promise?'

'Most certainly it is a promise, Madame,' said Yasmin.

'I have written my telephone number and address on this card for you. When school is not open, I live in Geneva. You must visit me whenever you have a chance. And I would be most happy, if you would write to me now and then and tell me what you are doing. I suspect that your progress will be very interesting to watch.'

'Why thank you, Madame. You really flatter me more than I deserve, I think,' Yasmin said, slipping the card into her purse.

Madame Duchamp walked over to the window and glanced out. 'I believe your father is here to collect you, Yasmin,' she said. 'Don't forget your promise, now.'

'I won't,' said Yasmin, kissing Madame warmly on the cheek. 'And have a lovely, quiet summer.'

'I certainly hope so,' Madame said as she gently closed the door behind her.

Alone in the room again, her home for the last three years, Yasmin felt a small wave of sadness creep over her. She walked to the window and looked down to where André was standing next to the car. Unaware of her gaze, he stood with his hands jammed into the pockets of his khaki twill trousers. They had obviously been tailored just for him. The casual elegance of his pale blue silk shirt, open at the neck, and the careless way he leaned against the side of the dark green Mercedes, sent a delicious thrill through her body. Hillary's sly remark came back to her. 'He may be your father, but he's not mine.'

And Yasmin thought, as the shiver of feeling intensified, 'He's not my father, either.'

She quickly glanced around the room, making sure that everything was collected, and then closed her suitcase and shut her trunk. Most of her things were in the trunk – all her books, sweaters, and overcoats. The articles of clothing she might need on the trip back to Tangier were in the suitcase. Her skis and ski boots were strapped to the top of the trunk. It looked as if everything was ready.

She turned and examined herself carefully in the mirror to make sure she was presentable. The scalloped hem of her denim skirt belled out around her slender legs. Her blouse was sheer white cotton, with sleeves constructed of layers of pointed fabric that fell to her elbows. Gone was the frightened girl in the Eastern robes that he'd brought to Paris. Yasmin hadn't grown, but she'd changed. The soft rounded curves of her face had lost the baby fat that had made her look so young. Now the delicate line of her jaw was more defined, and the sweep of her almond-shaped eyes above her fine cheekbones added a piquancy to her face that hadn't been there before.

Even though she'd wanted to cut her hair many times, she'd never done it. The mental picture of André's face when he told her never, never to cut her hair, had stayed with her for the three years. But it had been hard. She'd wanted so much to look modern, and long hair was impossible. Hillary had stayed up one night until three o'clock in the morning tying the long coils up in rags. Yasmin had wanted her hair to look different for a change. In the morning, when they'd brushed out the fat corkscrew curls, she'd been pleased with the effect. But the weight of the hair straightened them out before noon. So, most of the time she'd worn it in braids wrapped around her head, or in a thick knot at the back of her neck. Today she let it fall freely down her back.

Picking up her suitcase and her purse, Yasmin gave the room one final farewell glance.

She must have been one of the last to leave, because the building was eerily silent. Her footsteps on the wood of the stairs rang out with a hollow sound like the *drbouka* in the Medina. The smell of the school filled her nostrils with wax, dust, and books. Grinning happily, she ran out the door and into the brilliant sunshine.

4

Raising her hand to shield her eyes from the sudden glare, Yasmin stopped on the front steps. At that moment André looked up. Seeing the heavy leather suitcase she lugged, he swiftly covered the ten feet between them.

'Let me carry that for you,' he said, taking the bag from her. 'It's far too heavy. *Mon Dieu*, what have you got in here, bricks?'

'Yes, that's exactly what I have.' Yasmin giggled. 'I've been working on a collection of them. You'll be very impressed when I show them to you.'

'I'm already impressed,' André said, smiling ruefully as he heaved the bag into the trunk of the car. Slamming the trunk closed, he turned to look at her. Yasmin had placed a hat squarely on her head, to shade her eyes, but his glance was not at her face. The day before, she had been wearing the traditional graduation cap and gown. He hadn't been able to catch so much as a glimpse of anything but her face, her slender ankles, and her feet. As he drank in every contour of her small, finely boned body, she suddenly launched herself across the space that separated them, catching him unawares in an exuberant hug.

'Oh, how glad I am to see you!' she whispered.

Extricating himself from her grasp, he quickly placed his hands on her shoulders and held her a bit away from him. He had been totally unprepared for the sensations he felt when she pressed herself against the length of his body. It had been three long years since he'd seen her. He'd thought himself finally immune. His relationships wiht Claire and with all the other women during that time had been cool, sophisticated affairs that were easy to handle, easy to enjoy, and easy to extricate himself from. Now it seemed to him that Yasmin still had the ability to overwhelm him and throw his veneer of civilized behavior to the winds.

'And I'm glad to see you, too, *chérie*,' he said a bit gruffly. 'Especially out from under that funny hat with the cardboard on the top.'

'That wasn't cardboard!' she said, pretending to look chagrined. 'Aren't you proud of me for graduating with honors?'

'Of course I am, and you know it, but you almost knocked me down with that hug.'

'Erich Fromm says it's better for your health to express affection in physical ways. A hug can only improve your liver,' she replied archly.

'*Dieu me garde!*' sighed André. 'What have they turned you into in this place? A psychiatrist? That was not precisely what I intended when I sent you here, you know.'

'Life is full of little surprises, isn't it?' laughed Yasmin as she walked around the car and opened the door on the passenger side. 'Where are you taking me, chauffeur? I am impatient to begin my life.'

André got into the car and turned the key in the ignition. 'It's even worse than I thought. Not only a psychiatrist, but a pushy one, besides. Are you also a backseat driver?'

'Don't be silly. You can see perfectly well that I'm sitting in the front seat.'

'*C'est vrai*, I can certainly see that,' he said, chuckling despite himself. 'And where would you like to go, Mademoiselle?'

'Anywhere you want,' Yasmin teased. She didn't understand why she was talking in this light, provocative way, but decided not to worry about it now. They were off, driving down the long, tree-lined driveway, and she felt inexplicably happy, perhaps as happy as she'd ever been. She wondered if it would last.

'Well, if it pleases you, Mademoiselle, I thought we would drive through the Alps into France, and then down the Mediterranean coast until we cross the Pyrenees. From there we could wander through Spain, touching on Barcelona, Cartagena, and Valencia, until we reached Algeciras. Then we could always take the hydrofoil to Tangier. Does that suit Your Majesty?'

'Perfectly,' Yasmin sighed, a smile on her lips as the wind blew through the window, making her thick mahogany hair fly about her face. She blew lightly to get rid of the long strands that caught between her lips.

There were so many things she wanted to say to him, but there didn't seem to be a proper opening. Was he going to take her back to Tangier? Was she going to live with him? What about school? Was this it? Was she finished now?

Part of her had wanted to go on to college with the rest of the girls, but she'd never had the nerve to bring it up to him in her letters. Madame Duchamp had told her she should seriously consider going to college. Yasmin had done so well in her schoolwork, Madame had been horrified when she'd discovered that Yasmin wasn't planning to apply anywhere. But Yasmin had said she'd like to wait, take some time off before deciding. She'd claimed she wanted to go home for a while before she started another long stretch of time away from her country. Madame Duchamp had let it go at that, thinking the girl was homesick, which was understandable since she hadn't been back to Morocco for three years.

Yasmin had tried to bring up her college ambitions in subtle ways. She'd written André all the details of Hillary's plans to go to Radcliffe, and she'd told him how all the girls were waiting for their acceptances from schools with agony and desperation. Yasmin had hoped that André would rise to the bait and ask her if she wanted to go to college too. But his replies had been the usual bland letters about the weather, the state of his business, whether he was planning a trip – nothing more. He'd either not understood, or had chosen to ignore the entreaties buried between the lines.

As they drove, he talked aimlessly about his stop in Paris for a meeting on the way to pick her up, and a play he'd seen while there. She'd replied with equally innocuous things about the theater group at school and the silly show the graduating class had put on as their swan song.

They skirted the north side of Lac Léman until they came to Geneva. There, André guided the car through the traffic, which was getting increasingly heavy as the afternoon progressed. He stopped briefly to check a road map, then pointed the car toward a highway. Soon they were climbing into the mountains. On either side dense forests obscured much of the view, but occasional gaps in the trees showed her expanses of exceptional meadows. They were filled with a carpet of meadow flowers and alpine shrubs, a riot of hues, colors, shades, and variegations that delighted her.

The forests and meadows soon gave way to pine barrens, and then to firs, and finally, as they passed the timberline, Yasmin saw the rocky desolate wastes cluttered with boulders. Jutting, snow-covered cliffs gave way abruptly to sheer drops filled with rocky debris, which spoke of frequent slides. Beyond, she could see the rocky slopes of yet higher mountains, and hanging glaciers. As André skillfully negotiated the hairpin turns, Yasmin closed her eyes in fright.

Each time she opened them again, she was increasingly aware of his long, blunt fingers, and the curly hairs that sprung from the backs of his hands as they gripped the leather-encased wheel. She was also aware of the hard muscles of his legs outlined through the twill pants.

As he drove, André talked about everything except where they were going. He asked her about her trip to Greece, and about her summer at the Sorbonne, and what her favorite subjects were. Yasmin was beginning to feel like a little girl on an outing with her uncle. At one point she asked where they were headed, but André had simply smiled a mysterious smile, saying, 'That's a surprise.'

Yasmin wondered how long they were going to be able to avoid talking about important things. She was bursting with questions, but it was obvious André didn't want to talk about anything but Lautremont and the geological points of interest skimming past. Then the road got more dangerous. The turns got tighter, and sheer drops out the side of the car made him devote all his attention to driving, as Yasmin examined the smooth planes of his face at leisure.

What an even, sculptured profile, she thought – just like some of the Classical bronzes she'd seen in Athens. The line of his jaw was strong; it jutted out almost defiantly. His elegant, aquiline Gallic nose, with the flared nostrils, spoke of centuries of careful breeding. At times she wanted to touch him, to trace the line of his jaw or feel the muscles in his arm as they rippled under his shirt. But she sat in silence, her hands in her lap, gazing at him and then the stunning landscape spread before her eyes.

As they climbed higher into the Alps, a cloud bank began to move in. Soon they were enveloped in a soft, muffling blanket of moist air. They couldn't see more than three feet ahead. André slowed the heavy car to a crawl. Suddenly, without warning, they entered a long, pitch-black tunnel. It seemed to go on for miles until, at the end of the murky cone, she could see a flat white circle that signaled the other side of the mountain they were crawling beneath.

When they emerged from the tunnel, the mist was much lighter. Ahead, perched high atop a sheer cliff, there rose a pure white castle. The turrets, spires, and crenelated walls resembled a fairy tale.

'Oh, look!' Yasmin said, pointing. 'How incredibly beautiful.'

'Glad you like it,' André said, smiling, 'because that's where we're going.'

'What is it? Someone's castle?'

'Well, at one time it was a rebellious medieval knight's stronghold in the mountains. Now it's a hotel run by an order of Cistercian monks. It just opened for the season, and I thought we'd spend the night there.'

'Why isn't it open all year round?' asked Yasmin, almost breathless at the magical beauty of the castle.

'There are heavy snowstorms during the winter that make travel up here impossible. Otherwise I'm sure it would be, although perhaps the monks prefer it that way. They have peace and quiet for their devotions and meditations in the winter.'

André drove the car across a stone bridge that spanned a gorge, and under a high, curved stone archway that gave into the inner courtyard of the castle.

'This stone bridge was once a wooden drawbridge. The knight could make lightning raids and then retreat into the safety of his castle, pulling up the bridge behind him. No one dared to try and negotiate that gorge, so he was safe.'

'What kind of lightning raids did he make?' asked Yasmin, curious. 'The Robin Hood variety?'

'More likely the Bluebeard variety,' said André, glancing at her, the blaze of his blue eyes becoming pinpoints of light. 'Why build such a beautiful castle except to delight the maidens he captured and brought here?'

Before Yasmin could answer, a bellboy in a scarlet uniform hurried out of the ornately carved entrance to the hotel. He held open the door on her side. Clasping her purse, she stepped out of the car. André opened the trunk and handed the keys to the young man.

'He'll bring in our luggage and take care of the car,' he said, taking her by the elbow and steering her into the main lobby. 'First we will check in, and then we'll rest and have dinner.'

Inside, the magnificent hall was all white marble and crystal chandeliers. Elegant tapestries hung on every flat surface. On them, medieval lords and ladies playing lutes, viols, and psalteries lounged in glades of stubby trees; silver pears, crimson apples, and glowing purple plums dotted round fruit trees with short, slender trunks; and fat doves sat in the branches, while delicate whippets played at their feet.

The glowing threads were as brilliant as the day they had been woven, and Yasmin could barely tear her eyes away. André signed the register for the concierge, a tall, stoop-shouldered man who then handed the keys to the bellboy who had just come inside carrying the luggage.

André followed him to the small elevator next to the curving balustraded staircase, and Yasmin trailed after them silently, suddenly nervous. The little elevator creaked up slowly, the doors opened, and the bellhop lifted out their bags, placing them in front of two arched oaken doors off a small landing. To the right Yasmin could see a dark stone staircase with a low ceiling that curved down into nothingness.

'*Merci*. That will be all,' said André as he took the large brass keys from the bellboy, slipping a folded bill into his hand. The boy nodded and stepped back into the elevator. The ironwork grille slid shut, and glided down out of sight.

André slipped the key into the lock, swung the door

open with his foot, and Yasmin stepped into the room. It was a tower room formed in a great semicircle. The windows looked out on all three sides over a precipitous drop. They resembled long gun slits in the wall. Through one of them they could see a crenelated balcony which probably was once part of the catwalk that went around the entire castle. Each window had long interior shutters carved in high relief with designs that resembled the illuminated letters in ancient Celtic manuscripts.

Aside from a high mahogany wardrobe against one wall, the only piece of furniture in the room was a large four-poster canopied bed, hung with pearl gray curtains. The posts were carved with the figures of *putti* – podgy angel babies. The *putti* wove heavy garlands around each post as they flew into the canopy. The underside of the canopy was lined with sky blue satin caught in folds at the corners. A huge fireplace, high enough for a man to stand upright in, was sunk into the one wall that had no windows.

Yasmin glanced around her. Seeing that André had not moved, a momentary panic took hold of her as she wondered if they were supposed to share the giant bed. It was certainly far too big for one person alone. Her knees began to tremble, and she turned to look up into his eyes questioningly. Again she saw that intense, burning gaze that pierced through her with almost knifelike harshness.

Abruptly Yasmin turned to look out the windows, and saw that the pea soup fog they had passed through before entering the tunnel, had moved in, obscuring everything outside the windows in a thick blanket of white.

Suddenly he was standing next to her. She could almost feel the heat from his body strike the cool flesh of her bare arm. He bent his head and kissed her lightly on the cheek.

'*Ma petite*, why don't you rest, and have a bath before dinner,' he said softly. 'My room is right next to yours, and if you should need me for anything, just knock. It's unlocked.' He gestured briefly to a narrow oaken door set in the wall next to the wardrobe. 'I'll come for you at seven, and we'll have drinks and dinner downstairs.'

He backed out of the door, his eyes still locked on hers and his expression unreadable. Feeling just like a bird before a snake, Yasmin did not move until several seconds after she heard the gentle click of the door catch slipping into the lock. Turning to take stock of her surroundings, she shivered slightly, but it wasn't because she was cold.

Her eyes traveled swiftly around the room, locating a small door next to the bed. Opening it, she discovered that it led into a bathroom that looked as if it had once been a chapel. Perhaps it had actually been the private chapel of whoever lived in this tower room so very long ago, she thought.

The tub was a circle of pink marble set in the center of the floor. Two globular gold faucets sat on the wide, flat edge. There was a delicate oval sink over which hung a gold-leaf oval mirror, and a full-length mirror was set against the wall, reflecting the bathtub and the door to the bedroom in its silvery sheen.

Briskly, Yasmin set the plug and turned on the faucets. She adjusted the temperature, then went back into the bedroom and opened the suitcase André had put on the folding rack. She took out the dress she would wear, hung it in the wardrobe, and returned to the bathroom, where the tub was close to overflowing. She quickly shut off the water and stripped away her skirt and blouse.

Steam filled the room as she pinned her thick dark masses of hair up on top of her head. Catching a glimpse of herself in the mirror, arms upraised, she turned slowly, allowing her eyes to wander the length of her body. Her breasts were delicately shaped small mounds of flesh, balanced lightly on her rib cage. The length of her smooth flat stomach was indented with a shallow line that ran down to her belly button, and her hips were rounded curves that showed the faint outlines of her pelvis underneath. Her smoothly muscled legs, like those of a dancer, ended in small, shapely feet. Cupping one breast in her hand, she wondered whether André had someone he was in love with. Suddenly it seemed very important to her to know whether there was someone in his life at the moment who was prettier . . . more worldly . . . more sophisticated. Perhaps that was why he had stayed so far away from her. Probably, she told herself. It would certainly explain why he had avoided her so carefully. Even now he seemed distant – nervous in her presence. But, of course, there was no way to know. She couldn't just ask him about his love life, could she?

Yasmin stood, gazing in the mirror until the slight chill in the air raised goose bumps on her flesh. Then she lowered herself into the steaming water, relaxing for the first time since the day before. Soaping herself quickly, afraid that she wouldn't be ready when André knocked on her door, she pushed from her mind the worries that plagued her. After rinsing herself, she stepped out of the tub, and reaching for one of the fluffy white towels, was delighted to find that it had been warmed by the heated towel rack.

Rubbing her skin briskly until it began to glow with a rosy tint, Yasmin took the dress she'd decided to wear out of the wardrobe. She had bought it thinking it would be light and cool for hot summer evenings. Now, at the top of a snowcapped mountain, it was anything but hot outside. The white chiffon skirt fell just below the knee in five scalloped layers of sheer fabric. It reminded her of the curls of sea foam left high on the beach after the waves had receded. The bodice, also five sheer layers of fabric, bared her collarbones and then dripped off the shoulder.

Looking at herself in the glass, Yasmin decided to

leave her hair pinned up. It looked more grown-up, more sophisticated. As she put the tiny pearl earrings into her pierced ears, tendrils of hair escaped at her temples and the nape of her neck. Yasmin tried to make them obey, but they continually arched out, giving her face a soft, gaminlike quality.

Then, rummaging through her things, she found her traveling clock buried in the bottom of her suitcase. Seeing that it was almost seven, she quickly yanked her white sandals out of the suitcase and slid her feet under the delicate satin straps. After a year of practicing, with Hillary's hysterical guidance, she'd finally mastered the higher heels. Yasmin went into the bathroom to examine her reflection in the full-length bathroom mirror and was pleased to see the effect of the added height she'd gained with the slender pointed shoes. She looked tall and slim, she thought, almost like the models in the fashion magazines.

Pleased, with nothing to do but wait, she seated herself on the plumply quilted bedspread, when there was a light knock on the door. Before she could answer it, André pushed it open and stood framed by the arch. He stared at her. For a moment she was afraid she'd chosen the wrong dress. He was much more casual than she was. Under the black silk shantung suit, he was wearing a snowy white turtleneck shirt. But then he smiled, and her worries evaporated. Involuntarily her breath caught as his dark blue eyes swept over her. But his look of dark possessiveness lasted only a second.

'Come, *chérie*. You look lovely,' he said as his eyes became bland once more. Holding his hand out to her, he led her from the room.

When they stepped out of the elevator and walked into the dining room, Yasmin had the odd sensation that the entire castle was deserted but for the two of them. Then the maître d' materialized at André's elbow and led them past the empty tables into an alcove at the far side of the opulent room.

The long windows looked peculiar, and she realized they were blanketed in white. The fog had moved in with all its enveloping majesty, and the light from the tall silver candelabra in the center of the table reflected softly off the glass panes. Yasmin glanced around at the two huge fireplaces, where crackling blazes danced, casting shadows around the room. The tapestries on the walls receded into the flittering shadows.

'Would you like something to drink?' André asked as the waiter appeared next to the table.

'Perhaps a gin and tonic,' she said, trying to sound sophisticated.

'I thought we'd have champagne,' said André. 'In honor of your graduation . . . to celebrate how well you did in school.'

'Oh, yes, that would be lovely. Of course.'

Glancing over the wine list, André frowned, then said, 'The Perrier-Jouet, 1929, *s'il vous plaît*. And would you also bring us a basket of cherries?'

The waiter nodded briefly, and disappeared.

'You know, not one of these people looks the slightest bit like a Cistercian monk,' whispered Yasmin, nodding her head in the direction of the disappearing waiter.

Surprised for a moment, André did not answer. But then his delighted laugh filled the room.

'None of them are, *chérie*,' he said finally. 'They are hired by the monks to run the hotel. The monks only do this to raise money for the order. They don't wait on tables.'

'It's a lucky thing they're monks with a vow of poverty,' she said, glancing at the empty tables. 'Because they certainly aren't going to make much money. There's nobody here.'

'Don't worry. This is the middle of the week, and it's

84

the very beginning of the season. Right now I don't think there is anyone here but us. But by midsummer this place will be crowded with people. I suspect that poverty is the least of their worries.'

The waiter returned carrying a deep silver tureen filled with ice. He lifted the bottle, wrapped in snowy linen, gently out of the tureen. Partially unwinding the cloth, he held it up for André's approval. After André's nod, the waiter proceeded to slowly unwrap the wires and peel the lead down over the cork. Deftly pressing the cork upward with his thumbs, he extracted it before it flew across the room. This done, he held the cork out to André, who sniffed it briefly and nodded again. Then sparkling liquid bubbled into their long-stemmed glasses. André slowly raised his glass, sniffed it, and took a small sip. Finally he nodded his approval, and then raising his glass to her, murmured, 'To you, my little desert flower.'

Yasmin raised her glass and smiled at him across the rim. The bubbles, maddened by their sudden freedom, fizzed up and tickled her nose. She watched as he drank deeply, before she took her first sip. His eyes never left hers, and again she felt herself drawn deep into a slowly whirling abyss. But for some reason, this time it didn't frighten her. She took another long sip.

'Now I'm going to show you something,' André said, reaching for the basket of cherries. Carefully he pulled off the stems and dropped them, one at a time, into her glass. As each cherry sank and then resurfaced, it became covered with bubbles. Finally, when the last cherry bobbed up and no more would fit on the flat surface of the champagne, he dropped in one more. It sank down, collected is bubbles, and then came to rest underneath the layer of cherries already there.

'Now watch,' he said. The last cherry pushed its way up, displacing another cherry, which was pushed down to take its place; then that one pushed its way up, forcing down yet another cherry. Delighted, she watched as the cherries in the glass fought over which one was going on the top.

'How does that happen?' she asked, smiling with pleasure.

'Elementary, *chérie*. The bubbles are all rising. As the cherry that is underneath is coated with more and more bubbles, it becomes lighter than the ones above it. It pushes to the top, and the same thing happens over and over again, as another cherry is forced down and coated with bubbles. You see, in nature, things are always in balance, and when an imbalance exists, it is always righted.'

'You are a philosopher,' said Yasmin, smiling as she lowered her eyes. 'And are things that way in life too?'

'Only sometimes, it seems,' he said grimly, reaching across the white tablecloth and taking her hand in his. 'Now tell me about all the things you learned. I want you to tell me everything you left out of your letters.'

'But I didn't leave anything out,' Yasmin said.

A sharp feeling of incomprehension made her frown slightly. What was he asking her? Suddenly he was so serious, Yasmin felt the abrupt shift in the tenor of their conversation almost as if it were a physical blow. The blue of his eyes had changed to a smoky violet, and the tension around him was almost palpable. For a moment she had the feeling that he was seeing her as a piece of property he had neglected, but was rediscovering. She felt the tentacles of his proprietary interest in her start to wrap themselves around her from across the table.

Why, it's almost as if he's checking up on me, she thought briefly. But the thought passed. If he'd been so interested in what she did, he would have kept her closer. No, it must be something else, she thought.

But what could it be? Yasmin knew that there had been a gulf between them ever since that first night in his villa, but she had always been at a loss to figure out what had caused it. The only answer she'd ever arrived at was that it was something she'd done, something about her that had driven him away. She started to withdraw from him, and pull back inside. She had the sinking feeling that somehow she was about to do it again, whatever it was. He seemed almost angry, and she didn't know why.

'You left nothing out?' he said. 'Are you sure?'

'Of course I'm sure.' Yasmin took another drink of the champagne. She felt as if the bubbles were going straight up into her head instead of down her throat. André's eyes seemed to bore into her.

'Really?' he said, turning her hand over in his, but not releasing it. 'But I thought perhaps you might have made some interesting friends . . . or met a nice young man.'

Unable to remove her hand from his grasp, Yasmin laughed, suddenly nervous at his touch.

'Boys!' she exclamed. 'If only you knew how difficult it was to meet boys! Most of the girls at school were wild to meet some, but Madame watched us like a hawk. That's why they all called her the Hawk, you know.'

'Did they?' André chuckled, and relaxed his grasp on her fingers.

Yasmin sighed gratefully. His grip had gotten tighter and tighter as he questioned her, though perhaps he'd been unaware of it. Now he lightly ran his thumb across her palm. His smile looked dangerous, and made her uneasy.

'And did any of them manage to escape her watchful eye?'

'Only one or two ever tried to sneak out,' answered Yasmin, unable to drag her eyes from his. 'The more desperate ones.'

'And were they successful?'

'I guess they were,' she answered, still nervous. Why did he keep questioning her in this funny way? Did he think she was one of the ones who would occasionally sneak out of the window in the middle of the night? That she had –

'And did *you* ever sneak out?' he asked, his voice low and his eyes narrow.

Yasmin was tongue-tied when she saw the look on his face. But the waiter rescued her when he returned to fill their empty glasses and asked if they were ready to order yet.

'Not yet,' André snapped peremptorily, his thumb tracing light circles on Yasmin's palm. 'But we will have another bottle, if you please.'

He quickly drained his glass.

'Perhaps *you* felt like escaping now and then? It's only natural for young girls to do that, yes?'

Yasmin took another sip, and gazing at him, suddenly realized what was troubling him. He thought she had spent her three years at school chasing after excitement. A small laugh shook her shoulders as she smiled up at him.

'Escape? But I never wanted to escape. I liked it very much at Lautremont. The only thing I missed was seeing you. Why didn't you ever visit me, or have me come home for the *vacances*?'

The waiter returned with another bottle of champagne, filling their glasses once again. André adroitly avoided answering the question by asking him what was recommended for dinner.

'I would suggest the *chevreau rôti aux herbes*, the *foie gras de canard en brioche*, or the *assiette de poissons blancs*. That is a combination of bass, young turbot, and gray sole.'

'We will have the fish,' André answered, 'with *escargots* as the hors d'oeuvre.'

Yasmin was thankful that he'd ordered for her, because

her head was becoming increasingly fuzzy from the champagne. Inexperienced in drinking alcohol, she gazed happily at the pleasant haze that filled the room.

André continued to question her about her studies, the other girls, and how she had enjoyed her summer tours. He jumped from one subject to the next with alarming speed. She couldn't remember what her answers were, but as she ate and sipped at her champagne, she thought with a guilty giggle that it felt just like an examination at school. She wondered whether she would get a passing grade.

And then suddenly André was standing beside her, holding her elbow, escorting her out of the dining room and into the little elevator. As they stepped out onto the landing, she was overcome by a wave of vertigo. She sagged against his arm as she felt herself begin to whirl down a cone of light.

'I think what you need is a little fresh air,' he said, putting his arm around her waist to prevent her from falling. He slid the key into the door and pushed it open with his foot. Inside, she saw that someone had come and laid a fire in the fireplace. The flames cast the only light in the room, and darting shadows crept along the walls. André marched her across the room without a glance at the shadows, and flung open the long windows that opened onto the balcony. A blast of moist air struck her face, and she felt her head begin to clear.

'We'll stand out here until you feel a little better,' he said, leading her to the edge of the walled parapet.

Yasmin leaned her elbows on the wall. But when she saw the sheer drop below her, she abruptly pulled back and found herself nestled in André's strong arms. Leaning her head back against his chest, she felt his arms encircle her tightly. Then she felt him release her, but it was only for a second. He turned her around to face him, his arm around her waist like an iron band. With his other hand he tilted her chin up. His voice, soft and hissing, rasped across her nerve endings.

'Shall it be now, *ma fleur*?'

Before she could figure out what he meant, his mouth came down on hers, enveloping, rapacious, draining away what little strength she'd held in reserve. Yasmin felt her mind begin to fade away as the sensations in her body took over. A knot of desire was building deep within her, consuming her insides and replacing them with a writhing feeling close to pain in its intensity. She became aware of a hardness pressing against her pelvis, and involuntarily felt her legs begin to part, welcoming, straining to receive him. André's mouth on hers was demanding as his hands slid across her back, clutching her and pressing her in to him with bruising intensity. He released her mouth and let his lips wander over her neck, down to her collarbone. Then he grasped her head, and she felt the combs that held her hair in place come loose. A cascade of silken curls fell over his hands and down her back. With a shuddering groan he pulled the neckline of her dress down over her shoulder, allowing his lips to capture her pointed nipple. His tongue brushed across it, causing her to exhale suddenly.

Covering her mouth again, he slid his hand down the flatness of her stomach and cupped the mound between her legs. His fingers pressed into the material of her dress and she felt her most sensitive flesh become unaccountably swollen and molten with yearning. Unable to continue and still remain upright, André picked her up in his arms and carried her through the doors. He placed her on the bed without removing his mouth from hers. As she sank back into the depths of down and satin, she felt him slide her dress over her shoulders and down her hips. His mouth traced a pattern across her skin. Then he was no longer touching her, and her eyes flew open. He was standing in the flickering shadows before the fire, removing the gold cuff links from his shirt. His eyes were like hooded sparks. The swirling mists of vertigo that had assaulted her on the landing returned. She felt herself being pulled down into a long black revolving tunnel that was bottomless.

His clothes in a heap on the floor, André lowered himself onto the bed and ran his hand down the silken length of Yasmin's body. Her bare skin was warm, the texture sleek and almost glossy. Bending his head to kiss her pouting lips, he slid his hand down her stomach to cup the yielding warmth between her legs. That's when he became aware of the sound of even breathing from her slightly parted lips and realized that it could only mean one thing.

She had fallen asleep.

Cursing himself for giving her too much to drink, he groaned at his lack of judgment once again. Silently picking up his clothes, he drew the quilt up to cover her slender form and left her dreaming peacefully.

5

For what seemed an interminable length of time, Yasmin continued to fall down the twisting, turning length of tunnel, until finally she was engulfed in welcome blackness. A friendly warmth crept up as she slipped into a deep sleep. But then dreams came. She dreamt of hands touching her lightly and a voice murmuring in her ear. The voice kept repeating her name, whispering softly, as the hands insinuated themselves into more and more private places, probing, searching.

'You must forgive me,' the voice hissed through the mists in her sleepy head. 'But I cannot help loving you. I don't understand this feeling I have when I touch you. The pleasure of it . . .' The voice continued to whisper as the hands touched her breasts, the fingers lightly pinching her nipples. And the swirling mists began to dissolve even though Yasmin fought to stay asleep.

But the insistent mouth, the probing fingers, and the whispering voice didn't go away. They forced her up to the surface of consciousness as she realized vaguely that this was no dream.

Opening her eyes, she saw André's long, muscled body stretched out alongside her. One leg was thrown across hers pinning her to the bed. His head was supported by one hand, and the other was caressing her lightly. At the window the sky was a pale purple, the color right before dawn, the quietest hour of the night.

'So, you are awake, then?' he whispered against her ear. 'I couldn't sleep. I only meant to come in and watch you, but I couldn't help myself.' His lips moved across her cheek then pressed down against her mouth. His hand snaked across her thigh, moving her legs apart, and she could feel him shift his weight so that the length of his hard body rested over half of hers. Suddenly she gasped as he slowly buried his finger inside her, rotating it slightly. But the gasp was muffled by his mouth, alternately gentle then hurtful as his tongue snaked between her teeth. His fingers slid out of her and began to exert a delicious pressure, pinching and stroking as they brought her to a pitch she would not have thought possible.

She moaned softly, drawing her knees up, spreading them and opening for him as he pulled his body over hers. He pressed a hard, hot length against her swollen throbbing flesh for a moment. Then sliding downward, kissing first her breasts, rolling the nipples with his tongue, then probing the ticklish hollow of her belly button, he forced her legs even farther apart with his shoulders. Spreading the sensitive flesh between her legs with his fingers, his tongue thrust hard and demanding against the distended little button nestled there. Yasmin screamed, arching against him, so intense was the pleasure. It was almost pain, and she tried to get away from his flickering tongue and fingers, but he held her immobile as he explored her quivering swollen flesh. Knowing just how long to maintain the pressure and just when to stop for a second, his fingers and tongue moved together, teasing, wandering, prying.

And then just as abruptly, lifting himself over her shuddering length, he tried to push inside her with maddening slowness. But a sharp pain drove all sensation of pleasure from her. She reached for his hips and shoved hard, trying to dislodge the thickness that was causing her so much suffering. But she was pinned, trapped beneath his weight. He withdrew again almost completely, only to thrust into her again. Each time he moved with greater pressure, grinding into her pelvis. And then gradually the pain began to fade. Each thrust was a little less hurtful, until she felt herself beginning to rise to meet them. Feeling the different textures of his body over hers, rough, smooth, hard, pulsing, she was caught up in a vortex of sensation that threatened to fling her off into space. And inside her, every nerve was stretched taut, tingling, shuddering until, with the sudden magnitude of a starburst, she was caught by a spreading flood of pleasure that engulfed her completely, urging her to move her hips in rhythm with him. She was only dimly aware of the sounds André made as he groaned and thrust into her with great shuddering lunges. Then he grew still.

She hadn't noticed the wetness on her cheeks until André's hand came up to gently brush it away.

'I'm sorry if I hurt you, *chérie*,' he said looking at her with concern in his eyes. 'Are you all right?'

Slowly Yasmin returned from the reaches of inner space where she had been whirling out of control. She became aware of the crumpled satin of the quilt beneath her, the bruised throbbing between her legs, and the weight of André's body on hers. Licking her lips slowly, she nodded.

'*Comme tu es belle*,' he murmured, his lips against her forehead. 'You are so lovely this way, with your eyes so velvet, so soft. *Et que je t'aime*.'

She slid her hands down his shoulders, into the muscled hollow of the small of his back, caressing him lightly with her fingertips.

'I was afraid when I saw how beautiful you'd become, that somehow I had lost you,' he continued, his voice hoarse. 'All those young girls were so . . . I don't know how to describe it . . . so flashy and coarse. I was afraid that by sending you away, I'd merely turned you into one of those gum-chewing teenage nymphomaniacs.'

Yasmin began to laugh softly. 'You find them so repulsive?'

94

'No. They're just not like you. The Yasmin I love, that I've loved all this time, has an indefinable grace. It would have been dreadful if you had changed.'

'But I thought I *had* changed.'

'Indeed you have, *ma chére*. But you have lost none of the quality that I love most.'

'Nor have you.'

'Then I didn't frighten you? Hurt you too much?'

'No,' she murmured, turning her face away as she felt a hot flush creep up from her throat. 'I wanted you too. But there was no way I could tell you, let you know. Actually, I didn't know what I wanted. I didn't know it would be like this, but I think my body knew, even if my mind didn't. Do you understand what I mean?'

She shifted slightly under him, and he moaned softly.

'*Mon Dieu!* You are so tight, so velvety.'

He began to swell inside her again, thickening, filling her with a voluptuous hardness that made her gasp.

'Ah, God! You do things to me that I do not understand,' he purred, kissing her harshly. Gripping her hips with his hands, he began to move slowly at first, then more quickly. She stung a bit, but the stinging gave way to a pulsing throb of pleasure. Lifting her slender hips, he slid one of the pillows under her, raising her more effectively for him.

'This time, I want to watch you,' he murmured as he sat back, on his knees. 'The sun is up, so I can see now. I want to see the changes on your face, see the pleasure take you.'

Yasmin flushed scarlet and closed her eyes. Turning her face away from him, she whispered, 'No. Please don't. I am embarrassed.'

But he just continued to move inside her as his hands gently stroked her flesh and tangled in her silken hair. Resting his hand on the mound of her pelvis, he pressed

95

his thumb into the soft, slick flesh. Yasmin opened her eyes and her gaze was caught in his.

Then his breathing grew more ragged, and he thrust harder, deeper. And Yasmin, finally caught up in a spiral of delicious sensation, began to rock with him. Her hands grasped his knees and she tasted the saltiness of his sweat on her lips. Deep within her a pulsing throb began to build, until it became an undulating wave that engulfed her with spasm after spasm.

Later André bathed her in the round pink marble tub, gently soothing her bruised flesh and drying her with the warm towels. Then he ordered breakfast sent up to their room.

A white-coated waiter pushed a small table on wheels across the floor and left it beside the bed. On the snowy linen tablecloth were two dishes covered with silver domes, a silver coffee pot with ebony handles, and two fragile porcelain cups with gilded rims. A small vase of luminous blue glass held a single white rose.

Lifting the silver covers, Yasmin saw that on each plate were three delicate crepes filled with cheese, ham and eggs, a sprinkle of dill on the top.

'This will never be enough,' she sighed. 'I'm starving.'

'Don't worry, love. I also ordered cheese and fruit for you.' André produced a basket from the shelf underneath the table. It was filled with grapes, peaches, raspberries, strawberries, and small blood oranges from Spain. Another held a large wedge of brie and a thick round of camembert, covered by a glass bell.

Sitting naked on the bed while she ate, Yasmin basked in the sun that glowed through the long windows, tinting her flesh golden.

'I don't like to rush you, *chérie*,' said André as he gazed at the sinuous stretch of her legs, 'but I thought we might get started soon. We have some travelling to do before we reach our destination.'

Yasmin yawned luxuriously and stepped off the bed. 'And where are you taking me next, Monsieur le Baron?'

'I am taking you to Picasso's favorite town,' he answered, looking pleased as a cat. 'Mougins. It's about five miles north of Cannes on the Riviera. I thought we would stay at Le Mas Candille. It's in a beautiful park, and I also think it has a swimming pool.'

'Are we close to the Riviera? It seems impossible up in these snowy mountains.'

'Not so close, I'm afraid. It's about a hundred miles, so we have at least a three-hour drive ahead of us.'

The proprietor, at André's request, packed them a snack of fruit, cheese, wine, and a long loaf of French bread. As they drove, winding slowly down the mountain passes and past the incredible vistas of the French Alps, Yasmin alternately nibbled, chattered, and slept. André didn't seem to suffer from the lassitude that overcame Yasmin. She kept drifting in and out of dreams filled with fingers, mouths, and bodies. Periodically she apologized guiltily. But André told her not to worry about it as he smiled at her or reached out to fondle her hair. It's just as well, she thought, coming out of a particularly delicious dream. After all, we can't both be asleep. Someone has to drive the car.

Then suddenly they came out of a pass and below them lay a little town so pretty, it looked like a composition board set for a play.

'It's beautiful!' Yasmin gasped, rubbing the sleep out of her eyes.

'In the ninth and tenth centuries this was a fortified town. That was when the Saracens were marauding their way through France. Then in the eleventh century the Comte d'Antibes gave it to the Lérins monks. The monks made the townspeople pay them tribute, or protection, by bringing grains, fruit, and wine. Food has been of utmost importance in this town ever since. They make a *suprême de volaille* here that is unsurpassed.'

'I can certainly see why Picasso loved it,' said Yasmin, as they entered the flower-splashed town. Everywhere there were clumps of roses and bursts of daisies and geraniums. And behind every bush Yasmin was delighted to see cats, hundreds of cats, stretching themselves languorously in the late afternoon rays of sun. Most of the tiny streets were closed to traffic, so it was with difficulty that André threaded the car through a maze of signs and finally found their hotel.

After they had checked in, Yasmin grabbed up her straw hat and they went off to explore. They walked up the hill of Notre-Dame-de-Vie, which had the same kind of reputation among the faithful as Lourdes. After exploring the church, Yasmin pulled André down a path that followed a gurgling canal winding its way through honeysuckle vines and wild greenery.

'There it is!' said André, pointing to a little house deeply covered in vines. 'You have found it all on your own.'

'Found what?'

'That's Picasso's house, and this must be the Siagne Canal. How delightful.'

'I'm starved,' said Yasmin, suddenly overcome by hunger pangs. She tried to hide a yawn as she realized she was also tired.

'*Mon Dieu*, you are awfully physical! I show you the house of the world's most magnificent artist and all you can think about is your stomach and a nap,' André scolded. Taking her hand, he began to walk back along the path. 'We'll go to this little place called Le Bistro. Maybe you'll get to see a movie star there. It's where many of them eat when they're at the Cannes Film Festival.'

He led her back down into the town and through the

winding streets until they came to an ivy-covered wall. What had looked like a black hole at the bottom of a few steps, turned out to be a door. Brushing the vines away from her head, André ushered Yasmin into a barrel-vaulted stone cave filled wth small tables set with candles and flowers.

Though she stared hard at each of the faces around the bar, she recognized no one. No movie stars today, she thought sadly. But soon she forgot about everyone else, her attention absorbed by André and the *vin d'orange* in her glass.

'Do you like it?' asked André as she sipped at the licorice-flavored cocktail. 'It tastes just like your lips did, the night you first came to me.'

Yasmin blushed furiously as she sipped. She lowered her eyes.

'Every part of you tastes delicious,' he continued, taking hold of her hand. He ran a finger around each of hers, tracing the line of her thumb, the soft pad of her palm. 'Your mouth, behind your ears, your neck, your – '

'Stop it,' Yasmin begged, embarrassed and strangely warm. 'If you talk about it, I won't be able to eat my dinner.'

'Well then, perhaps we'd better order, because when I sit here looking at you, I can only think of one thing,' he said, smiling lazily. 'Perhaps I won't let you finish your dinner at all.'

And it seemed to Yasmin that he indeed was not planning to let her finish the bouillabaisse. His eyes fixed on her, unblinking and unwavering. He held her hand imprisoned in his as his fingers laced patterns on her palm and between her fingers. Frissons of pleasure trickled through her, and she barely tasted the magnificent concoction. She had just swallowed the last of the *gâteau glacé au chocolat*, a cold chocolate mousse, when he pushed back his chair and stood next to her expectantly. As she rose, he slid his arm around her possessively, and his fingertips brushed against her breast as he led her back out into the sparkling, lamplit street.

'Now, it's time for *my* dessert,' he whispered in her ear wickedly, and traced the shell-like curve of her earlobe with his tongue. The sensation bolted through her with devastating force. Yasmin was thankful for his supportive arm around her waist, because her legs threatened to crumble beneath her. She just wanted to lie down and give herself over to the sensations washing through her.

As they walked he kept up a softly whispered litany of what he intended to do to her, all the different ways he would take her, until she thought they would never get back to the hotel. Her knees were trembling violently as he opened the door to their room. Once inside, crushing her to his chest, he stripped off the little silk dress she wore without taking his mouth from hers. Then, when she was finally naked, he held her away from him.

'I knew you would be like this,' he said as his eyes bored into hers. 'These last three years I have waited for this.'

'Then why did you send me away? Why didn't you ever come for me?'

'I wouldn't have been able to keep my hands off you. Don't you see? You were too young then. You didn't want me.'

'Yes I did.'

'Perhaps. But not like this. Then you were a child. Now you are a woman.'

And with that he picked her up and carried her to the bed.

Their drive down the coast of France and over the Pyrenees into Spain was a blur of beautiful vistas by day and long sensuous nights. Exhausted by the nights, Yasmin dozed in the car as drove her from one town to the next, from one bed to the next. They stopped at Beaulieu and Cap Ferrat, where André insisted that she stop at each of the boutiques and buy whatever took her fancy.

'I want you to look like a princess,' he said as she stood before him in a skirt and a double silk crepe de chine blouse unbuttoned practically to her navel. Her reflection shimmered in the long mirror. 'You are a beautiful woman, and you should always wear beautiful things. Now, try this on,' he said, handing her a beguiling black chemise that was all weightless, ruffled silk.

They bought lacy underthings – some quite shocking – and delicate sandals, Yves Saint-Laurent suits, Givenchy and Balenciaga dresses. The trunk of the Mercedes was stacked with boxes as they wandered along Port de Plaisance, stopping at cafés to have champagne framboise and watch the boats in the marina, their fingers intertwined, both suddenly eager to return to the hotel room to make love.

They stopped in Albi, where Toulouse-Lautrec was born, and spent a lazy afternoon in the Toulouse-Lautrec Museum, looking at the sketches and paintings that hung there. And then they went farther south to Carcassonne, a medieval fairy-tale city surrounded by a high wall and sitting on top of a hill.

After leaving Carcassonne they climbed into the Pyrenees, heading for Viella with its old granite houses, shuttered windows, and wooden balconies. The black slate roofs angled in all directions, and behind the town rose the magnificent mountain of Baqueira-Beret.

'Do you ski well, Yasmin?'

'Of course.'

'Would you like to come back here for New Year's and ski this mountain?' André asked as they drove down. Yasmin nodded enthusiastically, thinking how very lucky she was.

'There is a wonderful New Year's Eve celebration on the slopes that you would probably enjoy.'

'I'd probably enjoy anything as long as it was with you.'

'Anything?'

'Yes, anything.'

He still didn't understand how she felt about him, she realized, knowing she would enjoy living anywhere if he was with her. Even though they were spending all their time together in this delicious idyll, Yasmin often wondered what André had planned for her. Did he even know? His mention of going skiing with her in the winter had been the first time he'd said anything concrete to her about the future. Perhaps he thought there was no need to articulate it, that she was supposed to sit back and let everything just wash over her. But she couldn't help but wonder if he was planning to keep her as his mistress or to introduce her to all his friends as his future wife.

The word wife made her shrink inside. André would want to marry a woman from his own class, she suddenly thought, filled with misery, not a little Arab girl from the Rif. Perhaps he had a woman who was just right, waiting for him in Tangier. Perhaps that woman was aching inside right now, wondering where he was and who he was with. Maybe she was beautiful and intelligent, and loved him just as much as Yasmin did.

She was abruptly filled with an overpowering wave of longing. Even if this was just a side trip for him, she thought – a side trip in every possible way – as long as he kept her close to him and loved her a little, she would always love him. How could she feel otherwise? she asked herself. Wouldn't any woman feel the same way? And Yasmin wondered what the other women in his life had been like, but she still couldn't bring herself to ask him.

Driving out of the mountains, they crossed eastern Spain and spent several days in Valencia. There, Yasmin

102

was amazed at the merging of expected, and unexpected delights. Along with the factory smokestacks, there were orange groves, crowds, paella, and sangria. On the Calle de Caballeros she saw the palaces of grand families with liveried servants standing outside. There were Flemish paintings, Baroque churches, and monumental gates. And there were beaches, the overwhelming noise of traffic, and the women who deftly held fans before their faces as they sat in cafés, gazing at men whose dark, classic features and hooded eyes made them look like birds of prey.

Each night she slid into the other world she inhabited, the world that didn't show to people they passed in the street in the brilliant light of day. That world was a black cavern of pleasure, which seemed to take all rational thought and send it reeling off, to be replaced with pure physical sensation. Although they ate lunch in magnificent restaurants – delicious arrays of the most exquisite food – they spent most nights alone in the closed circle of whatever hotel room they happened to be in. The rooms blended in her mind, as did the food delivered by discreet room-service waiters. Sometimes they collected fruits, cheese, and wines on their excursions during the day, bringing them back to feast on at intervals during the long, luscious nights of exploring each other's bodies.

It was when they finally drove into Algeciras that Yasmin felt an inexplicable sadness envelop her as she gazed across the Straits. This idyll would soon end, and they would be thrust back into the real world of André's friends, André's life. The demands of business would intrude on their days, and the nights wouldn't be the same.

'What is it, little one?' asked André, concerned at her withdrawal. They had just checked into the Reina Christina and were downstairs for an evening drink on the main terrace. The late afternoon sun was hot, and the

103

light breeze springing off the bay brought with it the scents from the garden below – luxuriant hibiscus, magnolias, and bougainvillea. A band was playing at the end of the terrace. The lilting sounds were reminiscent of the 1930s. Since it was so warm, Yasmin wore only white moire pants and a soft gold mesh jacket with short wide sleeves. The little pearl earrings that were always in her ears, like drops of dew on a morning glory, glittered in the cloud of thick dark hair that hung loose and flowing.

'Nothing,' she said, lowering her head so he couldn't read her thoughts the way he always seemed to. 'It's just that I don't want this to ever end.'

'And why should it end, *ma petite fleur*?'

'Tomorrow we will go back to Tangier, that's why it will end,' she said quietly. 'That's when you will go back to your life, and I will somehow have to learn to fit mine into yours.'

'But isn't that what you want?'

'Yes, that's the only thing I want. But it might not be as easy as you think. This trip is not exactly a replica of our real lives. It is removed, set apart from everyday things. It is the everyday things I'm afraid of. It is all your friends and what they will think of me, that frightens me,' she confessed.

'But you have no reason to fear them, *chérie*. It isn't as if you have come straight from the Medina, you know. That's why I sent you to Lautremont, or one of the reasons, at least. Don't worry. You will handle them all with ease. Believe me, they will be no match for you, your loveliness, or your cleverness.'

'It is easy for you to say,' she mumbled.

'You have stage fright, love, that's all,' he said, stroking her bare arm inside the elbow. 'And besides, I will always be there with you. I will protect you from all the beasts of prey that you seem to think are waiting to feast on you.'

Yasmin laughed. 'You make me feel so silly, but I suppose you're right. Beasts of prey? What kind of people do they let into your clubs? I thought they were supposed to be very exclusive.'

'They are very exclusive,' said André as he gently placed a kiss behind her ear. 'They only let in beasts of prey, the kind that eat delicious young girls like you. I've had a few conversations with them, and that's all they talk about.'

'I'll bet that's all they talk about,' said Yasmin, smiling.

'There is one thing I've neglected to tell you all this time,' André whispered, his breath hot on the side of her face. 'I happen to be a beast of prey myself. That's what I wanted you for – to devour, to feast on.' He bit her earlobe hard. Yasmin shivered at the sharp pain that somehow blended into pleasure. 'I intend to start here with your sweet ears and then work my way down as the evening progresses.'

Yasmin felt herself begin to slip out of the gloom. The fears she'd experienced ever since they'd set foot in Algeciras and she'd caught sight of the Rock of Gibraltar, began to slip away. It seemed André could drive almost any thought out of her head with the ease of a hunter, scattering frightened birds up into the sky. And all with his mouth. He had only to touch his lips to her hand, her wrist, her cheek, and she was transformed into an odalisque, existing just for his pleasure. She wondered how long that could possibly last, that constant descent out of free will, her knees weakening, her body turned to molten heat. But then she could no longer resist the pressure of his mouth on her flesh, and she opened her lips as he placed a raspberry into her mouth from the *confit de fruits* set on their table. With a smile he ran the tip of his finger around the delicately molded contours.

'But every condemned prisoner gets to enjoy a last meal,' he said, his eyebrows arched lightly. 'Let's go to

El Meson. I want every man to see you just like this, with your eyes so wanton, and know that you are mine, that you belong to me, and that I am going to take you back to my bed and make love to you all night long.'

They walked through the streets into the old part of Algeciras. The old town was an atmospheric little confine that smelled and looked like the sordid nest of pirates and spies it had once been. Inside the restaurant, freed from the hungry gazes of the dark-eyed unruly denizens of the streets, he ordered Cazuela de Langosta. He cracked the spiny lobsters open, and after dipping the sweet white flesh into the cup of butter, fed her by hand as if she were an exotic bird. After each mouthful she licked the excess butter from his fingertips, causing his eyes to glow harshly, his breath to come in short rasps.

'Ah, what you do to me, *mon amour*. I don't know if I will be able to stand up without causing a sensation,' he said, glancing down at his lap ruefully. 'I'd better wait a bit before we leave, to collect myself.'

'The executioner awaits his own execution,' said Yasmin, a sly glint in her eyes. She captured his hand across the table and slowly sucked his thumb into her mouth. Her eyes glittered as she watched the play of expressions across André's face.

'I don't care if you cause a sensation,' she whispered. 'Take me back – now.'

André stood slowly, took out his wallet and dropped a five-thousand peseta note on the table. The waiter, hovering nearby, smiled a knowing smile as he watched them leave the restaurant. It did his heart good to see lovers in such heat they had to get up and leave before they'd finished their dinner. The men always left much bigger tips because they weren't thinking straight, either. The bill would have come to, perhaps three-thousand-five-hundred pesetas. But when a man is thinking with his cojones, not his head, he rounds it off to the next highest

106

denomination. Yes, he thought with a smile, love is a wonderful thing.

Halfway back through the lamplit streets, Yasmin suddenly stopped. 'Kiss me again,' she said softly, pulling André into a dark, recessed doorway. 'I don't want to wait until we get back to the room.'

Groaning, André lifted his hands to her head. Running his fingers through her hair, he grabbed two handfuls of it and pulled her head back, baring her throat. His tongue traced the delicate line from her shoulder to her ear, and then his mouth found hers as he pressed her into the studded oak door. One of the iron studs was pressing against her back, but she didn't even notice it as his tongue thrust into her mouth, snaking along the roof of her mouth. His lips enveloped hers, sucking gently and then harder. His teeth cut against her flesh, making her insides melt. Pulling away from her a second, André allowed himself to gaze into her eyes. He began to lose himself in the soft, absorbing depths, then kissed her eyelids gently. But Yasmin ached for his lips on hers. Taking hold of his head, she pulled his mouth back down and sucked his bottom lip in between her teeth. Her pointed tongue rasped across the flesh, teasing lightly.

André gripped her more tightly as he pulsed into hardness against her body. He slid his hands down her back until they cupped her buttocks, then he raised her slightly so she could feel the hard length pushing between her legs. With a moan Yasmin lifted her leg slightly so she was balanced on the ball of one foot, and rubbed herself against him. She felt the wetness soak into her panties.

'Take me now,' she moaned. 'Now. There's no one who will see.'

'*Mon Dieu*, Yasmin. I can't do that – just because there's no one on the street now, doesn't mean someone might not pass.'

'I don't care,' she keened. Her breath was coming quickly as she rubbed herself rhythmically against him.

André slid his hand up the inside of her thigh and stroked her skin in long, smooth sweeps.

'Oh, please, André . . . please, I beg you . . .'

Her legs quivered uncontrollably as he moved his hand up until it touched the elastic around her leg, then he ran his thumb along the outside of the damp silk underwear. Rubbing lightly on the outside of her panties, the wet material clung to the folds of her flesh, almost feeling like flesh itself. Yasmin raised her leg higher to give his hand easier access, then André's mouth came back down on hers. He sucked at her lips, pulling at first the upper and then the lower one. He matched the rhythm of his mouth with the rhythm of his fingers, and Yasmin began to rock back and forth against his hand, arching her body.

His mouth muffled her thin wail of delight as he pulled the wet material away from her, insinuating first one, then two fingers inside. Tugging lightly at the crinkly hair on her mound, he slowly delved into the slick folds of flesh, rubbing and teasing the delicate lips apart. Yasmin's breath drew in sharply as she tried to shift herself so his fingers would find the spot that screamed for his attention. His thumb finally grazed against the swollen flesh he was looking for, and gripping her hard so she wouldn't fall, he began to rasp his finger across it, first back and forth, then in slow, delicious circles. With deliberate care he shifted her body so her side was pressed against his chest, allowing him free range of movement. Still holding her head with handfuls of long silken hair that fell across his wrist, he bent her backward. With his mouth still covering hers, his tongue traced slow, achingly sensitive patterns on her swollen lips. Arching even farther, Yasmin's fingers bit into his shoulders as he tugged and played with her flesh. Abruptly, her quivering turned to great quaking shudders as she screamed her pleasure into his mouth.

André felt the shudders against his hand, and as she opened, he thrust two fingers inside the warm, enveloping folds of her body repeatedly. Her hips thrust back and forth as the throbbing slit sought to suck his fingers deeper and deeper.

'Come inside me,' she moaned softly. 'Your fingers aren't enough. I want . . . I want – '

'Not here, my love. This will have to satisfy you for the moment,' he said, rolling his fingers inside her as the shudders calmed. 'I'll give you a minute to rest, and then I'm taking you back to the room. You forget – I, too, have needs in this relationship.'

Holding her gently, André slipped his hand out of her clothing and sucked slowly on his fingers. 'Umm,' he said with a wicked smile. 'Now come back with me. I still haven't had my dessert.'

Even though her legs were weak, André propelled her back through the streets. The sudden bright lights in the lobby made her blink her eyes closed. But no one seemed to notice her tousled hair and sleepy look as they got into the elevator and rode up, staring at the silent back of the elevator operator.

That night they did not sleep at all. Fed by Yasmin's anxiety, her nerves raw and taut, she teased at him, arousing him again and again, pushing him to take her back to that mindless place he'd shown her. The fear of returning to Tangier made her ravenous and clinging.

Late the next afternoon they packed the car and drove to Tarifa where they would catch the evening boat across the Straits of Gibraltar to Tangier. As Yasmin looked up at the Castle of Tarifa calmly gazing out across the Mediterranean, the Moorish architecture brought back a fresh torrent of the fears she'd had in Algeciras. But this time she said nothing to André. She kept her face carefully masked.

'You see that castle up there?' he said as they waited for the boat. 'There is a gruesome story attached to it. The Spanish commander, Alonzo Perez de Guzman, sacrificed his young son, who was being held hostage during a long siege in the thirteenth century. He said that he "preferred honor without a son, to a son with dishonor." He outlasted the siege, and his descendants later became the Dukes of Medina-Sidonia.'

'How cruel!'

'Much of history is the story of human cruelties.'

But before she could comment on his cynical answer, it was time to board. Yasmin gazed out at the white walls of Tangier, resting like a glittering tiara of pearls and diamonds on the opposite coast. The wind riffled through her hair, and she thought she could smell the familiar scents of the Medina wafting across the miles separating them from the country where she had been born.

It was much better to be coming back like this, of course; better than the way she'd left. But still she trembled. It would have been even better not to be going back at all, she thought. How she would have loved to stay in Europe, living anywhere but Tangier. There were too many memories, too many old associations, like rotten fruit forgotten in the corner of a cupboard. How easy André thinks it will be for me to just slip into his life, she thought. The old terror began to grip her as she wondered how she would ever deal with those people. Would they accept her? Did they already know who she was and where she'd come from? Probably. And if they did, wouldn't they be cruel? Probably. She shivered and longed for Lautremont. At least there she'd been safe. Everyone thought she was André's daughter. They would think no such thing in Tangier.

But then André's arm slipped around her and he hugged her tightly against his side, sending his warmth into her body, calming her for the moment. She leaned her head against his shoulder and tried not to give in to the strange shiver of apprehension that crawled up her back.

Suddenly he pulled away from her. Looking down into her troubled eyes, he started to smile. 'There was one little thing I wanted to ask of you,' he said softly.

'Anything.'

'Would you mind awfully marrying me, Yasmin? I know I'm much older than you are, but it would make me so very, very happy if you would be my wife.'

'Mind?' Yasmin felt a euphoric laugh bubble up inside of her. 'How could I possibly mind? I love you more than life itself.'

'You don't have to answer me now, darling. Think about it. Meet my friends, fit yourself into my life, and then decide if that's what you want.'

'I know now. That's what I want.'

'But it may not be what you want in a few months. I just wanted to know if you would consider it.'

'In a few months I'll only want you more, not less.'

He hugged her, and Yasmin smiled happily. Then the engines rumbled and the boat slowly backed out into the harbor. Turning in a half circle, it began to ply its way through the rosy evening sky, the waves slapping against the bow.

6

The waves danced before the pointed prow of the boat, and the lights ahead of them got brighter as Yasmin and André stood on deck watching. Leaning against the rail, they watched the rose of the sunset turn violet. Then it swiftly gave way to night, fading into dark velvety blue. The stars began to come out. It almost looked as if the brilliant lights of Tangier had been flung up to fill the sky.

A full moon hung low over the black mountains of Africa, and the sky turned brilliant with its light. High on the cliff Yasmin could see the flashing of the lighthouse. Now and then the boat hit choppy water. As the warmer currents of the Mediterranean hit the colder ones of the Atlantic, the waves would slap against the sides with an angry sound.

Then the pier could be seen clearly, the small figures moving quickly about growing larger and larger. The boat reversed its engines and slowly came alongside the dock. Yasmin watched the men below who were catching the heavy lines thrown down by the sailors on board. They skillfully made the boat fast against the dock.

It was then that Yasmin realized she hadn't heard Arabic spoken in three years. She had certainly thought in Arabic now and then. But increasingly, as she got closer to Madame Duchamp and Hillary, she had begun to think in French and speak in English. How far away and long ago school seemed. In the short space of two weeks Yasmin felt as if she had become another person – a person who might even become bored with Hillary's chatter.

As she watched the men begin to roll the ramps down to the dock, and listened to their guttural voices, a flood of longing for Lautremont and Hillary washed over her. What a safe haven it had been. There she had finally been given the chance to be a carefree child, a notion they only had in rich Western countries. Here in Tangier there were no carefree children.

What a pleasure it had been to sink into the ivory tower world of studying, basking in silliness with other girls her own age. But that was over now. They waited in the Mercedes as the cars ahead of them were maneuvered into position to drive off the boat. A stream of bodies was spilling off the passenger ramps and into the line of waiting taxis. Small boys were hawking their services as guides to the tourists, and the taxi drivers were fighting in loud, high-pitched voices for the attention of potential riders. Even though it was late, it seemed the city was pulsing and lively, just beginning to move after a slow day of waiting for the heat to lift.

Over the salt and fish smell of the harbor Yasmin could detect the smell of meat and the perfume of flowers. Her nostrils quivered as she realized how close she was to the Medina. With a shiver she fought against the memories that accosted her along with the smell.

Then it was their turn to be guided out of the boat, and André slowly maneuvered the Mercedes down the ramp and out onto the noisy, busy dock. Avoiding the crowds that scurried alongside and in front of the car, they were finally out of the mayhem and on the streets of Tangier. André swiftly drove past the station and headed around the western side of the Medina. He passed the Grand Socco and went straight up the mountain road. Yasmin gazed out the window in silence.

Her altered perception made the sights and sounds that assaulted her senses seem new and wondrous. She remembered Madame's favorite saying: '*Plus ça change, plus ça reste la meme.*' At the time Yasmin hadn't understood. It was Madame's way of telling them that growing up changes everything, when in fact, nothing has changed. Yasmin now felt the real meaning of that phrase as she looked at all the sights – so familiar, yet so foreign at the same time. The city hadn't changed, but she definitely had.

And then they made their way up along the coastline, the bent cypresses on one side and the mountains on the other, until the car slipped through the gate. Zayd held it open for them, then closed it behind the car as they pulled in front of the villa. André jumped out, threw the keys to Zayd, then went around to open the door for Yasmin.

Zayd hadn't changed at all. If time had passed, it seemed to have passed Zayd by. He still wore a gray djellaba, and his hooked nose and low forehead with its heavy brow ridges were no more lined than when she'd first seen him. His expression was also the same. Yasmin assumed that he knew everything about her and wasn't pleased to see her back. Typical Arab male behavior, she thought grimly, determined not to let it get to her.

As she stepped out of the car, she smiled at Zayd. She thought she saw a flicker of distaste cross his face as he nodded, acknowledging her greeting. But then his usual impassive expression quickly replaced it. Yasmin wondered if perhaps the look had been only her imagination, but decided it hadn't been her imagination at all. She had seen that expression many times – usually on her grandfather's face. But this time it was going to be different, she told herself. This time she was coming into the house as a woman who would give orders, not as a woman who would take them. It would be very difficult for Zayd to deal with. It would be difficult for her too. Yasmin wondered if she *could* deal with it. The way she felt at that moment, she didn't think so.

As Zayd opened the trunk and removed the luggage, André led Yasmin into the house, to the main foyer, with the long curving stairway ahead of them.

'Would you like anything to eat or drink before we go to bed?' asked André, stopping in front of the library door.

'No, thank you,' she said, subdued. 'I'm exhausted, and I think maybe I prefer to deal with all this after a good night's sleep. Strange memories have awakened. If I have one more thought about being back and what it all means, I will have a nervous collapse.' She attempted what she hoped would pass for a lighthearted smile, since she didn't want André to see how depressed she felt. But he seemed to notice nothing.

'Well, I think I'll have a drink sent upstairs. Zayd will have the bags in here in a moment, but we'll leave the unpacking for tomorrow.'

'Why, look. My trunks and boxes from school got here before we did,' said Yasmin, noticing them carefully stacked in the corner near the big door.

'They didn't take the scenic route,' chuckled André. 'You can deal with those tomorrow too. One more day in the foyer won't hurt them.'

'I bet it hurts Zayd to have them sitting there, though,' she said with a tired smile. But she was thinking that it probably hurt Zayd even more to have her back in the villa.

'What makes you say that?' said André, looking at her sharply.

'Nothing, really. It's just that he is so very neat. I feel as if each thing that is out of place, or not where it belongs, bothers him immensely.'

'That's why he is such a good butler. I wouldn't have hired him otherwise.' Yasmin saw that he obviously didn't catch the double meaning in her words.

Just then Salima appeared from the doorway to the

kitchen. Yasmin noted that she looked older and seemed to have lost weight. Her blue and white striped underdress hung on her shoulders, the warm brown eyes appeared to have sunk a bit in their sockets, and her high, wide cheekbones were more prominent. But the apron Salima always wore wrapped around her midriff hid any changes that might have occurred in her waistline. Her face was more lined than Yasmin remembered. Salima started to smile broadly when she saw André, then stopped abruptly at the sight of Yasmin.

Yasmin had often longed to be back in the villa, back with André. She had spent three years fantasizing about how wonderful it would be when she finally returned, and to her, Salima represented home and the closest thing to a mother that Yasmin had left. She'd forgotten that Salima had never warmed to her, had never wanted to talk with her or make friends with her.

With a cry of delight, Yasmin quickly crossed the space that separated them, flinging her arms around the older woman with unrestrained warmth. At first Salima was taken aback by the young girl's obvious happiness to see her. Salima's arms hung at her sides. But then Yasmin's enthusiasm communicated itself to the woman, and she had no choice but to hug Yasmin back.

'Oh, Salima,' Yasmin said softly. 'I'm so glad to be home.'

It was a delicate moment, and in another place between other women, it might have worked out differently. But in Morocco there is an unspoken community among women, who are faced with the same insurmountable obstacles presented by the exclusively male-dominated culture. And, too, Salima's basic, strong motherly instincts – the ones she focused on André – finally overcame any reservations she might have had about this motherless girl who had been dropped into her household.

'Mmm,' Salima mumbled as she rocked the slender

116

body against her. She was not quite ready to let go of her position, yet was unable to resist the affectionate warmth that poured from Yasmin. 'You must be tired. You must be hungry. Go upstairs . . . I will make you something. Zayd will bring it to you.'

Then, pushing Yasmin gently away from her, she turned – almost embarrassed – and disappeared into the kitchen. Yasmin noticed that André had already started up the stairs, and quickly caught up with him, and followed him up the curving staircase. When she reached the landing, he slipped his arm around her and led her into the room that had been his.

'You will keep your things in your room, but I want you to keep yourself in my room,' he said, lightly kissing her on the forehead. 'If it's all right with you, that is.'

'I would be delighted,' Yasmin said, snuggling into his arms, relaxing in their familiar comfort.

'Ah, you rub against me like a kitten.'

There was a low knock on the door, and Zayd came in with the suitcases.

'Would you please take Yasmin's bags into her room,' said André. 'And also, bring me a scotch and water when you're through. I could use a drink. Oh, yes, and take all those boxes into her room too.'

Zayd nodded, and avoiding Yasmin's eyes, picked up her things and left the room. Then André collapsed in the Morocco leather chair near the window and rubbed a hand over his eyes.

'I don't know why I feel so tired,' he said as he leaned back against the chair.

Concerned, Yasmin stepped behind him and massaged his neck and shoulders. 'I don't know why you don't know,' she laughed huskily. 'I think you have stayed up all day and all night for the last two weeks.'

'Don't be silly. Umm, that feels good. I went to bed when you did.'

'I know,' said Yasmin. 'It wasn't the sort of thing I could possibly have missed. However, when you went to bed you didn't sleep. And you drove all day, while I slept. I really don't know how you managed it.'

'You give me the strength of ten,' murmured André.

'Rather more like the strength of twenty, I think.'

Yasmin continued to rub the tense muscles in André's neck. He relaxed, and his eyes closed. He didn't move when Zayd returned with his drink and set it down on the table at his elbow. Then Zayd looked up at Yasmin, his eyes impassive, expressionless.

'Will that be all?' he asked in Arabic.

'Yes, thank you, Zayd,' she replied, meeting his gaze. The Arabic came easily, but the words felt strange on her lips. He nodded unsmilingly and turned on his heel.

It suddenly dawned on Yasmin, as she watched Zayd leave the room, that she had been harboring a strong dislike for Arab men, and Zayd was not helping to dispel any of her notions about them. He was arrogant, pompous, and as far as she could see, unfeeling. He used his position as a man to make her feel worthless and insignificant. As her thoughts began to crystalize, she realized that this was, in fact, the way she'd been treated by every Arab man she'd ever come in contact with. Maybe some were different, she thought, but she had yet to meet them. The first time she'd been treated with any care or affection by a man at all, had been when she'd met André. Then, at school, there had been some pleasant teachers who were men . . . Monsieur Derain, for one. He taught history and economics to them.

Small, round, bald, and about fifty, Monsieur Derain had made her think. He'd pushed her to use her mind. Delighted with her quick understanding of his subjects, especially economics, he'd taken Yasmin under his wing. And Monsieur Becher who taught art history was always kind and friendly. He never made her feel insignificant.

Yes, it's true, Yasmin thought sadly. I really don't like my own countrymen – men that is, not women. She wondered how she'd manage to fit into the life in Tangier if André's friends and acquaintances couldn't stand her. She shook her head quickly. Enough, she thought. It would work out. She'd make it work out if it was the last thing she did.

After Zayd had silently closed the door behind him, she focused on André. How perfect his features were, she thought, yet how tired he looked. The tiny lines etched around his eyes seemed deeper, and she had never noticed the dark smudges beneath them.

'Zayd brought your drink, darling,' she said softly, but André's eyes stayed closed.

To give him time to awaken by himself, Yasmin decided to turn down the bed and use the bathroom first. Stepping out of her pants and cotton chemise, Yasmin went into the bathroom to shower away the layer of salt crystals that had adhered to the exposed parts of her body during the crossing.

As she stood under the strong jets of water, she was suddenly grateful for the time alone, and realized with a start that this was the first time she'd been alone since André had picked her up at school. He had been with her every second. He held her when she slept, bathed her when she woke, gazed at her when she ate. It seemed he was always touching her, however lightly. When he drove, he rested a hand on her thigh or her shoulder, and when they walked he pressed her body against his hip, matching his rhythm to hers.

At home with her grandfather and uncles, Yasmin had always been surrounded by bodies. The times she'd been sent to watch the goats had been delicious. But then, in the compound of Abdul Khadir, she had never been left alone for a moment. There was always a watchful eye or two, making sure she didn't do anything unacceptable.

She wondered idly if they had thought she was going to run away. But why would she do that? What would she have done if she'd run away? Where was she supposed to run?

She was surprised to realize that the thought of escaping from the brothel had never crossed her mind. In fact, the concept of freedom had never crossed her mind, until Madame Duchamp had begun teaching her the concepts of freedom and choice. Her grandfather and Abdul Khadir would be horrified if they knew all that she had learned, she thought with a smile.

Yet even her situation now, she mused, did not precisely constitute freedom either. As the picture of André flashed through her mind, she rinsed off the soap and stepped out of the shower. Quickly drying herself, she opened the door, looking to see if he still slept.

'Ah, there you are at last,' came his voice from the direction of the huge walk-in closet. He emerged wearing a silken bathrobe of glossy maroon with satin edging. 'Now I see what they mean when they complain so bitterly. They say a woman spends all her time in the bath.' He chuckled and smacked her lightly on the bottom. 'I'll only be a moment.'

Hanging the towel on the back of the door, Yasmin slid naked into the welcoming coolness of the sheets and waited for him to join her. She looked around the room as she lay there, taking in the masculine grace of André's furniture. Certainly no example of a woman's touch, but handsome, tasteful, and comfortable all the same.

A perfect man in so many respects, she thought as she lay listening to the splashing water. She could just see into the bathroom, and caught his reflection in the mirror. What more could she want? He took care of her, he didn't use her, he loved her and gave her anything she desired. Yet in some ways he treated her like a little doll, or a child, she thought. But could she fault him for that?

she wondered. After all, she was still a child in many ways. He was so much older than she was, it was probably hard for him to think of her in any other way. And yet he also treated her like a woman. She slid her hand down along her flat stomach under the sheets.

Then it came to her: It was her body that he treated as adult. But her mind? It was as if he thought of her as two individuals instead of one. Perhaps at one time she had been two people, not one. But her years with Madame at Lautremont had melded the two. Now, she thought, it was necessary to show André that she was indeed worthy of being treated like the adult she had become. But, of course, that would be hard here in Morocco. On the other hand, perhaps not, she mused. Perhaps it would be simple. *I have to make myself think more like Hillary now, and less like myself,* she told herself, knowing Hillary wouldn't be bothered by a few old English biddies at a stuffy country club.

'Ah. You're still awake, *chérie,*' André said as he came out of the bathroom, switching off the light. He placed his robe over the chair. The moonlight illuminated his muscular body as he lowered himself onto the bed, next to her. 'And what were you thinking about, my little love?' He gathered her close to him, resting his leg possessively across hers, and breathed deeply the scent of her hair. 'I can still smell the sea on you, and the other scents of the harbor. To me you are just like Morocco, and it is so good to be home. Europe is too civilized. Sadly, I will never know all the facets of Morocco, and I will never plumb all the depths within you. That is the reason I cannot rest. That's why I didn't sleep for these last two weeks. I wanted to explore every nuance, every inch of you.'

'But now that you are home, you have time, time for everything,' she replied. 'I don't want you to get bored with me. What if you've already explored every facet of me?' Yasmin turned her head to gaze into André's face. 'What if there are no facets left? Will you still go over the ones you know endlessly, or will you tire of me?'

'Never. Because you will grow and change with every experience. There is so much left of you to explore that I am sometimes frightened.'

'Well, you needn't be, because I am really very dull,' she murmured softly as she snuggled deeper into his arms. She lay there for a while before realizing he had fallen asleep, his deep, even breathing warm against her ear. She listened to the sounds of the waves against the cliffs as she drifted off to sleep herself, her head pillowed on his gently rising and falling chest.

The next morning she was awakened by baritone singing in the bathroom and the supercharged rays of sun that poured through the windows. Stretching luxuriously, Yasmin swung her legs over the side of the big bed and listened to the words that came booming out of the cascading rush of water, garbled, yet joyous.

'*Quisas, Quisas, Quisas!*'

She recognized it as one of the songs she'd heard belted out of the Spanish cafés in the Petit Socco, and thought how fitting a song it was for this city. Who knows, who knows, who knows? No one ever knew what to expect. No one ever knew anything they didn't want to know, either. A pleasant way to run your life. Very existential. Walking to the window, she gazed out past the cypresses and the eucalyptus trees and caught a glimpse of the sparkling sea in the distance. Boats were filing slowly out of the harbor, fishermen off for their daily catch. A cool wet arm slid across her belly, making her gasp with the shock of coldness.

'If you stand there naked like that, every eye in Tangier will be on you. Those fishermen will never catch a fish, commerce will grind to a halt, and what is worse, the gardener will not trim the hedges and the neighbors will talk about what a slovenly place I keep here.'

'Don't be silly.' Yasmin laughed as André tumbled her onto the bed, kissing her throat and breasts. 'No one can see me up here.'

'Eyes are everywhere, *ma chérie*. Do not be mistaken. You have no idea how telepathic some men can be. If there is a naked woman anywhere within fifty miles, they will find a way to look at her. Especially if she is as beautiful as you are.' Resting on his elbows, he looked down at her with pleasure, and bent to tease her lips with his tongue. Then he pushed her away and sighed.

'*Chérie*, I cannot stay. I've been away for two and a half weeks and it's time I took care of a few minor things. You understand, don't you?' he asked.

'Will you be gone long?'

'Yes, my love, I'm afraid I won't be home until this evening. But you have some things to do, too, if I'm not mistaken.'

'Yes, all those boxes and trunks. I don't know if I can face them.'

'Well, throw it all out,' André said as he deftly knotted his tie. He shrugged his shoulders into his suit jacket. 'We'll get you more tomorrow.' He kissed the nape of her neck, and left.

Yasmin listened as the echo of André's steps receded down the stairs, then she sat on the bed again and tried to organize her thoughts. She supposed it would be a good idea to go downstairs to Salima – find out what had to be done in the way of settling into the rhythm of the household. She wondered whether or not she was supposed to help manage the house. Her precise position here was not defined. Would she insult Salima and Zayd by giving them orders? Should she choose the menu and then direct someone else to do the shopping? Or would Salima be insulted to have her domain intruded upon?

123

Perhaps she should wait and ask André. There were definitely things to do. She would write to Madame, and also to Hillary, unpack her trunks and boxes, and explore the house.

She turned the knob that connected to her room and was grateful to find it open. As she stepped into the room, the wonderful beauty of it hit her again. The delicate pieces of furniture were just as they had been when she left three years ago. The inlaid ebony wardrobe, the soaring four-poster bed, the cream-colored satin drapes, and the Persian rugs were as lovely as they had ever been. The colors sparkled in the sun, making the floor look as if it were covered with a carpet of precious jewels. With a sigh of pleasure she crossed the floor, her bare feet sinking ever so slightly into the plush wool of the rugs as she moved toward her bathroom. The gleaming marble room was still like a luscious greenhouse, and she decided it should be filled with singing birds in cages. How lovely it would be to be serenaded by finches and cockatoos while she bathed, she thought.

As the water filled the tub, she recrossed the room and flung open the doors of the wardrobe. There, hanging inside, was the dress she'd worn the night she had been delivered to André by Khadir. Briefly she was flooded with a strange mixture of embarrassment and sadness as her fingers traced the floral embroidery of the diaphanous material and the shedded fabric. It was so very sheer, she thought, as she slid her hand beneath it. Why, she could see through it almost perfectly.

She remembered how André had become a different man before her eyes. One minute so polite and reassuring, the next so deaf, so uncomprehending of anything outside of his need to touch her. How much she had learned since then. She turned and sat down on the bed. Suddenly tired, she leaned against the pillows, giving herself over to her thoughts.

Yes, indeed, she had learned a great deal since that first night. Allowing her hands to gently touch herself, she wondered at why she had been so frightened when André had first tried to make love to her. She wondered why the very same fear had been replaced by longing as the years had passed. When he finally made love to her for the first time, how ready she had been to accept him. Just the thought made her nipples stiffen and her loins warm. She touched the tiny button that was the seat of all the pleasure André gave her, and it swelled in anticipation.

Good Lord, I've been turned into a wanton, she thought, an insatiable creature who can never get enough of pleasure. How amazing to have one's body exert such an enormous influence over one's mind. She thought of André's mouth and what unexpected delicious thrills it brought her. Who would ever have thought that a tongue and lips would be able to enslave an otherwise reasonable human being? She continued to stroke the quivering, demanding flesh, and her body began to arch with pleasure.

Who would have thought that this part of her, so hidden away, could give such unequaled delight? It was almost as if once awakened, it lived a life of its own, made demands that had to be heeded, and would not be denied. But it demanded so much, she thought, as an aching void began to open up inside her. She slid a tentative finger into the pulsing center of herself and found that she hungered for more, for the thickness and length of André thudding deep inside her. Her other hand slid down of its own volition and encircled her burning flesh, pinching and stroking rhythmically. Suddenly a cascade of crimson flashed across her vision as she plunged into the delicious spiral she so adored.

It was with some annoyance that she slowly returned to consciousness and felt slightly cold. *What on earth am I turning into?* she thought. My brain has been unhinged by my body. Perhaps she really was two people inside of one. She sat up quickly, trying to avoid the memory of the slick, oversensitive spot between her legs, telling herself she had to get on with the day, that she had things to do. Ah, but it was so delicious, she thought.

Her thoughts drifted back to the girls who used to sneak out of the hotel rooms on those summer nights in Greece, sneaking out to meet those dangerous men who waited for them. And all that time, Yasmin had had no idea of the delights they experienced. Laughing to herself at last, she took her shower and stepped out onto the thick bathmat. Wrapping the towel around her tingling body, she strolled back into her room, glancing at the dress in the wardrobe. She would keep that dress forever, she thought languorously. It was her only link between the self that was, and the new self that had come to live inside her.

The heat of the day was beginning to rise, and her hair dried quickly. Slipping into a pair of shorts and a halter, she tentatively opened the door and peered into the hall. There seemed to be no one about, and the house was still. But she heard faint sounds coming from the kitchen, and so quietly walked downstairs and opened the door. The big room was empty, the stoves and sinks gleaming. The back door was open, and the sunlight danced on the flowers that grew in profusion around the edges of what appeared to be a small kitchen garden.

Making her way across the kitchen, she stood on the back step, shading her eyes from the sun with her hand. Suddenly she became aware of someone standing next to her and turned with a start to find Salima, gazing in horror at her shorts and halter top. Yasmin laughed at the expression on her face, then realized it was the wrong thing to do. Throwing her arms around Salima's

126

shoulders, she kissed her warmly on the cheek, trying to make up for her mistake.

'*Rahhalatun!*' clucked Salima. 'Look what the world traveler comes back wearing!'

'You should wear these too,' Yasmin said. 'They are cooler in this weather.' She plucked at the bottoms of her shorts. 'There really isn't much sense in wearing a woolen bathrobe in the desert!'

'Humph,' Salima snorted. 'I would never be able to bring myself to go to market wearing such an outfit. I wouldn't advise *you* to go walking about in those in public, either!'

'But the tourists wear them all the time,' answered Yasmin. 'What's the difference?'

'They are tourists and you are not,' said Salima, superior wisdom coloring her words. 'If they choose to behave like monkeys, I'm sure that is their choice. An Arab girl should know better.'

'Well,' Yasmin said, wheedling and smiling at the same time, 'if you promise to get me something to eat, I will go put on a dress. Will that make you feel better?'

Salima snorted again, and walked into the kitchen. Yasmin had to laugh. If only the American or European girls could hear the way the Arab women spoke about them. They thought they were so civilized, and the women with their veils and haiks so buried in ancient history. Yet Arab women thought those girls behaved like rabbits, weaving no sense of mystery and allure with their clothes.

Upstairs she finally found something Salima would consider acceptable – a loose shift of white knitted cotton. Thin spaghetti straps held the chemise up, and it flared gracefully at the hem just below her knees.

When she returned to the kitchen, Salima had a plate of yoghurt and a dish of raisins, fresh figs, and sliced oranges waiting for her. Yasmin ate ravenously. Salima pretended not to notice her as she moved around the kitchen.

'Is Zayd here?' Yasmin spoke to Salima's back. 'I need him to help me take my books down to the library.'

'Books!' snorted Salima. 'There is nothing useful in books. He's out in the garden somewhere, but I'll tell him when he comes in.'

Yasmin knew it was unlikely that Zayd would be in very shortly. The kitchen and the house were a woman's domain, and the Moroccan men avoided the house whenever possible. Every free minute they had was spent in the company of other men – in cafés, along the shore, anywhere but where the women could voice their demands and be heard.

'Oh, well,' she sighed. 'Don't bother him. There aren't that many, and I can carry them down myself in a few trips. It will give me something to do until André comes home.'

She slipped out of the kitchen and went back upstairs to collect the first armload of books. When she had all the books stacked in the library, she carefully placed each in its proper place and soon was covered with fine smudges of dust. She had no idea how much time had passed, but occasionally the big clock in the corner would chime.

There was a light knock on the door. That's probably Zayd, Yasmin thought contemptuously. He's going to offer to help me carry down my books, knowing full well that the work is done. 'Yes?' she said sweetly.

The door swung open and Zayd appeared. Behind him she could see the outlines of a tall man, but the details were obscured by the darkness of the foyer. Zayd nodded at her disdainfully and stepped aside, ushering the man into the library.

7

As Zayd closed the door behind him, Yasmin was transfixed to the spot by two midnight black eyes that held her immobilized where she stood. Her thoughts suddenly scattered as she stared into the dark pools which seemed to burn her skin as they slowly traveled around her face and then down past her shoulders. They took in the cotton shift and the cloud of mahogany hair she suddenly realized was loose to her waist. Then they continued on down to her bare feet, where they lingered briefly before they began their scalding journey up again. She was immediately aware of the fine hairs on her body raised in goose bumps, and the fact that her breasts were unrestrained by a brassiere, the nipples pushing against the fabric of her dress. A hot flush crept up from her throat to color her cheeks.

The man was elegantly dressed in a dark silk suit that fit him beautifully, close without being tight. She was immediately aware of his muscular body beneath it and the animal strength the clothing failed to hide. It reminded her of a panther, graceful and yet immensely powerful. His hair was black, thick, and cut close to his head. The harsh planes of his face were only marginally relieved by a molded, sensual mouth curved in a slight smile. His nose, long, slender and sharp, gave him a feral quality that caused her to shiver slightly.

'So, you are the new lady of the house?' The hissing softness of his voice reminded Yasmin again of a great cat, and the way he emphasized the word *lady* left no doubt in her mind of his disdain for her and whatever her present position was in André's house. With a start she realized that he had spoken to her in Arabic, and impulsively decided he was one of those insufferably arrogant men she instinctively hated with every fiber of her being – one of those who saw fit to buy her, sell her, use her, and treat her like a chattel.

He continued with a sneer, 'Does the lady of the house dust the shelves in addition to performing all her other duties?'

Yasmin snapped out of her reverie, embarrassed that she had been staring like an awestruck adolescent. Slamming shut the book she held in her hand, she tried to control the anger that flooded through her.

'Is there something that I can do for you, Monsieur . . . ?' She deliberately spoke to him in French, sarcasm dripping from her lips as she said *Monsieur*.

'Quite a few things, I imagine,' he said, his voice low and ominous as he smiled. His eyes had turned stonily flat, as they flickered across her breasts and returned to her face. The muscles in his jaw tensed, then his insinuating smile returned.

'Because, if not,' Yasmin continued in French, despite the fact that he insisted on speaking to her in Arabic, 'I have many things to do. You will excuse me, I'm sure.'

'Most certainly not. A delicious little thing like you shouldn't be wasting her time in a library . . . especially when she is obviously made for more exciting things than books.' Something dangerous flared in his eyes that made Yasmin drop her gaze. The deep cleft in his chin made her feel suddenly weak in the knees.

Allah, she thought, what is happening to me? She abruptly directed her attention to the shelves, carefully replacing the book she was holding. Without turning, she said, 'I can only assume that you're here to see Monsieur le Baron. Unfortunately he is away, but if you give me your name, I will tell him you were here.'

'Hassan Jalifa, at your service,' he answered, bowing

slightly. The thin veneer of civilization barely covered the animal quality of the man as he moved to her side. Catching her hand in his, he raised it slowly to his lips. 'And your name, Mademoiselle?'

Yasmin almost cried out as he turned her hand over in his and pressed his mouth against her palm. His lips seemed to burn her skin. Quickly snatching her hand away, she was barely able to suppress a shudder. Her eyes flew up to meet his, and she saw such intense forceful power in them that she was almost sucked into their whirlpool depths.

'My name is Yasmin,' she snapped as she collected herself back into the safety of her civilized world. The man is like a snake, she thought. Why doesn't he just leave? 'I'll tell André that you were here.' She hoped he would get the message, but if he did, he obviously chose to ignore it.

'So you speak French, and you catalog libraries. You are obviously a very talented young lady. What else do you do?'

Yasmin fought back the surprising impulse to slap him, and decided not to answer.

'You make me very curious,' he said. 'You are obviously Moroccan, but you speak French and dress like a Parisian. Has the Rif changed so much in the six months since I've been there, or do you come from a place that I have yet to hear about?'

'Oh, I come from the Rif,' she snapped, her head tilted up disdainfully. 'But you might say I've had the advantage of getting away from domineering, tyrannical men like you.'

'I see that,' Hassan Jalifa said, his voice deceptively sweet. 'And I suppose you went to a proper French boarding school, and all your clothes are from Balenciaga too.'

'What difference would it make to you? As far as men

131

like you are concerned, a woman is just another beast of burden, regardless of what she knows or what she wears. Am I right?'

'Not so fast, little fig. Some women, and I emphasize *some*, are only good to be donkeys. But there are others – and I believe this is where you come in – that are good for a great deal more.'

Yasmin gasped. 'You are insulting! But I suppose I shouldn't have expected more from a man like you. Arab men are all the same with their idiotic, pretentious claims to superiority.'

'But I certainly did not mean to insult you.' He stepped forward quickly, with the feline grace of the panther he resembled. He gripped her shoulder and she flinched as his hand touched her, his voice a menacing purr. 'I only meant that some women, like some men, are not meant for higher things. You obviously are a spirited, intelligent creature, and it is the women like you who must be nurtured and encouraged.'

'You expect me to believe that,' Yasmin snapped, wrenching herself from his grasp. His honeyed tones merely put her further on her guard. 'I suppose you have a harem of spirited, intelligent creatures tucked away somewhere that you are nurturing and encouraging by locking them in a walled garden.'

'God help me!' Hassan laughed wryly. 'Such a thing casts terror into my heart. One woman would be bad enough, but a harem? No thank you!'

Yasmin tapped her foot impatiently, hoping he would understand that she wanted to end this interview. But he was insistent. 'So please tell me, then. Where did you go to school?'

'Switzerland.'

'And do you ski and ride horses and spout Spinoza and Kierkegaard too?'

'When it suits me.'

'Ah, that André is such a clever fox. Who would have thought he had such a delicious and intelligent morsel hidden away. I wonder how long he will manage to keep you all to himself. I think perhaps that it is only a matter of time before some handsome, dashing type makes off with you.'

'I sincerely doubt it, thank you.'

'Well, well, well . . . and properly grateful too. Unlike most young ladies these days. And don't you think he's a little too old for you?'

'Do you mind?' Yasmin was rapidly losing patience with the demeaning questions he pressed on her.

'You know what they say about these May-September romances. Or is it an April-October romance that we're talking about here?'

'Would you please leave?' Yasmin stamped her foot with vexation. 'I will certainly tell André that you came by. Now really, I have things to do. Good-bye!'

'But, of course. Please forgive my intrusion, Mademoiselle.' Hassan stepped toward her as if to touch her again, but Yasmin glided out of his reach. 'We will certainly meet again . . . and often,' he continued, his voice purring malevolently. 'Tell André that I will come by this evening. There are matters which must be dealt with quickly.'

Before she could move away, he was next to her, his hand on her chin, tilting it up, forcing her to look at his face. His eyes glinted black and threatening as his fingers imprisoned her face.

'And you and I will continue this conversation, rest assured.' Abruptly, he released her. His hand dropped faster than the eye could follow and again caught hers, raising it to his lips, palm up. 'It has most certainly been my pleasure, as it will soon be yours,' he murmured, pressing his lips on her palm. For a second Yasmin was convinced she had felt his tongue flick across her skin.

133

The sensation was so intense that she gasped aloud as she snatched her hand back to cover her mouth.

'*In-shallah,*' he hissed, and then was gone.

'What a presumptuous pig!' Yasmin muttered to herself, hoping André didn't have too many acquaintances like him. Smoothing her dress and her hair much the way a hen would smooth her ruffled feathers, Yasmin quickly finished putting the books away.

Glancing up at the clock, she realized with horror that it was late – almost six o'clock. Where had the time gone? Wasted on that miserable Arab and his high-handed remarks, she thought. What effrontery! But she must hurry, she told herself, and get ready for dinner. André would probably be back at any moment, and she was covered with dust and dressed in a smock!

Taking the stairs two at a time, Yasmin dashed into her room and quickly washed her face and hands. After twisting her hair up on top of her head in a heavy knot, she chose a dress from her wardrobe and slid it over her head. She thought with satisfaction that at least she got the books put away, and without waiting for Zayd to help. If that wretched person hadn't appeared, she mused, I probably wouldn't have laid eyes on Zayd all afternoon.

Feeling hungry, she wondered what Salima was making for dinner. Probably something delicious, she thought, since this would be André's first dinner back home. She knew that Salima took excellent care of her employer and would go out of her way to impress him on his return.

Glancing out of the window, Yasmin saw the Mercedes turn into the gate and pull up in front of the house. She watched as Zayd opened the door and André uncoiled himself from behind the wheel. For a moment he rested his hand against the roof of the car, leaning his weight as if exhausted, and Yasmin felt a flash of panic rip through her. But then he straightened up and strolled insouciantly into the house. She heard him call her name as the door banged shut behind him.

'Coming, darling,' she called as she swiftly crossed the room. She almost flew down the stairs into his arms. They folded around her like huge wings, and she felt a delicious sense of security wash away the anger and tension of her meeting with Hassan Jalifa: as long as André was there for her, she had nothing to fear. His head bent over hers and he placed a long, exquisite kiss on her lips.

'What a delightful hors d'oeuvre to have greet me at the door,' he murmured against her mouth. 'And did you have a good day, *ma chérie*?' His hand caressed the small of her back as he led her into the drawing room.

'Yes, I accomplished quite a bit,' answered Yasmin, her head leaning against his arm. 'And you, my love?'

'Ah well . . . it was not too good and not too bad. Some of the things I am forced to do to make my money are tedious and idiotic.'

'Someone came to see you today,' said Yasmin.

'Oh, yes? Who?'

'He said his name was Hassan Jalifa and that he would return this evening because there are some things that must be taken care of quickly, whatever that means.'

André groaned, and extracted himself from her arms. 'I think I'd better have a drink. I can see this is going to be a long night.'

'Who is this man?' asked Yasmin, trying to control the irritation in her voice.

'Ah, Hassan is very important to me, and quite brilliant. Without him, I would be a hopeless mess. At least my finances would be.'

'I find that hard to believe,' Yasmin said, no longer able to hide her annoyance, and unable to get rid of the bitter aftertaste of Hassan's visit. 'He seemed to be a very unpleasant person.'

'Unpleasant?' André said absentmindedly. 'Not really. Actually, he's very interesting. He's the second son of a fairly powerful chieftain from the Goulimine area on the edge of the Sahara. His father was a very farsighted man and sent both his sons to school in England. After the Second World War he sensed that the old ways of rule were going to change in Morocco. He wanted his sons to be able to enter the government – deal with the European nations and Western businessmen. Hassan's brother went home after his father died, but Hassan decided to go to America. He went to Harvard, and got his PhD in Economics.'

'Sometimes a PhD makes a person more unpleasant, not less,' Yasmin snapped. She couldn't rid herself of the feeling that Hassan Jalifa was a dislikable person, no matter what André thought of him.

At the tone in her voice, André threw her a curious look, then smiled. 'I think you're prejudiced. I think you're letting other things stand in your way of seeing Hassan clearly.'

For a moment she wanted to tell him what he'd said to her. But she realized that Hassan's words had been fairly innocuous. It was the way he'd looked at her that made her so angry. André would probably think she was being silly. She decided to say nothing.

'I met Hassan when he was working in the Credit Française. He was handling a portion of my investments, and I found him to be brilliant. Eventually I hired him away from the bank. As it turned out, he's a perfect manager for me. Hassan is my right-hand man. He understands my entire Tangier-based business, yet he would rather live in Paris. He also handles my estate in France and the financial aspects of the vineyard. He's much happier in Paris, where I was born, and I'm much happier in Morocco, where he was born. It works out perfectly for both of us. Funny, yes?'

136

'Well, if he's based in Paris, then what is he doing here?' Yasmin asked.

'I don't know yet,' André said with a tired smile. 'But it probably means there's something wrong, which I will find out about later when he comes by.'

'It all sounds very mysterious.'

'It isn't, really. All very mundane. But I left at a difficult time, and my affairs require a great deal of attention. I wanted to meet you at school and take you with me on a trip, so I decided to let them all go to hell for a few weeks. Delicious, but not without its consequences, *ma chérie*.'

'Is there anything I can help you with? Madame said I had a very good head for numbers, you know.'

'How sweet of you,' André replied, glancing at her. 'But it really isn't anything you should bother your pretty little head about. I suppose we should eat dinner quickly so I can talk with Hassan when he comes. Did he say anything about what time he was expected?'

'No, just that he'd come by this evening.'

'Ah, well,' sighed André, reaching for the bell rope. 'I guess we should get on with it, though I must say I have very little appetite. My lunch this afternoon does not seem to be agreeing with me. I suspect I have a touch of indigestion.'

'Perhaps Salima will be able to fix you something,' said Yasmin, suddenly concerned. 'Why don't you sit down, and I'll see what she has ready.'

Yasmin had quickly crossed the room and opened the door, when she heard a thud behind her. For a second her heart stopped beating, then she whirled around. She didn't see André. Then with a sinking feeling, she let her eyes drop to the floor. There, crumpled in a heap near the chair, his body lay twisted.

Yasmin screamed, and paralyzed with fear, screamed again and again. The sounds reverberated in the room, bouncing off the walls like bats gone mad. Then, just as suddenly, she stopped herself, grabbed hold of the scattering fragments of her mind, and moved across the room. Her sense of unreality was so strong, it seemed to her she was in a slow-motion movie as she knelt beside André's still, unmoving form.

At that moment the door was flung open and Zayd rushed in, followed by Salima, wringing her hands in fright. Yasmin looked up, stark terror in her eyes.

'I don't know what happened,' she said. 'But someone should phone a doctor immediately.'

Salima backed out quickly, and Yasmin could hear her placing the call. All the noises and motions around her were enhanced, her senses heightened, more aware – like waving antennae receiving signals at a much greater rate.

'What happened?' Zayd asked as he bent down. Picking up André's limp wrist, he placed two fingers over the pulse spot. Yasmin waited in suspended animation, watching André's waxen face. His skin looked cool, gray, clammy. She waited for Zayd's words.

'There is a pulse, but it is very weak.'

'Thank God, he's alive,' murmured Yasmin. But she herself felt cold, as if there were a giant block of ice lodged in her stomach, slowly dripping its frigid water through her veins.

'I think he's had a heart attack,' said Zayd. He rose quickly and walked to the doorway. Calling to Salima, he said, 'Did you call for an ambulance?'

Salima nodded, unable to speak. Bunching her apron in her twisted hands, she rushed into the kitchen, her shoulders shaking.

'Did he say anything, or complain of anything before he fell?'

'Yes. He said he had a touch of indigestion. I was just going into the kitchen to see what Salima had prepared for dinner. If it was too heavy, I was going to ask her to prepare something simple and light for him, but I never got there. He fell when I reached the door.' She felt her insides begin to collapse as the tears welled up in her eyes, and her body was shaken with silent, racking tears. 'Allah, please let him be all right . . . please, please . . . !'

The whining two-note wail of the ambulance came wafting into the room. Zayd swiftly left to open the gate for them. Yasmin looked at André. He was perfectly still, and it seemed he wasn't breathing. Although she knew Zayd had found a pulse, she had a sudden shattering fear that somehow he'd slipped away while they were talking. But she was afraid to touch him, afraid that any movement on her part would chase away what little life was left in his body, and so remained perfectly still.

The wailing grew overpoweringly loud, then stopped abruptly. There was a clatter of footsteps in the foyer and the clanging of metal as the stretcher, hastily rushed into the house, knocked against the doorjamb. Suddenly she was surrounded by people. The stretcher was opened and two medics in white coats were kneeling beside André, one listening to his heart and holding an oxygen mask to his face as the other prepared an injection. Just as quickly they lifted him onto the stretcher, strapping his chest and legs down with wide black belts that had frightening-looking silver buckles.

'You'd better come with us,' said one, nodding to Yasmin as they wheeled the stretcher out. She hurried to catch up with them, waiting anxiously as they loaded the stretcher into the back of the ambulance. The medic reached out his hand to her and pulled her inside, then motioned her to sit at André's feet. The doors slammed shut, and the vehicle began to move. Yasmin, still in shock, watched dumbly as the medic did things that were partially blocked by his impassive white back.

As they careened down the road, she was thankful that the hospital was so close. But though she knew in the rational part of her mind that it would only take five minutes, the part of her that was not controlled by intellect or words or intelligence was in agony. 'Is he still alive?' she asked, numbed, as they pulled into the hospital grounds.

'Yes, but we must move quickly,' said the attendant. He flashed her a brief smile, then stood up, prepared to get out of the ambulance as it pulled to a stop. The doors were flung open and another set of attendants grasped the end of the stretcher firmly. They rolled it down the ramp and through the swinging doors of the emergency unit. Yasmin followed as quickly as she could, into the glaring, screaming lights of the hospital. Then a hand touched her arm as a nurse indicated to her that she must wait. Watching, grief stricken, she saw André disappear on the rolling white bed through another set of swinging doors.

The nurse who had stopped her motioned for her to sit down in a row of brightly colored plastic chairs.

'Please stay here,' she said. 'The doctor will be out to speak with you as soon as he can.' Then she handed Yasmin a series of forms saying, 'You can fill these out while you are waiting. Are you a relative?'

Shaking her head no, Yasmin stared at the forms, but the tiny print blurred before her eyes. Even if she were able to distinguish the letters, she might not know any of the information called for. How could she explain her relationship to André? She'd known him for three years, and yet she'd only known him for two weeks. She loved him, but she knew very little about him. She wasn't even sure how old he was.

Allah, what an impossible situation, she thought. She didn't know the name of his lawyers, or anyone who did. She wasn't related to him, but she had been his chattel, his thing, his human. She knew he'd asked her to marry him . . . someday. But who would believe her? Would the doctor believe her? She doubted it. André at least owned her, though. Didn't he? Did that make her some kind of relative?

Instinctively she realized that in fact he didn't own her. He owned her in the sense that he'd bought her freedom. But that only left her with less of a connection, not more. She dreaded answering the doctor's questions, and dreaded having to wait for him to come and ask them. And what would happen to her if André were to die? Her heart clenched with foreboding as she began to grasp fully her untenable position, her absolute helplessness.

Then the doctor was at her side, looking grim. 'I am Dr Calvados, Monsieur le Baron's personal physician. He is not dead, Mademoiselle' – a look of embarrassment crossed his face – 'but his condition is extremely serious. He has had a heart attack – acute pulmonary edema. We have given him digitalis, which may reverse some of the damage. He is in an oxygen tent now and breathing with some difficulty, but he is conscious and would like to see you.'

'Oh, thank you,' breathed Yasmin, rising unsteadily. 'Then he is going to live?' A sensation of exquisite relief began to wash over her, but her knees weakened. A wave of blackness threatened to close off her vision as the doctor steadied her, gripping her elbow firmly with his hand.

'Perhaps you could tell me what happened before he collapsed,' he asked, shifting his eyes away from hers. A slight flush crept up his neck. 'It might help me to handle the total diagnosis.'

'Well, he had just returned from a day devoted to business,' Yasmin answered, noticing his discomfiture. 'He complained of being tired and having indigestion from his lunch, he thought. Then he just fell to the floor.'

'He said nothing about pain?'

'Nothing.'

'And has he had any similar complaints recently?'

'None that I know of. We have just returned from a trip by car from Geneva. Perhaps he was overtired?'

'Perhaps. But it is more likely that the pressures of work affected his heart in some way. Vacations are usually relaxing, not exhausting.'

It was Yasmin's turn to color, and she looked away, unable to meet the doctor's frank gaze. He thinks I have killed him, she thought in dismay. That's what they'll all think.

'You may come with me, but please do not stay with him for very long, and say nothing that will excite him. His condition is relatively stable at the moment, but anything could happen during these critical few hours . . .'

Yasmin followed him quickly through winding corridors, then into a plain white and chrome room. A great plastic tent covered the bed, and she could see André's waxen face propped up on pillows, wires and tubes attached to his forehead and mouth, and running out of the tent to several machines lined up next to it.

She moved as close as she could, and his eyes fluttered open, lost their focus, then regained it as they came to rest on her face. He looked old. The smooth skin of his face seemed now to cling to his fragile bone structure, hanging against it, making it look somehow shrunken. His eyes were deeply embedded in the sockets, and he was pale, so very pale. Speaking in short, breathless bursts, he whispered, 'Come closer, there are some things which I must tell you . . . .'

Yasmin leaned her head as close to the oxygen tent as she could, barely able to make out his words. He has to live, she thought, but how can he live when he looks like this?

'The safe . . . you must go to the safe. There is cash in there which you will need in the next few weeks. It is . . .

142

it is behind the portrait of my mother in the library. The combination is – write this down – 32-20-14 . . . left, right, left . . . .' He stopped, gasping, and a dreadful railing sound issued from deep within his chest. Yasmin found a pad on the night table next to the bed and quickly wrote down the numbers.

'Ah, Yasmin . . . I'm so sorry, *ma chérie* . . .' He gasped again, his eyes closing with the effort of speaking. 'But if anything should happen to me . . .'

Yasmin shuddered, frightened by his obvious weakness. 'Oh, no, darling. Nothing is going to happen. The doctor said – '

'No . . . listen . . . I cannot speak much longer, *chérie* . . . if anything should happen to me, you must contact my lawyers. They have all the documents, all the papers, they will know what to do . . . The firm is – '

Suddenly his face flushed a deep red and his hand flew to his chest. Yasmin's eyes darted to the machines at his side and saw with horror that the needles were moving wildly across the dials. The door burst open and the room was filled with white coats. They surrounded the bed, obscuring him from her sight.

She backed from the room and waited outside the door, leaning against the wall, her eyes squeezed shut. After what seemed an eternity, Dr Calvados was at her side.

'The crisis is over and he is sleeping, but I don't think there is anything more that you can do here. Why don't you go back home?' Yasmin nodded dumbly as she stared up into his face. 'I am going to stay here, and I will also take care of all the paperwork. If anything should change, we will call the villa immediately. You should try and get some sleep, Mademoiselle. Come back in the morning, if you wish.'

Yasmin slowly turned and walked in the direction of the exit. Then, with a sinking sensation, she realized she had no way to get home, no money with which to pay a taxi. With a small sigh of relief she realized that Zayd and Salima were at home. They could handle it for her when she returned. Going to the main desk, she asked the gray-haired woman there to call a taxi, then went out into the night to wait. The stars twinkled merrily at her, and the soft breezes caressed her skin. A very romantic evening, she thought numbly. Pain twisted her insides.

The taxi arrived, and she rode in silent horror through the night. Zayd was at the gate when they pulled up. She asked him to take care of the driver for her, then walked into the library. Salima came quietly in, her face a question mark.

'He is still alive,' Yasmin said softly, 'but his condition seems very precarious.' Zayd had entered the room as she spoke, his stony face a mask of dislike. 'He has had a heart attack, acute pulmonary edema, I think. They said I should come home because there was nothing I could do for him in the hospital. But they will call me if his condition changes.'

'Did he speak?' asked Salima.

'Yes, he did for a few moments, but he . . . he couldn't continue. He was in an oxygen tent . . . he has a great deal of trouble breathing.'

Salima began to weep. Zayd, an accusing look on his face, turned and left the library without speaking. Yasmin sank into a chair exhausted, defeated, and alone with her thoughts as Salima followed on his heels. It was then that she became aware of the slip of paper in her hand, crumpled and damp with sweat. She opened her palm slowly, then raised her eyes to the ornate gold-framed portrait of a woman that hung behind André's desk.

She got up, crossed to the desk, and raising her hand to the portrait, began to lift it off the wall when she discovered that it swung aside easily. Underneath it there was a gunmetal gray square with a numbered dial in its center.

The safe, just as André had described, she thought, deciding it would be practical to take some money for herself. Tomorrow would in all likelihood be a terrible day, and she knew she was going to have to take several taxis and couldn't expect Zayd to be around to pay for them.

Carefully she read the numbers off the slip of paper, then began to twist the dial. With a barely audible click, the lock released and the door swung open. In the dark interior were several large manilla envelopes, some smaller white envelopes, some loose papers, and a thick wad of bills wrapped in a rubber band. Lifting it out, she saw it was a collection of dirhams and francs. Slipping some of the dirhams off the top, she quickly put them into the pocket of her dress

I haven't even the slightest idea how much I'm going to need, she thought, feeling like a simpleton. She didn't even know how much a taxi cost, or how much she took as she returned the rest of the money to the safe and closed the door. After carefully twisting the dial, she again pressed the portrait back against the wall. The woman in the painting continued to eye her suspiciously, but Yasmin paid no attention. Sighing with relief, she returned to the chair and collapsed wearily.

Oh, André . . . I need you too much for this to happen, she thought as she closed her eyes.

8

Yasmin was drifting in the murky world between sleeping and waking when she realized with a start that the door to the library had opened. Someone was standing there, framed in the light from the hall. Blinking her eyes, adjusting them to the sudden glare, she tried to remember when she'd fallen asleep. She must have been so tired, but no . . . it was probably some form of shock that made her body gratefully shut down to give her over-loaded mind a rest. But who was here?

'Is that you, Zayd?' she said sleepily. But a nagging worry was trying to reconcile the profile. It was taller, broader, and not wearing Zayd's usual djellaba.

'Hassan Jalifa,' came the soft, caressing voice in the darkness. 'Zayd just told me about André. Is there anything that I can do?'

Yasmin quickly stood up, trying to shake off the clinging vestiges of sleep that clouded her thoughts and judgment. She wanted to be fully awake if she was to have even the shortest of conversations with this man.

'Nothing, thank you,' she replied quickly. 'I am trying to get some rest. The hospital said they would call in the event of any change in his condition, but as far as I know, at the moment there is nothing to be done.'

'Well, perhaps I will stay a while with you,' he said, an unexpected note of kindness creeping into his voice. Yasmin's heart sank. 'You must be very upset, and it is often hard to be alone at a time like this.'

'Thank you for your concern,' she said coolly, 'but I am quite all right. There is no need for you to keep me company.'

146

'Perhaps the reason I'd like to stay is for you to keep *me* company,' Hassan said quietly as he crossed the room to where she stood. 'Actually, I am extraordinarily fond of André. I am very distressed at what has happened.'

'I'm sure you are, but I really should get some sleep.'

'Why don't you turn on a light or two,' he continued, ignoring her words. 'It's depressing to sit around in the dark.'

Yasmin could barely control her urge to scream at him to leave her alone. But he moved across the room, turning on all the lamps, and she was momentarily thrown off by the need to accustom her eyes to the light. Hassan, satisfied with his changes, settled himself comfortably in the chair she'd just vacated, crossing his legs in a graceful motion.

'Well, make yourself comfortable, then,' Yasmin snapped sarcastically. 'Don't feel that you need a special invitation from me.'

'I have known André for many years and I would appreciate it if you would please tell me what the doctors said.' Hassan's eyes raked her cruelly, making her feel thoughtless for not telling him about his friend.

'Oh, all right,' she said, sitting down in the chair opposite him. 'But then I really must lie down soon.'

She carefully went over all that had happened that evening, starting when André had arrived home. Occasionally Hassan interrupted her with short, sharp questions, which pointed to his genuine concern.

'And you say that he seemed to have another attack while you were in the hospital room with him?' he asked, his voice turning a little harsh.

'Yes,' she replied. 'But the doctor, Dr Calvados, said before I left that he was over it and resting comfortably.'

'That isn't too good, I'm afraid. André is fifty-one, and although that isn't particularly old, it is still a dangerous age for a man whose heart is weakened.'

147

'I'm sure he will be all right,' insisted Yasmin, speaking not so much out of conviction, but out of fear. 'He has to be all right.'

'I want him to recover as much as you do, but we must look on the practical side of these matters. What precisely is your interest in him, anyway?'

Realizing the direction his words were leading, Yasmin suddenly bristled. 'My interest in him? What do you mean by that?'

'Well, as a lover he will be of little use to you if he lives. If he doesn't, did you expect some monetary compensation for your services?'

'Why . . . you – '

'Please forgive me for being so blunt, but it's obvious that you are new in his life. I wouldn't want you to get an incorrect impression of what your present position is, that's all.'

'I am not new in his life. How dare you suggest such a thing? I have known André for three years.'

'If you say so . . . but that still leaves a few things that are not explained.'

'Such as what, you arrogant – '

At that moment the desk telephone rang sharply. Yasmin leapt up, her heart thudding like a drum, and grabbed the receiver off the hook. 'Yes?'

'Mademoiselle,' a tinny, impersonal voice spouted out of the black instrument. 'Dr Calvados calling. Please hold the wire.'

Yasmin's grip tightened and her knuckles went white with tension. For a second she thought she would faint, and it was only through the sheerest effort of will that she remained standing. Why was the doctor calling so soon? Surely nothing had gone wrong.

Then his voice came onto the wire, explaining in terms she could not comprehend, cold words that were beyond her grasp, that André was dead. He'd had another massive attack, followed by a stroke, and there was nothing they could have done. Then he was asking her kindly if she felt the need of a visit from him, some sedatives perhaps to allow her to sleep. No longer able to hold on to the telephone, dropping it from her hands, Yasmin heard from a great distance the tinny voice repeatedly saying her name as she slipped into unconsciousness.

The next thing she was aware of was a sensation of intense grief so crushing, so debilitating, that for a moment she, too, wished herself dead, away from this massive loneliness and fear. Gradually she allowed herself to make some tentative stabs at taking in her surroundings. It was at this point that she became aware of another sensation. Someone's arms were around her. Her head seemed to be pillowed against a hard, bruisingly muscular arm. With a certain amount of dread, she opened her eyes to find them caught in two obsidian black pools, which stared at her intently.

'Did you hurt yourself?' It was Hassan. What was he doing holding her like this? she thought with a start. Feebly, she tried to struggle out of his grasp, but he would not release her. 'No. I don't believe you should stand up yet. You would probably only fall down again, and this time you might hurt yourself.' He smiled at her. 'I spoke with the doctor after you so unceremoniously dropped the phone. I know.'

'Please let me go,' she muttered weakly, again trying to twist away from him. 'I'm fine, really I am. It's just that the shock was so sudden.'

'Do you think you'll need a sedative?'

'No . . . no. Just leave me alone.' She turned her face toward the wall as slow tears began to slide down her cheeks. But Hassan continued to hold her close.

'Perhaps it is better if I stay with you for a little while.

149

But I can't stay long. There are things I have to do, now that it is over.'

'Well, please go do them, then.'

'And where will you go now?'

'What do you mean, where will I go now? I have nowhere to go. André is . . . was all I had in the world.'

'I'm sure. But since you didn't love him, I had thought perhaps that you had something in mind.'

Yasmin marshaled all the strength she had, wrenched herself from Hassan's grasp, and moved away from him. *'Didn't love him?* Of course I loved him!'

'Loved his money is more likely, I suspect.'

'Money! How can you talk about money at a time like this! You are horrible! Absolutely horrible!' she shouted, and hurried across the room.

'And I suppose you think André loved you, too, eh?'

Yasmin stopped, and whirled to face him. 'Yes, I do,' she answered.

'He didn't love you, you stupid little cow.' The eyes that held hers were cold, black with cruelty. 'He was fifty-one years old, and what are you, eighteen? Seventeen? A child. Don't you know what happens as a man gets older? He starts looking for younger flesh to stroke. It makes him forget for a moment how the years have gone. They think that somehow they can regain their own lost youth through yours. He didn't love you, he loved your age, your beauty, your smooth clear skin. It was a purely physical obsession, and not a very unusual one at that.'

'That's not true!' The rising note of hysteria in her voice made Hassan smile cruelly.

'You know nothing about men and how they think,' he said calmly.

'André loved me! He asked me to marry him.'

'Oh, for God's sake.' Hassan laughed. She almost expected him to slap his knee, he laughed so uproariously. 'You all say that when cornered. And even if he *had* asked you to marry him – which I doubt – it would be typical. Men all say that too.'

'Why, you – '

Suddenly he was next to her, quickly catching her hands before her nails raked across his face. Forcing her body against his, he folded her arms behind her and held her tightly trapped against him. Gone was the amused twinkle in his eyes. It had been replaced by a look of barely controlled, subterranean violence that made Yasmin gasp. She wondered at the wisdom of trying to hit this man, and was glad he'd managed to prevent her from scratching him. It was obvious he didn't like being opposed – especially by a woman.

For a second, Yasmin thought, it looked as if he might kill her, but then the black, hooded expression faded, and his left eyebrow slowly went up, and he said, 'But don't worry, little one. You will have no trouble at all finding another protector. They are crawling all over the city. And if it's money you like, that will be just as easy for you. The pretty ones like you have no difficulty . . . at least until they, too, begin to get long in the tooth.' He smiled wryly at her ragingly furious face, then abruptly dropped her hands. 'Why, even though you are such a little hellcat, I am considering you myself.'

'Get out of here before I call Zayd,' she hissed quietly, barely able to control her words.

'I am on my way, little one. I must contact the lawyers at once. Now don't disappear. Who knows, if you really did know him for three years, as you claim, perhaps he left you a token in his will. And in the event that he didn't, I would consider it an honor to take care of you myself.'

With that, he strode from the room. She listened as his shoes made crisp, clicking noises on the marble floor. Then he was gone.

A torrent of tears left her suddenly breathless as cold

151

terror crept over her skin. The double shock of André's death and Hassan's insinuations hit her with renewed strength. Of course, his allegations were something she would have to consider. He was, in all likelihood, not the only one who would think precisely the same thing. Nothing but a gold digger, after André's money. And André's feeling for her? Lust, pure and simple. What a cold analysis they had of all the loveliness between them. An old man's lust, nothing more.

She also remembered those giggled conversations late at night in school. The girls talked about sex and petting and going all the way. Yasmin had never contributed. She had been afraid to open her mouth for fear of letting something slip. Turkana had told her quite a lot about life and love, and André had warned her never to mention Khadir or anything at all about the brothel. But the girls also talked about whores. Whores were girls who did it for nasty old men, and got paid for it too. Whores lived in whorehouses. A brothel was a whorehouse. Yasmin had looked it up. The memory of that shame flooded through her as she realized what everyone would think of her when it all came out in the end. The mortifying shame pounded up through her temples.

And Dr Calvados? He had even insinuated that Yasmin had been instrumental in André's death, albeit unwittingly. Perhaps it was already a joke around the hospital. He had asked her what André was doing at the time of his attack, hadn't he? Yasmin blushed crimson as the enormity of the world's ugly opinion flooded her with devastating accuracy.

But in a way it was true. She *had* killed him. He had not slept for weeks, and it had been all her fault, however innocent. Now here she was, alone, with nowhere to turn, cut loose from her own world, and still with no connections to André's world.

She straddled a very sharp cultural fence, especially

here in Tangier. She no longer felt like an Arab, but she was still not a European. Neither side would want her, nor could tolerate her. She could always take Hassan up on his suggestion – find a protector until she was too old even for that. What a disgusting thought! Yasmin ran her fingers through her hair distractedly. Perhaps a protector was what she *had* to have. She had never been free, despite everything that Madame had taught her. She had never taken care of herself, never handled money, never even shopped for food or bought clothes for herself. There had always been someone else to do it for her. First her grandfather, then Khadir, and finally André and the protection of Lautremont.

She could try and find a job, but what could she do? She would need someplace to live, but how would she pay for it until she got the job? Her mind was reeling with shock, fatigue, and the insurmountable problems that she faced. And there was no one who could give her advice. The thought of asking Hassan for help made her stomach flip with nausea. Was there no one?

Oh, André! How could you leave me alone like this? But her wordless plea fell on an empty room. Zayd? He obviously didn't like her. Salima? She probably had problems of her own, and was in no position to help anyone, least of all Yasmin.

Suddenly she thought of Madame Duchamp. Hadn't she said that Yasmin could come to her if she ever needed help? Where had she put that card with Madame's address and telephone number? Yasmin ran out of the library and quickly climbed the stairs to her room.

Flinging open the ebony wardrobe doors, she dragged out the purse in which she'd put the card on that last day of school. She prayed it was still in there. It would have fallen out anywhere during their travels. Oh, please let it be here, she begged silently. Allah, if you are there, and ever cared for me at all, please let it be here!

And then, miraculously, the card appeared: Madame Solange Duchamp, 13 Rue Saint Victor, Genève, Suisse, tel. 341319. She kissed the card, and flew back down to the library.

How does one place an overseas call? she wondered. She stopped, terrified as she held up the receiver. Then the operator's voice came through the little mouthpiece, and she had no choice but to go ahead. Giving the number, Yasmin waited until the operator came back, saying there would be a slight delay in completing the call.

'How long?' asked Yasmin, her voice high-pitched with anxiety.

'*Cinq minutes*. Shall I ring you back, or would you care to wait?'

'If it's only five minutes, I will wait, thank you,' Yasmin said, her grip tightening. She didn't want to lose her tenuous connection with Madame, even for a second. Surely Madame would know what to do, how to help her, she thought.

Yasmin followed the plodding course of the minute hand on the clock near the door. The time ticked by with agonizing slowness. Then she heard the sweet, bell-shaped tones of Madame's voice coming through the phone.

'Yes? Hello?'

'Oh, Madame Duchamp . . . it's Yasmin.' Yasmin's voice was almost a cry. She struggled to keep the trembling in her stomach from interrupting her.

'Well, hello, my dear. How delightful to hear from you.'

'Madame, the most terrible thing has happened. I must talk to you.'

'What is it, Yasmin?' Madame's voice was suddenly serious.

'André is dead!' Yasmin could no longer control the

sobs that had been lurking below the surface. She burst into tears, no longer able to talk because of the racking sobs.

'Dead? What do you mean, dead? Yasmin, try and control yourself, and talk to me.'

Yasmin drew three long shuddering breaths deep into her lungs and began again.

'André had a heart attack and he died in the hospital just now. They phoned me about an hour ago. Madame, I don't know what to do. You must help me somehow.'

'But, Yasmin, isn't there someone there who can help you?'

'No. There is no one . . . .' Her shuddering breathing was coming in rasping pants.

'But surely he has lawyers, friends – '

'Madame, you do not understand. There is no one. The relationship was not what you thought. I can't tell you about it now, it is a very long story. All I know is that I have nowhere to turn . . . and I'm frightened.'

There was a brief silence on the other end, then Madame's reassuring voice came through to her. 'Yasmin, do you think you could get yourself onto a plane and come to Geneva? You are obviously in no condition to manage a thing like this on your own. I can help you better here. Do you think you could do that?'

'Yes, Madame. I think I can do that.'

'It doesn't matter what time you arrive, my dear. I will be here waiting for you. Just get a taxi at the airport and give the driver my address.'

'Oh, Madame, I don't know how to thank you or what to say.'

'I know, my dear, I know. Just come, and we will straighten everything out in no time. Things are, I am sure, not as bad as you think. I am quite certain that Monsieur le Baron would never have neglected to arrange things so that you would be taken care of. After all – '

'Madame, you do not understand, but I will talk to you when I see you.'

'Yes, dear, of course . . . now, when you hang up, please call the airport and make a reservation on the earliest flight to Geneva. If you have any problems, just call me back and I will see what I can do. Is that clear?'

'Yes, Madame.' Yasmin was beginning to feel less muddleheaded as Madame's dulcet voice calmed her, assuring her that everything would be taken care of.

'I will see you soon,' said Madame, her confidence pouring through to Yasmin. 'And don't worry.'

'I won't . . . I'll try not to, Madame,' answered Yasmin. '*Au revoir.*'

'*Au revoir*, my dear.'

The click at the other end of the wire signaled the end of the conversation. Yasmin carefully placed the receiver in the cradle and sat down.

Now what? she thought. I must get going. Call the airport. Yes. Money? How to pay? Oh, yes, the safe. Is that stealing? Probably, but there is no help for it. Otherwise how to get to Geneva? No way.

She made herself get up and pick up the telephone again. Almost mechanically, like a wind-up doll, she asked the operator to connect her with the airport. A metallic voice told her that there was a flight to Paris at six o'clock in the morning and that she would have to transfer for the connecting flight to Geneva. Otherwise she could wait until five in the afternoon for a direct flight. Yasmin, feeling frightened and pressured, worried that Hassan would return or that the house would be sealed, made a reservation on the six o'clock flight.

She crossed to the portrait, alarmed and guilty, as she felt the almost living eyes of the woman in the picture gaze at her with accusation and contempt. Sharply, she pulled the painting away from the wall so it couldn't stare at her anymore, and twisted the dial. She reached inside the safe for the bundle of money and carefully counted out three thousand francs and five hundred dirhams. That should certainly be enough to get her to the airport, she decided, and if it didn't cover the flight, she was sure it was possible at the airport to change some of the francs to cover the rest. Putting back what remained of the money, she quickly closed the door and moved the portrait back into position.

Looking back into the steady gaze that seemed to be directed at her, she thought, Don't worry, I will return it when I can. Then she rolled the money up, holding it in the palm of her hand, and left the room.

Upstairs she looked around quickly, then pulled out a suitcase. It was small, and wouldn't hold much, but she didn't want to lug the big heavy one with her.

She could decide in Geneva what to do about the rest of her things. Quickly throwing into the bag what dresses, pants, and blouses she thought would be useful, she took up her purse again. As she closed the doors to her wardrobe, the caftan and haik she'd worn when she first came to the villa caught her eye. They were on the curved wooden hangers, so delicate, so much a part of another world and another life. The sight of them suddenly made the thought of leaving unbearable.

A knot of misery filled her throat. I will not cry, she thought, I will not cry. But her hand reached out to touch the fabric lovingly. One last memory she never wanted to lose, they would remind her of what once was, she thought, and slipping the garments out of the wardrobe, folded them across her arm. There was no room in the suitcase, so she had to carry them. She closed the wardrobe doors finally, bowing her head in grief.

Looking around one last time, Yasmin felt the awful wave of anguish that she was trying to quell again rise up in her breast. What a beautiful room, and what a lovely life it would have been. But not for her. Not now. All of that was lost, gone, snatched away by André's death. For a moment she wished she had never known this existence, never known André. That way it would have been easier. She wouldn't have had an inkling of how wondrous life could be. But now, once shown the delights, she would never be able to forget. Better to have never known at all, she thought, than be forced to compare everything to this.

She fought back the tears that threatened her once again, opened the door to her room, and glanced out to see if there was anyone to observe her. Relieved to find the house empty and silent, she made her way down the lovely curving staircase, her eyes caressing the rows of paintings. She quickly went back into the library, closing the door behind her. Thinking it wise to call Madame and tell her what plane she was going to take, she picked up the telephone.

Then her ears picked up another sound, at first faint, then louder. Seconds later she heard the crunch of tires on the drive. A car! But who could be coming there at that time of night? Carefully, she placed the receiver back on the cradle and listened. The car door slammed and she distinctly heard the heavy thud of shoes on the gravel. Then she heard Zayd, speaking to someone . . . that voice, that purring, sensuous voice. Hassan Jalifa!

Without reasoning, she picked up the suitcase and her purse, and crossed the room quietly as a cat. Opening the wide French windows that led out onto the veranda at the side of the house, she slipped out into the night, and made her way across the lawn to the eucalyptus trees bordering the wall. Once lost in their shadows, she slipped the haik over her head. The voluminous folds covered her completely and obscured what she carried. Drawing the hood up over her head, she slipped along the wall until she came to the high grilled gate.

With a last glance back at the house, Yasmin saw the

tall, broad-shouldered figure of Hassan silhouetted in the light from the library windows. But he would never find her now. Even if he were to pass her on the road, he would never guess who she was. Under the enveloping robe, she would look like any other Arab woman walking along the road at night. She silently thanked Allah for reminding her to bring the haik along.

No doubt someone would soon discover the missing money, but she told herself she would return it someday, to someone. Just not now. They would probably want to lock her up for stealing it in the first place. And besides, after the initial furor had died down, who would care to track down an anonymous Arab girl that André had briefly befriended? No one. Feeling safe but anxious, Yasmin hurried down the mountain road. She breathed the cool night air gratefully into her nostrils and walked swiftly under the tall, bent cypresses.

Slipping along from one shadow to the next, she drank in the sound of the pounding surf at the base of the cliffs. The salty air felt suddenly good to her. Far below, the twinkling lights of the city beckoned, filled with an unspoken promise. For the briefest of moments, intoxicated by the night and the smell of jasmine and the sea, she felt lighthearted with freedom. As the lights of the city spread out before her, it seemed her life was spread out before her as well. But then the nagging doubts and fears returned, obscuring the quick flash of delicious freedom she had felt. A chasm of fear yawned below her, threatening to swallow her up in its maw. Pulling the haik closer around her body, Yasmin fled down the hill as if pursued by demons.

As she drew near the city a car suddenly went hurtling down the road. Watching the red taillights blink and disappear around a bend, she wondered if perhaps that was Hassan looking for her. She quickly dismissed the thought. It had no relevance to her life anymore. She was free.

Her only concern now was getting to the airport, getting the ticket, and getting to Geneva and Madame Duchamp. She knew she'd get to the airport long before the plane left, but it didn't matter. She could sit in the lounge and wait however long she had to wait. At least for a while she was in control of her own destiny – and whatever it held in store for her.

PART THREE
Geneva, June, 1975

9

Later Yasmin would wonder how she'd ever gotten through the ordeal. Sitting in the deep, comfortable armchair in Madame Duchamp's sunlit apartment in Geneva, the tension-filled hours seemed to drop away and for the first time she relaxed. She ached all over from the strain of clenched muscles, the exhaustion of being up all night, and the agonizing loss of André's death.

Madame Duchamp's face, so elegant, so cool, and so sympathetic, had calmed her.

After the taxi had left her in front of the apartment house with its graceful Belle Époque scrolls and tendrils sculpted around each window, Yasmin had thought she wouldn't be able to drag herself the last few feet. But hoisting her bag, she forced herself to climb the steps. A small elevator paneled in mahogany carried her squeakingly up to the fourth floor where she gratefully put down her things and rang the bell.

The door was opened immediately, and she was hugged warmly by Madame Duchamp. 'Thank goodness you are finally here,' Madame said, ushering her into the apartment.

Yasmin slid into the comfort of a handsome wing chair, leaning her head against its cushioned back. 'Oh, Madame, you have no idea how glad I am to be here,' she sighed, as she let herself rest.

'First of all, please call me Solange, my dear. We are on a different footing now. I am no longer your headmistress, but your friend.'

'Thank you so much, Solange . . . how strange that sounds . . .'

'Think nothing of it, my dear. Now please, I will get you something to drink . . . tea, perhaps? And some food. Then you will tell me everything.'

Yasmin closed her eyes and listened to the faint sounds that came from the kitchen as Solange prepared a quick meal for her.

'Come and sit down,' she called, and Yasmin pulled herself out of the chair, following the voice into a small breakfast room that looked out over the street. Sun poured in through long, many paned windows, bathing the delicate wicker furniture in a golden glow.

'Now tell me . . .' Solange waited expectantly as Yasmin took a sip of her tea, feeling its warmth course through her. 'Why is it that you must come to me? What is it that I do not understand?'

As Yasmin ate, she told Solange everything. She talked about her family in the Rif, and André. She couldn't bring herself to tell Solange about Abdul Khadir, not just yet. She felt too ashamed, and didn't want to give anyone reason to think she was anything more than just a poor Moroccan child who'd found someone to help her through school.

She told Solange how André had decided to take care of her and send her to school after her mother's death. She told her how they had become lovers on the trip back to Tangier, described André's death, and with a barely perceptible shudder, described how people in Tangier had reacted to her since she returned.

'So you can see why I couldn't stay there. Without exception, they all thought I was a whore, a gold digger, or possibly worst of all, a murderess.'

'Well, I think perhaps you exaggerate,' Solage replied. 'Certainly no one would accuse you of murdering André. These unfortunate things happen, my dear. It is certainly not the fault of the woman involved. But still, I can see your point about the other. Perhaps if you had been there longer, gotten to meet people and know them socially, you would have been in a better position. As it is, I think the best thing for you to do is stay here in Geneva. I doubt that there is any reason, or even any point, for you to return to Tangier. I'm sure that in time Baron de Saint-Clair would have made some financial arrangement for you, but of course he had just returned. *C'est la vie.*'

'Oh, thank you, Ma – I mean Solange. But I don't want to be a burden to you.'

'You will certainly not be a burden, Yasmin,' Solange said. 'We will just have to get you settled and give you some time to recover from this sad occurrence.'

'I'll try and get a job somewhere. I am really not trained for anything, but at the very least I can be a waitress or something.'

'Please. I do not think you should rush to get a job. You have a few things to get over, my dear. You must rest, collect yourself.'

'No. I can't just sit all day. I have to be busy. I have to be so exhausted at the end of the day that I have no time to think, no time to remember.'

'Mmm, I see what you mean. Well . . . I don't really agree, but perhaps you know best.'

'And I also want to be able to return the money I took from the safe. Don't you see? They will find out and think I am a thief. It occurred to me on the plane that they may even accuse Zayd or Salima of taking the money, and that would be terrible.'

'You know,' said Solange, a faraway look appearing in her eyes, 'I have just had a thought. Perhaps I know of a job for you.'

Yasmin was silent as she watched Solange.

'I have an acquaintance, Oskar Von Rothenburg, who just asked me if I knew someone who could handle the paperwork for his private collection. He is a very wealthy

165

man with a magnificent private collection of art and antiques. They are constantly on loan to museums and galleries. He attends auctions all the time, looking for new acquisitions. He travels most of the time, but he needs a secretary of sorts to handle the permissions, the publications, and the shipment of his pieces. It is really a very delicate job, and he asked me if I knew of someone who was trustworthy and at the same time intelligent enough to keep track of everything for him.'

'That sounds wonderful, but do you really think I could do it?'

'Of course you can, my dear. You can type. You have had excellent training in art history and antiquities. Think of all those trips you took, that summer course at the Sorbonne. You would be perfect!'

Solange stood up and went to the telephone. 'I will call him immediately, just to make sure he hasn't hired someone in the meantime. If that is the case, we will just think of something else, won't we?'

Solange was gone for what seemed a long time, but Yasmin was thankful to just sit and drink her tea in peace. She basked in the sun, and watched the cars and people down in the street. The light filtered through the leaves on the tree-lined street, making dappled patterns on the sidewalk where people hurried back and forth. It was a lovely, peaceful scene, and in a way, she felt totally at home. If only André hadn't wanted to return to Tangier, she thought. If only he'd decided to stay in Europe with her, then he wouldn't have had the heart attack and everything would be as it should have been . . . not like this. The creeping lassitude of despair again began to coil its numbing tendrils around the edges of her thoughts. As if the sun had slipped behind a cloud, she continued to sit staring out the window, but the brightness had disappeared.

She didn't hear Madame's footsteps as she came back

into the room. Only when she spoke did Yasmin snap her head forward, forcing herself to focus on the words.

'Well my dear, we are definitely in luck,' said Solange cheerily, 'Oskar hasn't hired anyone. In fact, he said he was waiting for *me* to come up with someone. Isn't that ridiculous? The man is using me as some sort of employment agency. Humph!'

'He probably won't want to hire me,' answered Yasmin, her voice low and dull.

'Don't be silly. By the way, I took the liberty of saying that you were André's adopted daughter, Mademoiselle de Saint-Clair. It's easier all around to describe you in that way. I explained about André's unfortunate death – he's bound to hear about it in his circle anyway, and I said that you wanted a pleasant job, not too taxing, to give you something to do, chase away the doldrums, etcetera.'

'You mean . . . I got the job based on my supposed connection with André?' Yasmin felt somehow diminished by the knowledge, as if without that mention, a sort of bona fide reference, she would have been unacceptable.

'Certainly not, my dear. You don't have the job yet. Oskar would like to interview you tomorrow. I'm sorry I couldn't put it off for another day, but he is going to Paris next week and would like to get you started if he thinks you qualify.'

'Qualify? What am I supposed to do to qualify?' Panic filled Yasmin's voice.

'Probably nothing. At the very least it's a formality, since you were recommended by me. At the very most he probably wants to see whether you are pretty or not. They are all the same, my dear. Don't forget it for a minute.'

'I would rather work for a woman,' Yasmin said sullenly.

'I'm sure you would, and you needn't take this job if you don't like it or if you don't like Oskar. But I assure you he is a very dear friend of mine and a most delightful person. You will see tomorrow. We still have to deal with today, however, so come with me.'

Solange opened a door in the rear of the apartment, saying, 'This is the bathroom,' then she opened the one next to it showing Yasmin into a small room furnished with a bed, a small Regency desk, and a long low bureau. The bed was covered with a soft blue quilt and piled high with pillows.

'That looks inviting,' said Yasmin, then walked to the bed and lay down, letting herself sink back against the pillows.

'You must be exhausted. I suggest you try to sleep.'

When Solange left, Yasmin's thoughts were still in a whirl. She was afraid she would never be able to shut them off. But before she could worry about it, her overloaded senses shut down without any prompting and she fell into a deep, healing sleep.

'It is a perfectly delightful day,' came a voice, and Yasmin felt herself being lazily drawn out of a soft, enveloping cocoon as her eyes opened to dazzling bright sunshine. Forgeting where she was for the moment, she was unprepared for the pale blue curtains and the sounds of cars honking in the street. 'I know that you're tired, but you've slept almost around the clock, my dear. It's time to get up!'

Yasmin stretched lazily and rubbed her eyes. When Solange said 'around the clock,' she suddenly remembered. Geneva, of course. Goodness, she must have been tired. She'd never slept that long before in her life. Swinging her legs out of bed, she stretched again.

'What time is it?'

'Why, it's almost eleven-thirty, and we're to be at

Oskar Von Rothenburg's after lunch. You must hurry.
I've pressed your clothes and they're hanging in the
closet. Now you go and take your bath, and then we'll
eat something and leave.'

Yasmin stood in the shower, rubbing her body clean of
the grit that had accumulated since that disastrous day in
Tangier.

Was that only the day before yesterday? she thought.
Now, under the strong jets of water after her leaden
night's sleep, those events seemed far away, as if they
had happened months ago. Yasmin wondered at the
resilience of the human mind. Perhaps it wasn't possible
for a person to withstand that much pain without shoving
it into the background. She hoped it stayed in the background because she had to force herself to get on with
the business of her life. She had no time to wrap herself
in thoughts of what might have been. To do so would be
to fall into a quicksand of sorrow, and she couldn't afford
that.

After rinsing she stepped out and rapidly toweled
herself dry, she dressed quickly, then went into the
kitchen.

Solange shooed her away, and Yasmin took a cup of
steaming coffee and a croissant into the dining room and
sat before the open window. She rubbed her hair dry
thoughtfully as she sipped, wondering what the day would
bring. It was actually an interesting sensation – not
knowing. Before, she had always known what to expect.

Solange came in with an omelet and began to talk
about her plans for the day and the places Yasmin should
see. She didn't mention André, and Yasmin was thankful.
She only wanted to eat her omelet and let the flow of talk
wash over her. The sun shining in the window dried her
hair as she ate, and the soft breezes of early summer –
breezes carrying the delicate scent of flowers mixed with

169

the exhaust from cars – wafted over her. After breakfast they left the apartment.

'I thought we should take the bus,' Solange said, 'so you'll learn how to get around by yourself. The number eight Rive bus stops at the next corner and lets you off about a block from Oskar's residence.'

Yasmin looked out of the bus window as the shifting shapes of the city flowed past her. It was so pleasant to just sit still and let the images fly past. But when it was time to get off, it was with a certain amount of trepidation that she followed Solange out into the solid world so soon, and up to an imposing building with an inlaid green and white stone facade.

Solange pulled the bell. The door, a heavily carved oaken slab with brass fixtures polished to a high sheen, was promptly opened by a liveried footman. He bowed slightly. Solange gave their names, he ushered them into the huge foyer. The polished black and white tile floor smelled of wax, and the walls were covered with a profusion of paintings hung two and three high. The ceilings seemed to rise up forever, ending in a trompe l'oeil oval framing a painted blue sky filled with wispy clouds. Little sculpted angels peered over the rim of the oval, their faces brimming over with mischievous good humor.

Yasmin was enchanted. Beyond the foyer she could see into a huge sunlit room with polished wood floors and stark white walls. There seemed to be a profusion of statues in the room as in a museum.

Then the door to their right opened and a very large, florid-faced man emerged. He was wearing a cream-colored linen suit that made him look even larger, a shimmering mauve ascot carefully arranged at his throat. Yasmin almost expected a monocle to drop out of his eye. But he merely swept across the intervening space, his arms spread out like a huge airplane about to land.

'Solange, how delightful to see you,' he boomed, and after kissing Madame's hand in the continental fashion, he directed his attention to Yasmin. 'And here is Mademoiselle de Saint-Clair. I am delightful to meet you, and most distressed to hear about your loss,' he rumbled, bowing over Yasmin's hand.

'Thank you so much,' Yasmin murmured, startled at his grip on her hand. But he dropped it instantly and spoke again with Solange.

'You have saved my life again, my dear friend. I don't know what I would have done if you had not come up with Mademoiselle de Saint-Clair. I have so many things to do, and I am a dreadful judge of people. I was at my wit's end, but if you say that Mademoiselle –'

'Please call me Yasmin,' she interrupted. 'I would feel much more comfortable.'

'But, of course,' continued Von Rothenburg with a brief smile in her direction. 'Why don't you come into the study. I'm sure you want to see what I need done. It's so . . . well, you'll see what I mean.'

Yasmin suppressed a smile. It was true that the poor man seemed to be at his wit's end. She wondered how he ever managed to acquire such an extensive collection, one so vast it needed cataloguing, if his mind was always this scattered. It occurred to her as she and Solange followed him into the huge room lined with leather-covered partner's desks, Chippendale armoires, and glass cases filled with smaller pieces of pottery, that perhaps it was this very impression of addled simplicity that threw his competitors off. Perhaps they expected him to miss the good pieces because he was so inattentive. Apparently he saw more than he let on.

He motioned for them to sit down, then realized there wasn't an uncluttered chair in the room. Hurriedly he picked up the papers lying on two of the delicate Empire chairs and placed them on the pile that obscured his desk. A couple flew off the top and landed on the floor, but he ignored them.

'I haven't had time to file any of these. It's relatively simple to do, but I just can't get myself to do it. You can see what my problem is, can't you, Mademoiselle? I mean Yasmin.'

Yasmin looked around her with a smile. 'Yes, it seems that you could use a little help organizing this.'

'Do you know the alphabet, my dear?'

'Of course!' Yasmin was shocked at the question, not realizing he was joking with her.

'Well, for the first few weeks, that's all you will have to know. I need my files put in order, and all you need for that is an extensive knowledge of the alphabet. That isn't too alarming, it is?'

Yasmin allowed herself to laugh, saying, 'I think perhaps I'll be able to manage it, Monsieur.'

'Please call me Oskar,' boomed the bearlike man jovially. 'You're hired!'

'I am?' Yasmin was incredulous. 'But you haven't asked me anything about art, or typing, or previous experience!'

'Madame Duchamp has told me all I need to know, my dear. And furthermore you know the alphabet. When can you start? The sooner the better.'

Yasmin looked to Solange for help.

'Well, Oskar, I think she can come tomorrow for half a day. After that she will be with you full time. Is that acceptable?'

'It would have been better if she started right away,' he answered owlishly. 'But I can see that it's a conspiracy to keep my office in a mess that much longer. Yes, tomorrow would be fine. What time should I expect you?'

'Perhaps at ten o'clock,' Yasmin said quickly, surprised at her self-assurance. 'We can work for two hours before

172

lunch, and then for two hours afterward. That way I will not have to assimilate too much at one sitting.'

'Perfect!' Oskar Von Rothenburg boomed.

For a moment Yasmin thought she felt the vibration shudder clear through the delicate chair legs. But then she decided it was her imagination. If it had been true, she felt certain the chairs would never have lasted a year in that study. 'Then I will see you tomorrow at ten o'clock. We will immediately start our mining operation in this stack of papers!'

Solange and Yasmin rose together. As they walked out into the foyer, Von Rothenburg offered to show them his gallery before they left. Ushering them into the sun-washed room, Yasmin saw that the light came from a huge skylight in the ceiling. The filtered whiteness of the glare shone down on a superb collection of large Greek bronzes and terra-cotta urns.

'I call this the Greek room, and I presume you can see why.'

'I had no idea that there were so many of the large bronzes outside of museums in Greece,' said Yasmin, her eyes wide with wonder. 'I thought – '

'Yes, I know what you thought,' he rumbled happily. 'So do most other people. But there has been a fantastic market in these for at least a hundred years. Salvage operations that are somewhat on the quiet side – if you catch my meaning – are bringing them up all the time. Now, with the new developments in underwater work after the Second World War, there has been a veritable flood of them. Of course, none are from the truly great fourth-century sculptors – Praxiteles, Scopas, Lysippus, and the rest. But they are quite lovely, and a boon for the private collector.'

'But they're magnificent!' Yasmin breathed rapturously.

'We have the Romans to thank for this treasure trove.

After they conquered Greece, they were so enthralled by the great masterpieces, they took most of them out of the country to grace their estates in Italy. The vagaries of winds and storms on the Mediterranean sank innumerable ships. Only now is the sea beginning to give up the great treasures they carried on board. But if it hadn't been for the outright thievery of those conquering demagogues, these bronzes would have been melted down for weapons in later centuries. That's what happened to so many of those that survived the trip or were left behind.'

'You see how odd the workings of fate can be?' said Solange, gazing at Yasmin with understanding. 'Sometimes what appears to be a disaster ends up being the thing that saves you in the final analysis.'

'This is one of the reasons that I *must* have a secretary. So many new books are being put together by historians on the basis of these' – he waved his hand possessively around the room – 'and others like them. Photographs must be taken, permissions for the use of them given out to deserving scholars, special exhibitions set up. It's endless, the problems these beauties have caused me.'

'It's going to be exciting to work in such exalted company,' said Yasmin, nodding toward the statues. 'I can't think of a nicer way to spend my day.'

'You see?' Von Rothenburg said, turning toward Solange. 'I was right to wait. I knew you would find just the right person for me.'

Once out in the street Yasmin could have whooped with joy. 'Oh, Madame – I mean Solange – what a wonderful job! I don't know quite how to thank you.'

'Your happiness is all I require, dear Yasmin. I think that the real thanks belongs to Oskar. He hired you. But you will be in an excellent position to thank him yourself by managing his affairs properly, and I have no qualms about your ability to do that.'

'I think it will be easy. That doesn't sound right, does

174

it? What I mean is, it won't be difficult because it is so much easier to work with something you love.'

'I know. That's exactly what I think. Now let's get the bus back to the city. I have an idea. Would you like to visit Grand Passage before we look at Lake Geneva? It's a department store of sorts, but you might be able to get a few things you need there. Let's take a look, shall we?'

As they climbed into the bus that had just wheezed to a stop before them, Yasmin wondered at the tricks fate seemed to be playing on her – making such a terrible impasse almost turn into an adventure. Surely there must be some mistake, but she didn't want to know what it was. She was content to watch the buildings whiz by and mask her grief for now.

10

'Now that you have looked at every file in these cabinets, you've got a general idea of where things should go. So just take this small pile here,' said Von Rothenburg, a droll expression on his large, cheerful face as he handed her a teetering stack of papers, which was easily a foot high, 'and start putting each one where it belongs. If you have a question, just ask me.'

Yasmin, seated on a swivel chair facing the yawning drawers of the file cabinet, had a momentary flash of dismay as she took the pile onto her lap. She picked up the first sheet. 'Philadelphia Museum of Art,' it said, and the one underneath said, 'Yale University Library.' Beneath that were two letters from the Department of Antiquities in Athens and a thick sheaf of papers from a Professor at Columbia University.

'Do any of these need answering?'

'That's what I'm doing now, separating the ones I've dealt with from the ones that still need replies.'

'Where are the letters you sent in response? All I find here are the requests.'

'I don't know, my dear. I can only hope they'll turn up. I assume that everything is buried in there someplace.'

'Should I file them together . . . that is, if they turn up somewhere?'

'You do it any way that makes you feel most comfortable. After all, when I need one of these letters, I'm going to ask you for it. Since you are the one who is going to have to find it, you had better be the one who works out the system.'

'I suppose,' Yasmin said softly to herself, and decided

to make a few changes. She bent her head to the task of sorting the massive amounts of paper before her, and the time seemed to slide away.

At noon Hilde, the housekeeper, brought them sliced roast duck and endive salad for lunch. Yasmin ate hungrily while Von Rothenburg talked at her in rapid-fire sentences about his future plans for portions of the collection.

'And, of course, the majolica plates are beginning to be recognized too,' he said. 'For many years they've graced some of the most fabulous collections, but only the true connoisseurs knew about them. They were Italy's finest contribution to the decorative arts – tiny, elaborate gemlike enamels – but the public was not really aware of them until recently. I have managed to unearth as many of Nicolo da Urbino's works as I can, and these are soon to travel around the museum circuit. That is if you, dear Yasmin, can collect all the appropriate papers and make the arrangements.'

'Do you have anything modern?' asked Yasmin, swallowing the last of her salad. 'I only hear you talking about Classical and Renaissance pieces.'

'Quite frankly, my dear, I don't like modern art. Oh, I realize it's an excellent investment, if you can find the right artist to back. But I do not collect purely for investment. I collect because I love the things I own. And I find as I get older that my feelings about modern art are less than charitable. I prefer to stick with what I like to look at,' he chuckled, pleased with himself. 'But, of course, this could be my downfall – collecting only what I personally like. I am reminded of a friend of my father's who went to Paris just after the turn of the century to look for interesting paintings to buy. Of course, he was shown all the new works by upstarts like Picasso and Braque. But he thought them repulsive, and refused to even consider them. Instead he bought a whole stack

177

of English hunting prints – the ones that were so popular at the time. He knew they were a good investment because he liked looking at them. His son is still bitter about it. He is now the proud owner of a least two hundred of the worthless things. I know – how could they be worthless? They turned out to be copies of the originals that were so valued. And in the meantime just one Picasso is worth millions. Amusing, yes?'

Yasmin chuckled as she returned her attention to her work. Shaking her head at the trials and tribulations of the rich, she thought briefly about the 'collections' of her people: a string of beads, a chain of coins, a few bolts of cloth, and a herd of goats! No matter what you have to worry about, it causes its own problems, but still, as Mark Twain said, 'Rich or poor, it's good to have money!'

Shortly before two o'clock she had managed to make an impressive dent in the papers before her. Standing up to stretch from the cramped position, she raised her arms over her head and yawned.

'Are you tired, my dear?' asked Von Rothenburg, looking guilty as a child. 'I hope I haven't made you work too hard.'

'Not at all,' said Yasmin, smiling. 'It's just that I needed to stretch. Actually, the time has gone very quickly, no doubt because I was enjoying every minute of it.'

'You only enjoyed it because it was something new,' he answered. 'Soon it will just be another boring job.'

'I doubt it,' said Yasmin. 'How could it be boring being surrounded by such beautiful things!'

'We shall see, we shall see. Now, I really think we should stop for today. I have an appointment in an hour, and I think you've had enough,' Von Rothenburg said, rising awkwardly from the delicate little chair that had somehow managed to hold his great bulk all this time without breaking. 'What time do you think you will come tomorrow?'

'Why, I think at nine o'clock, and stay until five o'clock, if that is all right with you.'

'You are joking, of course,' he chuckled. 'All right with me, indeed. Of course it's all right with me. I'll have Hilde prepare lunch for us again.'

'That would be delightful. With lunches like those, it would be an honor and a privilege to work for free!'

'That I doubt, young lady,' he said, his mustache bristling comically. 'And I wouldn't say such a thing around an old skinflint like myself. Who knows but that I might take you up on it.'

He walked her to the door, which was immediately opened by his butler Franz, and she waved as she walked down the stone steps and out onto the short walk to the street. At the nearby bus stop she swung her purse in carefree exuberance and felt the warm summer sun sink deliciously into her skin. Deciding it was too pretty a day to take the bus, she began to walk back home. Solange had mentioned an appointment that afternoon, so she wouldn't be there anyway.

Yasmin walked along the tree-lined streets, heading toward the lake. She planned to skirt the lake until she came to Pont du Mont Blanc, where she could cross over and start home. Perhaps, she thought, she might see some nice shops in the business district as she passed by. But none of it mattered. The day was so warm and sunny she just wanted to enjoy the sights and sounds of the city. She could bother about shopping another time.

Out on the lake sailboats were coursing along ahead of the wind, and swans and ducks were floating lazily on the slightly choppy surface. She strolled past young lovers who seemed entranced with each other, unaware of the outside world. They wrapped their arms around each other, trying to merge into one, as lovers always do.

Suddenly Yasmin was overtaken by such a wistful sadness that she sat abruptly on one of the benches facing

179

the water. The aching in her chest tore at her, and she thought her heart would burst from the pain of her memories. Staring at the water without seeing it, she tried not to remember André and his arms, his lips on hers. She had forced herself not to think of him while she was immersed in working or talking with Solange. But alone . . . alone she was too open to the devastating memories.

I have to keep constantly busy, she thought sadly. Then standing, she took a deep breath, straightened her shoulders resolutely, and continued walking. She crossed the bridge, gazing down at Ile de Rousseau, where swans were clustered near the hanging ivy, their great arched necks looking like graceful reeds.

The sun was lowering in the sky, and Yasmin realized it must be getting on toward four o'clock. She strolled off the bridge and made her way past the lovely English Garden on the other side of the lake. Deciding to do more exploring, she crossed Quai General Guisan and then Rue de Rive, heading for the smaller streets in the older section of Geneva.

As she walked, drinking in the lovely old buildings and watching the children at play in the streets, she passed a sign – Rooms to Let – hanging outside a dilapidated building. She entered the courtyard and gazed at the staircase inside, which wound up past each landing. Through a glass doorway she could see the old, carved marble fountains that had probably once been used to water the horses. Now they were filled with plants. Around the fountain were several large marble tubs planted with trailing ivy, the leaves partially obscuring the relief carvings that danced around their sides.

Yasmin rang the bell and waited several minutes. An elderly woman, her face seamed with wrinkles, slowly shuffled to the door and opened it a crack.

'S'il vous plaît?' she said, peering at Yasmin over the

tops of her gold-rimmed glasses. Her worn purple velvet dress was trimmed with antique lace at the wrists and throat. Without doubt it had once been very elegant. Now the velvet was worn away in places and hung on her bony frame. A delicate cameo was pinned at her bosom, depicting the profile of a pretty young girl with her hair hanging in loose, winding tendrils around her shoulders.

'You have a room to let?' Yasmin asked, wondering at her own audacity. Well, she thought, it couldn't do any harm to look. Even if she didn't rent it, she could get an idea of what was available and for what price.

'Ah, yes' the woman answered, and opened the door wider to admit Yasmin. 'It is on the second floor, and looks out over the street.' Her voice sounded like a breeze rustling through cracked parchment. 'Follow me, Mademoiselle.'

Laboriously the woman climbed the stairs ahead of her, resting briefly about every fourth step. At the landing she stopped again to catch her breath, then led Yasmin to the end of the hall, where she extracted a large, ornately scrolled key from her pocket and opened the narrow door. Yasmin walked into the room and surveyed the three long windows that let in the rosy light of afternoon. Along the wall, partially hidden by folding doors, was a kitchenette. A half-size refrigerator was under the countertop, and the sink and stove were right next to each other, crammed into the tiny space.

A small, round drop-leaf table was set near the windows, and two cane-backed chairs nestled against the worn wood. At the other side of the room was a single bed, a bureau, and a large overstuffed easy chair. Hanging against one wall was an exquisite, huge, gold-leafed mirror about five feet tall and four feet wide, with carved climbing vines and leafy tendrils lacing their way around the edges of the frame and occasionally dripping down across the silvery, pocked surface of the glass. The gilt was worn in some places and the mirror darkened in large spots, but it spoke of a bygone era in a way that no other piece in the room did.

'Isn't that mirror worth a lot of money?' she asked, struck by its obvious elegance.

'Sadly, no,' answered the woman. 'I had it appraised once. The gentleman told me that it would be worth about eight hundred francs at auction, but it would cost six hundred francs to have it packed in a special case to get it there, so I just leave it. It appears to be far too much trouble to try and sell.'

'Actually, I'm glad,' said Yasmin, gazing at her silvered reflection in the glass. 'It's a beautiful thing to have in one's room.'

'Yes, I rather thought someone would like it.'

'It makes the room seem much larger too,' said Yasmin as she looked at the reflection of the room in its depths.

'The bathroom is through that door,' said the woman, pointing her gnarled finger, 'and the closet is over there.'

'How much is it?' asked Yasmin, mentally trying to figure out how much she could afford.

'Four hundred francs a month,' answered the woman, her mouth pursed. She pushed her glasses back up her nose as she waited for Yasmin to reply.

Thinking of the four hundred and fifty francs a week she was paid by Oskar Von Rothenburg, and rapidly calculating the bus fare at about eighty centimes each way, plus food, Yasmin decided it was a very good price.

'I'll take it,' she said precipitously.

'I will need one month in advance, and one month as security,' said the woman, peering at her hopefully.

'Yes, of course,' said Yasmin, 'but I must go home and get the money, if that is acceptable to you. You will hold it for me?'

'*Naturellement,*' said the woman, smiling happily. 'I am Madame de Goncourt. And what is your name, please?'

'Yasmin de Saint-Clair,' she answered.

'Very good, Mademoiselle de Saint-Clair. When will you return?'

'In about an hour?'

'That will be fine,' said Madame de Goncourt. 'I will be waiting for you.'

Yasmin took one last look around the room that would soon be hers, said good-bye, and hurried down the stairs into the dark, slightly crumbling courtyard, then out into the street. A group of boys were chasing a soccer ball along the sidewalk, and they stopped briefly to watch her as she passed. She waved at them, smiling happily, and hurried along to Rue Saint Victor to tell Solange her exciting news.

Fortunately, she thought, she was only about five blocks away. How nice to be so close to the only person she knew in Geneva, with the exception of her employer.

As she burst in the door, she found Solange seated in the comfortable wing chair by the window, sipping Campari and soda.

'I had a wonderful day,' Yasmin said in a singsong voice, 'and I have also found a room to rent! What do you think of that?'

'I think that's wonderful,' said Solange, rising slowly out of her chair. 'But you know that I am not rushing you away. You are a delightful guest, and you needn't feel that you have to leave.'

'Oh, no, I don't feel that way at all,' said Yasmin, 'I just happened to walk by the sign. The room is near here and very nice . . . and not too much money. I thought I should take it.'

'How much is it?'

'It's four hundred francs a month. Is that expensive?'

'No, it is surprisingly inexpensive. What street is it on?'

'It's right off Cours de Bastion. It's an older building

with a courtyard. The woman who lets the rooms is named Madame de Goncourt.'

'Yes, I think I know the one.'

'I told her that I would return in an hour with the deposit and one month's rent in advance,' said Yasmin. 'Why don't you come with me and see what you think?'

'That's a good idea,' answered Solange, placing her glass on the table. 'And what are you intending to use for money?'

'I have the francs I took from the safe – oh, goodness! I just remembered. Those are French francs, and Madame de Goncourt will probably want Swiss francs!'

'Well,' said Solange, 'why don't I bring my checkbook with me. I will pay the advance and then you can give me the money tomorrow. I think you should have it all changed into Swiss francs, anyway. That will give you something until Oskar pays you.'

They walked to the apartment and Yasmin and Solange climbed the double flight of stairs. When Yasmin had opened the door, Solange swept into the room, her gaze taking in all aspects of the now dimly lit space in one great sweep. After swiftly crossing the room, assessing the size of the closet and the condition of the bathroom, she slid open the door that hid the kitchenette.

'It has definite possibilities,' she said musingly. 'Of course, you are going to need drapes for those windows. I have a set of linen ones that will do very nicely.'

'But Solange, you really don't have to – '

'Don't be silly. They're folded up in my hall closet, and I certainly have no use for them. And that bedspread is rather ancient too. But I have one for you.'

She opened the wooden cabinets over the sink and stove, taking stock of the few plates, cups, and glasses deep in its recesses. 'Musty,' she said, sniffing slightly. Then she opened the oven and located a collection of pots and pans. 'These will probably do for now. Unless of course, you are planning on gourmet dinners for twelve?'

'Not this week,' laughed Yasmin.

'This is really very exciting, my dear. You know, my secret passion is decorating, and I have all sorts of things I can give you. This room will be delightful when we get through with it.'

'Then you approve?'

'Approve? Of course, I approve. You did very well finding this place. Let's go back downstairs and seal the bargain, then we'll return home and eat something. After that we can collect all the goodies I have for you.'

After making their arrangements with Madame de Goncourt and wishing her a pleasant good night, Yasmin and Solange returned home. Solange almost burned the dinner, since she continuously remembered something else that would do well for Yasmin's new apartment. She dropped what she was doing to dive into one closet after another, rummaging wildly in their depths.

It was close to midnight when they stopped, exhausted, next to the growing pile of tablecloths, linens, bath mats, curtains, vases, lamps, potted plants, and rolled-up posters that threatened to block the door.

'We'll have to finish this tomorrow,' sighed Solange. 'Otherwise you'll never be able to get out the door to go to work.'

'Are you sure about all this?' asked Yasmin as she eyed the pile. 'After all – '

'Don't be silly. I can't bear the thought of throwing things out, and this is the perfect answer. I'm really the typical thrifty Frenchwoman, so it's the only solution to the overwhelming problem in my closets. The things inside there have begun to develop personalities. Everytime I open a closet door, they all start shouting "Put me someplace else!" and I cannot stand it another second.'

'Well, I feel a little better then,' said Yasmin with a

yawn. 'But let's go to bed. I have to attack that pile of papers tomorrow and I suspect they will be yelling the same thing at me too.'

Exhausted, Yasmin fell asleep almost as soon as her head touched the pillow. She didn't even have time to think about what she would do the next day. The next thing she knew, the angry buzzing of the little clock next to her ear on the bedside table woke her rudely, and the sun was streaming in her window. The sleep she'd been getting these past couple of days had been odd, dreamless. When she woke up it felt like being awakened from the dead. There were no dreams, just nothing – a deep, flat nothing.

She caught the bus at the corner, and once in her seat, devoted herself to mentally rearranging the furniture. She tried not to think about André, refused to think about him, actually, and was grateful for any excuse. Arriving on Von Rothenburg's doorstep promptly at five minutes of nine, she took a deep breath and rang the bell.

'Good gracious,' Von Rothenburg sighed as he joined her in the library about half an hour later. He sounded like a walrus blowing water out of his nose. 'You are viciously prompt, aren't you?'

Yasmin laughed, but didn't look up from the papers. 'I am almost finished with all this filing. Soon we will be able to get down to work.'

'You are far too efficient, my dear,' he muttered. 'Soon you will work yourself out of a job. Remind me sometime to explain to you the politics of working.'

'Hah,' said Yasmin. 'That would be a fine idea, but I wouldn't advise telling too many people about it.'

'I don't have to, I'm afraid. Most of them already know it. The book I've been planning to write would simply never sell.'

'When are you leaving?'

186

'Day after tomorrow. But I'll be back after the weekend, so don't worry. I'll leave plenty to keep you busy.'

For the remainder of the morning they worked clearing off the papers, putting the books and catalogs where they belonged, and sorting through the correspondence that had to be answered. In the afternoon, after an elegant lunch of leek and potato soup with little watercress sandwiches, they viewed their handiwork.

'This is truly quite amazing,' said Von Rothenburg, stunned at the number of clear surfaces that greeted his eyes. 'I don't know if I'll ever be able to work in this room again. Too many clean surfaces make me nervous.'

'Pshaw,' Yasmin chided as she picked up the manilla folder containing the correspondence. 'You must tell me what has to be written to each of these people.'

And so they passed the remainder of the day until the lowering sun, and the lengthening shadows in the room, indicated that it was time to stop. As Yasmin picked up her jacket, she wondered at how abruptly her life seemed to shift from one path to another. Well, it may be upsetting, but at least it isn't boring, she thought, briskly picking up her purse.

Yasmin made her way to the bus deep in thought. She paid no attention to her fellow passengers and found herself praying that her life would now move along on the even keel she was so desperately trying to establish here in Switzerland. She just wanted a nice, repetitive life with quiet, repetitive days.

It was only the beginning of June, and in the last month she'd graduated from school, fallen passionately in love, lost her virginity, toured the south of France and the Mediterranean coast of Spain, had the love of her life drop dead – leaving her alone, forlorn and penniless – escaped to Switzerland after stealing the money to do it, gotten a job, and found an apartment. That was enough, she thought.

Frowning as she stared without seeing out the window, she wondered how long it would take until she no longer missed André. The pain of his loss was so deep. Solange had said that time would heal this wound just as it healed all others, and Yasmin supposed she was right. But from her present vantage point it hardly seemed possible to forget.

PART FOUR

Geneva, October, 1975

11

Allah, thought Yasmin as the buzzing of the alarm clock dragged away the last wisps of her dream. She pounded the top of the clock, hitting the button that switched off the alarm. As she lay there, recalling it was 6 October, she thought about Von Rothenburg coming back the day after tomorrow and that she hadn't finished the correspondence, made the arrangements for the luncheon on the 10th, or picked up her dress from the cleaners.

Sighing, she slipped out from under the covers, walked to the windows, and pulled back the heavy cream-colored drapes. The sunlight flooded in, and the sounds of early morning traffic floated up from the street. She put some water to boil on the little stove and went into the bathroom.

When she emerged, a billow of steam surrounding her, the tea kettle was whistling angrily. Padding lightly across the soft carpet, Yasmin muttered a mild curse. She turned off the gas, staring malevolently at the kettle, which continued to whistle in a desultory fashion, its high-pitched note getting lower and lower.

'Do this, do that!' she snapped at the smooth round shape, her reflection glinting back at her from the polished metal surface. It almost looked as if the distorted mouth and eyes belonged to the kettle, and not to her. 'Everybody wants me to do something for them. Even my stupid tea kettle screeches at me!'

She stomped off, dropping her robe on the chair, and rummaged through her bureau drawers looking for her underclothes. After laying them out and straightening the bedding, Yasmin poured the water into the coffee pot, then went into the bathroom to put on makeup while she waited for the rich coffee to steep. She'd had to comb Geneva to find the little shop that sold good, strong coffee, the kind she was used to. Finished, she slipped her robe back on and got a croissant out of the bread box. Carrying her coffee cup and the delicate, crumbling pastry to the table, she sat down to relax for a few moments before the rush began.

Yasmin wondered, as she ate, whether the fabric of her days was going to be like this forever. Up in the morning, rush around, do what she was told, rush home, eat, read, sleep. She wasn't bored, certainly, but this wasn't quite what she had in mind either. She wanted more out of life, but she didn't know how to go about getting it.

She was free to take whatever direction she wanted to take, she thought, though of course she had to work to eat and have a roof over her head. Between nine and five she was caught. After five she could do what she wanted, but only until bedtime: she needed her sleep so she could go to work again the next day.

Perhaps money was the key, she thought gloomily. And if that's the case, I'll never have any freedom. Not unless I can figure out a way to become something besides someone else's secretary.

It occurred to her she could go back to school, but her time was so limited that she could only take a few courses, and at that rate she wouldn't get her degree for ten years.

What a miserable trap, she thought, taking a long sip of her coffee. Maybe Solange could think of something. Maybe Oskar could provide her with some new way of looking at things, though she doubted he'd do anything to risk losing his new assistant. In any case, neither was around to talk to.

Solange had gone back to Lautremont two weeks before, to administer the opening of school, and Oskar had been away for a month. By the time he'd left early in September, she'd had three months to get a good grasp of what had to be done in his office. But things just seemed to pile up all the time.

Nearly every time she sat down to take care of the correspondence, the phone would ring. Then she'd have to deal with the consequences of the phone call. Before she knew it, it would be after five o'clock. She wondered how Oskar had gotten everything taken care of before she came to work with him. No wonder he spent most of his time traveling. You can't answer the phone if you're four hundred miles away, right? Sighing, she bit into the croissant.

Yasmin refilled her coffee cup, and started to get dressed. But still, she mused as she buttoned her blouse, she adored the work, no matter how hectic and frenetic. Each day she was surrounded by beautiful things and interesting people. Von Rothenburg's collection was even more exquisite than she'd realized. He had huge Ming dynasty vases, medieval tapestries, antique bronzes, Sialk pottery, Macedonian ironware, and a magnificent collection of icons, which were at the moment touring museums in the United States.

She was totally immersed in her work, and Von Rothenburg was delighted with her enthusiasm and her knowledge, which became more extensive each day. Amazed at her prodigious memory, he often referred to her as his 'little computer.'

It was true that Yasmin loved her job and being around beautiful art, but looking at pretty pictures and shuffling papers was beginning to pall. What really attracted her as she got further into Von Rothenburg's world was the business end of it. Sometimes he'd asked her to help him with his complex financial maneuverings, but only in the capacity of an assistant bookkeeper, and she wanted more than that.

The numbers held a fascination of their own – establishing patterns and weaving intricate webs that clearly dictated every move he made. Of course, that was only if you knew how to look at them. For some reason Yasmin could look at the rows of numbers, and a picture would begin to form rapidly in her mind. She saw in the numbers things Von Rothenburg didn't talk about, such as how the value of his pieces could be enhanced depending on how he sold them, and to whom. She saw the immediate connection between interest from a museum and interest from private collectors. That often hung on an obscure PhD thesis that found itself in the right hands. And because of the shift in the value of gold, suddenly other things were taking on added value – things few people had cared about before.

Art, Yasmin had realized, was just like money, soybean futures, cattle, horses, gems, or precious metals. Supply and demand. The two had to be diametrical opposites. High supply and low demand equaled low price. Low supply and high demand equaled high price. In terms of the marketplace, art was no different than nickel or platinum or pork bellies. It was just nicer to look at.

Yasmin also enjoyed watching Von Rothenburg's low-key salesmanship. The more he wanted to get rid of a piece, the less he seemed to want to sell it – at least in the presence of a prospective buyer. Supply and demand again. Sometimes, listening to the drone of his voice from the other room, Yasmin had to suppress a laugh. It wouldn't do to have the help howling away in the next room while he made his pitch, would it?

That was the trouble: she really was just the help, and she wanted to get into the money end of Von Rothenburg's world. She wanted to be privy to his decisions, wanted him to teach her why, explain how and what and where. But Von Rothenburg didn't seem to have the time, or the inclination, either. Each time she'd tentatively put the suggestion, he'd changed the subject. She hadn't pressed him. This time when he comes back from his trip, she thought vehemently, I'm just going to ask him outright.

Riding on the bus, she gazed out the window at the changing trees and thought of the week she and Solange had spent on Ibiza in August, exploring the island on bicycles each morning, then lolling in the sand and sea all afternoon. Refreshed and glowing, Yasmin had returned to Geneva, leaving Solange on the island for another week alone. But Yasmin hadn't minded. Her apartment was cool and comfortable, and she was glad to bury herself in work. Gradually her numbness had fallen aside, and she was able to direct her thoughts away from André when she was alone.

As her heels clicked up the crisp stone walk to the house, she thought how lucky she had been in having Solange and Von Rothenburg. Both had been patient, sympathetic, and understanding. They had waited for her to emerge from her cocoon of grief, even when she'd been convinced that she never would. But they'd waited, and sure enough she had finally, tentatively, taken the first steps. Now she was definitely on the way to recovery. She had even found a stable in Rive that wasn't too expensive. Spending each weekend riding, giving herself over to the glorious sensation of the wind in her hair and the powerful muscles of the horse as they rippled under her, had been the best medicine of all.

With a sigh she stepped inside, said good morning to Franz, and entered the study. Deciding to get as much done as possible before the telephone began ringing, she attacked the typewriter. She *had* to get the correspondence cleared away before Von Rothenburg returned, she told herself, knowing from past experience that he always arrived with a huge stack of new work.

As she pounded away at the last letter, she heard the

door to the study open behind her. Since Hilde usually brought in the mail sometime in the late morning, she didn't bother to look up.

'Thank you, Hilde,' she said, hoping that the pile wasn't too large. 'Please just put it on my desk, and I'll look through it when I'm finished with this.'

But when Hilde didn't answer her, Yasmin snapped the swivel chair around to see what was the matter. Her heart plummeted as her eyes met those of the figure standing in the doorway.

Hassan Jalifa!

Smiling charmingly, he strolled across the distance that separated them, his hand extended and his eyes drilling into hers. She had forgotten the catlike grace with which he moved. But he seemed different somehow. The subtle sense of threat that floated around him the last time they'd met didn't seem to be there. Could he be masking it? she wondered. There was an unreadable expression in his hooded black eyes that didn't match his smile.

He leaned down, resting one hand on the desk. 'Well, well, well,' he said slowly. 'At last, we meet again . . . and under far more pleasant circumstances.'

'What are you doing here?' Yasmin gasped. Her voice trembled as she pushed her chair back from the desk, back from Hassan. But she wasn't able to get as far from him as she would have liked. 'How did you find me?'

'Believe me, it wasn't easy,' he said with a smile. His sensuous mouth curled up pleasantly.

'What do you want?' she asked sharply, rattled by this sudden intrusion from another life.

'You, little one, are what I want. And I've had a devil of a time finding you too. We looked for you everywhere, even at your old school. But unfortunately it was closed for the summer. It wasn't until your friend Madame Duchamp returned that I was able to track you down.'

'I'll give you back the money,' Yasmin snapped. Then

she turned back to the typewriter, praying he would disappear.

'I haven't the faintest idea what you're talking about,' Hassan said, straightening up. He placed a leather brief-case on the desk. Opening it, he took out a thick, creamy white envelope scrolled with elegantly embossed letters. With a disconcerting grin he held it out to her. 'I have a letter here for you from the law firm of Baron André de Saint-Clair. You remember him, perhaps? I presume the name rings a bell.'

'Lawyers? A letter from André's lawyers?' Yasmin's heart thumped with renewed fear. So they knew about the money after all, even if Hassan didn't. She knew she should have sent it sooner, but she'd needed to buy some clothes first. Oh, what a stupid mistake, she told herself.

Hesitantly she reached for the letter. For a split second Hassan's disturbing gaze clung to her possessively, but it faded into innocuous blandness almost instantly. The man has incredible nerve, she thought as she turned the envelope over in her slightly shaking hands, not wanting to open it.

'Since it's good news, I specifically asked if I could deliver it in person,' he said.

Her eyes dilated with amazement. Good news? Was he being sarcastic? She wanted to retreat from him, from his penetrating gaze.

'Thank you,' she said in a weak voice. 'I will read it later, when I am alone.' She hoped he would take the hint, but his eyes continued to hold her.

'I think you'd better read it now,' he said as he lowered himself into the chair next to the desk. Crossing his legs, he folded his hands and waited.

Annoyed at his persistance, Yasmin proceeded to open the letter with an ornately carved ivory knife, thinking if she read it quickly, he'd have to leave.

A slight smile hovered on Hassan's lips as he watched

her. She glanced up at him, startled to see how handsome he was and startled at the almost physical shock his presence in the room gave her. But she also remembered how vicious and cruel he'd been the terrible night André died.

Turning her attention back to the letter, she slowly pulled it from the envelope. She didn't want to read it, but told herself she had to. She unfolded the heavy sheet of paper, and read the raised, elegant black letters at the top: 'Fauquier, Renan, et La Tour.' It was dated the day before.

As she forced her eyes to follow the print, Yasmin's amazement increased. The letter requested her presence in their offices in Paris as quickly as possible. It was necessary to read André's will and have her sign certain papers that would enable them to execute its provisions. She must advise them on how to handle certain matters relating to the late Baron's estate, it said, and take over his businesses, which were badly in need of attention.

'I don't understand,' she whispered, staring at the letter. 'Why do they need . . .?'

'You, my dear, are the sole heir of his estate,' Hassan answered. 'You've even inherited the title. From now on you are Baroness Yasmin de Saint-Clair.'

Stunned, Yasmin carefully placed the letter on the desk and stared sightlessly in front of her.

So they hadn't hunted her down as a thief after all, she thought. And how terrified she'd been, how guilty. What a strange twist of fate. If she'd stayed in Tangier that night instead of running like a frightened rabbit, none of this would have been necessary. She dragged her eyes up to Hassan, who was watching her with an odd expression on his face.

'I must speak to Madame Duchamp,' she said numbly.

'There isn't much that Solange can help you with,' Hassan said coolly. Yasmin's eyebrows shot up at the familiar use of her friend's first name. 'After all,' he continued, 'I am André's investment counselor. I am the only one who understands all phases of his business, his holdings, and his investments. And let me tell you there is a great deal to be done. All this has had to hang fire while I looked all over Europe and North Africa for you. Nothing can be done without your signature, and time is now of the essence. We will discuss it tonight over dinner. In the meantime I would suggest that you leave work and make arrangements to go to Paris tomorrow morning. Settle all your affairs and take care of whatever you have to take care of.'

'But – I can't leave work until five,' gasped Yasmin, stunned at the suddenness of his request.

Hassan stood, brushing off his pants, and Yasmin's eyes were drawn to his strong, blunt fingers with their cleanly cut nails. He stopped, then laughed softly as he leaned over the desk. 'Little one, you can leave any place you want at any time you want. You are a millionairess. Aren't you happy? Isn't this every girl's dream come true?'

Yasmin gasped again as her hands flew to her throat. She stood up, knocking a pile of correspondence to the floor.

'The letter said nothing about money, only that they needed me to sign . . .'

'Believe me,' Hassan said, 'you will see that everything I have said is true when you are with me in Paris tomorrow.'

'There is no need for you to go with me,' Yasmin said. She was troubled by what she remembered of Hassan. She couldn't forget his cruelty that night when André died. But now he seemed so different. It was almost as if the man she remembered was someone else entirely. Could she have been so wrong that night? she wondered.

Perhaps. She'd been in shock. 'You don't need to trouble yourself,' she said.

'Ah, but I must. And it will be no trouble at all. I am the Saint-Clair investment counselor, and I've handled the accounting for years. I'm the only one who can teach you how to manage his businesses. You will have to put up with me,' he said, winking broadly. Snapping the briefcase shut, he walked to the door. Then, his hand on the knob, he turned again. 'So do whatever you wish, but I will pick you up at your apartment at seven. I look forward to it.'

He smiled pleasantly, and Yasmin was again shocked at how smoothly elegant he was. Why did she have this persistent picture of him as a panther? She was suddenly having a hard time remembering.

The door closed behind him, leaving her standing at the desk. She looked down at the letter that had so abruptly changed her life, once again. She sat down hard, feeling faint both from the startling news and the shock of seeing Hassan. What a strange person, she thought, and tried to regain her bearings. I must call Solange, she thought, and reached for the phone. The way he had used Solange's first name in such a familiar fashion! And the look on his face when he said it!

Yasmin had an awful thought, but just as quickly, she pushed it out of her mind. Solange was a lady . . . a cultured, sensitive lady who would never be attracted to someone like Hassan. Or would she? Yasmin had to admit that he was very handsome, and he'd been extremely pleasant. Perhaps she'd just read him wrong in Tangier. Here, in this room, he had all the gloss and mannerisms of a cultured, sensitive, and, she had to admit it, virile man. It would be understandable if Solange were attracted to him.

Quickly she placed the call to Solange, knowing that as ever, her friend would advise her. She was still unable to completely grasp the ramifications of being André's sole heir. A millionairess? And a baroness on top of it? It didn't seem real. What exactly did being a millionairess mean? To someone who had only recently begun to deal with the most minimal amounts of money – enough to pay a small rent, take the bus twice a day, and buy a few dresses – it had almost no meaning at all.

'I knew I'd be hearing from you shortly,' came Solange's voice over the telephone. Yasmin thought she could detect amusement behind the words. 'Did your ardent admirer finally locate you? I presume that is what this call is all about. I'm very sorry if I sent him on to you without your permission, but under the circumstances, I thought it best.'

'I'll discuss that part of his visit with you later,' said Yasmin, 'but what I have to say is far more important.'

'Well, I can only assume since he came to you with a letter from André's lawyers – that much he told me – that you have come into an inheritance of some kind. Is it enough to help you out at all?'

'It is more than enough, but I don't know whether it will help me or not,' Yasmin said. Her voice was quivering. 'I'm his sole heir, Solange. Everything . . . the money, the houses, the businesses – whatever they are. I don't even know the half of it, but he tells me I'm a millionairess, so that should give you some idea. Oh – and the title too.'

Yasmin could hear a sharp intake of breath at the other end of the phone.

'Well, that is certainly good news. I hardly know what to say.'

'There isn't much to say, I'm afraid. Except that I have to leave for Paris in the morning to sign papers and . . . I don't know what else.'

'Good heavens. What does Von Rothenburg say?'

'That's the other problem. He's not here. He won't be

201

back until next week. And there is so much to be done here. I really can't leave.'

'But you must! There is no question. Simply place a call to him. Where is he?'

'Belgium.'

'Just call him and explain what has happened. He'll understand. You are just throwing up inconsequential barriers. You must take care of André's affairs, and that is your first priority. Besides, you may have fun. You will be traveling with Hassan. I must say, he is perfectly charming.'

'Do you really think so, Solange?' Yasmin found it hard to express her misgivings. 'You see, he may be charming now, but he was ugly and vile to me the night André died.'

'Well, perhaps you misunderstood him that night,' said Solange soothingly. 'I found him quite delightful, and brilliant too. Did you know that he has a doctorate in economics from Harvard? In many ways I think he is like you, my dear. You could certainly choose a much worse man to spend time with.'

'I don't know, Solange. Maybe you're right,' Yasmin replied. It was obvious that Hassan had charmed Solange outrageously – but then again, it was true he seemed quite different.

'As a matter of fact I almost wish he didn't seem so interested in you. That's how fascinating I found him.' Solange laughed. It was decidedly uncharacteristic throaty laugh which Yasmin found very strange. 'At any rate, you must do everything he tells you to do. He is eminently trustworthy, at least as far as money matters are concerned. Go to Paris and speak to the lawyers. You can decide what to do about your job with Von Rothenburg then.'

'But won't he be upset?'

'Of course he'll be upset. You can always offer to train

your replacement. But there's no sense in worrying about these little things until you have more information. Am I correct?'

'Yes . . . I suppose so,' Yasmin replied sullenly. 'You always are.'

'Good, then. I'll speak to you in a week. Get going, dear, you have a lot of things to do. You can't talk on the phone all day, you know.'

Yasmin hung up, feeling touchy and out of sorts. But Solange was right, she thought, so she placed the call to Von Rothenburg, apologizing profusely. But he refused to accept the apologies, and told her not to think about the office even for a minute. Feeling more and more irritable – everyone was making it far too easy for her to just pick up and leave her comfortable existence – she put the desk in order, wrote a few notes to Von Rothenburg, and prepared to leave.

It was close to four-thirty when she gave Hilde instructions for handling the phones and the mail. Hilde smiled broadly. Yasmin could see she thought Hassan was her lover come to whisk her away on some romantic adventure, and Yasmin found her conspiratorial smiles disconcerting.

She walked to the bus stop. Seven o'clock! That was too soon! Too many changes, too quickly. She lifted her chin resolutely, deciding to try and get through it as best she could. After all, it would only be for a week at the most, and then she could return to Geneva and get on with her life. At most she'd only have to correspond with the lawyers by letter or phone now and then, she told herself.

She got off the bus feeling peevish. Actually, she thought, looking around her room, it isn't as exciting as one would think to get handed a huge lump of money. Her room, which she had found on her own, worked hard to decorate and pay for, was so much a part of herself – it had far more meaning to her than something chosen and paid for by someone else. The small apartment gave Yasmin the sense of being at home that she'd never had anywhere else.

André's villa belonged to André. Lautremont was school, not home. Khadir's compound was . . . was so long ago that she couldn't remember how she'd felt about it. She'd probably had no feelings about it. And home? After her mother had died, leaving her alone with her grandfather and her two mercurial uncles, considering *that* her home was out of the question.

Her bad temper continued to plague her. Examining each of her few dresses in turn, she discarded them in a heap on the bed. The dress she should have gotten from the cleaners would have been perfect. But naturally she'd forgotten to pick it up, and now it was too late.

She tried to remember the exact words Hassan had said to her that night. But it wasn't the words that came flooding back so clearly as the visual memory. The way he'd stared at her, hungry, sensual, and possessive. Could he have changed so radically in four months? Maybe, but she wished desperately that she had the black silk with the high neck and long, prim sleeves. It was obviously what this evening called for.

But she didn't have it. That only left the rose-colored knit. It had a high neck also, which was good, and the sleeves were long. But the dress also clung to her whole body, she realized when she stared at her reflection in the mirror, seeing the curves of her hips and breasts outlined against the fabric. Her nipples were pressed against the material, clearly visible.

Then with a stridency that startled her and made her jump, there was a heavy-handed knock on the door. Her eyes flew to the clock at her bedside.

It was only quarter to seven! Allah! Hassan was early!

But I'm not ready, she thought, when the persistent

thumping forced her to move suddenly for the door. Her lustrous hair was still loose, cascading over her shoulders and down her back. She looked, she realized, too sensual, too provocative. She didn't want to look this way for him. It was wrong. Somehow, someway, he might use her exotic beauty against her.

12

'Good. I'm glad to see that you're ready,' he said, striding past her into the room. His presence there suddenly made it seem smaller, more cluttered. He looked around, frowning as he quickly assessed her few possession. Then he turned to her for the first time and flashed his hooded smile. 'You look lovely.'

Yasmin flushed and quickly turned her head. 'Well, thank you, but I'm not ready. You're early, and I haven't done my hair yet.'

'Don't,' Hassan said brusquely, his dark eyes lingering on her. 'Leave it. I like it. You should not hide your beautiful hair in one of those silly knots.'

Yasmin was surprised by his intimate words. Then his expression changed and the probing stare was replaced by a calm smile. He picked up the lightweight black linen coat draped over a chair and held it toward her. 'Put this on,' he said mildly, 'and let's go.'

In truth, she was just as glad to leave. He filled up the room, made it seem close and stuffy. Maybe it was because he was so tall. Maybe it was because there had never been a man in her room before.

Out on the street he walked briskly. His legs were long and she had difficulty staying alongside him.

'I'm sorry,' he apologized, when he realized. 'Shall I walk slower?'

'Yes, please,' she answered. She kept her eyes lowered.

'You probably think I'm walking this fast because I'm used to having woman walk ten feet behind me,' Hassan said with ill-concealed humor.

Yasmin looked up at him, surprised. He was making

jokes about being an Arab. Most Arab men didn't make jokes about anything, much less themselves.

'Actually, women no longer walk ten feet behind. That's all changed since the Second World War,' he continued. 'Since so many of the landmines still haven't been found and detonated, the nomads ask their women to walk twenty feet ahead in case of an unfortunate discovery.'

'I'll bet they do,' she said indignantly. 'That's the thing I've always liked about Arab men – their tender consideration for others.'

'We're not all like that,' Hassan said smoothly, adjusting his step to hers. The night was surprisingly warm for October, and Yasmin didn't feel the need for her coat. Abruptly Hassan took it from her and folded it with elaborate care over his arm. 'There's no need for you to carry that.'

Yasmin began to protest, but he interrupted her. 'I found a nice restaurant across the bridge which overlooks the lake. I thought we would walk, since it's such a pleasant evening. However, if you're feeling tired, we can take a taxi.'

Wondering if there was a challenge in his words, Yasmin nodded. 'Walking would be fine,' she said.

The sun had already set behind the mass of surrounding mountains, and the purple sky seemed to be lit by the water plume. Hassan unexpectedly halted in the middle of the bridge and stared at the huge jet of water. Yasmin, startled, stopped alongside him.

'Truly magnificent,' he murmured. 'It would be nice to have such a thing in the harbor in Tangier.'

'I doubt it would be sanitary. Tangier is a backward city. Everyone uses the harbor as an open sewer.' Yasmin sniffed in disgust. 'The bacteria level in the water would make it impossible. Imagine spraying all that filth in the air.'

'True,' he said thoughtfully. 'But don't be too hard on them, Yasmin. They have a long way to go. After all, it's taken Europe five hundred years to get out of the Middle Ages. We've only just started the process. Morocco has done amazingly well in the last thirty years, don't you think?'

Yasmin pursed her lips, wondering why she disliked her homeland so much. She wondered it she'd ever feel differently. She started walking again, not wanting to answer. With two strides Hassan caught up with her and slipped his arm across her shoulders. His hand continued to slide down until it rested on the small of her back. Yasmin jumped as it struck with a jolt of electricity.

'Stop that!' A shudder reverberated through her as she stepped quickly out of his grasp.

'I'm so sorry,' he said quickly, removing his hand. 'I didn't mean to frighten you.'

'I'm not afraid of anything!' she snapped indignantly. 'I just don't want to be touched, thank you.'

'You're tense tonight,' he said as he watched her irate profile. 'Try and relax, and I promise you that by the end of dinner you'll feel much better.'

Why will I feel much better? she thought. And what's that supposed to mean, anyway? She decided to remain silent as they walked along the glittering lakeside. With great relief she heard him say, 'Here we are . . . it's just across the street.'

Raising her eyes from the pavement, Yasmin saw they were heading toward a hotel. She tried to pull back, but again his arm dropped around her shoulders, and she felt herself propelled into the main lobby.

'The restaurant is called Les Continents,' he said blandly. 'It's on the eighteenth floor. The view of the lake is superb.'

His fingers were caressing her shoulder lightly, and all her nerves felt as if they were being rubbed raw. Her face began to burn as they entered the crowded elevator. She couldn't pull away from his stroking hand without knocking into one of the other passengers. When they reached the top floor, Hassan ushered her out of the elevator doors and in the direction of the maître d'.

'I have reserved a table by the windows so the view will be that much more spectacular.'

Hassan gave his name, and the maître d' led them to a table on the far side of the room. Hassan pulled out an upholstered chair for her, then seating himself next to her. She felt his thigh press along the length of her leg as he settled himself comfortably. He appeared not to notice, however, and ordered champagne. Yasmin watched as he tasted the tiny amount poured in the glass before allowing the wine steward to fill both glasses. Then he raised his glass to her, and looked at her with a sensual smile.

'I thought we should celebrate your little windfall with a good champagne,' he said before taking a deep swallow. 'Taste it. I think you will approve.'

He watched her with his peculiar gaze as she slowly raised the glass to her lips and drank. 'You must have been a delightful companion to have earned such a princely sum in payment.' His eyes flickered across her.

Yasmin couldn't tell whether he was being pleasant or sarcastic. She took another quick sip of the champagne to give her strength. 'I loved André very much, and I still do. No man will ever mean as much to me as he did.'

Suddenly the tenor of his look changed, and his eyes seemed to sink into a glittering black vortex. 'Nonsense. I know at the moment you won't accept what I'm about to say, but as you get older, you will see that I am right,' he said, never taking his eyes from her. She felt hypnotized. 'What you felt for André was not love, but you're too young to know it, that's all. At the very most it was puppy love, and at the very least it was some form of exaggerated gratitude.'

His hand swiftly shot across the table and captured hers in a hard grasp. 'Now listen to me. André was obsessed with you. That much is obvious, and the consequences of being the object of someone else's obsession are often confusing. The object begins to partake of the obsession. But partaking of an obsession doesn't involve will or choice. It can easily be confused with love because of the very subtle nature of obsession, but it is still one-sided. Obsession behaves like love. Even though it comes from only one of the people, its intensity is enough for two. Do you understand? André thought of you as the child he'd never had. In addition he thought of you as a plaything. His guilt merely fed his obsession. You merely absorbed it.'

Unwillingly Yasmin listened to his voice coming at her as if through a tunnel. She heard every painful word, and it hit her in the pit of her stomach. She also felt his thumb as it licked across the palm of her hand, sliding firmly between each of her fingers, caressing her. She began to tremble, and was unable to pull her hand away, mesmerized the way a moth is by a flame, knowing full well the lethal consequences. She shivered as the sensations flashed through her like jagged bolts of lightning. She was reacting to what he was saying, but knew he assumed her reaction was to what he was doing. Barely able to breathe, she heard his voice almost without hearing it, and fought to think of some way she could extricate herself.

'You see?' he murmured softly as he felt the shiver run through her hand. 'You are a very sensual little creature. All André did was tap some of that sensuality. It's perfectly understandable that you should become confused. But don't invest his memory with too much. It can only stand in the way of your leading a happy and fulfilled life.'

Then he let her hand drop. Startled, Yasmin was thrust back into the real world of the humming restaurant. Quickly she hid her burning hand on her lap. She tried to shift her chair closer to the window, but it was impossible. The legs were caught in the thick carpeting.

'Could we please order?' she asked, trying to pretend that his words had no effect on her. She thought of André, beloved André who had meant so much to her, and wondered if what Hassan said was true. Perhaps that *was* what he felt for her. Maybe he had told Hassan those things, she thought. But no. It couldn't be. André *did* love her. She had felt his love envelop her. Hassan was wrong. He was just too arrogant to know it. Well, that was his problem, she thought, not hers.

'Certainly,' he said, smoothly refilling her glass. 'We should feed you before the champagne goes to your head.'

She refused to answer, and turned her gaze out to the lake as he motioned for the waiter. Without consulting her, he ordered for them both and waved the man away with an impatient brush of his hand. She didn't even hear what he'd ordered.

'We must also discuss some of our business. I will lay out the groundwork for you, so you aren't overwhelmed once we get to Paris.'

Yasmin turned to face him and nodded briefly. She kept her gaze carefully focused on his chin, not wanting to deal with what lay in his obsidian black eyes. But he seemed uninterested in her as he plunged into a description of the workings of André's estate.

'The most important things you will have to deal with are, in descending order – the vineyards, the real estate, the mining investments, and the factory. The factory will be a simple decision. It involves either selling the building

211

and the machinery or finding a suitable tenant, if you wish to hold on to the property. I personally would advise holding on to it, but that will require a certain amount of management on your part. The real estate is just a matter of bookkeeping – unless, of course, you want to buy or sell anything. However, I wouldn't advise either. The mining investments don't need any attention right now. The vineyards, unfortunately, are another matter. André had planned to start distribution in the United States this year. I advised him against such a move, and I will advise you to do the same. If you want at some later date to make such a decision, wait until you understand more of the business before you put his plans into effect. The marketing and distribution of this year's wines must be dealt with immediately, though. We have already had to hold things up while I scoured two continents for you.'

Yasmin listened, dazed, to his words; they flowed over her like water. Their food was served, but she barely tasted it as she mechanically brought each forkful from her plate to her lips. She felt herself nodding each time he stopped talking, but only because the pause seemed to indicate that he wanted some response before launching into another detailed speech. As they ate, he scribbled figures on a pad and mentioned impossible sums of money.

Overwhelmed with the quantity, if not the texture, of his words, she could find nothing to say. Finally, after a long pause, it seemed that he became aware of her again and understood that she was unable to grasp the complex details he was telling her.

'Don't worry,' he said, his voice unexpectedly kind. ' I will help you with everything. What I'm doing now is just laying the foundation. Over the next few years it will gradually come clear to you, so don't feel pressured.'

'Years?' Yasmin tried to hide her dismay. 'But that's such a long time.'

'A few years is nothing, my dear. You are now a baroness – a very wealthy one, and you're going to be dealing with this for the rest of your life! You're going to have a great deal of help from me, so take even longer than a few years if you wish.'

The waiter returned, asking Hassan if they would care for coffee and liqueur. Hassan declined for them both. 'We should leave,' he said. ' We have an early plane to catch tomorrow and you need to get a good night's sleep. So do I, for that matter.'

After he had signed the check, he rose and pulled out her chair so that she could stand. He moved too quickly, and she lost her balance for a moment. But Hassan took hold of her elbow firmly, in a proprietary way, and they walked to the elevator.

'I think I'd like to walk back,' he said, breathing in the moist, fresh wind blowing off the lake as they stepped into the street. 'Do you mind?'

Yasmin *did* mind. She suddenly wanted to spend as little time with him as possible, but before she could say no, he'd already started ahead of her. Deciding it was pointless to argue, she followed.

As they walked along the edge of the lake, he questioned her relentlessly about her life, where she'd come from, her family, what school had been like. He fired questions at her with machine-gun rapidity. She wondered why he never bothered to ask her about Khadir. He'd once implied that she was only André's mistress – his Moroccan whore. But perhaps he knew as much as he needed to know, she thought, since she doubted he was trying to avoid an issue she might not want to discuss.

Finally, breathless from the pace and the talking, and slightly annoyed at his prying, she stopped. It took him a few paces to notice that she was no longer beside him.

'And what about you?' she said as he turned questioningly, wondering what had happened to her. 'Why don't you tell me about yourself?'

213

'Of course. Anything you want to know,' he answered, looking surprised. 'I thought you weren't interested in me.'

'I'm not, but anything is better than being interrogated hour after hour,' she snapped. 'Did you get married yet? A quadruple wedding, perhaps, to fill a nice little harem back in Morocco, waiting on your every whim?'

Hassan roared with laughter. 'Great God, no. What a ghastly thought. There's probably only one thing worse than having a wife, and that's having more than one wife. But I already told you that, didn't I? I have a brother. I let him marry. I'm quite happy with my present state, thank you.'

'That's what all Arab men say,' she said. 'But in the end they get four wives anyhow.'

'I doubt it. I prefer the Western approach, personally. They only allow you one wife, and it keeps you out of trouble.' Hassan laughed again. 'My uncle once took me aside when I was about fourteen years old and explained the facts of life to me. He said that you married your first wife, and for a while everything was wonderful. Then he said that suddenly, after the first baby, she complains there is too much work for one wife, she has to take care of the baby and cook and collect the wood, do the shopping, carry the water, clean up, do the wash . . . and on it goes until you break down and get another wife. Then the two of them get on you, and before you know it, you have four wives to feed and clothe, and they all complain that there's too much work. This, of course, is after they've spent the whole day in the baths. The Western approach is much better, right?'

Yasmin sniffed indignantly, saying, 'More likely, you will probably succumb to the influence of your upbringing. Then, before you know it, you'll have four wives.'

Hassan burst out laughing. 'Perhaps you're right. If I lived at home with my brother, I might just do that. But I have not lived at home for years. I really didn't like it there. My brother is now the sheik, and the life suits him just fine. For me, I would rather live in Paris.'

'Then why don't you?' Yasmin asked.

'I do. I've lived in Paris almost exclusively since I started working for André. As far as I'm concerned, I would never live anyplace else. The sophistication and the cosmopolitan atmosphere suits me.'

'Denying your heritage, eh?' Yasmin couldn't help turning his answer round.

'Why not,' Hassan answered, 'if you prefer another? And what about your heritage?'

'My heritage has no meaning for me, and never has,' Yasmin snapped. 'Perhaps if your father is a sheik, you can find something good about it. But I have no father. There is nothing good about that.'

Hassan glanced at her during her short outburst, but said nothing. Yasmin focused her attention on the crystal night, with its flickering lights. Her words had a greater effect on her than she'd expected. She'd often wondered about her father, but she'd never thought of him as being 'no father.' But once the words had been flung out in the open, she realized how true they were. Suddenly the void deepened, and she felt strongly her need for an anchor. She missed André terribly. He had been her anchor for a while. But no more.

Yasmin could think of no other questions to ask Hassan, so she said nothing. She was grateful that he didn't resume his questioning either. But though the questions had made her angry, the silence was making her as nervous as a cat.

When they finally arrived at her apartment house, she could hardly wait to get upstairs. She turned to say good night to him at the bottom of the stairs, but he brushed past her and walked up briskly. She followed, and found him standing at the door, waiting for her with a lazy smile on his lips. Slowly, filled with dread, she took the key from her purse.

'Well, thank you for a lovely dinner,' she said unsmilingly. She turned away from him as she slid the key in the lock. But she didn't turn it. 'Good night.'

'You're not going to invite me in for an aperitif?' he said as he stepped closer.

She could almost feel the warmth of his body radiating across the distance between them, and bent her head, pretending to look in her purse for something.

'Well, as you said, it's late and – '

'Why are you afraid to be alone with me, Yasmin?' He moved even closer as he spoke.

'Don't be ridiculous,' she said. 'It's just that this has been a very long day and – '

'But you are a very lovely woman, and it's hard for a man to tear himself away from you.'

'It's late . . .'

'Somehow I get the feeling that you don't like me. Or could it be that I've made you angry?'

'Angry? Yes, you did say a few things that made me angry, but it's also true that I'm tired,' she said, trying to control the trembling in her voice. Why doesn't he just leave? she thought desperately.

'But surely you feel the same electricity I feel,' he murmured, his voice silky. 'I've noticed that this kind of sexual tension goes two ways. Even now you're excited. I can see your nipples standing out against the material of your dress. Or perhaps you will tell me that you are cold?'

He raised his hand with almost blinding speed, and before she could step back, he lightly brushed his fingers across her breasts. A coiling thread of pleasure shot down into her belly. She was mortified. She didn't want to feel that way about anyone but André.

Yasmin gasped, and tears of vexation started to fill her

216

eyes at this outrage. She opened her mouth to scream at him, but before she could get the sound out, he had taken her gently in his arms. He placed his soft lips against hers.

The kiss drew her breath out like a succubus, draining her of will and strength. Then, as if sure of his effect on her, he began to lightly, tenderly kiss the corner of her trembling mouth. Taking her lower lip gently between his teeth, she was torn between wanting it to continue and wanting it to stop. An uncontrollable trembling had begun to shudder through her as he softly murmured against her mouth.

'You see, this is quite nice, isn't it?'

It was the tone of his voice that brought her back, and she pushed away from him. Then swiftly raising her arm, she slapped him as hard as she could.

Frightened, startled at her own action, she at first thought he would be angry. But to her amazement, he laughed harshly instead.

'Why you . . . you . . ,' she sputtered, helpless with rage.

'That was a fairly plausible imitation of outraged virginity!' he taunted her, his eyes black, unfathomable. 'I didn't know you were an actress.'

'Damn you!' Yasmin ground out, her teeth clenched with heart-swelling exasperation, her breath coming quickly.

'You must forgive me,' he said, his face saturnine. 'When you come to me willingly, it will be much more exciting for both of us.'

'That will never happen,' Yasmin hissed, her burst of anger beginning to ebb. She moved away from him, only to find herself backed up against the door. Reaching behind her, she touched the key, still reassuringly there. But he was obviously through playing with her.

'It feels as though you've lost weight since you've been

217

living on your own. I'll have to fatten you up a bit . . . make sure you eat properly. Now, remember – we are catching the eight o'clock plane to Paris tomorrow morning, so I'll pick you up at six-thirty.'

His voice was light and bantering, but his tone was contrasted by the harsh planes of his face. She could easily detect the enormous control he was exerting over the turbulence she had felt in his kiss. Then he seemed to relax, and turning on his heel, started down the steps.

'Good night, little one,' he called, not bothering to turn around. 'And pack riding clothes. That is, if you ride.'

Yasmin felt limp as she stepped into the safety of her room. She bolted the door behind her and let out a sigh of relief.

Riding clothes indeed, she muttered as her head hit the pillow. What do I need riding clothes for? Do André's lawyers have their office in a stable? The sooner we get this business taken care of, the better, she thought, and resolved to pay close attention so that she could learn everything as fast as possible. The less time she spent around Hassan, the better.

13

Yasmin felt utterly numb as Hassan helped her into the car outside the offices of Fauquier, Renan, La Tour. She was hardly aware of anything going on around her – not the noise of the traffic, or the bustling people. Nor did they seem to notice her.

She wondered how anyone could possibly *not* look at her, how they could avoid seeing the aura she was certain hung over her head as she stepped out into the sunlight. Perhaps this buzzing in her brain was the result of getting up so early and flying to Paris. But she was certain that a little hop like that wouldn't be responsible for jet lag. No, this was something different.

Fortunately André's lawyers were elderly, and very sweet. There was another man there too – Henri LaMarquette, André's banker from the Paris office of the Credit Française. He was also elderly, but apparently not so sweet. Yasmin had wondered about him when she first came into the office. About sixty years old, he was very elegant, beautifully dressed, slim, snobbish, and cold. Instead of looking at her, he seemed to prefer examining his perfectly manicured nails. He barely acknowledged her presence when she was introduced to him as Mademoiselle, the Baroness Yasmin de Saint-Clair by Monsieur Fauquier. He and the other two lawyers were delighted to meet her, delighted that she had been found, delighted at her good fortune, and just generally delighted about everything. Henri LaMarquette didn't seem delighted at all. He had merely nodded his smooth gray head in her direction wordlessly, not meeting her gaze.

All three of the lawyers had been involved in drawing

up André's will, and each of them smiled graciously as they explained the phenomenal terms and the even more phenomenal estate. When Henri LaMarquette had any questions – and he seemed to have quite a few – he addressed himself to the men in the room only. Yasmin sometimes felt as if she wasn't there. He even seemed to show mild distaste whenever his eyes would accidentally rest on her. At first she was frightened, embarrassed, and appalled. But soon it ceased to matter to her what he thought. She was too caught up in trying to understand the vast complexity of the business she'd inherited.

She found herself staring at Hassan several times, noticing how relaxed and at home he seemed with these four distinguished men. With increasing appreciation she noticed his elegant bearing as he sat coiled in the deep leather chair, carefully listening. He looked so very different from them, she thought – especially the lawyers.

Monsieur Renan was about sixty and balding, with blue eyes, which were barely visible behind his thick wire-rimmed glasses. He handled the proceedings, while Fauquier and La Tour listened, nodding every now and then. Monsieur Fauquier was short, slim, and had a bush of iron-gray hair that stood straight up. His eyebrows were long and curled up toward his forehead. He looked like a puckish leprechaun, she thought, wearing a Savile Row suit. Monsieur La Tour was very fat, very red-faced, and very jolly. Hassan, on the other hand, was young and sleek and dark.

This was the first time Yasmin felt she could quietly observe him without being noticed. She decided that he must be about thirty and had the bearing of a prince. She also realized his family must be very rich and powerful, otherwise why would he have been sent to Harvard? She remembered what André had told her about Hassan, and knew that some of the more powerful sheiks, even though they had no intention of leaving Morocco or shifting their power base into industry, sent their sons abroad to be educated. They wanted to keep a hand in the running of the country and needed Western-trained and educated men to do it. Only they could deal with European and American politicians and businessmen as equals – even though these small sheiks had more personal power than any businessman could ever hope to have, it made no difference across the bargaining table. Their sons came home looking like exactly what they were – highly educated, but barely civilized small kings with an Ivy League gloss. It was a perfect meld of the two cultures. It was with a new appreciation, at least for his business sense, that Yasmin looked at Hassan today.

As Hassan had told her, she'd inherited the vineyards in Auxerre, the family estate, the mining investments, and the factory. At the moment the factory was empty, but it could always be rented out to another small manufacturer, or even sold.

There was also a small house on the water in Ibiza – if only she and Solange had known that when they'd gone on vacation! – the villa in Tanzier, several buildings in Paris – including one that was André's private residence – and some vacant lots in the suburban area outside Paris. And, of course, as Hassan had said, she also inherited the title. From now on she would be formally know as Baroness Yasmin de Saint-Clair.

After reading the will, they starting handing her paper after paper, giving her instructions on what should be done with each. After that they had asked if she would like to continue Hassan's services as investment counselor. No one was particularly surprised when she nodded yes.

Henri LaMarquette had suggested that Hassan also be appointed acting director until such time as Yasmin was able to take the reins. With a sigh of relief Yasmin said that would be fine, and signed a clause to that effect. She had been appalled to discover, as they had been giving her papers to sign and instructions to follow, exactly how much she didn't understand. She had also realized during those hours exactly how important Hassan was to the firm, and was relieved to know she didn't have to figure everything out and make the right decisions for a while yet.

Finally, at four o'clock in the afternoon, after what felt like an eternity, she was driven somewhere in a big green car. On her lap she held a bulging briefcase containing papers she was supposed to start reading that night. She had to decide what to do with the factory – rent it or sell it – but it couldn't be done until she'd gone over the figures. As if that would make any difference to her in her present state! she thought.

She also had to decide whether to go ahead with André's plan for distributing the wines in the United States. Considering the unfortunate delays and the fact that Hassan thought it was a mistake since André wasn't there to direct his plan, she knew she should wait a few years. But again Hassan said they had to go over the figures first.

Her sense of unreality, which crowded out everything else, even extended to the passing scene as the car twisted and turned through the mounting traffic. She stared blankly out the window. The blur of stonework, ironwork, and bodies mingled in a hazy kaleidoscope of color.

'. . . and then after dinner we'll start looking at the numbers,' Hassan was saying. 'I don't know if we'll finish, but we must try, because tomorrow we'll drive to the vineyard. You'll meet Bertrand Labiche, André's manager, and his wife Cecile, of course. Bertrand is one of our most trusted managers, and one of the great wine makers in France.'

Yasmin nodded, trying to pull herself back down to earth as the car pulled to a stop in front of a small but distinctive town house. Two enormous lanterns stood on either side of a great carved oak door, and handsomely worked iron grilles covered the first-floor windows. Smaller stone balconies graced the two upper stories. As Yasmin looked up at them, she could see window boxes full of red flowers. Before she could absorb the flawless white marble balustrades and mantels, Hassan had taken her arm and marched her up the steps. The door was opened by a plump red-cheeked woman before they could ring any bells.

Yasmin guessed she was about fifty, but her fair unlined face seemed that of a young child. Wreathed in smiles, she hugged Yasmin warmly, like a long lost friend, saying, 'Ah, Mademoiselle Yasmin. I have waited so long for you to come here. Welcome home, *chérie*.' And with that she ushered them briskly through the foyer and into the main salon.

'Now you sit down right here,' she said, 'and I will bring you both a glass of sherry.'

Yasmin found herself almost pushed into the deep, down cushions of the sofa. She could think of nothing to say or do, so she smiled back.

'That's Françoise,' Hassan told her as the woman bustled out of the room. 'She isn't happy unless she has someone to fuss over.'

Yasmin nodded and looked around the room. What an exquisite room it was. The furnishings were definitely eclectic. Each piece was from a different country in a different period, and yet the whole was harmonious and graceful. Handled in any other way, the room would have looked like a museum interior, cold, unlived in. But this room had the warmth and humanity of sumptuous domesticity. Hanging on the walls were huge portraits of what must have been André's family. It looked to Yasmin as it they went back to the fifteenth century. She was in awe that all this was being handed down to an eighteen-year-old Arab girl from the Rif. She wondered, staring at each painting, what the previous holders of this title would think of the terms of André's will.

Leaf and dart moldings encircled the room, and carved garlands of flowers were draped around the window and door frames. The thick Persian rugs scattered on the parquet floors gave it friendly warmth without obscuring the beautiful craftsmanship of the wood. A delicate Art Deco desk stood under the windows. The light illuminated the coiled tendrils and vine shoots that miraculously held it up. And cut flowers were everywhere – obviously Françoise's touch. It was apparent that she, too, loved the room.

Drained, Yasmin sighed luxuriously and leaned back against the lemon yellow couch cushions. Françoise returned carrying a delicate silver tray on which two glasses filled with rich amber liquor were balanced.

'Now, drink this, and you'll feel much better,' she said as she served first Yasmin and then Hassan. Yasmin noticed that she seemed especially glad to see Hassan. She patted his shoulder tenderly as she handed him his drink. 'And as soon as you finish, I'll run you a nice warm bath before dinner. *C'est bien?*'

Before Yasmin could reply, she bustled out again.

'Did André always own this house?' Yasmin asked, glancing out the window as she sipped her drink.

'No. Actually, he bought it about a year and a half ago. Up until fifty years ago or so, the family always had a town house in Paris, but there were some very hard times during the Great Depression and the Second World War. For a while they had only the manor house that adjoined the vineyards. But that fell into great disrepair because there wasn't enough money to keep it up. It's the same story for many noble families. André's father began to build up their holdings before he died, and then

André continued. He was quite successful in recent years, as I presume you have already gathered. He bought this house, intending, I guess, to live in Paris. Or maybe he just wanted to use it as a *pied à terre* when he was visiting. Who knows?'

Yasmin wondered whether André had bought the house because of her. Maybe he realized that she might not be happy in Tangier, but had waited to see how she would react. Too late, she mused as she looked around. Just a little too late.

'Why don't you go up and rest a bit,' Hassan said. 'Françoise will make us something for dinner, and then we can work straight through, all right?'

'Sounds fine to me,' Yasmin answered coolly as she stood up and stretched.

'Don't fall asleep,' he said as she walked to the door. 'We have too much work to do.'

Yasmin didn't answer. She opened the door into the foyer and slowly climbed a long curved staircase, pausing to look at the statues standing in arched niches that graced the walls. At the landing she stood still, uncertain what to do next.

Françoise poked her head out of a door at the far end of the hallway. 'In here, *chérie,*' she bubbled. 'In here. This is your room, and I have your bath all ready for you. Hurry up, I must go downstairs and finish my sauce.'

The room was all pale yellow, chrome, and glass. A tall antique secretary decorated with stylized marquetry roses enclosed in octagons stood against the wall, and a Chinese screen was near the windows, its delicate colors catching the light.

Françoise had unpacked her suitcase and hung out her clothing. Scented steam from the bath billowed fragrantly out the connecting doorway.

As she undressed, Françoise chattered away, asking her questions without waiting for answers, answering them herself, then commenting on her answers. What would Mademoiselle like for dinner? What time does Mademoiselle wish to be awakened in the morning? How nice it is to have someone to look after and cook for. How long does Mademoiselle think she will be staying in Paris? How dreadful about Monsieur le Baron – he was such a wonderful man. Yasmin felt tears spring to her eyes at the mention of André. All the people she had spoken with since his death hadn't the slightest inkling that she'd been destroyed. Solange, though very sympathetic, had treated the whole thing as if it were a slightly less than successful affair that should be forgotten, swept under the rug with all the other less than successful affairs. But it had been more than that. It had been her whole life. Von Rothenburg never mentioned it. In Tangier they had considered her at the least an embarrassment, and at worst, a whore. And André's lawyers . . . well, they were very sweet, but seemed amazed.

At least, she thought, Françoise was behaving toward her as if she belonged, had some right to exist within the framework of André's life. That was very comforting.

As Yasmin lay soaking luxuriantly in the warm, scented water, she realized that for the first time since André's death, she felt free; free to do and say whatever she pleased. Now, she told herself, she would finally be able to figure out who she was, to find herself. She was startled at the thought. What a ridiculous concept, she thought with a smile. Find myself? I've been right here all along. Me. Yasmin.

Her thoughts drifted to André. He had been in her life for about three weeks, she realized, and if counting the time before Lautremont, maybe six weeks all together. Not much to base a relationship on, she mused. Of course, she'd known him for over three years, but most of that time they had communicated through letters. Not very intimate letters either. Hers had been about what she was doing in school and things that happened to a few friends; his letters had to do with how pleased he was with her schoolwork, why he couldn't come and see her during vacations, and what arrangements he'd made for her during the summers. Pretty thin stuff.

Yasmin wondered if Hassan had been right about her feelings for André. Could all that intensity really have been just gratitude combined with a newly awakened sensuality? It hardly seemed possible. Yet there was so little else. Yasmin sighed audibly as she tried to pull together the scattered pieces of her emotions. On the one hand she was André's woman, André's thing, now set adrift. One the other hand she was Yasmin, her own person, and had always been Yasmin, with Yasmin's thoughts and dreams. For the past six months she hadn't dealt with herself as a separate entity. She had tried to collect the tangled skeins of her life and knit them into something cohesive.

It had never occurred to her that those threads had never been unraveled. Perhaps that's what Solange had been trying to tell her, but she hadn't understood. Oddly enough it was Hassan who had helped her see it. It certainly would have been nicer if he could have done it with more grace, she thought.

A small scowl creased her forehead. He is, without any doubt, the single most complex man I've ever met, she thought. She slid deeper into the water, so that it covered the bottom of her chin. Just thinking about him made the adrenaline start to throb in her veins and her body stiffen with tension. At times he was insufferable, arrogant, thoughtless, but at other times he was gracious, witty, cosmopolitan, and charming. It was disconcerting. Just when she expected one Hassan, she got the other one. His split personality was disturbing.

Yet at the same time, she remembered how his hands

had affected her – and his kisses. How was it possible for her to have so powerful a reaction to him?

It was very strange. She didn't really need him or want him. There was plenty to do, and plenty of perfectly nice men in the world, if it came to that. She just hoped that he wouldn't touch her for the next week, because if he did . . . if he did, what?

Oh, Allah, she thought. If he did, she was afraid . . . afraid that her physical reaction would make her actually . . . Why did the thought make her feel as if molten lava was moving through her veins? Why did she feel that sudden swollen longing? Maybe she was lonely. Maybe everything André had taught her and showed her had become a physical necessity, something she needed instead of something she'd given to him and him alone.

Sliding her hands down her body at the memory, she delicately touched herself. Perhaps she'd enjoyed Hassan's touching her, holding her, and that thought frightened her. It was probably just that it had been so long since anyone had touched her at all, she told herself. Then, almost imperceptibly, she became aware of another presence in the room.

Snapping her head around, she saw him in the doorway, leaning insolently against the frame. His body was loose, and yet coiled at the same time. Like a wolf ready to spring, she thought. A smoldering light flickered in his eyes, carrying with it a dangerous message, a message that wasn't at all difficult to read.

'You are beautiful,' he said in a low voice. His eyes slid over her, penetrating the water in which she lay. Yasmin didn't know what to do. He was obviously aroused – she saw the telltale bulge in his clothing.

'What are you doing in here?' she said, her voice piercing as its pitch rose.

His face grew dark for a second, then the scowl

228

vanished. He smiled with his mouth, but not with his eyes.

'I'm sorry. It's just that I wondered what was taking you so long,' he apologized. 'I would have sent Françoise, but she was busy with her sauce and didn't want to leave it for a second. I came myself . . .' All the while he talked to her, his eyes were traveling down her body with tantalizing slowness. They lingered on her mouth, on her breasts, then came to rest on her hand. She blushed furiously, realizing what he must be thinking. Then, with a knowing smile, he said, 'I didn't mean to disturb you.'

'Just get *out* of here,' she hissed, unable to stand his presence, or his thoughts, or the implications of his words for one more second.

He didn't say anything as he turned on his heel and walked out of the room.

At last, certain he was gone, Yasmin lifted herself out of the tub and grabbed one of the towels. Wrapping the warm folds of material around her, she dashed into her bedroom and quickly flipped the lock on the door.

She dried and dressed herself as quickly as she could, unable to keep from blushing at the thought of his surprise visit. Why couldn't he just leave her alone? She wondered how she'd get through the evening, knowing she still had to review the papers with him. Perhaps he would devote his attention to work, and only work, she thought, but doubted it.

After zipping her slacks and smoothing her sweater into place, she checked herself in the mirror. Annoyed, she saw that the flush of red on her face hadn't gone away yet. Instead of making her look ridiculous, however, it gave a certain glow to her face that made her feel even more uncomfortable. He'd probably misinterpret that, too, she thought as she reluctantly left the room.

Forcing one foot to follow the other, she walked back downstairs. Through the open door of the study she could

229

see Hassan seated at the desk. His head was bent over a sheaf of papers spread before him, his clean, aquiline profile hawklike in its concentration. A stray lock of his thick black hair had fallen across his forehead, which was creased in thought. She was consumed with embarrassment as she forced herself to enter the room.

Hassan looked up at her briefly as she entered, his eyes blank and uninterested. 'Good. Now we can get down to work,' he said as he gestured toward the chair next to him. 'Sit down.'

14

The pale, pinkish light of the early morning sun was filtering through the drapes when Françoise cheerily bustled in.

'*Bonjour, Mademoiselle*,' she chirped as she set the tray she was carrying down on the bedside table, then bounced over to the windows. With a sweep of both arms, she opened the drapes, and light poured into the room.

'What time is it?' Yasmin mumbled, turning over to bury her face in the pillows. It felt very early, and Yasmin didn't want to get out of the pleasant warmth of her bed. 'It feels like the crack of dawn.'

'It is! It is!' warbled Françoise. 'The best time of the day, don't you think?' She bustled back and pulled the covers down from Yasmin's shoulders to her waist. 'Now you just sit up so I can put your breakfast tray down.'

Yasmin rolled over and pulled the top half of her body into a sitting position. Françoise proceeded to plump her pillows, setting them up to make a backrest. Then she turned to pick up the tray.

'Why so early? What time it is?' Yasmin asked as she leaned back. Françoise pulled the legs of the folding tray and expertly placed it over Yasmin's lap. Handing her the linen napkin, she replied briskly, 'It is six o'clock, Mademoiselle, and I have brought you café au lait and croissants.'

'Six o'clock!' she yelped.

'Yes, Mademoiselle. Monsieur Hassan asked me to awaken him at five-thirty and you at six. There is more *café* in this pot, and hot milk in this pitcher,' Françoise

231

answered, ignoring Yasmin's outraged protest. 'Since you go to the vineyard today, it is necessary to get up early.'

Yasmin sighed, and picked up the delicate crumbly pastry, tearing off a small piece.

'Thank you, Françoise,' she said, smiling briefly. 'I didn't mean to sound angry with you, it's just that I'm so tired.'

'Of course, *chérie*, but you have a two-hour drive ahead of you. It is necessary.'

'I know. I'll sleep in the car if I'm tired,' Yasmin said, then she popped a buttered piece of croissant in her mouth. 'Umm, this is delicious!'

'If you would like something more for your *petit déjeuner*, tell me,' said Françoise. She stood watching Yasmin eat, her hands folded across her round stomach and an expression of pleasure on her face. 'I wasn't sure what your habits were.'

'This is lovely,' answered Yasmin. She reached for the coffee, washed down the croissant, then she proceeded to butter another piece.

'Now, what do you plan to wear?' asked Françoise.

'Oh, I don't know. Slacks and a blouse, I guess.'

'May I suggest riding clothes?' said Françoise. 'I noticed you brought them with you when I unpacked your things, Mademoiselle.'

'Are there horses?' asked Yasmin, brightening visibly.

'Yes, indeed, Mademoiselle. Monsieur André has a stable at the vineyard. He always rode when he went there. Monsieur Hassan also. It is one of his favorite pastimes.'

So that's why Hassan told me to bring my riding clothes, thought Yasmin as she chewed the remainder of her croissant. Perhaps today won't be such a disaster after all. There's nothing like a thousand pounds of horseflesh to keep a man from grabbing you, she told herself, grinning.

'That's wonderful,' she said aloud, 'Would you please take the tray, Françoise? Now that you've told me there will be horses, I'm ready for this day. I should dress quickly.'

'Very good, Mademoiselle,' said Françoise, smiling more broadly now, as she saw the smile on Yasmin's face. 'I'll lay out your clothes while you're in the bath.'

Yasmin leapt out of bed and made a beeline for the bathroom. When she came out, briskly brushing her hair, she saw Françoise had made the bed and laid out her jodhpurs and a white silk blouse. Her boots were standing next to the bed.

She pulled on her jodhpurs and tucked the blouse into the waistband. Then, standing before the mirror, she twisted her thick hair into a knot at the back of her neck, pinning it deftly in place with combs. A few strands at her temples refused to accept the confines of the combs, and curled around her face. She frowned at them, noticing how they detracted from the clean severity she preferred. But there was no helping it. Yanking on her riding boots, she pulled a long lavender scarf out of the wardrobe and wrapped it around her neck.

Isadora Duncan, she thought as she looked in the mirror, or perhaps a lady flyer from the 1920s. Oh, well, down we go . . . into the waiting arms of Bluebeard. Laughing at herself, Yasmin left the room and quickly ran down the curving staircase.

As she reached the landing, she could see Hassan standing by the door. A slight quiver of apprehension did a glissando down her spine. He was wearing khaki pants that fit him like a glove and a pale blue shirt that was open at the throat, the sleeves rolled up. His hair curled wetly, as if he'd just showered. He lifted his eyes up at the clatter of her boots on the stairs, and she could see them widen briefly, then narrow at the sight of her.

She took the rest of the steps with more decorum.

After all, she was now a baroness, she told herself, aware of Hassan watching her descend, his eyes lingering on the snowy silk blouse that clung to her body revealingly, then sliding down to the slim-fitting jodhpurs, which outlined her almost boyish hips and slender legs.

'I see you didn't forget to bring those,' he said as he gestured at her boots. 'You're so stubborn, I thought you had probably not done as you were told.'

Yasmin smiled sweetly. She was annoyed at his condescending tone, but covered her true feelings and shrugged nonchalantly. 'I always bring riding clothes with me, no matter where I go.'

'Good', he said, smiling. 'Then it is safe to assume this will not be the first time you've been on a horse.'

'Hardly!' she answered haughtily, and realized she sounded more like a dowager empress than a baroness. This new part was going to take a little getting used to, she thought, and said, 'Shouldn't we get going? Or do you intend to stand around in the hall all morning?'

Hassan didn't answer, but continued to gaze at her thoughtfully.

'I'm practicing to be a baroness, so you'll have to excuse me,' she said, 'I'm working on haughty today, if you don't mind.'

'Is that so?' Hassan said with a crooked smile. 'Well, in that case . . .' He grasped her arm at the elbow, and ignoring her muffled protests, marched her out the door, saying, 'Your car, Mademoiselle la Baronne.'

A sleek maroon Mercedes sports car was parked in the street. Without saying another word, Hassan opened the door and gave her a gentle push. She snatched her arm from his grip and settled herself in the front seat, staring straight ahead. The door slammed loudly, and a moment later he slid in next to her on the driver's side. The engine started with a low purr, and they pulled away from the curb.

'I should use this time to fill you in on the history of Saint-Clair,' he said, suddenly all business again. All trace of arrogance was gone from his voice, and Yasmin could see that it was a subject that interested him.

'Saint-Clair Vineyard is in Auxerre, about a hundred miles from Paris. It was one of the best known wine regions of France in the twelfth century, and even before. Before Bordeaux and Burgundy came into recognition, the wines of Auxerre were considered the very best. When King John wanted payment from his nobles, he asked for casks of Auxerre wine.

'The vineyards are spread along the banks of the Yonne, and the monks of Chapître de St Martin began cultivating the vines on the slopes above the Serein. They looked for the place where the winter snows melted first, as does any good wine grower. But more important, they planted their vines where a layer of Kimmeridgian clay emerged. This clay is made of the fossilized remnants of tiny crustaceans that died in the sea covering the area during the Jurassic period. The brittle, shattered, rocklike substance gives rise to one of the great wines of the world.'

'So it is the soil that affects the grapes?' asked Yasmin.

'Well, it is many things – the soil, the climate, the proximity of water, the exposure. However, in this case the soil makes a significant difference. The mass of tiny shells, cockles, conches, and winkles gives the Chablis a persistent delicate flavor that is unmatched. In the area there are seven *grands crus* and twenty-nine *premiers crus*.'

'And these vineyards have been in existence since the twelfth century?' asked Yasmin, awed at the weight of history they represented.

'Since before, actually,' replied Hassan, warming to his subject. 'Auxerre Chablis was known at least three hundred years before that. By the early sixteenth century there were seven hundred vineyards in the area, the vines growing primarily on the Kimmeridgian soil. However, in the eighteenth century the consumption of cheap wine by the French population grew to such massive proportions that new varieties and practices began to be introduced in order to boost production. The loss of grain fields and pastures resulted from the indiscriminate growing of more prolific vines. In order to protect the Chablis, a royal edict in 1731 forbade the starting of new vineyards and also required the uprooting of any recent vines. By 1759, however, there was such an uproar that all decrees regarding land use were swept aside. The French Revolution went even further, and Chablis was almost drowned in a flood of common grapes.

'Then, during the spread of the phylloxera louse in the nineteenth century, Auxerre died as a cheap wine center. But the expensive Chablis was saved by two things. One was the cost of transportation by cart, and the other was that the narrow valley traps the cold spring air and easily kills the tender May vine shoots. It wasn't worthwhile to risk the loss of two or three consecutive crops to the cold or the louse, if the end product couldn't command high prices. So the few growers who remained, the Saint-Clairs among them, stayed faithful to Chablis grapes.

'At the turn of the century their holdings had been depleted by André's profligate grandfather, and in a way this turned out for the best. Perhaps André and his father would have continued in that wastrel's footsteps, gambling and whoring away their family's tradition. But André's father, faced with his meager inheritance and the prospect of a life in the military or the civil service, decided to risk everything and keep the land. He mortgaged it to the hilt and began producing wine in earnest. He studied everything there was to know, hired expert managers, and put Saint-Clair back on the map. His knowledge, and his fascination with the grapes, were prodigious, and he taught André everything he knew.

'In the sixties his last big battle was a result of the new frost protection techniques. One would have thought it was a godsend, but it turned out to be a double-edged sword. Since the risks of growing were significantly reduced, the growers of common grapes began to struggle for appellation status. Even though these growers didn't have land with the Kimmeridgian clay, they wanted appellation as Petit Chablis. André's father died fighting tooth and nail, and André carried on the battle. But they lost. The extension of the appellation was granted, the twenty-five hundred acres originally carrying the status have now been increased by an additional fifty thousand acres, and they no longer have to be called Petit Chablis. Those additional fifty thousand acres are called Chablis, even though they don't have the benefit of the soil.'

'But what does that mean for Saint-Clair?' asked Yasmin.

'That is what prompted André's decision to market in the United States. He felt there is a growing snobbism about wines, and despite the intrusion of the California Chablis – something that had stopped him in the past – he decided that there is a specific market that can command extremely high prices. That would cover the losses he was suffering here because of the enlarged appellation.'

'You mean he was planning to appeal to the wine snobs?' asked Yasmin, intrigued.

'You might say that,' Hassan answered. 'But more than that, I think he wanted to appeal to the money. There are, after all, wine snobs and wine snobs. Pehaps I should call them connoisseurs instead. They make up the bulk of the new market, my dear, and you shouldn't go around insulting them.'

'You are so right,' laughed Yasmin, entering into his

spirited comments. 'We wouldn't want to offend their delicate sensibilities.'

'Now André is dead. There is no one connected with the vineyard who knows as much as he did. Just you and me, and we unfortunately are not as experienced as we should be. I understand all the financial aspects, but that is not enough.

'Bertrand Labiche is running it now, and he's the best,' Hassan said, turning his impassive gaze on her. 'But now it all rests on your shoulders, Yasmin. A thousand years of great tradition and a little Arab girl, forbidden by the Koran to drink alcohol, inherits the lot.'

He laughed, throwing his head back as he succumbed to a fit of humor Yasmin didn't comprehend. Did he think her a total incompetent? she wondered. Obviously he did. Well, he would see. If André could learn from his father, she could learn from Bertrand Labiche. She would show them all!

Yasmin shrank back into the seat, again returning her gaze out the window. Hassan was obviously finished with his lecture, and directed his attention to the road. Out of the corner of her eye she thought she could see him glance at her periodically, but she didn't turn.

After a while she reached over and flipped on the radio. The station was playing a popular French love song, and she let the bland rhythms fill her mind.

'What do you intend to do with the villa?' Hassan asked, breaking the silence. He didn't take his eyes off the road.

'You mean in Tangier?' Yasmin kept her response as wooden as possible.

'Yes,' he answered. 'Will you sell it or keep it?'

'Sell it,' she replied flatly.

There was a long silence that seemed to fill the car. Yasmin saw no reason to discuss her feelings on the subject, so she kept quiet.

'I wouldn't, if I were you,' said Hassan. 'Just from a financial point of view, of course.'

'Well, I have no use for it. I doubt if I'll ever go back there,' she said. 'I wasn't happy about living there with André, and I'm certainly not going to live there without him. So that's that as far as I'm concerned. Why don't you buy it, if you like it so much?'

She crossed her arms and stared fixedly out the window.

'I'd still think about it if I were you,' he said in a strange tone of voice. 'It doesn't pay to be too precipitous.'

'I suppose you're right,' she replied, wondering why Hassan thought she should keep the villa. She didn't think she'd ever be able to bear going back there. She sat in silence.

The car swung smoothly off the road, into a long driveway. The road reminded her of a painting by Van Gogh. A symmetrical double row of trees faded into the horizon, and on the other side of the trees, she could see row after row of low vines. They were tied to wires strung between wooden stakes in the ground. Bare of fruit, their leaves were beginning to fade. She wondered whether the harvest had been a good one, but no one had bothered to mention anything to her one way or the other. She had a lot to learn, she thought, and the largest part of her problem was not even knowing what she didn't know. Yasmin could see it was going to be another day filled with too much information for her to assimilate. Her head began to buzz at the thought.

Hassan stopped the car with an abrupt jerk and flung open the door. Yasmin saw a large two-story stone manor house with a maze of chimneys on the slate roof. As she climbed out of the car, a man emerged from around the side of the house. He whooped and strode to Hassan, grasping him with his thick arms in a warm hug. Slapping each other, they kissed on both cheeks and then turned to face Yasmin. The man was about five foot eight, with the heavy-boned, hard-muscled build of a French peasant. He looked to be about fifty, his darkly tanned face seamed with wrinkles from hours in the sun. A close crop of short, gray hair covered his head.

'*Ah . . . mais elle est charmante,*' he said, winking in Hassan's direction as he smiled broadly. 'But you are delightful, Mademoiselle.' He walked toward her, his arms outstretched, and Yasmin felt as if she were being stalked by a huge smiling bear. Then he stopped. 'This *is* Mademoiselle de Saint-Clair, is it not?'

Hassan nodded, and watched as the man continued his lumbering progess forward. 'Yasmin,' he drawled, his words barely covering his laughter as he observed the look of dismay on her face. 'This is Bertrand Labiche.'

Yasmin relaxed and held out her hands to Bertrand, catching them in hers just before he had a chance to grab her in the same bear hug he had given Hassan.

'Monsieur Labiche, I am so glad to meet you,' she said with pleasure. 'I've heard so many wonderful things about you.'

'Please, call me Bertrand,' he answered, beaming with pleasure at her compliment. He dropped her hands and bellowed in the direction of the house. '*Cecile! Viens ici!*' Come here!

In a matter of moments a very pretty woman of about forty-five emerged from the house, wiping her hands on her apron. '*Cecile! Mademoiselle de Saint-Clair est ici!*'

Before Yasmin could utter a word, she had been caught up in an affectionate hug. Then the other woman stood back and looked in Yasmin's face. 'You are quite lovely,' she said with a sly smile. 'I had thought you would be, but one is always curious, you know.'

'Of course she is pretty,' boomed Bertrand. 'Le Baron had excellent taste . . . in everything.'

An odd expression crossed Hassan's face as he listened to this interchange, but it faded just as quickly. Bertrand suddenly turned and gripped Hassan by the arm, dragging him toward the side of the house. 'You must taste this bottling,' he said. 'Tell me what you think.'

They all headed into a low back door, and Yasmin found herself inside a large old kitchen. The walls were tiled with blue and white painted squares from the floor to about midway up the walls. Two huge cast-iron commercial-size stoves covered with gray enamel stood side by side. Copper pots and large tin pans hung from black hooks in the ceiling, and there was a tremendous stone fireplace that took up one entire wall. A long slab of marble made up the counter, and two deep sinks with wrought-iron legs stood on either end. On the long oak table in the center of the room stood a smoky green bottle and four delicate wine glasses.

'This is the batch we will ship,' said Bertrand. 'Just taste it and tell me what you think.' His face was wreathed in a smile, and Yasmin thought she could detect a smug complacency in his eyes. He knows perfectly well that it is good, she thought to herself. He just wants to show off for Hassan. Really, under the circumstances Bertrand should direct his comments to me. After all, I'm the owner. Yasmin sighed audibly, telling herself Bertrand was just another example of a man who could only talk seriously to other men. How could she break that down? How could she ever get these men to take her seriously?

Bertrand deftly poured some of the golden liquid into one glass and handed it to Hassan who took a sip. To Yasmin's amazement, after swirling it around his mouth, he spit it into the fireplace. Before she could say a word, however, he'd taken another mouthful, and this time after savoring it, swallowed. Bertrand and Cecile never took their eyes off him. Suddenly he smiled and slapped Bertrand on the back.

'It's fabulous, Bertrand. Absolutely fabulous. I think perhaps it's the best we've ever had.'

241

'Bertrand already knows that,' said Cecile as she gazed at her husband primly. 'He's not interested in your opinion, he only wants your praise.' She proceeded to pour wine into the remaining glasses, handing one to Yasmin, who dutifully took a sip.

She knew nothing about wine, but this was as good a time as any to start learning. The liquid had an unusual silky perfume. It was a delicate dry flavor. There was even a slight sparkle to it. Not bubbles precisely, and not even effervescence. She drank the entire glass, and Cecile happily poured her another before she could even set it down.

'Now,' said Bertrand, his chest puffed up with pride like a pouter pigeon, 'come with me and we will check the casks.' He took Hassan by the arm and propelled him out of the kitchen. Hassan had to stoop as he went out the low door so as not to bang his head.

For a moment Yasmin expected them to ask her to follow. She stood there expectantly, but the two men didn't turn back or call her name.

I don't believe it! she thought helplessly. They're supposed to be showing me the vineyard, and instead of taking me with them, they've left me in the kitchen for girl talk! Incredible!

She'd started to trail after the two men when Cecile put her hand on Yasmin's arm. Not wanting to act as if she were angry at Cecile, Yasmin made an effort to control the irritation on her face and smile at the woman.

'Would you like to see the stables, Mademoiselle?' asked Cecile as her eyes swept over Yasmin's riding clothes. 'I see that you are dressed for riding.'

'I'd love to,' answered Yasmin, and began to set down her glass.

'Oh, you can bring it with you, that is no problem,' Cecile said, smiling as she walked to the door. 'You haven't finished it yet, and the horses certainly don't mind wine in their stalls.'

Yasmin took her glass and followed Cecile out the door. They walked back around some smaller buildings. Through the door of one of them, she could see Hassan standing with his back to them.

'He is very handsome, isn't he?' said Cecile, winking conspiratorially as she saw the direction of Yasmin's gaze. Yasmin shrugged. She didn't much feel like talking about Hassan. But Cecile didn't notice. 'Just looking at his hands,' she continued, her voice a low whisper, 'and you know he is a magnificent lover . . . oooh la la!' A throaty giggle emanated from her. 'Always you can tell by a man's hands, you know. The fingers are so broad and thick . . .'

She sighed and smoothed her dress across her stomach in a gesture that was full of significance. 'You are a very lucky young lady,' she said, looking at Yasmin candidly, her clear blue eyes opened wide.

'What kinds of horses did André keep?' Yasmin wanted to get off the subject of men and their hands, and especially Hassan.

There were wide double doors at each end of the stable. The doors at the back led to a small enclosed pasture of hardpacked brown earth. Small tufts of green grass lined the outer edges of the fence where the horses' hooves hadn't been able to reach. Inside the long stone masonry building, small, high windows ran along the side walls.

There were two windows for each stall, and golden shafts of sunlight cut across each other, making a geometric play of light and shadow. The air was redolent of fresh hay and fresh horse droppings.

'Are these riding horses or race horses?' Yasmin asked as she looked around the warm, dark building.

'Ah, Mademoiselle,' Cecile said, rubbing her hand

along the velvety nose of a dapple gray that poked its head out of the stall as they came in. 'Riding horses, of course. What would Monsieur Hassan do with race horses? You can't ride them, you can't even get near them usually. They are very high-strung and skittish. Besides, race horses require much attention. He just likes to ride for pleasure.'

'I thought these were André's horses,' said Yasmin.

'*Vraiment*, Mademoiselle, I suppose technically they were,' Cecile said. 'But you know, Monsieur André hardly ever came here. It was Monsieur Hassan who kept the stable in operation. He lives in Paris, and comes here all the time. He is the one who loves to ride them. Bertrand and I ride them too.'

Yasmin stopped by a small chestnut and looked into its glistening brown eyes. Though extraordinarily powerful animals, horses always seemed to be creatures she could deal with in a completely straightforward manner. Yasmin always felt most relaxed and happy when she was with horses. They didn't care where she'd come from or why she was talking to them.

The earthy smell reminded her of Lautremont. Riding had been an integral part of her schooling as a proper young lady, and the stable was one of the first places where she'd felt at home. The big warm animals with their stamping feet and silken tails swishing at flies reminded her of the goats she'd watched as a girl growing up in the mountains. They were friendly, uncomplicated, and responded automatically to a soft voice and gentle hands.

Cecile and Yasmin walked slowly back into the recesses of the stable, stopping in turn to pat or stroke each of the five horses in their stalls.

They had been in the stable for about ten minutes when Bertrand and Hassan entered and were blinded by the sudden darkness after the glare of the full morning sun outside.

'Cecile? Are you in here?' called Bertrand, squinting. 'Bring La Baroness to the office.'

They returned to the house, and this time went through the kitchen and up a narrow back stair that led them into the main part of the house. Off the broad entrance, Bertrand led them into a room that could have been either the library or the study. The walls were paneled in rich brown wood, and long wine-red velvet curtains hung at the windows, giving the room a dark, almost ecclesiastical feeling.

Bertrand drew Yasmin over to the desk with a pile of papers, and stack of ledger books, and two boards with acetate overlays on top.

'Oh, these,' he said with a disdainful sneer. 'Some silly *cochons* from an advertising firm submitted designs for new labels. What do you think, Mademoiselle?'

He lifted the sheets of clear plastic so she could look at the mounted squares. One was a rich cream color with ornate raised black-scroll lettering. Next to it was a plum-colored one with red and white lettering on it.

'I don't like that one at all,' said Yasmin, lifting the plum one up and squinting. 'Too raucous. Too loud. The label should not be loud.'

She set it down again, allowing the acetate to flip back, dismissing it altogether.

Hassan stood to one side with an amused expression on his face. Bertrand rubbed his chin with a gnarled hand. Funny, she thought, how these things work out. She knew nothing about the wines, nothing about the vines, and nothing about the financial aspect of the vineyard. However, she did know how to look at graphics and read what a picture could tell you. Feeling somewhat more confident, she straightened her spine and continued.

'Yes. I think it has to be the cream and black one,' she said firmly.

Bertrand nodded, and Hassan smiled at her, his eyes glinting with humor. Obviously he thinks I'm play acting, she thought, but it didn't matter to her. She returned his gaze defiantly, knowing they had to do whatever she said because she was Baroness Yasmin de Saint-Clair now. Feeling a bit silly, she tossed her head and tried to look serious.

'You picked the right one, Mademoiselle,' Bertrand chuckled. 'It's the one we've used for one hundred and fifty years.'

Yasmin felt angry. What kind of a stupid test was that? she wondered. She opened her mouth to tell Bertrand what she thought of his silly game, but before she could speak, Hassan put his hand on her shoulder.

'Don't take it personally, Yasmin. Bertand does that to me all the time. It was just one of his quizzes. It's a wonder Cecile doesn't hit him with the frying pan sometimes.'

'She does,' Bertrand said, and hooted with laughter again. 'But then I make love to her, and she isn't so mad anymore.'

Yasmin blushed furiously.

Hassan noticed her embarrassment and quickly changed the subject. 'Bertrand, why not take Mademoiselle down to the cellars,' he said lightly. 'Perhaps she would like to taste some of the other vintages we have down there.'

'*Bien*,' he said gruffly. 'You come, too, Hassan. I have a few other things to show you.' He quickly made a few notes on the pad that lay on the desk, then turned and left the room.

They circled to the back of the house and went into a doorway set in the moss-covered stone foundation of the house. Crisp, shining ivy hung around the lintel, brushing

246

Yasmin's hair as she followed them down a short flight of stairs into a long, cool, moist hallway lined from floor to ceiling with round wooden kegs. Each keg had a small spigot set in its face. On the ceiling hung a rack that held glasses pointed downward, suspended by their stems. Hassan stepped aside to let her walk ahead of him as Bertrand gestured to each cask, telling her the grapes and the year they had been pressed. Hassan followed very close behind her, and she could feel his breath stirring the few strands of hair that had escaped from the knot she had made that morning. Then Bertrand suddenly stopped, and Yasmin almost ran into him. He pulled one of the glasses loose from the overhead rack and held it under the spigot.

'Everything down here looks as if it's been the same for hundreds of years,' Yasmin said as she watched him.

'And that's the way it should be,' Bertrand answered with a pompous sniff.

'But aren't there ways of modernizing parts of the operation?' Yasmin asked, looking around. 'I don't necessarily mean aluminum kegs or anything that would change the taste of the wine. I mean things that would make it possible to produce more of it?'

'Perhaps Bertrand has his reasons,' Hassan said, giving her a warning glance. 'After all, if you've got a good thing, it's best not to play with it too much. Right, Bertrand?'

'Right.'

'You mean the old ways are the best ways?'

'Oh, we try something new now and then,' Bertrand said smugly. 'This is a new grape that André wanted to try,' he said as he turned the little knob, filling the glass half full. 'I think it's rather nice, but you try it.'

He handed the glass to Yasmin and proceeded to fill one for Hassan. Yasmin tasted it slowly, keeping her eyes on Hassan to see whether he did anything odd, such as spitting it on the floor. She didn't want to look too stupid now that she was, at least nominally, in charge. But he just swirled it around his mouth and then swallowed it, nodding. Yasmin did the same, and found that this wine, although not too far away from the one she had tasted earlier, had a slightly smokier flavor and a more definite sparkle.

'Why, it's almost champagne!' she said. Then, again embarrassed at her lack of knowledge, asked, 'Is it champagne?' For a moment she though she'd made a dreadful mistake. Was this another one of his tests? She hoped not. But Bertrand smiled at her, his expression one of satisfied complacency.

'No, it's not supposed to be champagne. It's a bit too light for that, and too smoky. But we wanted it to be close,' he said happily. 'I believe that it is as close as we could come with our soil.'

Hassan nodded, complimenting Bertrand on bringing it along so well. Then he drained his glass, so Yasmin drained hers too. Abruptly Bertrand snatched it from her, proceeding to fill it again while Yasmin shook her head. She already felt a strange buzzing in her head from having had three glasses of wine on what was now an empty stomach. She had last eaten hours ago, and it was lunchtime. Perhaps the others didn't feel its effects, but *she* certainly did. She waved at him, shaking her head no, but he ignored her. Bertrand pushed the glass into her hand. Not wanting to be rude, and in fact rather liking the taste of the wine and the gentle floating sensation, she accepted it.

Slowly sipping at its contents, she followed along as Hassan and Bertrand continued to discuss the various casks on the racks. Yasmin didn't pay very close attention, even though she knew she should be soaking up every word. But the wine was going to her head, and the cool, dank mustiness of the underground room made concentration impossible. Another time, perhaps, she thought, giggling slightly. After all, Hassan said I have my whole life to learn this business, so I can allow myself at least today. And a life is a good deal longer than one day. I'll learn all this tomorrow. She took another sip and followed the two men, allowing their words to wash over her in a fizzy amber haze, just like wine.

15

Because of the wine Yasmin no longer felt particularly hungry. She also didn't mind floating around in the wine cellar while Bertrand and Hassan talked an endless stream of incomprehensible terms. The grain of the wooden casks, the rows of spigots, and the mixture of odors all combined to make her feel pleasantly euphoric. She was almost sad when Bertrand said it was time to go up for lunch. Following them out into the bright sunlight, her gaze flickered around the collection of buildings, then beyond to the long rows of vines in the distance. Behind the house a tangled forest of trees, bushes, and scrub formed a protective barrier against the cold north winds of winter. Mine, all mine, she thought. How odd. How –

Her thoughts broke off as they came around to the front of the house and she saw two horses saddled and waiting at the bottom of the steps. One was a large black stallion that stamped its hooves fitfully and pawed the ground. The animal's head was held high, the strong arch of its neck powerful and arrogant. As it tossed its head, she saw that one eye was brown and the other a disconcerting pale blue. The other horse was a chestnut filly with a long silky mane and large liquid brown eyes. Her head was beautifully molded, and her nostrils quivered sensitively as Yasmin drew near. With a delicately moody wave of her head, the horse tossed her mane and went back to grazing. Yasmin was about to ask who was going riding, when Cecile came out of the door carrying a picnic basket. She set it down on the steps and said to Bertrand, 'Why don't you go and wash. I have prepared a picnic for Hassan and Mademoiselle Yasmin. I thought

250

pehaps it would be a perfect opportunity to show her around the grounds.'

Bertrand's smile looked conspiratorial, Yasmin thought, as he patted Cecile on the backside. 'Excellent, *ma chérie,* excellent. It is the only way to get an idea of the size of the vineyard. Horses can go where cars cannot, eh, *mon petit chou*?' He winked, then disappeared into the house.

Hassan expertly mounted the black stallion. 'Hand me the picnic basket,' he said briefly, allowing his glance to rest on her for only a moment, and Yasmin slowly carried the basket down the steps.

Cecile had packed them a cold herbed chicken, tender string beans soaked in lime, a loaf of crispy French bread, a thick wedge of brie, and a bottle of wine. Two glasses were carefully wrapped in linen napkins, and some strawberries and pears were tucked into the side.

After handing the basket to Hassan, Yasmin unwrapped the filly's reins from the stone balustrade. Slipping her foot into the stirrup, she pulled herself into the saddle. The horse stirred under her.

'What's her name?' she asked as the horse danced sideways, glad to be ridden on such a beautiful day. The animal's anticipation communicated itself into Yasmin's body as well. It had been too long since she'd ridden, she thought, suddenly filled with a heady pleasure. There had been so much work lately, and she needed this respite, this little oasis of relaxation. She patted the horse's neck, calming her a bit.

'Her name is Athene,' answered Hassan. 'You're sure she isn't too frisky for you?'

Yasmin laughed. She patted the horse's neck, then tested Athene's mouth for sensitivity and noticed that she was indeed a wonderful horse. Athene responded instantly, and Yasmin was pleased. Patting the horse's neck again, she answered Hassan, arching one eyebrow slightly, 'You needn't worry about my ability to handle her, thank you. But that horse you're on looks like a real handful. Are you sure you can manage him?'

'If I have a problem, I'll trade with you,' he said, and stated off at a canter into what looked like a wall of underbrush behind the house. Yasmin turned Athene and followed.

Just when it looked as if he were planning to enter an outgrowth of raspberry bushes, Hassan turned and cantered off along the edge of the trees. Then, as if by magic, the wooded area ended and a broad field stretched before them. Seeing the expanse, Athene gave in to joyous freedom after the confines of the stable, and took off with a burst of speed. Feeling the horse's abandon, Yasmin rode with it, the wind tugging at her shirt.

Yasmin was hardly aware that she'd passed Hassan in that first ecstatic burst of motion. She and the horse felt like a single body in graceful flight as she bent low over Athene's neck to allow her the greatest possible extension. The smell of the horse and the newly broken earth filled her nostrils. The liquid yellow sunshine on the fields made them undulate before her eyes. She forgot about lunch and Hassan altogether and gave herself over to the sun, the wind, and the horse's rippling muscles against her thighs. The wind whistled in her ears, drowning out all other sounds in a kind of white noise that smoothed over her thoughts.

Then she became aware of another noise. Whipping her head around, she saw Hassan thundering up beside her.

Yasmin reined in her horse. 'What's wrong?'

'Are you all right?' Hassan shouted.

'Of course,' she answered. 'Why?'

He laughed shortly. 'I thought the horse had run away with you. I can see now it was only youthful exuberance.'

Yasmin looked into his eyes and was startled by what

she saw. Then the look of masked annoyance – so different from the words she was hearing – faded and was replaced by bland concern. Maybe she hadn't seen that look at all, she thought. She turned her head away, trying to clear it, but by now both horses were bored with the unexplained stop.

'Now at least I know you're in control of the horse, so let's get moving.' he said. 'There's a lot to see.'

They skirted the edges of the Saint-Clair holdings for about an hour, and Hassan periodically pointed out things of interest, shouting across the space that separated them.

'How do you harvest the grapes?' Yasmin asked finally, seeing how many stakes and vines were on the estate. 'It seems like such a big job.'

'Manpower,' Hassan replied. 'It's a delicate business too. And often slow.'

'Isn't there a machine that could do it?'

'Perhaps, but Bertrand wouldn't be interested,' Hassan said. 'Each part of the process is very important . . . each thing must add to the flavor of the finished product. Machines could bruise the grapes.'

'But what happens if you don't have enough manpower?' Yasmin asked. 'What happens if there's a storm? Or a frost, or something that prevents you from harvesting the grapes when you're supposed to?'

'You lose the crop.'

'There really ought to be a better way,' Yasmin said thoughtfully. 'After all, a business shouldn't be solely dependent on the vagaries of . . .'

'If there were a better way, my dear,' Hassan said condescendingly, 'I'm sure Bertrand would already be using it.'

Then, as if tired of her questions, Hassan spurred his horse and galloped ahead.

Suddenly the fields ended. Hassan guided his stallion into a small opening barely visible through a stand of trees. Yasmin followed him carefully. Athene's delicate hooves picked their way along the path, avoiding stones and hollows, which could spell disaster for her slender legs. An occasional branch would swing back, and Yasmin would duck, wondering where Hassan was leading her.

Then, just as suddenly, the underbrush gave way to a small clearing surrounded by a thick wall of trees and undergrowth. Sunlight filtered through the leaves high overhead, and Yasmin thought she could hear the faint gurgling of a stream. Hassan reined in and sat waiting for her as the horse dropped its head to graze on the thick grass carpeting the ground.

'Shall we eat?' he asked. 'I, for one, am hungry.'

Yasmin glanced around her at the idyllic setting, and although she definitely felt rumblings of hunger in her stomach, wished he had chosen a less exotic setting for their lunch. Something a little less secluded. But before she could voice an opinion, he dismounted and was unfastening the basket from its strap on his saddle. Dropping it unceremoniously to the ground, he walked to the stream at the edge of the clearing, knelt, and splashed water on his face, cleaning off the dust from the fields. Then he whistled long and low to the horse, who slowly ambled over and drank noisily from the rushing water. Suddenly thirsty and hungry, and sensing Athene's desire to stop, Yasmin led her horse over to the stream too.

'Why don't you wash your face and hands,' Hassan said, his eyes glowing and a smirk wrinkling the corner of his mouth. 'You're a mess.'

He reached up and ran his finger lightly across her cheek, then examined it with feigned care. 'Dust. You're covered with dust, little one.'

'You make me sound like bric-a-brac on a shelf,' Yasmin said, and laughed. She swung her leg over the saddle and started to dismount, but with one catlike move Hassan was at the horse's side.

His arms reached up and caught her as she began to slide off. 'You need someone to take better care of you,' he said, gripping her firmly under the arms.

Then, with deliberate taunting slowness, he slid her down the length of his hard, muscular body, little by little guiding her down. Then, holding her feet just off the ground, he allowed her to catch on his body, her thighs pressed against him. Her eyes dilated and she squirmed, but instead of freeing herself, she found herself more firmly caught on the hardness between his legs. She gasped as a jagged bolt of pleasure shot through her. It was only intensified by her struggling.

Hassan slipped one arm firmly around her back, and holding her tightly, he caught her buttocks with the other and pressed her more firmly against him. His hair, rumpled by the ride, fell across his opaque eyes, and he grinned wickedly into her face. His eyes searched for and found signs of the molten yearning coursing through her body, betraying her. The pulse at her throat quickened with alarm, and an uncontrollable tremor set in under her skin as her breath caught sharply. By trying again to worm out of his grasp, she was merely ensnaring herself even deeper in a web of pleasurable sensation. A thick, swelling pressure filled her, and she couldn't decide whether to arch away from him or into him. His voice turned husky as he gripped her even tighter against him.

'Are you being deliberately provocative? Each of those little squirms makes it harder for me to let go of you.'

'Please . . . put . . . me . . . down,' she managed to get out, breathless, not only from being held so tightly, but from the silky, sensual feeling slipping so deceitfully through her.

'Of course,' Hassan studied her for a moment. Then with a chuckle he set her down hard on the ground.

Yasmin exhaled sharply with surprise and reached her hand up to push a few strands of hair out of her eyes. She tried hard to look nonchalant. Hassan just smiled knowingly then casually turned toward the picnic basket. 'You really should wash your face.'

He went from one extreme mood to another so quickly, she thought. Forcing one foot in front of the other, she walked to the stream. Kneeling, she dipped her hands into the sparkling water and splashed it on her face. To her dismay some accidently splashed down the front of her shirt. The frigid stream trickled across her breasts, making her nipples pinch with the cold. Still unsteady, she walked back and sat on the grass where Hassan was setting out their lunch. She purposely kept the picnic basket between them.

Hassan opened the wine bottle, poured some in both glasses, and offered her one. 'Drink this,' he said, his eyes moving down to her wet blouse where it clung to her breasts. 'You must be thirsty after your long ride.'

'Oh, no thank you,' Yasmin answered quickly, knowing she was still feeling the effects of the four glasses of wine she'd consumed earlier. 'I'd rather drink water.'

She began to get back up, but Hassan stopped her. 'You shouldn't drink the water from that stream, you know. Something might have died just around the bend, and you would get terribly sick.'

'Didn't Cecile pack any water?'

'Of course not. Wine makers never drink water. Here, drink this. You'll be fine.'

'You're telling me to trust you, right?' Yasmin said with a small smile. But she didn't know what else to do, and feeling very thirsty, took the glass.

Although she only meant to take a sip, she drained it, feeling twitchy under Hassan's constant stare. His black eyes were fathomless and heavy-lidded, his face hard and deliberate. Seeing him sitting on his haunches, his shirt open almost to the waist, the black hair curling from his chest, she felt awkward and frozen, unable to move. He was playing a cat and mouse game with her, she realized, and she was defenseless. Dropping her eyes to the basket, she reached for the hunk of cheese, and his hand shot around and stopped her.

'Why don't you just lie down, and I'll put everything out,' he said softly, his voice hypnotic. 'Rest for a little while. The sun will feel good to you.'

Yasmin felt the heat soaking into her skin, and without exactly knowing why, stretched and lay back in the grass, closing her eyes. The horses had wandered off and were grazing contentedly. The languor that had washed over her earlier began to creep back. The sun soaked into her body, warming her, making her limbs feel loose and boneless. I'm drunk, she thought.

Then a rustling sound made her open her eyes. Hassan was sitting on his heels next to her. But the glare of the sun was blinding, so she closed them again, unable to move. She felt him slowly begin to unbutton her blouse, his hands lingering at each button, brushing against her nipples through the thin material. But whether she couldn't move or didn't want to move, she didn't know, and allowed him to continue. When all the buttons were undone, he gently pulled her blouse out of the waistband and peeled it back, revealing her small, rounded breasts, exposing them to the pulsing warmth of the sun.

His hand slid up along her rib cage, molding each breast in turn, savoring the satiny texture of her skin. Their callused scratchiness caused her to shiver involuntarily. A sweeping tide of panic welled up inside her, urgent and piercing, but the limp unresponsiveness of her body kept her from moving and the heavy indolence grew more pronounced. Suddenly, without warning, she felt his mouth on her breast. His tongue slowly, agonizingly

257

circled her nipple, and she couldn't contain the moan that seemed to bubble up from inside her.

Then he moved to her other breast, nibbling delicately at her nipple, causing it to harden almost painfully, She arched her back against the soft, cushiony grass. A hand replaced his mouth on her breast, and his lips came down hard on hers, forcing them to open and receive his tongue. Greedily he caressed her mouth, then searched more deeply. His teeth ground against hers.

Yasmin was desperately torn. His slow exploration was wonderful, but she didn't know if she wanted him to touch her and kiss her like this. First his mouth was hard, then it grew gentle; first he forced her, then he drew back, accepting her response. She felt limpid and pliable as his hands glided down her stomach and gently began to unbutton her jodhpurs. Her mind screamed for him to stop, but her body throbbed with impatience. Not only was she unable to resist, she wanted to urge him on, tell him to hurry. But even her voice wouldn't work, wouldn't do as it was bid. He raised her hips slightly as he pulled the jodhpurs down to the tops of her boots. The sun struck the skin of her belly and thighs with delicious warmth. Hassan cursed softly as he pulled off each boot in turn. Keeping one hand possessively on the delicate mound at the top of her thighs, as if to keep her from bolting, he tossed the boots aside impatiently, then he gently pulled the trousers over her feet. She was completely naked, exposed to the sun, his eyes and his hands. She could feel the light breeze caressing her.

Hassan was no longer touching her. Feeling suddenly cool without his hands on her, her eyes flew open. She wanted to see where he was, what he was doing. With great difficulty she raised one arm and shaded her eyes from the molten intensity that seemed to glue her to the ground. Her flesh tingled as she saw him standing over her, arms akimbo, watching, gazing at her, consuming

258

her with his eyes, black and impenetrable, a slight smile was on his lips. He slowly began to unbutton his shirt.

Embarrassed, and yet feeling inexplicably wanton, Yasmin dragged her gaze away from him, overcome with shyness. Then she felt his hands on her knees. Her eyes widened as she saw him kneeling, still dressed, an obsessive look on his face.

'You're so perfect,' he murmured thickly. 'I can't keep my hands off your exquisite skin. It's like honey . . . all golden and sweet. I must . . .'

His hands slid joltingly up her thighs, touching the soft, sensitive flesh where they met. Teasingly, they began to roam, grazing her body lightly. A fierce, darting tongue of pleasure shot up her spine. Her lips parted with a small moan of pleasure and her knees dropped apart on the grass. A low noise came from his throat, and he was suddenly kneeling between her legs. She moaned as his thumbs opened the delicate shell-pink flesh. Then his darting tongue explored – biting, sucking, teasing, probing at her oversensitive cleft. Her moan turned into a keening wail as his rough hands gripped her hips and held her still as his mouth insistently assaulted her swollen flesh. She wanted more, yet begged him to stop. Her insides were turning into a twisting coil, demanding, totally apart from her.

She couldn't remember when he took off his shirt, but when she reached down for his shoulders, she could feel the springy coils of hair and a small scar at the base of his neck. His hands kneaded her hips, hurting and stroking, and his mouth alternated between softness and harshness, keeping a constant pressure on the distended nib of flesh. Just when she thought she would be driven mindless, out of her head by his diabolical tongue, the reverberating pattern he was tracing on her senses suddenly stopped.

Snatched so cruelly short of her pleasure, her eyes opened wide, dilating with panic. He knelt between her legs like an animal coiled to spring, his knees under her thighs, holding them spread wide, lifting her up. She could see the ripple of his muscles under the tawny glow of his skin, and she started to speak.

'Why . . .?' Her voice was unrecognizable, broken by a shuddering tremor.

Slowly his eyes narrowed to slits as he unzipped his trousers. She gasped at the size of him, and overcome by panic, tried to twist away, afraid she wouldn't be able to take all of him inside her. André hadn't been like that. How could it be possible? she thought as her teeth began to chatter. He lowered himself down to her slowly, so she could watch. Her eyes were drawn to him, caught in fascination mingled with fear. He dragged the head of his penis down the hollow between her thighs, wetting it with the slickness, then pulling it slowly back up. The exquisite tension she'd felt under his mouth returned with lightning rapidity, and her back arched with longing as he rubbed back and forth across her screamingly sensitive flesh. Then he pushed against her. Her head fell back as he slowly penetrated, lodging himself a short way inside her resisting body.

'Please . . . no more . . .I can't – '

But he covered her mouth with his, stopping her words, and she tasted the sweet tanginess of herself on his mouth. Then softly he held her in place, partially impaled on his thick pulsing flesh as he reached up to pinch one of her nipples between his thumb and forefinger. A jagged spear of pleasure shot through her as he plunged deep into her quivering body. Yasmin gasped for air as he filled her full, almost tearing, like a blow to her stomach. Then slowly drawing out, and thrusting sharply in again, he rammed shockwaves through her . . . shuddering rhythmic explosions that left her spinning out of control. Under the insistent pressure battering her insides, a swelling tide of mounting pleasure finally took over.

Afterward, as she lay limp under his weight, she felt raw, raw everywhere, raw and throbbing and swollen between her legs, raw in the throat. Had she screamed? She couldn't remember. She tentatively shifted one leg.

'Am I too heavy for you?' he asked, his voice husky. His breath against her ear was warm. He blew softly into the thick masses of her hair.

Hassan started to nuzzle at her throat, but then picked up his head to look into her eyes. Resting on his elbows, he pillowed her head in his hands, cradling it gently as he studied her with languid interest. She looked back and their eyes locked, merged, and held. She felt a stirring inside of her. He pulsed hard, rhythmically thudding against her soft insides. Her look of surprise made his eyes suddenly wrinkle with amusement.

'I'm still there,' he whispered softly. 'See?'

She gasped as the pulse inside her grew stronger.

'Anybody home?' he purred. His eyes looked amused as he watched the changing expression on her face. 'You like this, don't you?'

Then slowly, deliberately, he began to move inside her again. This time more in control of himself, he watched her face, calculating the effect of his every move. He smiled as he watched, and increased his thrusts – first teasingly slow, then hard and deep. Caught in a rising tide of electric shocks, she began to meet each thrust, until she forgot who she was and again gave herself up to the pleasure.

When Yasmin returned to awareness again, she realized Hassan was no longer on her, or in her. She sat up halfway, resting on her elbows, and noticed that the sun was low in the sky. Realizing it must be late afternoon, she listened as the whirring of insects in the glade rose to a hum. The breeze had died down, the leaves were still, and the sun had heated her skin. Then she saw him kneeling at the edge of the stream. The muscles in his back and shoulders rippled as he bathed in the sparkling water. He was naked, and as he walked back toward her, his body caught the late afternoon shadows.

Her eyes traveled languidly over his firmly muscled abdomen, which ended in a knot of tightly coiled hair at his thighs. His legs were long, a study in opposing curves, and she was reminded of those Greek bronzes in the National Museum. All the girls on that trip to Athens had stood at the statue's feet adoringly, their eyes firmly fixed on all the perfectly formed bronze kneecaps, too embarrassed to raise them any higher. Yasmin watched the way Hassan's walk was lithe and sure, like a jungle cat. Then he was back beside her.

'I think we should get back to the château,' he said mildly. 'Cecile and Bertrand will be worried about us.'

He held out his hand and helped her to her feet. That's when Yasmin remembered she was naked, and that her clothes were scattered all over the grassy little clearing.

Oh, Allah, she thought helplessly. That was easy, wasn't it? she thought, and wondered if he thought she would just lie down and spread her legs for any man. She looked around her unsteadily, then started to collect her things.

'Let me help you with those,' said Hassan. Moving quickly, he picked up her clothes. He watched her pull on her jodhpurs, then helped her with her blouse, slowly buttoning it for her. He bent down and placed a kiss on her forehead, which was surprisingly tender.

'You have made me very happy, Yasmin,' he said, lifting her chin up so he could see her eyes. 'You are everything I've ever wanted in a woman. We'll talk about what I have in mind back in Paris, though. This has been a day of many shocks for you.'

Tired and speechless, Yasmin couldn't find any words to answer him. Talk? she thought. Why did they need to talk? She could only stare back into his bottomless eyes.

16

When she and Hassan returned to the house, Cecile was in the kitchen slicing vegetables for dinner. A knowing smile flashed across her face at the sight of them. Yasmin had flushed red as Cecile's eyes quickly flickered over her, taking in the tousled hair and the grass stains on her silk blouse. To make matters worse, Hassan had winked broadly as he walked through, and given Cecile a light smack on the rear end. Cecile's laugh was delighted, not angry, and her eyes lingered on his back as he strode up the stairs two at a time to find Bertrand.

'Did you get to see everything?' Cecile had asked Yasmin sweetly, lowering her gaze back to the carrots she was slicing. A smile hovered at the corners of her mouth.

Yasmin, still too embarrassed to speak, mumbled something about it being lovely.

The two men came clattering back down the stairs, and after a dragged-out set of farewells, she and Hassan were in the car, gliding back down the long driveway into the purple evening.

Finally Yasmin had time to think as she sank back into the cushioned seats. It was dark and womblike in the Mercedes, the pale green, fishy glow of the dashboard lights illuminating Hassan's handsome profile. She was glad of the dark, because no matter where she tried to direct her thoughts, they kept returning to the things he'd done in the glade. And each time, she could feel the heat of a blush rise up into her face. Yasmin was relieved that he couldn't see it.

For the most part they drove in silence periodically

punctuated by some remark of Hassan's and the soothing music on the radio. When they were close to Paris, speeding through the outlying suburbs, Hassan began to hum abstractedly.

'You know,' he said, breaking off his humming abruptly, 'it's good that things have turned out this way.'

'What way?' Yasmin murmured, not really paying attention.

'Oh, everything,' Hassan continued. 'Finding you, finally being able to get work started at the vineyard . . . but more important, discovering how much I have in common with you, and seeing how much I need you and how much you need me. I'm pleased.'

'That's nice, but I probably need you more than you need me,' Yasmin said slowly, not certain she understood what he meant. She wondered if it always felt this awkward to talk to a man right after you'd made love. She didn't seem to remember it being like this with André, but that had been different. That had been a lifetime ago. 'I have no idea how to run everything,' Yasmin continued. 'I'm lucky I have you to take care of the important things – that is, if I don't want to lose them.'

'That's true,' Hassan said slowly, 'but not precisely what I meant.'

There was silence in the car. Yasmin didn't want to speak.

'When I said I needed you, I meant as a woman, not as a business associate. I don't need anyone as a business associate.'

'That's very nice of you,' Yasmin said slowly. 'But don't feel you have to say something you don't mean just because of this afternoon. I'd understand, really I would.'

'What are you talking about?'

'You know – about making love,' Yasmin said slowly. 'These things happen sometimes. You don't have to – '

Suddenly Hassan began to laugh. He reached over and stroked her leg gently. She shivered at his touch and the memory of how his hands made her feel when they were on her naked flesh. Then he pulled her close to him.

'Are you worried about what I might think of you?' he asked. 'Is that it? Do you think I won't respect you anymore, or some other little middle-class notion you picked up someplace?'

'No,' Yasmin said, trying unsuccessfully to put some distance between their bodies. 'That's not it. It's just that what happened shouldn't make you feel that you have to change our relationship in any way. After all, I'm going back to Geneva as soon as the legal things are finished, and – '

'No,' Hassan said, suddenly serious. 'First of all you won't be going back to Geneva – ever.'

Yasmin gasped. 'Ever?'

'That isn't what it sounds like, my dear. What I mean is, you are André's heir. You have to stay in Paris until the will is fully probated. The fastest I've ever heard of a probate going through is two months. After that you're responsible for his estate.'

'But I thought everything would be be taken care of,' Yasmin said. 'I thought you would act as director.'

'I will. But all the same, I want you here. You are still the head of the firm, for one thing. But of course I want you here for another reason as well.'

Yasmin didn't answer.

'I thought you understood. Back there, what happened in the glade wasn't just a passing thing, Yasmin. You are everything I've always wanted. I want you with me, close to me, always. Not just because of the estate and the vineyard, but because you are wonderful.'

'What about my job? My apartment?' Yasmin was still avoiding the full import of his words.

'You don't need any of that. You have a job here. You

have a town house here. I'm delighted with you. I've wanted you since I first saw you. But I knew I had to go slowly, not scare you. I hope I didn't scare you today, but I couldn't wait – '

'You didn't scare me.'

'Good. The time was right, and besides, I fed you so much wine, you couldn't possibly have felt scared. Now listen to me, Yasmin,' Hassan said. 'We are about to spend a tremendous amount of time together, you and I. I wouldn't have been able to keep my hands off you, I wanted you so badly – and you made me wait so long. It could have been just an ordinary little sexual adventure, and that would have been very nice. But it was much more than that – for me at least.'

Hassan stopped and peered through the darkness at Yasmin, as if trying to gauge her reaction or elicit some response from her. But the words wouldn't come. Yasmin was stunned. She picked up her hand where it rested lightly over the one he had so firmly laid on her thigh. She began to fidget with her scarf.

'Now, I want much more from you than I did this morning,' he continued slowly. 'I want you to spend your life with me. You and I are very much alike. Perhaps it's because you are from Morocco too. Perhaps it's because you are so beautiful, or because the chemistry between us is perfect. I don't know. I simply want to enjoy it, and you, forever.'

Yasmin was stunned. 'But – '

'Don't say anything yet. I know it's too soon for you. But don't worry. I've waited this long, I can wait a little bit longer.'

Hassan slid his hand slowly off her thigh and rested it between her legs. She felt the pressure intensely. She was still swollen and bruised, but his movement was a gesture of ownership more than one of affection. In the strange

266

green light of the car, Yasmin saw a half smile momentarily cross his lips and then disappear. Again she felt that events were out of her hands. She'd been feeling that way since Hassan had turned up at Von Rothenburg's house. That day felt so very, very long ago to her. How odd that it was only three days ago, she thought.

But it wasn't an altogether bad feeling to have everything taken out of your hands, Yasmin mused. In fact it was almost restful. To be taken care of was so easy. But then again, it was so soon. Was it too soon?

'You're tired,' said Hassan hypnotically in the dark. 'Go to sleep, little one. Soon we'll be back in Paris. We'll talk more after you've had a good night's rest.' He laughed shortly. 'I don't know if I'm going to let you have a good night's rest. But we'll discuss that later too. Sleep now. I'm driving a car, so I can't make love to you. This may be the last chance you get – take advantage of it. Go to sleep.'

It was almost as if the words were orders, but Yasmin gratefully closed her eyes anyway. Exhausted, she fell off into a deep, dreamless sleep. She was only vaguely aware of Hassan carrying her out of the car and into the house in Paris.

Somehow the days turned into weeks, and the weeks turned into months, and Yasmin couldn't bring herself to feel that she had anything to complain about. For three entire months Hassan seemed to know just what she needed, and when. He took care of everything, and did it with the grace of a true aristocrat. She felt as if she were wrapped in a cocoon of pampered idleness. But he never asked her opinion, never wanted to know how she felt, or what she liked. He assumed that he knew everything about her. And surprisingly, to a great degree he did.

During the day Yasmin was often on her own, and in the evenings, Hassan took her all over Paris. It was not the same as the sightseeing tour she had been given by André when she passed through on her way to Lautremont. They saw the city the way natives do, with leisurely strolls in the evening, scouting out little hidden restaurants, finding private spots to sit and watch the boats on the Seine. And they talked. Or rather Hassan talked, and Yasmin listened.

He was brilliant, sophisticated, and witty. There was very little he didn't know or have a strong opinion about. But mostly Hassan knew what he wanted and how to get it. He went after things the way a shark goes after a fish – with singleminded intensity. Just the way he talked to the people who worked in bookstores and antique stores sometimes made her shiver.

'How do you do that?' she asked Hassan after he'd managed to get a porcelain Chinese dragon plate that she'd liked from an antique dealer at half of what it was listed for.

'Haggling,' Hassan had answered. 'Nothing more to it than that.'

But Yasmin wasn't thoroughly convinced. 'It felt like more than that to me,' she said. 'That dealer thought so too.'

'Don't be silly,' Hassan answered with a sharp laugh.

But Yasmin could see that Hassan was very pleased with himself. He was pleased with his purchase too. It was as if he'd won something, caught the animal he'd been stalking. It was a hunter's mentality.

Yasmin sometimes had the sense that she was a quarry, too, or a prize. She sensed it in the calculating look that flashed across Hassan's face, as if he were mathematically weighing the odds of each and every one of his words. He seemed to refer to an unseen balance sheet before saying or doing anything.

But not all the time. Often she was swept off into an exciting, sensual world where money meant nothing and enjoyment everything. Meanwhile it got easier and easier to lose herself in the cluster of each day's activities. Even when Yasmin spent time wandering through the parks and along the Seine by herself, she didn't seem to be able to think. Or at least to think clearly about her situation.

She lived in the town house with Hassan and slept in the big bed in the master suite with him every night. She had her own rooms, as well, but they were for her daytime use.

Hassan certainly acted as if he loved her. But she felt there was something odd about his possession of her. Sometimes it seemed as if every time he made love to her, he was marking her, marking her as his territory. Their lovemaking was powerful, but Yasmin felt as detached from that as from everything else. The satisfied look on his face each time she had an orgasm seemed satisfaction that he'd once again proved to himself and to her as well, that she belonged to him. Hassan couldn't seem to get enough of her when he was home, she thought because perhaps he sensed on some level that he wasn't getting what he wanted from her. He wanted to possess her body and her soul. Her body he had, but her soul was not as easy.

Yasmin thought she was in a kind of shock. She had everything she wanted, everything André promised when they took the boat from Algeciras. But instead of living in André's house with André, she was living in his house with Hassan. The twists of her fate were unnerving her, and she had difficulty reconciling the man with the place, difficulty even thinking about it.

She'd tried telling Solange how she felt, but Solange would brush her doubts aside. 'What in heaven's name could you want to *think* about!' Solange would say over the phone, and laugh. 'You lead a Cinderella life, and with an incredible man too. And you're worried about it? Pshaw! Try and think like a Frenchwoman. So perhaps you're still a little in love with André. So perhaps you need a little time to shift your gears. Good. Take the time. But in the meantime, you *like* Hassan well enough, yes? He doesn't disgust you, does he? No. How silly young girls are sometimes!'

So Yasmin drifted with the pattern of her days, not even noticing that it was a pattern Hassan had designed for her. From the moment he'd carried her into the house, he'd taken complete charge. He never mentioned business, never again suggested they go to the vineyard, and he treated her with exquisite deference and respect. When she started to ask him questions, he put her off lightly or kissed her, as if he felt by stopping her mouth with his own, he also ended her need for an answer.

Yasmin's protected existence was very seductive. She almost felt the way she had when in school. She had a schedule that she had to meet, and she had no worries. She was fed, and driven wherever she wanted to go. She didn't have to think about her clothes or her laundry or the shopping or money.

And Hassan was wonderful. He was handsome, attentive, generous, thoughtful, and totally overwhelming. It was impossible to resist him. Not because he was pushy, but because he made sure that what he wanted was what Yasmin wanted – or thought she wanted.

After three months of this delicious existence, Yasmin had a flash of worry. 'You never talk to me about how the probate is going,' she asked uncertainly over dinner one night.

'I'm so sorry, darling,' Hassan said, suddenly concerned. 'Did you think I was withholding information?'

'Oh no,' Yasmin answered, looking down at her plate. 'Nothing like that. But it always seems so amazing to me that I could have inherited all this without there being some problem. I was afraid that you wouldn't tell me, for fear of upsetting me or something.'

'Well, you have absolutely nothing to worry about,' Hassan said. 'Things couldn't be going more smoothly. For a time I was afraid there might be some relatives that none of us knew about, that they would surface and start making demands. But that hasn't happened. The title searches are clear, and everything is being transferred into your name.'

'I feel guilty that I'm doing nothing and you're doing all this work for me.'

'Well, don't feel guilty,' Hassan said softly. 'I am being paid more than enough for my services during the day – even without your generosity in the evenings.'

He raised her hand to his lips. Turning it over, he placed a soft kiss on her palm as he watched her face soften in the candlelight. His tongue traced a quick pattern on her skin, causing her to shiver. Without another word he helped her to her feet. They left their dinner unfinished and went upstairs.

The next day, after leaving a group of galleries on Rue Saint Germain des Prés, Yasmin walked aimlessly through the streets. In the months since she'd been living in Paris with Hassan, she was oddly surprised that she'd been happy. She walked slowly. It was two-thirty in the afternoon and she didn't have to be back at the town house until five, when she would bathe and dress for their theater engagement.

Two and a half hours with nothing in particular to do and no place to go, she thought. It was cold. She pulled the fur coat close around her as she walked. The coat had been a gift from Hassan. It was Russian sable, and she always felt like a princess when she wore it. Hassan gave her many gifts – beautiful clothes and expensive jewelry; thick chains of gold and precious gems in elaborate settings. He liked it when she wore his gifts, and she realized he felt the pride of ownership.

She walked without knowing where she was going, passing small cafés, butcher shops, and boulangeries. There were Christmas decorations hanging in the windows, and the churches she passed had outdoor crèches set up, which she thought beautiful.

The neighborhood she was walking through became residential and more working class. Soon packs of shouting boys raced back and forth across the street, dodging cars and cursing at the worried drivers. Stupid-eyed young men lounged against the walls outside the shops. As near as Yasmin could tell, their main activity seemed to be lighting cigarettes and glancing up and down the length of the street. They had the air of waiting for someone or something they knew would never show up. Small groups of girls sat on the stoops of the houses. Their makeup was too heavy and their coats too light. They had the hard-eyed look of incipient whores.

Yasmin stood out because of her sable coat, but even though she realized she should be careful, she didn't feel afraid. This was a different world from the one she'd been living in for the last three months. It was also quite different from her world in Geneva, or her life at school. But it was not frightening to her.

It most resembled what she had come from – only the language was French, not Arabic. The clothes were different, but not the crushing sense of poverty, nor the feeling that these young people would do anything for money – anything at all. Not that there was anything wrong with that mentality, Yasmin thought. It was merely survival. On these streets there was no such thing as crime. There were only better and worse ways to earn a living. Some ways were just more dangerous than others. Crime, here, was a bourgeois concept. She sensed rather than saw the feral energy that emanated from cold young eyes, and the shifting glances that missed nothing and coveted everything.

For some reason, as Yasmin looked at these young people she suddenly broke out of the daze she'd been in for so long. Reality came bolting in through her senses, and along with it, the colors and sounds of the street seemed exaggerated. An energy she hadn't known she possessed seemed to flow through her body. She could almost feel her fingers start to tingle.

'That's it!' she said out loud. A group of boys stared at her. But she was walking so briskly, she was around the corner before they could hear her next words. 'I've been a child.'

Instead of letting the inheritance buy her the freedom she wanted, she realized she'd let it tie her to an overprotective guardian of a man. She recognized her behavior as part of a pattern she'd been in for her whole life. Aghast, Yasmin crossed the street, heading back to Rue Saint Germain des Prés.

She'd been afraid, she thought, so spineless that she hadn't even considered her alternatives. Now she had the same freedom as Oskar Von Rothenburg; she had the money to allow her the freedom to do what she wanted. All I have to do is figure out what *that* is, she told herself, and then I'll be truly free. With a smile, she suddenly realized what André had done for her. He had, as his parting gift, truly bought her freedom.

All this time, ever since the day Hassan had walked into the office in Geneva, she had been unable to think for herself. Suddenly a flood of all the things she had wanted to do came washing back like a powerful tidal wave.

She recalled that she'd wanted to learn the business angles of Oskar's life, wanted to see how the art got turned from art into money and then back into art again. Now she realized that the vineyards could be the same sort of challenge. Grapes got turned into money and then back into grapes. But would Hassan teach her?

Immediately Yasmin knew he wouldn't. Hassan didn't want a woman like that in his life. He wanted a courtesan, perhaps, an intelligent woman definitely, but not an independent woman, and certainly not a businesswoman.

But how could she learn? she wondered. That was the question. There was a second question too. Not for one moment had Hassan ever doubted that Yasmin was his property, his acquisition. He had never asked her to marry him and she had never said she would. Hassan had just assumed that she agreed. But as delightful in many respects as her life with Hassan was, it had numbed her. The indolent, sophisticated, pleasure-loving life had been an anesthetic, and Yasmin knew she had to get away.

The inheritance would carry her wherever she wanted to go. Her only real problem lay in getting away from Hassan, and trying to learn the business at the same time.

'Impossible,' she muttered.

Then Yasmin burst out laughing. It was all so simple! Why hadn't she thought of it before? she wondered. But, of course! School. She would go back to school. After all, everyone else at Lautremont had gone on to college. Hillary was at Radcliffe, and Yasmin could go there too.

But Radcliffe was in America, she realized. Too far.

Well, there was always the Sorbonne, in Paris.

But that was too near, she thought with a laugh. England? Why not?

But what about Hassan? she wondered. Did she love him? She couldn't say. She thought not. But it was true that she enjoyed his company. She enjoyed his lovemaking. But it wasn't love. Love had to be more than that. She remembered André and how she'd felt with him. Swept away. Perhaps that was love. But what she felt for Hassan was something else. Pleasant, but something else.

At a broad street filled with taxis, she hailed one. As the cab whizzed her back to the town house, she realized

274

how glad she was that she'd come to her senses, and felt exhilarated at the prospect of her life.

When the taxi pulled up in front of the house, Yasmin handed the driver a twenty-franc note, even though the fare was only seven francs. Without waiting for her change, she bolted out the door and up the steps.

Singing happily, she slipped into a turquoise caftan, and draped a string of pearls around her neck. She was already waiting for Hassan downstairs when he came in.

'Ah, good.' he said briskly as he put down his briefcase. 'You're ready. We can leave as soon as I change.'

'Oh, Hassan,' Yasmin said. 'I've poured you a drink. I've made a decision, and I wanted to tell you about it.'

'Really? So you've decided to marry me tomorrow. Is that it? I'm delighted, but I didn't need a drink to prepare me for that one.'

'No. I've decided to go back to school. It's what I'm interested in. All this time I've been trying to figure out what I wanted. Today I suddenly remembered, and I'm filled with happiness.'

Hassan didn't appear at all happy about her decision. For a moment Yasmin thought she saw cold fury in his eyes.

'No,' he said. His voice was hard. 'I want you here with me.'

'I'm not deciding against you,' Yasmin said. 'I just want to go back to school – in England.'

'What makes you think you can leave everything and have it be just the way you want it when you come back?' he asked, ice in his voice. 'Aren't you taking a lot for granted?'

Yasmin faltered slightly. This was harder than she thought it would be. 'But I always liked going to school,' she said softly. 'I wanted to go to college, too, but André never suggested it – there wasn't time.'

'Perhaps he didn't feel that it was right for you.'

'It doesn't matter what he felt,' she said lamely. 'But it matters what I feel. I would like very much to continue my education.'

'How were your grades?'

'Excellent, of course,' Yasmin said. 'I was valedictorian.' She stood a little straighter as she said the words.

There was silence in the room. Hassan stopped pacing around and sat down. He lowered himself into the wing chair with liquid grace. As usual Yasmin was taken aback by his resemblance to a big cat. Every movement he made was beautifully controlled, spare, and economical. He would have made a superior athlete if he had chosen to be one, she thought. He stared into his glass for a long time, and Yasmin felt the hair on her arm prickle, felt almost afraid. What was he going to say to her? she wondered.

Suddenly he looked up at her. 'Well, I suppose there is no harm in it,' he said, his voice suddenly soft. His words had a careful sound to them. 'After all, it would make you even more fascinating as a lover.'

'It would?' Yasmin was surprised at his sudden shift of mood.

'Perhaps not.' Hassan laughed. 'But it would make you a more interesting conversationalist. Besides it would be silly of me to stand in your way. After all, you might get there and decide you miss me, or decide that you're bored to tears by all that nonsense. Then you'll be back in a flash.'

Yasmin was annoyed. 'Were you bored to tears at school?'

'Of course not,' Hassan answered.

'Then I probably won't be either.'

Suddenly Hassan was out of the chair and standing by her side. He lifted a thick lock of her hair and blew softly against her ear. Yasmin shivered as the sensation threaded through her tense body.

'I will take care of everything for you until you decide to stop fooling around and come home,' he whispered against her forehead. 'I will guard your castle and all your pots of gold, little princess. But remember one thing.' He took her shoulders in his hands and held her pressed against him. Then he folded her into his arms and held her tightly. 'Remember that you are mine, always.'

Yasmin's temper started to flare. Why didn't he ever say anything about love? she wondered. Why always just ownership, or rights, or indebtedness? Maybe he doesn't know about love, she thought, but that doesn't mean I have to forget about it too.

Her thoughts were cut off as he tilted her chin up so he could see into her eyes. 'Are you sure you won't marry me right now?' he asked. A strange smile hovered around the corners of his mouth. 'I'll just ask you this once, and then I won't pressure you again.'

Hassan's hand slid down her back and pressed her hard against his body. His mouth came down over hers and began a soft and sensuous caress that was insistent and possessive. The languorous sensuality she always felt with him began to steal down through her body. She arched against him but he seemed remote, detached. It was as if he were purposely showing her the reaction she always had to him, wanting her to feel the power he had over her.

His mouth traced patterns on her lips and his tongue snaked between them, touching hers and then withdrawing. When he knew he had her, he slid his hands down and gripped her hipbones as if they were handles on a vase. Adjusting her slightly, he moved a hard-muscled leg between her thighs, then held her tight against his leg. Moving rhythmically, he purposely excited her.

'Now tell me what you want, Yasmin,' he whispered against her lips. 'Do you want to leave me? Leave this?'

Before she could answer, he picked her up and carried her across the room. He dropped her down on the yellow couch and lifted her skirt up, exposing her thighs to him.

'Perhaps I should remind you of what you will be missing when you're off with your dusty books,' he said softly. Her eyes were riveted on him as he slid her silk panties down over her ankles and then unzipped his pants.

He entered her without any of his usual caution, and with no foreplay. She was appalled at how ready she was for him. It wasn't fair, she thought, but then she couldn't think clearly anymore. He watched her carefully, still very much in control of himself, and moved with wicked slowness in and out of her slick body. As he moved, he slowly lifted the caftan over her head, exposing her breasts to his view. Tracing a circular pattern around each erect nipple with his thumb, he studiously excited her to the point of no return. It wasn't until her screams of pleasure subsided that he allowed himself to come too.

'Are you sure?' he said softly. This time he wasn't smiling.

Yasmin nodded her head silently. She didn't think she could trust herself to speak yet.

'All right, then. You can go,' he said, standing abruptly. 'But don't go running off to anyone else. You may want to go to school, and you may want to bury your nose in books, and I will allow you to do that. But I want your body for myself. Is that clear?'

Yasmin looked carefully at his face. 'Hassan, do you love me?'

Hassan, for once, was unprepared for her question. 'Love you?' His expression was startled, naked, and unguarded for a moment. 'Why do you ask me that?'

'I don't know,' Yasmin said. Suddenly she felt strong

278

and in control of the conversation. 'It seemed like a logical question to ask. After all, you want to marry me. You tell me what I can and cannot do with my body. I was just wondering whether or not you loved me. Is that so strange?'

But Hassan wasn't cornered for long. With his usual agility, he sidestepped the question.

'You read too many novels, my dear,' he said with a smile. Then he sat down next to her and gathered her into his arms in a hug. 'You want it to be the way it is in the books, don't you?'

'And what's wrong with that?' Yasmin asked. 'Are the books incorrect?'

'Of course not,' Hassan said. 'But we aren't animals either. What passes for romance with the masses may not be what passes for romance with people like us.'

'I don't fel any different from the masses, as you call them,' Yasmin mumbled against his chest. He made it so hard for her to talk sometimes.

'If it makes you happy,' Hassan said in a tender, but almost patronizing tone of voice, 'I love everything about you. I love your funny little mind and all its intellectual pretensions. I love your body. But most of all I love this . . .' He cupped his hand over the mound between her legs.

Yasmin wondered why he just couldn't say I love you. But at least he was letting her go, she thought. Ignoring his fingers, she started thinking about applications, letters of recommendation, and getting her transcripts from Lautremont. She would call Solange immediately. There was so much to do and so little time to do it. Perhaps she could start in the middle of the year. February was little more than a month and a half away. It would be hard, but not impossible.

As her mind flickered over the mental list that was rapidly getting longer, she felt as if she weren't quite herself. It seemed as if she was standing on the other side of the room, watching this large, handsome man make love to a small, dark girl. The girl was standing still, her eyes open, a small frown creasing her brow. The girl was obviously not paying close attention to what was going on.

Yasmin laughed low in her throat, and wondered if Hassan noticed her lack of participation. Well, at least he had something to keep him busy, she told herself, while she figured out how to extricate herself from the life he had so carefully planned for her.

PART FIVE

Gstaad, 1982

17

Huge wet snowflakes stuck to Yasmin's eyelashes, making it almost impossible to see. How would she ever find her way back to Oskar's chalet in that soup? she wondered as she ran across the picturesque street toward the car.

When she'd come into town an hour earlier, it hadn't been snowing. In fact, patches of blue sky seemed to point to clearing conditions for the day, and all the skiers had been busy getting their gear ready in hopes that the snow wouldn't come. Not that a little snow would keep many of them inside – but this was different. Even Yasmin, who was an excellent skier, could see it would be impossible to do anything in this swirling, blinding, unbelievable mess. It was more like flying slush.

'Oh, well,' she said to herself, fumbling with the keys to the Citroen she'd borrowed. She hadn't come for the skiing anyway, but to see Solange and Oskar.

It had been three years since she'd seen Solange, and even longer since she'd seen Oskar. In fact she hadn't seen Oskar Von Rothenburg since her whirlwind visit to Geneva six years before to clear things up right before she'd started at St Anne's College at Oxford, where she'd taken her degree in economics. Of course, she'd written letters, but it wasn't the same.

The minute Yasmin had made the decision to go back to school, she also realized that her stay in Paris with Hassan hadn't been helping her deal with her life. Although she hadn't known what was missing at the time, she now saw it had been a sense of direction. She didn't need or want to be taken care of anymore. She wanted to take hold of her own life and revive the strong sense of purpose that she'd been missing.

She also realized that sex was one thing, love another. She saw that she was still in love with André – whatever her reasons were for that love. Whether she was still clinging to her childhood fears, or that he was the first man in her life, didn't matter. What mattered was that she didn't feel ready to begin again. André's shadow hovered out of reach, just out of sight, and held her tightly in its grasp. No matter how physically satisfying Hassan was, she wasn't ready for him. He was powerful, but not powerful enough. And Yasmin needed to examine her feelings and sort them out before embarking on another love.

What's more, she realized she had to arrange her life – and fast. Her apartment in Geneva had to be dealt with, as well as all her belongings. And there had been Oskar Von Rothenburg too. Though it had been three months since she'd left him to claim her inheritance, poor Oskar, with typical absentmindedness, hadn't hired a replacement for Yasmin. It looked as if he were waiting for her to come back and start typing and filing.

Yasmin had felt guilty. She should have made her position clear to him from the start, she'd thought. She mentioned her guilt to Solange, who helped her pack her belongings in crates, getting them ready to be shipped to England.

'Don't be ridiculous,' Solange said with a laugh. 'You had no idea what to expect. How could you make your position clear to Oskar when it wasn't even clear to you? And besides, I keep telling you this and you keep refusing to listen – Oskar did very well without you for many years.'

'Very well, indeed,' Yasmin said, giggling. 'You saw what his office looked like!'

'And it looks that way again,' answered Solange. 'But

284

that's simply his way of working. Don't feel guilty. Besides, he said he'd like you to come and spend a few days with him and train someone. He's planning to hire a girl for three days a week.'

'Poor thing,' Yasmin sighed as she folded a sweater, placing it on the pile of clothes in the box.

'What time did you tell Oskar you'd come by?' asked Solange.

'Four o'clock.'

Solange looked at her watch. '*Mon Dieu!*' she said. 'It's three o'clock. I promised Martine I'd meet her for tea in half an hour!'

'Solange, please go,' Yasmin said. 'I can finish this tonight. I wouldn't want you to be late on my account.'

When Solange left, Yasmin put some water up to boil, thinking a cup of tea would wash away the smudgy exhaustion she'd been feeling for the last few days. She'd been forcing herself not to think about Hassan. She couldn't deal with it because she knew it wasn't Hassan she'd miss. She'd miss the solid security he offered her. But that was akin to a prisoner missing his jail cell because it was warm and kept the rain out. She would be succumbing to a weakness that she would regret all her life, she thought, if she didn't make this move.

After putting some of the cartons aside, she scanned the room, wondering at the massive changes that she'd lived through. Funny how unpredictable life was, she thought. Her earliest memories were of sitting on a sloping hillside in the Atlas Mountains, watching over a small flock of goats. The tinkling sound of their bells had been like music. It was a strange symphony of uneven notes, yet lovely all the same. Her own beads and bracelets would also tinkle as she ran, making her feel like one of the little goats that she played with on the scrubby hillside.

How she had loved it when her mother made *tajine*.

The tasty chicken cooked in oil and then covered with olives, apples, and carrots had been her favorite. Sometimes she got a pastry to take with her when she went into the hills with the goats. They were delicious, sticky things filled with crushed almonds and honey. The baby goats would lick her fingers, hunting for traces of the syrupy sweet. Finally giving up, they would race off to find their mothers and drink the warm, musky milk from their hanging teats.

It had all been so simple then. If her mother hadn't died from those terrible, hacking coughs, things would have stayed simple. Yasmin would probably have been married off to someone very much like her uncles. No doubt by this time she'd have four children and a fifth on the way – or be dead in childbirth like so many of the other women in the village. How strange were the twists of fate. Now she was the mistress of a small empire, a millionairess, and about to become a businesswoman.

Allah had definitely not been paying attention. He was Moroccan, and as Solange had said those many years ago to André, Arab men weren't known for their liberated thoughts regarding women. For Allah to make one of his own daughters a businesswoman was certainly an oversight on his part. It made her smile.

Shaking her head to clear away the cobwebs of her memories, Yasmin left to catch the bus, just as she had for so many months. Standing in the shifting shadows at the bus stop, the late afternoon sunlight washed everything in its crisp, winter clarity. With a jolt Yasmin realized that she could take a taxi if she wanted. Money certainly was no object. Then she realized that she *wanted* to take the bus, wanted to give silent farewells to her other life and repeat, as far as she could, the routine of her days on this last day before she took up the reins of her new existence.

Von Rothenburg had been delighted to see her, and

apparently not the slightest bit put out by the fact that she'd been gone for three months, or put off by the knowledge that she was now a baroness. He also didn't seem too upset that she was leaving for good.

'I assumed from the beginning that I wouldn't have you for long, my dear,' he said, chucking her under the chin. 'After all, a young lady as beautiful as you are usually gets married after three or four months. So, you see, I was lucky, I had you – with bits off here and there – for almost eight months. That's much longer than I expected.'

'Three months is a rather long "bit" to take off from work,' Yasmin said. 'The length of time I worked for you was closer to four months. You're exaggerating again.' But she flushed at his compliment, then turned aside to look through some papers.

'And besides,' Von Rothenburg continued, 'perhaps it will work out much better for me this way. I understand Saint-Clair had quite a nice collection himself. Perhaps – and mind you, this is only a suggestion – perhaps there are a few little knickknacks hanging around that you might consider selling. Something that would round out one or two of my collections, eh?'

'Knickknacks?' Yasmin laughed at the twinkle in his eyes and answered shrewdly. 'You may have something there. I don't think there's anything in the house in Paris that I'd want to sell, but maybe there's a knickknack or two in the villa in Tangier. I'll see if perhaps there's anything there you'd like.'

'Splendid, my dear, just splendid.' He had rubbed his hands together in such a ridiculous imitation of unrestrained greed that Yasmin had to suppress a laugh. For a moment he looked like a huge, crafty gnome.

'You should have been on the stage!' she said. 'You could have been a great actor.'

'Do you really think so?' Von Rothenburg was obviously pleased at the compliment, and he preened slightly. 'I doubt it, my dear, but not because I'm not good at it. I'm not the leading man type, I'm afraid, and that's the very least I would settle for. Furthermore, if the truth be known, I prefer to keep my performances for smaller audiences. That way no one will ever know that I'm really acting. They will always think I'm totally sincere.' He chuckled. 'Clever, don't you think?'

'Diabolical!' Yasmin said, laughing. 'Now I know how you do so well at all those auctions. You don't telegraph your intentions. That's what keeps the price down on what you want until the very last minute!'

Oskar glared at her sharply, his eyes narrowing for a second. But then he relaxed into an amused expression. 'And you, my dear, are very clever too. I hope I never run up against you at an auction!' He raised his eyebrows in mock alarm at the thought. 'Now, let's get down to work,' he said, picking up an untidy handful of papers and shaking them at the ceiling. 'I haven't the faintest idea what all of this is . . . do you believe that?'

'Not for a minute,' answered Yasmin. 'But I'll play along with you just this once. When does the new secretary start, by the way?'

'In two weeks,' Oskar said.

'But that's dreadful! I won't be able to stay and train her,' Yasmin said, looking miserable. 'I'll be in England in two weeks.'

'Don't worry about it,' Oskar said with a wave of his hand. 'She'll figure it out the same way you did. Perhaps it's better to let her work out her own system anyway.'

'I suppose you're right. But still, if there was some way – '

'Please, stop babbling about helping her. Start helping me instead,' Oskar said, trying to sound gruff.

They worked steadily for about two hours, then Yasmin kissed him fondly good-bye.

'And the next time I'm in England, I'll stop in and see you,' said Von Rothenburg at the door. 'You'll have to cook me a nice dinner to make up for all the trouble you've caused.'

'With pleasure,' Yasmin said as she stood on the steps. 'But you'll have to take me to the ballet to pay for it.'

That evening after dinner, she and Solange finished cleaning up the little apartment Yasmin had called home. After returning the keys to Madame de Goncourt, they carried the boxes downstairs and piled them into a taxi. Back at Solange's apartment, exhausted, Yasmin refused a glass of brandy and went straight to bed.

But she found it impossible to fall asleep. Her mind was filled with a shifting screen of pictures, a kaleidoscope of events she was unable to shut out. The most persistent involved Hassan, and she was assaulted by a strong physical longing. Even here, in the security of Solange's guest room, miles from his powerful presence, Yasmin felt torn. Her skin began to tingle as pictures flickered across the screen of her mind. With them came flashbacks of the physical sensations as well. She tossed fitfully as the memory of his mouth and hands caressed her with aching vividness.

And she didn't even love him! Yasmin was appalled at the physical response she had to the man. She had vowed to forget him, but it wasn't easy. She didn't want that aching place between her legs to make her change her mind about all the things she wanted for her life. She had to wipe that hunger away, she told herself, before she went running back to Paris.

Determined not to give in to the sensual madness Hassan had kindled, Yasmin tucked a pillow between her legs. Gripping it tightly with her knees, she fell into a dream-tossed sleep. What the dreams were, she didn't

know, but when she woke up, she was even more exhausted than she'd been when she went to sleep.

Solange's coffee helped, but she felt drained and unwill-
ing to face the day. How lovely it would be to just sink
back into the pillows and lose herself in sleep.

'Wake up, sleepyhead!' Solange gave her a brusque pat
on the shoulder. 'You're just trying not to think about
the changes in your life. All small children respond the
same way to change. But you're a grown-up now!'

'No, I'm not,' mumbled Yasmin dispiritedly.

'Picking through old possessions always does that to a
woman,' Solange said cheerily, waving her arm at the
stack of boxes in the hall. 'Why do you bother with all
this, anyway?'

'Because it's mine,' Yasmin said.

'That's like saying you want to climb Mount Everest
because it's there,' chided Solange. 'Why not just throw
it all out? You could drop in to the couture salons
tomorrow and buy everything you desire, am I right?'

'Solange! That's wasteful!'

'Perhaps,' Solange agreed. 'But you could do it if you
wanted to.'

Yasmin didn't even crack a smile. 'Do you really think
I should?' she asked, staring listlessly at the boxes.

'Should what?'

'Throw everything out.'

'Do whatever you want, my dear,' Solange had said.

But in the end Yasmin took everything with her to
Oxford. She decorated her small room with the posters
she'd so carefully chosen, and covered her bed with the
throw pillows and bedspread Solange had given her. It
made her feel nice and ordinary. All she yearned for
during those years was to be ordinary, because one of the
hardest things for Yasmin to get used to was *not* being
ordinary.

The concept of being rich was utterly alien to her. It was nice to have money, of course. It was secure. It was even exhilarating at times. But on the whole Yasmin didn't feel right about having *so* much money. She knew she hadn't earned any of it – she had it because of an unlucky accident, a windfall.

On top of it all, the windfall came as a result of something embarrassing and appalling. If she'd had to sit down and describe the sequence of events to anyone – starting with her mother's rape, continuing on through her sale to Khadir and working in his brothel, and culminating in her short affair with André and his immediate death – well, it didn't look too good, now, did it?

The less said about her wealth the better, Yasmin reasoned, and was relieved that no one at St Anne's College at Oxford asked her about it. Yasmin's desire to be anonymous had something to do with this reaction.

In Paris she had gradually, under Hassan's tutelage, become flamboyant in the way she dressed and the way she wore her hair. Hassan had often gone with her when she shopped, picking out the most interesting clothes for her. He liked her hair either flowing and loose, or in an elaborately coiled coif. Gradually he'd transformed her into a stunning, eye-catching woman. Often people stared when she walked by. Yasmin didn't like it, but Hassan loved it. She sensed that the more flamboyant she was, the more important and powerful he felt. If he could afford a stunning possession like her, she thought, it made him all the more masculine in other men's eyes – and no doubt in women's eyes as well. Of course, no one ever mentioned that it was her money that paid for all the stunning clothes. But no one ever asked either.

But here in Oxford, Yasmin pulled her hair back tightly in a bun at the base of her neck and wore brown corduroy pants. Over them she wore loose dark gray or brown sweaters. She faded right into the mahogany paneling, looking exactly like her own concept of an economics student – unobtrusive. Because she spent such long hours working, she'd strained her eyes, which led to the final cap on her disguise – she began to wear glasses. Choosing large tortoiseshell frames that obscured most of her face, she had finally achieved her goal of dissolving right into the background.

Hassan had laughed the first time he'd come up to Oxford to see her. It had also been the last. Yasmin had been aloof and withdrawn, and whatever it was that drew Hassan to her so strongly seemed to fade away in front of her eyes.

'You fit right in here,' he had said to her with a wave of his hand at the stacks of books.

'I know,' Yasmin answered briefly. 'That's why I'm here.'

'You can hide from me and from all your classmates, but you can't hide from yourself, Yasmin. Not forever.'

'I'm not hiding from myself. This *is* my self.'

Hassan had laughed. 'If you choose to think that, go right ahead, my dear. But I know you better.' He slid his hand across her cheek, then down to her collarbone. 'Yes. Much better than you think.'

'Really?' Yasmin had asked, thinking it might be interesting to see just exactly what he thought he knew. 'Tell me what I'm *really* like, Hassan. I'd be interested to hear.'

'Your sweet little personality is split right in two,' he'd said. His gaze had been mildly calculating. 'Perhaps it would be easier for you to grasp if I called it insecurity instead. You aren't comfortable with yourself as you are. You think you have to keep working, keep going to school, keep making yourself into something you're not. You think you are unacceptable as you are. André did that to you, you know.'

'He didn't make me insecure,' Yasmin said carefully.

292

She had an intuition that if she defended André with more than a casual tone, she would end up angering Hassan. 'He gave me an incredible opportunity. He plucked me out of the old ways of Morocco and brought me right into the twentieth century.'

'But you're saying the very same thing I'm saying,' Hassan said with a smile. 'You just don't hear yourself. When André bought you, you were perfect in all respects – '

'How would you know?' Yasmin retorted sharply.

'Oh, I didn't know you, but I can certainly imagine what you were like. You see, when he sent you away to school, to you, that was a rejection. Maybe he didn't understand what he was doing, but it marked you forever. Admit it, Yasmin.'

This was a very hard conversation, she thought. It wasn't a conversation she wanted to be having. 'It's true that at first I didn't know why he sent me away,' she said carefully. 'But I was a child, don't you see? I'd been sold to him for a purpose, and . . . and he didn't . . .'

'He didn't what, Yasmin?' There was a sly smile on Hassan's face. He realized that he was getting to her, and it was obvious he enjoyed the power it gave him. 'You know, all this time we've never talked about André. You've never really told me what actually happened between you. At first I thought that was because the relationship wasn't very important to you.'

Yasmin got up and walked over to the window. It was a cool, rainy day. The fog was blotting out the new leaves that had just begun to bud on the grassy square in front of her room. Everything looked misted, wrapped in soggy cotton wool.

'I loved André very much. But that's what I've always told you. He never hurt me. He was always wonderful to me.'

'No, I think you're wrong. I think his early rejection

hurt you terribly. Tell me something, Yasmin. Did he make love to you before he sent you away?'

It was a key question, and Yasmin didn't like where he was leading her. 'No,' she answered. 'He wouldn't. He didn't want to frighten me. He was thinking of my best interests, not just his own needs.'

'That may be so, but at the time you didn't understand, did you? It was what you'd been told to expect, right? Who told you? Khadir? No matter. You thought there was something wrong with you. I suppose it wasn't until he took you out of school that he consummated your friendship, so to speak.'

Yasmin spun around, her eyes flashing. 'That's right, and he waited until I was ready for the relationship. Quite frankly, I dislike being stalked. I'm not prey, you know. I'm a person. I know that may sound ridiculous to you, but sometimes I feel I have to come right out and say things that should be obvious. To anyone else but you, they probably would be obvious.'

'It's a question of vantage point, Yasmin,' Hassan answered. He pulled himself out of the straight-backed chair he'd been straddling and moved across the room to stand next to her. He glanced out the window at the thickening fog. The heavy coils of dampness wrapped themselves around the upper branches of the trees. 'I hate clichés, but sometimes they are so fitting. Sometimes you cannot see the forest for the trees. I still think that you try too hard. You are still reacting, albeit unconsciously, to André's rejection of you. That, coupled with the fact that you're Moroccan and trying to make it in the West, makes you especially vulnerable.'

Yasmin could almost feel the heat emanating from Hassan. More than anything, she wanted to be away from him. She shivered and wrapped her arms tightly across her chest.

'You can go to school forever, Yasmin, but it won't

make you better,' Hassan hissed softly, his obsidian eyes unreadable. 'It won't make you feel better about yourself either. The only way you're ever going to be happy is when you accept what you are.'

'And what am I?' she asked, looking up at him.

'You're a little girl who's been rejected by every male you've ever dealt with – your father, your grandfather, Khadir, and of course André – every man, that is, except me. I intend to prove to you that I won't ever reject you. I'll wait until you finally come to me of your own volition.'

'I don't consider André's death a rejection,' Yasmin said sharply, turning back to the room. She liked the sight of all her familiar things. They gave her a sense of place she desperately wanted right now. 'He certainly didn't plan his death.'

'Intellectually, death is not a rejection,' Hassan answered slowly. 'But emotionally, it takes a long time for people to reconcile what is actually the most final of rejections. It's a typical response, Yasmin: "If you really loved me, you wouldn't have died on me like that." You're not the first one who felt that way, and you won't be the last.'

'So what do you want from me?' Yasmin said. She felt his eyes stripping her, felt lost and vulnerable and cold.

'I don't want anything from you. I told you I'd wait, and I will. You'll eventually come back to Paris and to me, and you'll be much happier with me as a result.'

'You don't know that for a fact.'

'Yes, I do. Where else do you have to go? For you, Yasmin, I represent home.'

He'd left her with papers to sign, saying he had business to attend to. Later that week Hassan had picked up the papers, kissed her lightly on the forehead, and left for Paris.

'Let me know when you're ready,' he'd said. After that

295

Yasmin hadn't seen him again. She hadn't missed him, either. Odd.

In fact, sometimes she thought that he had been right – that she was hiding from herself, from things she felt she couldn't face. But it didn't matter, because she was happy. Her life fit her like her clothes – loose, warm, and comfortable. Her mind ranged fully around all the things she was learning at school. It had seemed only natural when she got her degree that she should go right on from Oxford to the London School of Economics, which was to become her real proving ground.

Economics had been engrossing, but applying it to actual business situations had been inspiring. Yasmin no longer felt as if she were hiding. She felt totally involved. By her last year she was ready to get involved with André's businesses.

Hassan had been sending her papers to sign, but had never come back to England. She'd never gone back to Paris, either, not on vacations or at any other time. Their relationship was suspended in limbo. Every now and then Yasmin would shake her head, wondering if it had existed at all. But of course it had. And, of course, her remembrances sometimes intruded.

Yasmin had deliberately asked Hassan to send her copies of anything that needed signing – not that she didn't trust him; she trusted him implicitly. But she wanted to be kept abreast of everything that went on. He had full power of attorney, and sometimes there were things that needed to be done too quickly for the paperwork to be sent to her in England. But Hassan always sent her copies, though he did it in an indulgent way, as if he were bowing to the whims of a child. Perhaps Hassan thought she didn't understand what she was looking at, she thought. But how could that be so? After all, she was getting her MBA. How could she not understand these things? But then she decided Hassan had little blind spots. He probably wanted to think of her as an ignorant Moroccan girl because it suited his purpose. So he treated her like one, and ignored all evidence to the contrary.

Each shipment of papers he sent was always accompanied by an exquisite gift, the kind of thing one would send to an expensive mistress, thought Yasmin, looking at that month's gift. It was a beautiful little inlaid, segmented fish, a piece of Chinese enamel work – very old and very rare. She loved it, as Hassan had known she would. But the gifts seemed to have another message, as if Hassan wanted her to feel like a precious toy, not a thinking, educated woman. Happily, they didn't have that effect on her.

Yasmin had opened a bank account in town and also rented a deposit box. This fish would go rest in there, next to all the other precious baubles Hassan sent to make her feel like an odalisque. He must have thought the presents formed links in a chain that kept her bound to him, she mused. She laughed quietly to herself as she slid the lovely object into its box. Then, pushing her glasses back up on her nose, she sat down to work.

Not only did Yasmin keep a close eye on what was going on at the vineyard, she also kept her own set of running books. She hadn't mentioned this to Hassan because there was no need, and also because she didn't want him to feel she didn't trust him. She just liked the opportunity to put what she was learning into practice on something real – something she was interested in. But it also made her laugh to think that even if she had told him, he would probably have forgotten. One thing that never stuck in Hassan's mind for long was evidence that she had a head for business. Well, he'd find out soon enough, she told herself.

It was during her last year in school that Yasmin finally came to terms with something important. Analyzing and reanalyzing her feelings for André, she had finally come to the startling conclusion that Hassan had been correct when he told her that her feelings for André had been infantile. Well, perhaps infantile was the wrong word to use, she'd amended, but it wasn't an adult love for another adult, that much was certain. Everything about her background pointed the way toward an overpowering attachment to someone older, someone who would protect her, promise to love her.

André was all she'd had. Of course she had been in love with him, but what she'd been in love with was not the man, but all he stood for. He was a father figure, as well as a lover, a teacher, and a brother – all rolled into one. Unfortunately André had treated her like a child – partly because she was one, but also partly because that was the only way he could see her.

She sometimes wondered whether, if he had lived, she would have been able to convince him that, indeed, she was a woman, and an intelligent woman at that. All he saw was the frightened beautiful girl Khadir had brought to him that night in Tangier, and that might have been all he would ever have been able to see.

'Ah, life is so complicated,' Yasmin said out loud as she guided the car slowly through the blinding whiteness of the snowstorm. 'But it all works out in the end, doesn't it?'

Only Yasmin wasn't sure yet, since she hadn't come to an end and she was willing to bet there would be a lot more unexpected events awaiting her. Although, by the looks of this storm, she thought, it may all be over in the next seven minutes.

As she drove, she thought about the odd shifts in behaviour Hassan had been exhibiting. A few months before she was to graduate, his attitude toward her changed once again. During a short telephone call he had asked her whether she was going to continue going to school after she got her MBA. It was the usual question in one respect: He had made a habit of asking her every few months whether she was tired of the 'nonsense,' and ready to come back to him. Each time she'd laughed, and said, 'Not yet.'

During that last telephone call, however, his tone had been less bantering. There was a tenseness behind the words, and Yasmin had been unable to pinpoint a reason for it.

'Can I expect you back in Paris, my dear?' he'd said. 'Or will you be devoting your talents to books rather than life for another two or three years?'

'I'll be finished with my thesis work next month, and my coursework in December,' Yasmin had answered. 'I'm planning to come back to Paris after New Year's.'

'What are you doing over Christmas, if I may ask?'

'I'm going skiing in Switzerland with Solange. I plan to stay with her at Oskar Von Rothenburg's. It will be good to see my old friends again.'

'You have many old friends, Yasmin. Some of them have waited a long time to see you again.' There was a long silence as Yasmin tried to think of an appropriate answer. Did he mean himself? But then he spoke again. 'You seem less than interested.'

'Hassan,' she finally said, keeping her tone light, 'you're being silly. I'll be back in Paris in a couple of months. Then I'm staying for good. Heavens! Who knows when I'll get a vacation after this.'

Hassan's tone quickly changed and became as light and bantering as her own. 'Wise decision, my dear. Once you come back you won't get another one soon! As far as I'm concerned, the last six years was a vacation for you.'

'Maybe I'd better get a job working for some other vineyard,' Yasmin had teased. 'I think you're going to be a terrible taskmaster.'

'I'll be sure to keep you busy day and night,' he'd said, chuckling. It was a throaty, gut-level laugh that made Yasmin shiver. 'You can tell me later whether you think it's terrible – or whether you love it.'

Yasmin had pretended not to understand the meaning of his words. She had laughed, and quickly said good-bye.

The call made her realize Hassan hadn't forgotten about her. He was just waiting patiently – like a clever cat in front of a mouse hole. Endless patience, with one paw raised in the air, waiting, eyes unblinking. Over the years she had almost forgotten about that part of his personality. Because he'd only seemed mildly amused by her scholarly pretension, even pleased that she was away, Yasmin assumed he'd found someone very pleasing to take her place, with his interest in her diminishing as a result.

Suddenly she realized that he must have found women to take her place – but not forever. He was biding his time. That was why this skiing vacation felt odd to her. She was up in the mountains, making the transition between the world of the intellect and the glittering world of the rich she would be returning to in a week. And Hassan was waiting for her in Paris. He was so very subtle, she thought, letting her enjoy her friends before he reclaimed her.

'I can't think about this anymore,' Yasmin muttered to herself as she maneuvered the car at five miles an hour around a deadly hairpin turn that she could barely see through the blinding snow. 'It took me fifteen minutes to get into town, and it's going to take me four hours to get back.'

Devoting her full attention to the winding road up the mountain to the chalet, she pushed the vivid images of Hassan out of her mind. She thought instead about seeing

Oskar and a houseful of very exciting guests in a couple of hours, and decided she wanted to look beautiful.

The brightly lit gates of the chalet loomed out of the blank whiteness. She gratefully pulled the car up in front, where the valet was waiting to park the guests' cars. From the unfamiliar Rolls Corniches and Mercedes limousines she saw parked, they had already started arriving. She gave him the keys, then slipped and slid through the snow around to the side entrance.

She was planning to wear a simple black sheath she'd had in Paris. It was six years old, but classically tailored. With it she would wear an impressive Egyptian necklace made of carnelian, lapis lazuli, and gold open work. It was one of Hassan's gifts. The necklace was very wide, and the dress very low cut, emphasizing her bosom. She would do something dramatic with her hair, she decided, knowing she would look superb.

For a long time Yasmin hadn't felt like being looked at. But tonight, for some reason, she thought she should go back out into the world of the glittering rich. She was about to turn twenty-five, she was the Baroness Yasmin de Saint-Clair, and she ought to be able to handle anything and anyone, she thought – in theory.

But as she turned slowly in front of the mirror, inspecting her reflection, she felt uncomfortable. It was too flamboyant – too striking. She'd hidden her body under baggy sweaters and loose shirts for so long, she suddenly felt exposed. She couldn't go downstairs and meet all those strangers dressed this way, she thought. It was the kind of look that Hassan had always encouraged her to have, but it simply didn't feel right.

Yasmin threw open her closet and quickly pushed aside the clothes she had brought, looking for something more subdued. Finally, she settled on a floor-length black skirt and a white satin blouse with a high neck and full, billowing sleeves that were caught at the wrist. Then she

301

pulled her hair back into the tight bun she was used to, put her glasses on, took one last look, and headed for the door. She knew she looked just as if she was about to make her piano debut at a small concert hall, but she didn't care.

The sounds of music slid up the stairs to greet her, and suddenly she was nervous. Stage fright, she thought, feeling silly. Maybe champagne would relax her.

18

'Darling! It's so good to see you again,' came a high-pitched nasal voice as Yasmin reached the bottom of the stairs. The party seemed to be going strong. Quickly glancing around the room, Yasmin could see dozens of beautifully dressed people milling around, holding glasses and talking animatedly. The main salon of the chalet was tremendous. Five black chandeliers hung from the vaulted ceiling, their hundreds of tiny lights sparkling merrily. At the far end of the room there was a huge fireplace, big enough for a man to stand in, and on either side of the tremendous opening, oversized statues of naked women held the mantel up above their heads. The sinuous curves of their lush thighs and breasts caught the light from the fire that blazed in the hearth.

Yasmin wondered if the wonderful mantel had come with the chalet, or whether Von Rothenburg had bought it at some auction and then had it installed. She could just as easily imagine that he'd bought this place high in the Swiss Alps just to possess that fireplace. It was the sort of thing Oskar sometimes did. The thought only served to remind her of how different it was to have money. Indulging such a whim would mean very little to someone like Oskar Von Rothenburg. Perhaps that was why he was always so cheerful, she thought affectionately.

She turned as she recognized the birdlike woman who stood a few feet away. Baroness Angela von Doningen, a close friend of Oskar's, was in her early sixties. The petite, elegantly dressed woman had flaming red hair, and beautiful bone structure that seemed to defy age. She'd often come to have a quiet bite of lunch with them in the days when Yasmin had been Oskar's assistant. An inveterate collector of art, and husbands, Angela had an inexhaustible supply of energy and money. She'd often told Yasmin that one could not have the first two without having the second two. Angela always had something wicked to say, and always seemed to have fun.

'Darling,' she gushed as she pulled Yasmin into the swarm of people in the room. 'You must come and meet my latest – he's an Italian count and he plays the most divine jazz piano you ever heard.'

Angela slipped effortlessly through the crowd, dodging liveried waiters balancing trays of crystal champagne glasses. She stopped for a fraction of a second to avoid knocking a tray of glasses to the floor, then continued. Yasmin caught up with her as Angela stopped in front of a tall, slender gentleman with a magnificently trimmed Vandyke. Prominent pale blue eyes stared out at her from under an expressively high forehead and dark brown hair. Startling wings of white hair smoothed back over his ears. Yasmin noted with surprise that he wasn't as young as Angela's usual husbands.

'Leonardo, you must meet Yasmin de Saint-Clair.'

The man bowed low from the waist, then picked up Yasmin's hand and kissed it.

'Isn't he courtly?' Angela said with a smile. 'That's why I love him so. I've decided that at my age, one should leave the cradle alone and find a man who complements one's decor rather than one's appetites. He's tremendously decorative, don't you think?'

Yasmin smiled, not knowing which question to answer. Probably yes to everything Angela said was the best way of handling it. But not knowing how Leonardo, the Italian count, felt about being discussed as if he weren't there, she decided silence was the best response. She supposed that he'd gotten used to it by now, or perhaps the benefits of being married to Angela far outweighed little annoyances such as being treated like a piece of furniture. Then Leonardo smiled at her as if to say, It's quite all right, Angela and I understand each other perfectly, and Yasmin felt less embarrassed.

Suddenly Solange materialized. 'There you are!' she said, planting a kiss on Yasmin's cheek. 'I was afraid you'd gotten stuck in a snowdrift.'

'I almost did,' Yasmin said, hugging Solange back. 'But I made it – despite terrifying odds.'

'It's all Oskar's fault – having a party in the Alps in the middle of the winter. Winter parties should always be held in tropical places. Now come with me,' Solange said, 'and I'll see that you meet all the right people. Why, it's been years since you've been out in the world. You'll find that so much has changed.'

'Did everyone switch husbands and wives?' Yasmin asked as they made their way around the room.

'A few switched,' Solange answered, 'but most of them elected to marry completely new ones. That's why these parties get bigger every year. If only people would marry insiders, then it wouldn't get out of hand this way.'

Yasmin laughed and then followed Solange as they made their way through the crowds. Solange introduced Yasmin to what seemed like a hundred different people. At first she was able to keep their names straight, but soon all the faces, names, and titles began to swim aimlessly around in her head. She'd also been handed another glass of champagne. Since she had very little to say to the people she was meeting, she'd been taking sips from her glass in order to cover the fact that she wasn't talking, and after a while felt herself in an alcoholic haze. That was when the rock music started. In a way the din of the band made it easier, she thought, since she could appear to be listening to the music.

She was surprised that Oskar had hired a rock group for a party like this one. The members of the band were wearing skin-tight silver and black jumpsuits that glittered as they moved. The lead singer was a black girl with a magnificent blond Afro that stuck out around her head like a halo. She was stunning, and she knew it. Every male head in the room turned to watch her as she belted out a slow, suggestive blues number. The rhythms began to seep into Yasmin's bones, and she felt herself swaying gently to the music.

How wonderful it would be to dance, she thought wistfully, the way she'd danced as a girl, with the *drbouka* tucked under her arm, alone in the center of the room.

Suddenly tired, Yasmin excused herself from the group she'd been left with by Solange and wandered through the connecting salons until she found a window with a comfortably cushioned seat to hide in. It was off to one side of a wall of French windows that let out onto a terrace with a beautiful wooden balustrade. Outside, the snowstorm was raging, and the tall fir trees that surrounded the chalet were weighted down with heaps of wet snow. The brilliant house lights lit up the falling snowflakes, making it look like a dream world of whiteness.

Leaning back against the edge of the window, Yasmin closed her eyes, thankful for the relative quiet of her private corner. She hadn't realized until now how used to peace she'd become during her years in England. She'd avoided gatherings like this one because they didn't seem to fit into her life. Now her life was about to change again, and she still didn't fit in.

Suddenly she had the feeling she was being watched, but when she looked around the room, it was empty. Then she heard a muted noise outside on the terrace. Snapping her head around, she almost screamed when she saw a tall man standing out in the snow, staring at her.

Dressed in ski clothes, the man's face was obscured by

a ski hat and reflective glasses. As he peered at her, a crazy smile creased his face, and he leapt out of sight. A moment later, in a burst of wind and snow, he entered the room through the French windows.

That's when Yasmin finally screamed.

'Surprised you, didn't I?' he said as he pulled off the glasses and ski cap. He spoke beautiful French. Yasmin couldn't help but notice his even, smooth features, in a handsome elongated face. High cheekbones gave him an almost Oriental cast alongside a regular nose and a wide, mobile mouth. A shock of blond hair fell across his twinkling blue eyes. She was reminded of pictures she'd seen of Russian students – big, blond, handsome cossacks, from the looks of them. It was the wonderful tilt to his eyes that held her attention.

'You certainly did surprise me,' she gasped. 'What in the world were you doing out there?'

'Arriving.' He laughed. 'I skiied down from the lodge where I'm staying. It's up the road about a mile.'

'You skied down in this snow?' Yasmin was aghast. 'But that's horribly dangerous, you know. You could have gotten lost or injured, and no one would have known where to find you. In a storm like this one, by morning you would have been buried.'

'You sound just like my mother,' the man said. 'Don't you know that if there's no risk, there's no thrill?'

'Suicidal slop,' Yasmin muttered under her breath. Louder, in a sarcastic tone, she said, 'Perhaps decadence has taken its customary toll. If life is so dull, you should try something more foolproof. I've heard that jumping off cliffs is the ultimate thrill of all time.'

'It is,' said the man smoothly. 'That's why they invented skiing and ski jumps. If you skied, you'd understand.'

'I do ski,' Yasmin said with a sniff. 'But I love it for other reasons.'

'Rationalizing, of course,' the man said with a laugh. 'I

know. You're going to tell me that you love the solitary freedom, the sensation of flying . . . the exquisite scenery, the lack of any noise but the sound of the skis skimming over the snow. Absurdities.'

'Those are the very things I love about, and it isn't absurd, it's true.'

'Bien. Then I'll meet you on the slopes tomorrow and we'll spend the day listening to the sound of your skis.'

'I doubt it,' said Yasmin.

'By the way, my name is Charles. Charles LaMarquette. What's yours?'

The name sounded familiar, but Yasmin didn't think about it. All names were sounding familiar to her after the hundreds of introductions she'd been through with Solange. She didn't recall meeting him anywhere else, either.

'Yasmin de Saint-Clair. Were you invited to this party, or are you crashing?'

Even though the question was supposed to throw the man off balance, he suddenly stared at her with wide eyes and a slightly open mouth.

'You're kidding,' he said, aghast.

'Of course I'm not kidding,' Yasmin said. 'It's a perfectly acceptable question, don't you think? After all, you just came in through the window. For all I know, you're a thief or something. Maybe I should call Oskar and see what he has to say.'

'First of all, Oskar never knows who's invited to these bashes and who isn't. And second of all, that wasn't what I meant. Are you telling me that you're really Yasmin de Saint-Clair?'

Yasmin was beginning to protest, but slowly raising her eyes to meet his, was caught by his strange, intense look.

'Of course,' she answered. 'Why else would I say that? And why do you ask?'

'Because I've wanted to meet you for years, that's why.'

She thought he might be joking, but could see from his expression that he was dead serious. It was unnerving. 'I'm afraid I don't know you,' she finally said. 'How could you have wanted to meet me for years, as you say?'

'Don't you recognize my name?' he said.

'No, quite frankly.' Then it came back to her, that day so many years ago when she sat with Hassan in the lawyers' offices, Fauquier, Renan, et La Tour. Henri LaMarquette, André's banker, was also there. He was the man who was so distant, so humorless. But this young man was nothing at all like that dour, disapproving man. 'Are you related to Henri LaMarquette?' she asked slowly.

'He's my father.'

'I don't believe it.'

'Try.'

'What a small world.'

'Delicious, isn't it?'

She had been in a fog that day, and everyone else in the room had been pleasant and helpful except Monsieur LaMarquette, who had treated her with disdain. Now here she was meeting his son, who dripped melted snow all over the Aubusson rug and looked at her as if she were an exhibit on display.

'Well, now you've finally met me,' Yasmin said coldly, as her thoughts raged inside her. Here was someone who might connect her past and her present. She wanted to be anyplace else but here, alone in this room with this man. 'I think it's time I joined the party. It's been lovely meeting you.'

Yasmin got up to go, but Charles LaMarquette blocked her path. His hand shot out and took hold of her arm.

'No, wait. Please.'

A shudder of panic shot through Yasmin, and for a

moment she wanted to run. But that seemed ridiculous. After all, he certainly wasn't going to harm her. He looked so forlorn, and big men look ridiculous when they look forlorn, she thought, finally relaxing a bit and smiling.

'Can't we just talk a while?' he said quietly.

'Of course,' Yasmin said. 'I just thought I'd like another glass of champagne. Wouldn't you?'

'In a minute,' he said. Charles hadn't let go of her arm, and he was gently guiding her back to the window seat, pulling her down next to him. 'It's just that I'm still a little stunned, and I've waited so long to meet you. I'll probably lose you in that crowd out there.'

Actually, it was exactly what Yasmin had been hoping for, but sitting here for a little longer would do no harm, she decided, and so said nothing.

'I thought I'd finally get to meet you when I heard you were living in Paris, but then suddenly you disappeared again. That was a long time ago too. Where'd you go?'

'Back to school,' Yasmin answered brusquely.

'Where?'

He was grilling her like a policeman, she thought. 'Well, I went to Oxford and took my degree, and then I went on to the London School of Economics,' she replied.

'Really?' Charles seemed incredulous. 'I can't believe it. After all, you are just – '

'Just what?' Yasmin snapped. She could hear the familiar words coming – 'You're nothing but a Moroccan whore' – and decided to face him head on.

'Well, you know,' he said. 'I mean your background is so . . . so different, if you know what I mean.'

'Different? What is that supposed to mean? That I'm supposed to be too stupid to get an MBA?'

'No, no. I didn't mean that. I just meant that it's unusual for a woman to get an MBA.'

310

'No, it isn't. Lots of women are getting degrees. Where have you been? Under a rock?'

Charles laughed. 'I can't believe how lucky I am,' he said. 'I've finally met you and you're even better than my wildest dreams – beautiful, and with brains as well! I've always thought that brains in a woman was the most erotic thing imaginable.'

Yasmin felt she'd lost the thread of the conversation.

'My father was in charge of the Credit Française in Tangier. Ever since he told me how André left everything to you, I have wanted to meet you.'

Yasmin looked down at her hands. No words came.

'That was the most romantic thing I'd ever heard,' Charles went on, obviously oblivious to her reaction. 'He sent you off to school in Switzerland, didn't he? Which school did you go to?'

'Lautremont.'

'That's near Lausanne, right?'

'Right.' Yasmin still felt lost.

'When André died,' Charles continued, 'my father had been transferred to the Paris branch. I felt certain I'd meet you then. But that man – Hassan Jalifa, right? – he looked everywhere for you, but you were gone. Where did you go? And why? What a fantastic mystery.'

Yasmin stood up again. She felt as if she were suffocating. 'I'd really like another glass of champagne, if you don't mind,' she said.

'Of course,' Charles said, staring at her with an odd look. 'How thoughtless of me.'

Not letting go of her arm for a minute, he walked out of the room with her and back into the throng of gyrating people in the main salon. Suddenly the din of the music and the voices took over.

A waiter slid by with a tray of glasses, and Yasmin quickly grabbed one. She drank the sparkling liquid down quickly. Charles immediately took the empty glass from her hand. He put it back on the tray and handed her another.

'You seem very tense,' he said, laughing. 'Have another. It'll relax you a bit, and then we can dance. The music is great, isn't it? Who's the band, anyway?'

I'm not tense, Yasmin thought. *I just can't stand this self-centered man!* She glared at him, but he had been looking around the room, and now focused on the singer. 'Look at that gorgeous woman,' he whispered in her ear. 'But, of course, she's nowhere near as beautiful as you are.' Then as if seeing her for the first time, he looked at her very hard. 'Why are you wearing your hair in that ridiculous bun? And what is this choir girl outfit?' Holding her at arm's length, he looked her up and down. 'This isn't the way I imagined you at all,' he said, frowning. 'You're supposed to be wearing veils and chains and brilliant colors! And your hair should be down. And you shouldn't be wearing glasses either.'

He reached up to take off her glasses.

'Don't!' Yasmin said sharply. 'My whole purpose in life isn't to live up to some adolescent fantasy that you have about me.'

Charles's arm dropped back to his side. He looked suddenly ashamed. 'I'm sorry. You're absolutely right. Will you forgive me?'

He looked so miserable that Yasmin couldn't sustain her annoyance. 'I suppose so. But please don't try to change my appearance in the middle of a party.'

'I wouldn't dream of it,' he said. Then his smile shifted again, and he pushed the shock of blond hair away from his eyes in a quick gesture. 'Later I'll rearrange you. Later I want to see you just the way I always have in my mind's eye. When we're alone.'

Yasmin started as the implication of his words sank in. But before she could speak, Solange and Oskar danced

312

by. Seeing her, Oskar abruptly stopped dancing with Solange and grabbed Yasmin around the waist.

'My dance,' he whooped, then dragged a protesting Yasmin out onto the floor. Before she could say a word, the crowd had swallowed them up. She could no longer see Charles or Solange. Dancing with Oskar took all her attention. He was moving like a Kodiak bear and she had to be quick to keep from being stepped on. So did everyone around them. The sight of other dancers dodging their huge host made her laugh.

'Dancing with you is better than going to a Marx Brothers movie,' she yelled, trying to be heard over the loud music.

'I intend to lose fifteen pounds tonight,' Oskar yelled back. 'By the way, who was that swain you were talking to? He looked smitten.'

'That was Charles LaMarquette. He claims you invited him.'

'Oh lord, so I did. All the LaMarquettes are staying in another chalet up the road a way. I invited them all, actually. Did he say the old man was here too?'

'He didn't say.'

'It's too loud to talk over this noise,' Oskar yelled back. 'Forget LaMarquette and dance. I have seven pounds to go still.'

But Charles LaMarquette wasn't forgetting about Yasmin. Before another three minutes went by, Yasmin saw him moving purposefully through the throng of twisting bodies with an alert expression on his face.

'May I cut in?' he said loudly, grabbing Yasmin around the waist.

Oskar didn't even lose a step, but bumbled up to a young woman in a flaming red dress who was dancing with her eyes closed. He cut in front of the short, balding man who was ostensibly her partner, and whirled her off.

Meanwhile Charles held Yasmin close to his body.

313

Yasmin could smell the fresh, clean soapy smell that emanated from his clothes. But the music was fast, and Charles wasn't dancing. He was standing perfectly still, pressing her hard against him. He buried his face behind her ear and inhaled deeply.

'What are you doing?' Yasmin asked, pulling back.

'I'm dancing,' he whispered. 'Can't you tell when you're dancing?'

'Of course I can. But this isn't a slow dance, this is a fast dance. You're supposed to be standing at least a foot and a half away from me for this kind of dance.'

'But I don't want to stand a foot and a half away from you. I want to hold you. Let's just pretend it's a slow dance.'

'This is ridiculous.'

'No it isn't,' Charles breathed in her ear. 'This is delightful. Where's your room? Let's go upstairs.'

'WHAT?'

Yasmin pushed hard, shoving him into the couple behind them.

'I did it again, didn't I?' he said, looking sheepish.

'Yes,' Yasmin snapped. By now the boyish grin was beginning to grate on her nerves. 'Do you always seduce women by apologizing profusely and then committing the same stupidity all over again?'

'It always worked before,' he said with a shrug. 'You must be a tough case.'

'I don't even know you!'

'Yes, you do,' he replied just as quickly. 'I introduced myself to you at least a half hour ago. Besides, this isn't 1940. And you can't claim to be a virgin, for Christ's sake.'

Yasmin gasped, then turned and fled. It wasn't until she was safely behind the door to her room that she stopped to catch her breath. The unmitigated gall! The nerve! What an awful man, she thought feverishly.

When she was finally thinking clearly again, she looked at herself in the mirror. It was obvious that no matter how hard she tried to hide, enough people knew about her history to make hiding impossible. A story such as hers was too interesting to stay buried for long. The reaction she'd gotten from Charles LaMarquette made it very clear, and he didn't even know the half of it.

Here was someone who'd never even met her, but who had heard the story of how André had left everything to an eighteen-year-old Moroccan girl. The reasons why, would of course be clear to anyone who gave it more than two minutes' thought.

Hardly a virgin, indeed, she thought with fury. But, of course, it was true. Except that no one would believe her side of it even if she told them. No matter what she'd say, the reality would fade behind the power of the fantasy, just as his thoughts of her were overpowered by the mental pictures he had carried around with him for ten years.

No matter where she went, Yasmin thought, no matter what she did, someone would appear and start the gossip. There was only one way to deal with them, she decided: make so much money, become so rich, that it wouldn't make any difference what they said or thought. That would also fill her time quite nicely. She could take the Saint-Clair enterprises and turn them into a multimillion dollar set of walls to hide behind. Then it wouldn't matter where her career had started. It would only matter where it ended. That would be enough to make the most obnoxious banker's son think twice before he tried to validate his ridiculous fantasies at her expense.

She lay back on the bed, trying to sort out her conflicting emotions. The life she'd just laid out for herself would be a lonely one. But it would be painfree, as well. It would be worth it.

There was a pounding on the door, and Yasmin sat bolt upright. 'Who is it?'

'It's me. Charles.'

'Go away, for heaven's sake.'

'Look, I'm really sorry. You have to let me in. You have to forgive me. I didn't mean to hurt your feelings like that.'

'Just go away, will you?'

'I won't go away until you tell me you forgive me. I'll stand out here and bang on the door until you open it. I promise not to lay a finger on you. Please just open the door so I can see your face one more time.'

Struggling to her feet, Yasmin walked to the door and flung it open. 'All right. Now you've seen my face,' she snapped. 'Is that good enough? Can I go to sleep now?'

'Won't you come back downstairs?'

'No, I'm tired. It's after midnight.'

'I'm terribly sorry. I'll prove it to you, somehow. I promise I'll leave you alone tonight, but please say you'll see me again sometime. In a few days, perhaps?'

'I'm leaving in a few days, and I'm really busy until then,' Yasmin said. He doesn't give up, does he? she thought.

'Where are you going? Don't disappear again.'

'I'm not disappearing now, and I never did. I'm going back to Paris to take over André's business.'

'All right, then, I'll come visit you in Paris. May I see you again once you're settled?'

'I doubt it, Charles. Now, if you don't mind, I'm going to bed. Good night.'

Yasmin closed the door firmly and slid the lock. Through the door, she heard a muffled 'Good night.'

She waited until she heard his footsteps go back down the hall, then wearily hung up her skirt and blouse, and slipped her nightgown over her head.

It wasn't until she was under the big eiderdown quilt

that she thought about returning to Paris . . . and Hassan, another hurdle entirely.

Judging from what Yasmin knew about men in general, and Arab men in particular, he would be less than easy to manage. She would have to handle him with kid gloves, and that would be less than easy too. Especially since Hassan was under the impression that he could control her with the flick of a finger.

Yasmin suddenly blushed in the dark. It wasn't going to be easy at all to take back control of the business. The flick of his finger was a very powerful thing. She wondered if she would be able to resist, once he really decided to put sexual pressure on her. Grace under pressure, she thought, is what will be called for. Very English. Her facade of English indifference was going to be put to a very severe test, indeed. She forgot all about Charles LaMarquette as she thought over the difficulties facing her in Paris.

PART SIX
Paris, 1983

19

But it hadn't been as difficult as Yasmin thought it would be. In Paris she threw herself into the work of learning all aspects of the vineyard and the wine business. She told Hassan that she wanted to know everything, and he obliged her. Not only did he show her how the Saint-Clair vineyard operated, but they also watched the day to day operations of other vineyards in parts of Bordeaux, Chamonix, Aix en Provence, Médoc, and Neuf Chapelle. She spent long hours in the library going over various histories of the regions, and everything she could find about wine production and distribution.

Yasmin also studied the development and distribution of California wines, and discovered that the California producers in recent years had begun using mechanical harvesters to pick the grapes. Hand gathering of the bunches could take days, and mechanical harvesting took only hours. A harvest could be ruined by an exceptionally heavy rainstorm, or a freak hail storm – and then an entire year's growth would be destroyed on the vines. The quick mechanical harvesting, Yasmin thought, might avert such a disaster.

Also, contrary to what the traditional French growers would have thought, the mechanical harvesters turned out to be much more selective about which grapes made their way to the presses. When the harvesting rods shook the vines, only the ripe fruit fell. The unripe grapes remained attached. What's more, the stems weren't torn off. The leaves which were shaken free during the picking were blown away from the grapes as they traveled on the belts to the crusher. Within minutes of being picked, the grapes were crushed, which protected them from additional oxidation and spoilage. Not only that, a mechanical harvester, unlike a human, could work just as well at night as during the day. That way the grapes could be picked when it was cool, which enhanced the flavor of the wine and made cool fermentation possible.

Although she mentioned these developments to Hassan and Bertrand, she saw that their resistance to change was too embedded to fight. It was too soon to press them, she thought. There was time. She still had much to learn before she could start making innovations.

She did, however, make note of the new packaging of California wines. Originally bottled in squat, earthenware jugs with thumb handles at the neck, one of the biggest producers introduced a graceful new flagon shape in the sixties, which was much more appealing to the market they were trying to crack. Yasmin wondered whether it was time to investigate a new shape of bottle and use that same marketing approach in the United States, in order to gain for the Saint-Clair market a share that could be lost to the California wines marketed at a reasonable price.

She was certain it would be possible without sacrificing quality. However, it would also require a massive amount of money, not to mention a lot of research and planning. It was obvious to her that it would take more than a new label to make a significant dent in America, but Yasmin strongly felt that America was where the future of the Saint-Clair wines lay. Their present distribution gave them a steady income, but in no way provided the increase she wanted. Meanwhile, however, she tried to hide her intentions from Hassan and Bertrand Labiche. In her day to day relationship with Hassan, she behaved like a serious student whose main interest lay in fully understanding the status quo. To indicate in any way that

322

she wanted to change that status quo would have been inimical to her plan.

With uncharacteristic sensitivity, Hassan remained helpful, yet aloof. It was possible that he had another woman in his life, she thought, and that kept him away from her. After all, he was a very handsome man, and from what she knew about him, a sensualist who wouldn't stay away from the pleasures of women for long.

Yasmin was living in the town house, and Françoise took excellent care of her. It felt as if no time had passed and nothing had changed. Francoise continued to treat her as if she needed mothering, and Yasmin delighted in her thoughtful sensitivity. Hassan lived in an elegant flat on Rue de Grenelle which ran almost parallel to part of the Boulevard Saint-Germain. He seemed content to live a fairly private life that didn't include Yasmin, except during the day at the office on Avenue Montaigne. They were rarely alone. A secretary worked with them, handling correspondence, and answering the phone.

Yasmin adored their office. It was on the second floor of an old mansion, with floor to ceiling arched windows overlooking the street. All the great couture houses, as well as some of the most famous jewelers, were right there. Winston, Gerard, and Cartier were close by Dior, Courrèges, and Pierre Balmain. It made Yasmin feel wonderful just walking to and from her office. Not only were the buildings beautiful, but the people were inspirational.

And the history of the street was wonderful. The thing that she liked the most about it was that at one time, Avenue Montaigne was called Avenue des Veuves, and by *veuves*, they didn't mean widows. It was named for the streetwalkers who frequented its darkened doorways. Some of the crown jewels belonging to Marie-Antoinette had once been found under a tree on that street one morning in 1792. Two thieves had carried them off, and then for reasons no one would ever know, had dropped them and then disappeared – forever. Avenue Montaigne had for many years been a well-known hangout of thieves and pickpockets. Now it was one of the most elegant streets in Paris. It was at number 1 that Napoleon Bonaparte met and fell madly in love with Joséphine de Beauharnais at a party given by Madame de Tallien.

But living with all the history, looking at all the shops, and seeing all the elegant women didn't make Yasmin want to change her own unobtrusive way of dressing. She was still much more comfortable in her quiet colors and loose sweaters and slacks. She chose to wear the big tortoiseshell glasses almost all the time now, because she could hide behind them so effectively.

Now, as she sat leaning over the hand-painted Venetian secretary that served as her desk, going over columns of figures from the vineyard, she thought about her conversation with Hassan the day before.

Tired, with a stiff neck, Yasmin had pulled off her glasses. Leaning back in her chair, she'd raised her arms high over her head in a sinuous, catlike stretch.

'Lord, I could use a massage,' she'd said. 'There was a girl at St Anne's who used to have a private masseuse come every day during exams. It sounds like a good idea right now. Margaret – that was her name – said it helped her to concentrate. Of course, no one believed for a moment that the massage was all she'd got.'

'Perhaps you should investigate that for yourself,' Hassan said, looking up at her sharply, his impenetrable dark eyes watching her.

'You do nothing for yourself, Yasmin,' Hassan continued with a slow, languorous smile. 'I've been watching you for the last five months. You have no friends, you don't go to the theater, you have no life – '

'I'm perfectly happy with this,' Yasmin said, placing

324

her hand firmly on the papers in front of her. 'I don't need anything else.'

'Perhaps not,' Hassan answered. 'But I don't think it's very healthy for you. Here you are in one of the great capitals of entertainment, food, sensual pleasures . . . life itself, and you don't partake. I think you should join in.'

'Well, maybe. Maybe next month.'

'What about tomorrow? I've had a cancellation so I'm unexpectedly free for the evening. I will take you out for dinner. We'll go to a nightclub. Anything to give you a change. You're too young to bury yourself this way. Give life a chance before you find it's too late.'

So Yasmin had agreed. But now, the next day, she was having second thoughts. There was so much to do, and she'd really wanted to finish looking at some papers. But if she was to be ready by seven, she'd have to leave. And there was also the problem of what to wear. Hassan didn't go to quiet bistros on the Left Bank for dinner. He'd probably take her to someplace impossibly decadent. The gray sweater and tailored skirt she was wearing wouldn't do for a place like that. She'd have to go through her clothes.

Best to stop work now, she thought wearily. Beatrice, the secretary, had already gone home. In a way, she knew he was right. She shouldn't exclusively bury herself in her work, but his statement that she should go out before it was 'too late' seemed melodramatic, she thought. Too late for what? Too late to find out that she was only fuel for other people's fantasies?

She carefully put the papers away, hoping that this evening with Hassan wouldn't end up being a late one. But she would try to be pleasant to him. After all, she and Hassan had to work together, so it was best to avoid a fuss.

* * *

325

After taking a bath, Yasmin was finally able to locate a dress in her closet that she thought would be acceptable. It was an emerald silk dress with a flared skirt and tight-fitting bodice. Elbow length split sleeves moved gracefully when she walked, and the color seemed to suit her skin nicely. She pinned her hair up in a smooth round knot at the nape of her neck, and thought she looked very nice. Then she went down to the study to wait for Hassan, and was just flipping through a newspaper when he strode into the room. She looked up and was surprised at his appearance.

Usually he was neat to the point of obsession, but this evening his hair looked mussed and his normally guarded expression was gone. In its place she saw the hooded predatory look that had so unnerved her when they first met. Again he was moving toward her with the smooth grace of a panther.

'Put that down,' he commanded, reaching out his hand and pulling her up slowly out of the chair. He took the paper from her and put it down on the desk. Then raising her hand to his lips, he kissed her palm.

'You look lovely,' he said as his eyes swept her from head to toe. 'A bit dowdy for my tastes, but your natural beauty shines above even your most impressive efforts at camouflage. You've spent too much time with the English. Their taste in food and clothes is awful. The hair I could tolerate, but do you really need those glasses?'

'No . . . I guess not,' Yasmin said, and took the glasses off. 'I really only use them for reading.'

'I'll do all your reading for you tonight,' he said. 'Now come. I have the driver waiting.'

'Let me get my coat,' Yasmin said, regarding him suspiciously. He seemed different, but she couldn't pinpoint where the difference lay. The words he spoke were gracious, but there was something dangerous about the way he moved. She went to the closet and began to put on her black linen coat when he stopped her.

'Not that, little one,' he said, reaching past her. He pulled out the mink jacket that hung next to it. It was one he'd given her six years before. 'Wear this instead. To please me, all right?'

Actually, the jacket looked much better on her, and the silken fur felt delicious against her cheek as Hassan slipped it over her shoulders. She'd almost forgotten how sensuous fur could be. But as they walked through the hall, she caught a glimpse of herself in the gilt mirror hanging near the door. The emerald dress belled out at the hem, making her legs look impossibly slim and delicate. The mink jacket framed her face and made her eyes, no longer hidden behind the glasses, look huge and dark.

Hassan pulled her out the door and handed her into the back of the big, dark green Mercedes. 'Number three, Rue Arsène Houssaya,' he said, settling back against the seat. 'It's a very nice restaurant that is *classique*, as they say around here. After that I thought I'd take you dancing. Or did you forget how to dance?'

Yasmin laughed. 'No, I didn't forget, but I'm not sure I feel like dancing tonight.'

'We'll see after dinner. There's no sense in making you decide right now.'

But after dinner, and the bottle of wine they shared, Yasmin was feeling lightheaded, and at that point, dancing seemed a good idea. So they made their way to a small club on the Left Bank.

Limousines lined the block, the chauffeurs all waiting patiently. Tucked in and around the big cars were little Vespas and big motorcycles. Leaning against the walls and seated on the surrounding stoops were all kinds of young people. Some were dressed in the latest punk styles, while others looked like struggling artists. Inside it was the same. There were very elegant women dancing wildly with men in tuxedos. Alongside them, gyrating just as wildly, were shaggy-haired, paint-spattered young toughs with their girls.

Hassan managed to get them a small table and asked her what she wanted to drink. 'That is, of course, if you want to drink,' he said, eyeing her carefully. 'You can get anything you want here. Would you like some cocaine instead?'

'Oh, no,' Yasmin said, surprised at him. 'A drink would be fine, thank you.'

The hooded eyes blinked, but his expression remained serious. 'Just checking. I didn't know what you'd learned while you were away. Cocaine is the latest craze, but I don't like it that much. It's good for some things, perhaps, but not for lovemaking. Hashish is better for that. Do you like hashish?'

'No,' Yasmin answered shortly.

'I thought not,' he said with a sharp laugh. It sounded hard to her ears, but she decided to push her annoyance aside as her eyes were drawn to the undulating mass of bodies on the dance floor. The blare of the music was unrelenting, and its rhythm suddenly made her want to get up and dance. But they hadn't ordered yet, and the floor looked packed.

Hassan followed her eyes. 'It's too crowded out there right now. Why don't I order a bottle of champagne. We'll watch the show for a while.'

Yasmin nodded. It was fascinating to watch everyone. One couple in particular caught her eye. The girl had a thick mane of blond hair that fell below her shoulders. She was wearing a dress that had large cut-outs. As she moved, the fabric shifted, giving people tantalizing glimpses of her breasts. The man she was dancing with seemed oblivious to her. As he danced, his eyes roamed around the room, fixing on one female face after another.

Yasmin wondered at his ravenous expression. She would have assumed the girl he was with was more than enough. But apparently not. It looked as if he wanted them all. No commitments, no attachments, no entanglements, just sheer physical pleasure.

She wondered what that would be like. Perhaps it was the best way, she thought with a small frown. One could easily take care of one's physical needs – without having to get into all the unpleasant, sordid messes that entanglements seemed to bring. No one could hurt your feelings because you would have no feelings about the relationships at all. It would be as if one were trying out a different restaurant every night. If one disappointed you, who cared? There was going to be another one the next night.

But what would happen if you liked one restaurant more than all the others? What then? No, she thought grimly. Better to be safe and not try any restaurants at all.

The waiter came, bringing the champagne and two glasses. After pulling the cork expertly, he poured some and left. Hassan didn't even bother to taste it before pouring the rest. He handed her a full glass.

'Perhaps this will put you in the mood for dancing,' he said with a quick smile. 'It's the best they have here, but it's not too good. Think of it as part of your education. This is what champagne *shouldn't* taste like.'

Yasmin sipped, and found she liked the taste. 'Well, that shows how little you've managed to teach me,' she laughed. 'As far as I'm concerned, this tastes delightful.'

She finished the glass while watching the dancers. The Hassan stood up and pulled her with him out onto the dance floor. They found a space just as the next song began. Not quite as hysterical as the ones that preceded it, Yasmin found she was very comfortable with the blues rhythm. In fact as she started to move, she realized how very sexual it was. Her pelvis easily slipped into the beat, as if her body remembered far more than she would have liked. As she became more and more involved in the music, she began to forget where she was. Soon her whole body was synchronized with the sounds as her eyes closed and her head tilted back.

Then, hardly aware of it, she felt Hassan's hand come up and one by one remove the pins that held her hair in the tight knot at the nape of her neck. Her thick main of glossy hair fell down her back like a cascade of water. Feeling the weight of it swinging against her back catapulted her inexorably deeper into the rhythms of the dance. Her arms slowly lifted over her head as she gave herself over to the music with complete abandon.

As if in a dream, she felt Hassan's hands grip her hipbones, pulling her against him. But she didn't stop her dance. She continued to move, bumping lightly against him. Hassan fit his own rhythm to hers and moved against her as if he was part of her. Then his mouth came down on hers, softly. She felt a sense of merging, one form sliding into another as they moved together for what felt like an hour. Then the music stopped.

'Let's go,' he said softly.

With his arm around her shoulder, he pushed through the throng, picked up her coat, and moved her out to the street. Yasmin shook her head, trying to remember why she didn't want to do this, but she couldn't. She had liked the dancing. She really wanted to dance more – dance all night. But before she knew it, she was in the back of the Mercedes and the tinted glass that separated them from the driver had slid across, closing them into the dark space in the back of the car. As the car began to move, Hassan's mouth came back down on hers in an absorbing kiss.

Yasmin was aware of nothing but the sensation of his lips moving softly as his tongue gently pushed its way into her mouth, expertly exploring it, claiming her. His hands slid from where they'd framed her face, down across her collarbones to cup her breasts. There, his thumbs gently tugged across her nipples, which hardened into sensitive peaks in response. It had been so very long since those sensations had been awakened in her body, that Yasmin almost gasped at their intensity. How could she have forgotten this? she wondered. How could she have lived without this overpoweringly delicious sensation?

She relaxed against the back of the seat as she felt Hassan delicately slip her skirt up across her thighs. Then, with practiced ease, he slid his hand inside the elastic of her silk underpants and down into the warm space between her thighs. With a will of their own, Yasmin's hips lifted up to meet his fingers and her legs parted slowly to give him easier access to that most sensitive spot. As if she were still dancing back in the nightclub, her body began to move rhythmically against his hand. She felt, rather than heard, his sharp intake of breath against her mouth. His kiss became suddenly more demanding, as if he intended to suck the very life out of her. His teeth began to cut into her lips as he pushed her slowly down across the leather seat and pressed the length of his body down on hers, pinning one of her legs under him on the seat while pushing the other leg out with his knee.

Fully opened for him, his fingers thrust deep inside of the slick wetness of her body, and Yasmin gasped with shock. Twisting her head away from him, she cried out as an agony of sensation flooded through her. Oh, Allah! she thought, as if from a distance. So fast. This is too fast. I have been so starved that I'm easy game for the slightest touch. But her thoughts were soon obliterated by the scarlet rush of pleasure his thrusting fingers brought through her. His mouth came back down on hers and muffled the cry that broke from her lips.

331

As the sensation quickly receded, she awoke to the reality of the backseat of the limousine, the shadow of the driver's head through the glass, and the slight smile of triumph on Hassan's face. His hand possessively cupped the slippery mound of her pelvis where his fingers were still deeply embedded inside of her. He twitched them slowly, bringing a round of aftershocks that shuddered through her.

'More?' he said softly. His hand began to shift into another more purposeful rhythm as his hooded eyes gleamed. Yasmin felt coldness seep into her blood as a feeling of deep embarrassment stealthily replaced the sensations of a moment ago. She glanced at the back of the driver's impassive head, and struggled to sit up.

'No, please, I – ' she started to say. But Hassan, sensing her discomfort, chuckled low in his throat.

'I understand, little one. Not here,' he said softly. Helping her to sit up, he smoothed her skirt back across her knees and settled her jacket around her shoulders. 'The car will be at my apartment in a few moments. Then we can continue at a more leisurely pace. I only wanted to give you a little taste of what you've been missing.'

As Yasmin looked into his smiling face, she suddenly wanted to crawl back inside herself. This wasn't what she'd wanted, yet she had fallen so easily. How could she have let this happen to her? She was mortified. She didn't want to go back to his apartment, didn't want to do whatever it was that he'd planned for the rest of the night. She felt the long tentacles of his willpower reaching out to envelop and crush her.

'NO!' she said, aware that the words came out much too loudly. 'I mean no, I'd rather go home, please. Forgive me, but I didn't mean for this to happen.'

The relaxed pressure of his arm on her shoulder changed to coiled tension at her words. 'Am I to understand that you're finished for the evening?' came his sarcastic voice through the dark.

'Please, I didn't mean for you to misunderstand me,' she said, trying hard to sound calm. 'I only wanted to relax a little for the evening . . . not this. I'm sorry.'

'I was under the impression that you enjoyed what just happened. Can you honestly tell me that wasn't the case?'

'Yes and no, Hassan. I did . . . but also I didn't, because I don't want our relationship back on that footing again. I don't feel that way about you anymore.'

'But you did once?'

'No. I mean, sort of, it just wasn't . . .'

'Wasn't what? Is there someone else?' Hassan burst out laughing, but the sound of his laugh wasn't pleasant. 'Of course, I should have known that you'd have someone else. A body like yours, which is made for pleasure, couldn't manage being alone for this long. Who is he?'

'There's no one else, Hassan. But it isn't that, it's that I – ' Yasmin was suddenly aware that the car had stopped. They had arrived at Hassan's destination, and she had to make it very, very clear that she didn't want to go up to his apartment. 'Please, Hassan, I have to think. Could you just take me home?'

There was an eerie silence in the car. After a moment Yasmin couldn't resist the impulse, and turned to look at Hassan's face. What she saw made her shudder. His jaw was clenched, the barely controlled fury on his face was frightening.

'If that's what you want,' came his icy voice. 'But you have hurt me very much, Yasmin. I will take you home because I only want what you want. That doesn't change the fact that I don't understand what has happened to you at all. You say there is no one else, but that only makes it worse. At least if there was another man, I would know what I was fighting. This way I am competing with an enemy that doesn't exist. That's a very difficult enemy to vanquish.'

He leaned forward and gave the address of the town

333

house to the driver. The car spun out from the curb and drove swiftly back through the night. Yasmin shivered, and drew the fur jacket around her shoulders. Suddenly the May night seemed cold to her.

Hassan's voice broke the silence again. 'Forgive me for losing control before,' he said, a pleasant tone threading around his words. 'I shouldn't have done that to you. Of course, you will have to think about this. I gave you no indication up until tonight that what I want is to have you back. We'll talk tomorrow.'

Before she could answer, the car had stopped in front of her town house. Hassan quickly stepped out and helped her out of the car. Planting a light kiss on her forehead, he said softly, 'Think about what I said, my darling. I'll talk to you tomorrow.'

Without another word he climbed back into the Mercedes. For a moment Yasmin stood on the steps, unable to move. He doesn't give up, does he? she thought. Tomorrow will be even worse than this evening was. I'm afraid I'll never make him understand.

20

'If what you want is a formal proposal of marriage, then that's what you'll get.' There was a slight twist to Hassan's smile. Then, with a dramatic flourish, he handed her a bunch of flowers that he'd hidden behind his back. 'Here.'

It was early, and Yasmin had just gotten into the office. She was in the middle of hanging up her coat when Hassan walked in on her. Fortunately Beatrice wasn't in yet, Yasmin thought, wondering what her reaction would have been to this intimate scene.

Yasmin was forced to smile, but her smile quickly faded when she saw that his expression was intensely serious.

'We are very much alike, you and I,' he continued, not giving her a chance to speak. 'I realize that you don't see it now, but someday you'll know how good we are for each other. We are both Arabs, but we've both been westernized, pushed out of our traditional places and roles. Our old way of life is no longer acceptable to us, and yet we have no acceptable replacement for it either, no other place to go.'

'That's not true,' Yasmin said quickly. 'I am here in Paris and I find this a perfectly acceptable place to be.'

'Do you really?' he answered, looking at her with an odd expression. 'I think not. I think that in fact you are very lonely. I understand you because I know you . . . I know everything about you, and I love you despite it. No, that's not right. I love you because of it.'

'You don't have to say these things.'

'Yes, I do. Don't you see? You will never be comfortable with someone who doesn't know your whole history.

335

But, in your own mind anyone who knows your whole history will instantly become suspect. You will cease to trust them, and you will constantly feel that either they love you because of what you once were, or that they tolerate you in spite of it.'

'That's not true.'

'Really? I think you know what I'm talking about. I, on the other hand, don't find what has happened to you so titillating. In fact I admire you tremendously for everything you've managed to accomplish.'

Yasmin could only stare at him. What was he saying? Did he know how others reacted to her? Had someone told him? But that was impossible. He was just casting about for a reason to make her believe that he was the only man she could feel close to. He was using words to force her to feel dependent toward him. His speech sounded prepared to her, it was delivered too smoothly to come from the heart.

'You need me, Yasmin. As much as I need you. I've loved you and needed you from the first time I saw you standing in André's library all smudgy with dust. That night when I came back for you and found you were gone, I thought I would go mad.'

Yasmin was stunned. That wasn't the way she remembered the scene at all. As she remembered it, Hassan had treated her just like the little whore he thought she was. If he had really loved her, she thought, he would have been far more compassionate. Why was he saying these things to her? she wondered. What could he possibly gain by telling her this?

'Even though I admired and respected André,' Hassan continued, 'I wanted you even more. In a way I'm glad that he died. Don't look so shocked, Yasmin. It's true. If he had lived, I would have taken you anyway. It would have ruined our friendship – or worse.'

'Don't say these things, Hassan,' Yasmin said softly.

She turned away from him and walked to the windows. Outside, the morning sun was glinting down on the small garden behind the office. Birds were frolicking in the carved stone birdbath set in the center of a bed of flowers just coming into bloom. Spring seemed to be flooding the world – everywhere but inside this room. Here it was strangely cold.

'But I have to say them. It's true that the attraction I felt for you then was purely physical, but that's only natural. You were a beautiful girl – so exotic, so tantalizing. Any man who felt less would have to be dead from the waist down. But now you are much more. You are a beautiful woman, yes, but you are also cultured, intelligent, witty. I don't know why you're putting me through this, but if it's what will convince you in the end, I don't care.'

'I think what you want is an Arab girl who will submit to you in the way that tradition demands, but yet not be so far away from you intellectually that you'll be bored – that's what I think,' she said coldly, turning her back to him.

'That's part if it, of course,' Hassan said quickly. 'But it isn't everything. I love you for yourself, Yasmin.'

She turned to face him. 'Perhaps that's what you believe, but I am not what you think I am,' she said. 'We're not as alike as you may believe. Perhaps once that was so. Maybe I was the girl you're talking about before I went to England. But now I'm different.'

'Not so different, I think.'

'I grew up. I don't want to be some sort of exotic odalisque all my life. I don't feel the slightest bit bound by Moroccan tradition. I happily kissed that part of my life good-bye years ago. Marrying you would be a step backward for me, not a step forward.'

'I don't expect you to be bound by Moroccan tradition.'

'That's what you say, but I could never believe you.'

337

'In time you would see that I'm right.'

'No. You just aren't the right person for me, Hassan. I have other things in my life now, and I don't want to jeopardize them – not for you, or anyone else for that matter. I want work to be the central motivation in my life.'

'Work? What work? You don't know what's good for you, that's all,' Hassan snapped, losing the control he had so carefully nurtured for this meeting. His eyebrows were low over his eyes and his mouth was becoming a hard line.

'I know exactly what's good for me,' Yasmin said. 'I have it all planned. What do you think I've been doing here for the last few months? Why do you think I spent all those years at school? Just biding my time until a man asked me to marry him and make babies?'

'What's wrong with that? Maybe you were improving your mind so you wouldn't bore a man to death. That's what all the most famous courtesans did. They educated themselves, of course, but for another's pleasure.'

Courtesan! Courtesan? Yasmin was outraged. He *was* just like everyone else. No matter what he said, that was how he thought of her and why he wanted her. Despite what he said, all he could see was that she had once spent some time in a brothel; after that, everything else faded. Well, she wasn't going to be anyone's 'woman' – much less his!

'Well, I'm sorry to have to tell you this,' Yasmin replied, containing her anger, 'but I'm no courtesan, and I educated myself for my own pleasure. I fully intend to take over the Saint-Clair vineyard, and I intend to expand the business, move into the American market, and become a real presence in the business world.'

'You'll never be able to do it,' Hassan said with a derisive snort. 'Better men than you – and I use the term advisedly – have tried to take on the California vineyards

338

in the last ten years. I don't have to tell you that they failed miserably.'

'They failed miserably because they applied French penury and age-old growing techniques to a task that cries out for innovation and brashness. I'm not bound by any of those traditions because I'm not bound by any traditions at all. I'm going to make my own damned traditions.'

'It'll never work, and you're a fool!' Hassan's face was icy and hard.

As Yasmin looked into his eyes, she saw something that could easily have passed for murder lurking in those inky depths. It could have been the face of a rejected lover, but she was willing to bet that it was much more than that. Rejection was something no man handled well, but by his expression, Hassan was dealing with the loss of something far greater.

Seeing him go from ardent to icy in such a short span of time made Yasmin wonder what Hassan really wanted. Maybe he wanted to run the Saint-Clair vineyards forever and to marry her in order to maintain his position. But if so, it wouldn't work. The vineyards were hers, and marriage to him wouldn't change anything unless she wanted it changed. And she didn't want her life changed by a man telling her what to do. She only wanted to do her work and run the vineyards in her own way.

She would have to move carefully, she thought, slowly, and ask for his help each step of the way. It was repulsive to have to do it, but it was the safest way. First, however, she had to defuse Hassan. Right now he looked like a bomb about to go off.

'I'll need your help, Hassan,' Yasmin said. 'Don't walk away from me now. It's not you I'm rejecting, it's a way of life. I don't want to be somebody's wife or somebody's mother. I want to be an autonomous person with a purpose and a life of my own. Don't you see?'

Hassan's expression remained unchanged. Allah, Yasmin thought. This wasn't going to be easy. She went on.

'If you would just listen, give my ideas a chance at least . . . I certainly wouldn't try to do something that would destroy the vineyard. I just wanted to make it bigger and better than ever . . .'

Yasmin tried her best to look at him with a meltingly feminine expression. It seemed to work. His rage was gradually turning into annoyance.

'Women,' he muttered. 'I can't stand it anymore.'

With that he turned on his heel and strode from the room. She heard to door slam shut behind him, and a sigh of relief escaped from her lips.

Yasmin immediately sat down and started to outline her expansion plan. This way, if Hassan continued his pursuit, she would have something else to talk about.

That whole day and half of the next she worked to prepare a presentation. Unable to decide whether to work in the town house or in the office – she didn't want Hassan to see what she was doing, or start talking to her about love and the future of their 'relationship' – she finally opted for working at the office because, unfortunately, all the files were there. As she went over the material she had compiled, along with the information on the latest machinery she'd gotten from manufacturers in America, she finally felt confident that she could make an excellent case for her proposal.

By the time she stopped for a break, it was about four-thirty in the afternoon and she felt exhausted. She wasn't used to working under such tension, had never faced a real life business situation that demanded her entire focus. What if she failed? she wondered. It was an odd feeling, one of insecurity and exhilaration at the same time. Yet it felt good, for at least the reins of her life were firmly in her own hands. This time there was the possibility of real success, and success meant so much this time. This time if she succeeded it would be through her own efforts, with no help from the outside. This time she would have only herself to thank for whatever happened.

Suddenly the door was flung open and Hassan stood framed in the light from the corridor. There was a strange set to his shoulders.

'I came to apologize for yesterday . . . and for the night before too,' he said slowly. 'It was my fault for pushing you. I understand perfectly how you must feel. I don't always take other people's feelings into consideration, but this time obviously I must. I'll wait however long I have to, and I promise not to pressure you. When you're ready to marry me, I'll be here for you.'

'Even if that never comes?' Yasmin asked quietly. In a tired gesture she brushed a lock of hair that had fallen across her eyes.

'Even if that never comes,' Hassan answered. She could see by his smug expression, however, that he didn't think it would take too long. So much the better, she thought.

'I won't keep you,' Hassan said shortly. 'When you want to discuss your plans with me, let me know.'

'I'll be ready to discuss them with you in a few days.'

'Why don't we make it next week? I'm afraid I have a few things to take care of,' Hassan said. Yasmin peered at him closely. She thought he was looking a bit odd, but that passed quickly. Perhaps it was just her imagination. 'Thursday?'

'Perfect.'

Hassan walked to the door, stopped with his hand on the knob and turned to look at her. 'I do love you, you know.'

'Thank you,' Yasmin said steadily.

He looked at her for another few seconds, an unreadable expression on his face, then left her alone in her office.

A week later Yasmin carefully outlined her plan for Hassan from start to finish. It included selling off some of the real estate in the Saint-Clair holdings. After using the cash to buy some machinery, the rest of the real estate was to be used as a guarantee against the bottling and an aggressive marketing campaign in the United States. The bottling would require new designs, and the plan was to cover a five-year initial period to start the following spring with a market test conducted through an American firm that had offices in Paris. She'd already discussed certain aspects of such a plan with them, in a hypothetical way. They had given her a rough estimate of the cost of a 'wet test' that would involve distributing the newly packaged wines in a small area before they expanded to a wider area.

If the market test was strongly positive, it would pave the way for further financing and cover most of the initial expenses. It would take a large initial outlay, but they would not have to pay for the entire operation out of their own funds. After an initial outlay, the banks could handle the major cost of the entire distribution. That way they were protected from too great a loss.

Yasmin thought the plan a good one, and as she spoke, she became more engrossed in her words, and more exhilarated. It seemed impossible to her that anyone could find fault with her proposal.

'No,' Hassan said, standing up and turning his back to her. He walked to the windows overlooking Avenue Montaigne, turned again and looked her directly in the eye. 'I'm afraid it's impossible.'

She was shocked. 'What do you mean, impossible?'

'It's far too aggressive. Out of the question.'

Yasmin was furious. 'Aggressive?' She could barely control her voice. 'You mean too aggressive to have been conceived by me, that's what you mean, isn't it? And why shouldn't I have an aggressive plan? The thrust of all

342

my training and education for the last six years has been in the direction of aggressive business tactics. And furthermore, this is, in fact, my company. I can't see what your objections could possibly be. Even if you have objections, I don't see why that should make any difference in the final analysis. It's mine to do with as I please.'

'Not totally. As your business manager, and acting head of the company, I feel I should have a certain amount of say in what you do.'

'It was understood that I was to have more control over the vineyards when I returned. I've been back for five months now, and I have been most circumspect about involving myself directly in the operation of the vineyard. But that was by choice, not by necessity.'

Yasmin stopped abruptly. She had the sudden awful thought that she'd gone too far. Perhaps she shouldn't have put it quite so harshly. She was about to qualify her last remarks when Hassan, who'd been staring at his hands, looked up.

'Actually, Yasmin, I think it's a magnificent idea. Forgive me for jumping to a decision so quickly. I'm not in the habit of listening to other people's ideas, so I was too quick to judge.'

Yasmin was shocked at Hassan's quick change of heart, but before she had a chance to register her surprise, Hassan continued.

'I'm behind you all the way, and I'll help you in any way you want. I also think it would be a good idea if you ran the entire thing yourself. After all, it's your idea, and you know best how it should be done. Sometimes people who've been doing something for too long get stuck in the old ways. They can't see their way clear to innovation and change. It's also good to do it yourself because it will throw you right into the center of the work. That way you'll be getting a wonderful introduction to running the vineyards. I couldn't have thought of a better way to do that for you.'

Delighted, Yasmin crossed the floor and put her hand on his arm. 'Then we're in business,' she said, starting to smile. 'Oh, thank you, Hassan. I'm overwhelmed with gratitude. I couldn't have done it without you, and I'm sorry I spoke so harshly before. You've been a wonderful partner for me all these years and I shouldn't take your knowledge and expertise for granted that way.'

Hassan gently shook her hand away and stepped back. He looked at her with a wry smile. 'No problem. You were angry, that's all. We all say things when we're angry that we're sorry for later. Look at me. I do the very same thing. Of course I understand, and you are definitely forgiven. Now I must be going. I think I should pull together some figures for you. That way, you'll have a good idea of exactly what you'll have as working capital.'

'But I already – '

'You made a good start, Yasmin, but let me do all the follow-up for you. There may be some things you overlooked.'

'Of course, and thank you again.'

Yasmin could barely contain herself after Hassan had left. Finally, everything she'd worked for was about to happen. She could hardly believe her success. And Hassan! What an about-face! she thought. Perhaps she'd been wrong about him. After all, it probably was just as he'd said – he wasn't used to listening to other people's ideas anymore. It just took him aback for a moment, she told herself. But he'd readily seen how workable the plan was, and would help her in any way he could.

The first thing she had to do was call the marketing firm. She would need a formal proposal with all the costs set forth. She also needed to figure out the dates and the time she'd have to work with. That meant going over, one more time, the vineyard schedule, and double-checking the bookings they already had for this year's bottling. It was possible that some of the wine could be diverted for the test. But, of course, that depended on what they had already had on hand in the casks. Then she would contact the lawyers and talk about the sale of the properties she had in mind.

Yasmin reached for the phone, humming lightly. But before she could pick up the receiver, the telephone rang.

'Hello?' came a strangely familiar voice. 'Who is this?'

What an odd question to ask, thought Yasmin. 'Who is this?' she replied.

'This is Hillary Branford, of course. Is this Yasmin?'

'Hillary!' Yasmin was stunned. 'Hillary, where are you?'

'I'm right here, silly. I decided to call every Saint-Clair in Paris to see if I could find you. You're the first one I called!'

'Hillary! I'm so glad you did,' Yasmin said. 'I wondered what happened to you. Why didn't you answer my letters?'

'Oh, you know me – I hate to write letters. I always planned to, but then I never got around to it.'

'What are you doing here?' Yasmin said, suddenly excited. 'Are you married? Do you have children? How long will you be in Paris?'

'Well, actually I'm not there yet. When I said *here*, I meant *here*, not there.'

'You haven't changed at all! So when are you coming? How long will you be staying?'

'So many questions!' Hillary giggled. 'I'm arriving next week. No, wait a minute . . . I'm arriving in *two* weeks. And no, I'm not married. Not anymore, at least. Not to my first husband, or my second one either. And no, thank heaven, I have no children, and how about if I stay for one month? I'll stay longer if I'm having fun, and I'll leave immediately if I get bored. Does that answer some of your questions? When can I see you?'

'Oh, this is so exciting, Hillary. You can see me whenever you get here, of course. Call me as soon as you get off the plane. Would you like to stay with me?'

'Oh, goodness gracious, no! Not that I don't love you, but I want to stay at the Ritz. It's fun to out-snob all the snobs. And I want to see your luscious father again too!'

There was silence for a moment before Yasmin could bring herself to reply.

'He had a heart attack. He's dead. Look, Hillary, I have so much to tell you. But we'll have to talk when you get here. It will take at least all night.'

'Ooh, it must be good! I can hardly wait.'

'Call me as soon as you get in, and we'll get together immediately. And Hillary – I'm so glad you called me. I've always wondered what happened to you.'

'Lots. I can see I might need to stay two months, not one. See you!'

Yasmin put the phone back in its cradle and stared at it. She often thought about Hillary and had written her a few letters for a year after André's death. None had ever come back, but none had ever been answered either. She'd finally decided that Hillary must have disappeared into a new life and been too busy to keep up.

Yasmin had often desperately wanted to talk to her friend, but there hadn't been any way for her to get in touch. Now Hillary was going to be arriving in two weeks. It would be one marathon conversation, Yasmin thought. How would they ever get all the spaces filled in?

It also meant that she had better get down to work! After all, she had a major project to oversee. But in her heart, she knew she would have no problem. The only problem had been Hassan, and now he was helping her. It would be smooth as butter, this plan. She could hardly wait to tell Hillary everything!

21

But the way was not as smooth as Yasmin would have liked. Things went smoothly enough with the marketing firm. That wasn't the problem. She had spent almost the entire week with them, laying out her plans, providing them with material from the company library, calling American farm-machinery manufacturers for prices and lead times on delivery. She'd had little time in the office.

One night, remembering that she'd forgotten a file she'd compiled to give to the marketing people, she quickly caught a cab to Avenue Montaigne. Opening the door, she was surprised to find the lights glaring. Who could be here at this hour? she thought, frightened.

Quietly, she padded across the floor, hoping she wasn't interrupting a burglary, realizing what she was doing could be dangerous. She knew she should just close the door and go downstairs to call the police, but she was furious that someone had the effrontery to invade her private office. Undaunted, she had flung open her office door to discover Hassan seated at her desk.

His great bulk looked funny sitting at her delicate secretary. His head snapped around, eyes wide and unguarded with surprise. A second later his eyelids half closed into his usual impassive stare. 'What are you doing here?' he asked abruptly, slamming the ledger books in front of him closed.

'Well, I can certainly see what *you're* doing here,' Yasmin said with a small smile. 'I didn't know you were in the habit of burning the midnight oil, and with so many account books too.'

A relaxed smile spread across Hassan's face. 'Of course,

I'm not in the habit of working late – burning the midnight oil as you so aptly put it. But I'm trying to help you with your plan. This, of course, means much extra work.'

Yasmin wondered why he had to sit at her desk, though. She knew he'd promised to figure out the working capital – even though she'd already done that – but why at her desk? After all, he had a desk of his own, and one that fit him better too!

She was about to ask, when she realized she'd probably had a ledger or two that hadn't been put away. Perhaps he'd just wanted to look something up, so it would be silly to carry it all the way to his desk, then return it to hers when he was done.

Yes, she thought, her suspicions melting away, he really is taking this seriously.

'You don't know how much I appreciate this, Hassan,' Yasmin said, gratefully. 'And you'll see. I've been working it all out, and I trust you'll be impressed. It's going to be exciting.'

'I'm sure I will,' he answered smoothly. 'Do you need something?'

'It's all right,' she said, walking across the room. Hassan watched her closely. 'Don't let me disturb you. It's just that I left these papers here. I need them tomorrow morning at nine.'

She walked to the couch and picked up the sheaf of notes. 'That was all. Just my absentmindedness, I'm afraid. You'll lock up?'

'I'll take care of everything,' he said.

Yasmin went home thinking how wonderful Hassan was being. She supposed he was only doing it so she would agree to marry him the next time he asked, but the reasons didn't matter. If keeping him on a string helped her get what she wanted for the business, then that was fine with her.

But a week later, just when she thought everything was

348

going smoothly, she was faced with a major snag. Hassan had researched the amount of available cash, and which pieces of real estate were not encumbered and could therefore be sold. That morning as he went over the figures with her, she saw there would never be enough to start.

'Are you sure?' she asked Hassan again. It seemed impossible that with so many holdings in the Saint-Clair name, none of them were liquid.

'I'm sorry, Yasmin, but I've checked every avenue. You don't have enough. There is a chance that next year, with proper juggling of stocks and holdings, you could manage it. Unfortunately, launching your plan this year is out of the question. I wish I had better news for you.'

'I don't understand how I could have figured it wrong.'

'You didn't figure it wrong. There were just some contractual aspects of the real estate holdings you didn't know about, that's all.'

'Back to the drawing board,' Yasmin said, staring disconsolately out the window.

'It will happen, just not right now,' Hassan said, trying to make her feel better. 'We'll work together to pull everything into place so that it happens as soon as we can make it work.'

But that night, unable to fall asleep, Yasmin went over every detail of her plans and every detail of what she'd learned from Hassan. Although it hadn't seemed possible, there it was, down in black and white – not enough money. But there had to be a way, there just had to . . .

Abruptly she sat straight up in bed. If she could get major financing from banks based on the results of the market test, she told herself, she could get a less significant sum in order to do the market test in the first place. There was no reason to use her own money for any of it. The real estate holdings that couldn't be liquidated could be put up as collateral.

Tomorrow she would go to the bank, she decided. All the data she had created for her original presentation to Hassan would work just as well for stuffy Monsieur Henri LaMarquette. She wondered briefly if Hassan should speak with him instead, but decided against it. Hassan wouldn't present the plan as well as she could. Besides, this was hers and hers alone. She recalled that Monsieur LaMarquette hadn't seemed to like her very much when they last met. He always dealt with either André or Hassan, both men. But maybe this time would be different. Also, the last time they'd met she was a good deal younger, and had yet to prove her worth. This time she had the weight of her accomplishments behind her. Certainly he would be able to deal with her now that they were on more common ground, she told herself, deciding to call first thing in the morning and make an appointment.

'*Un moment, Mademoiselle*,' the secretary said. 'I will see when Monsieur LaMarquette can see you.'

Yasmin drummed her fingers lightly on the desk, waiting as the woman put her on hold. She hoped he would be able to see her soon, but these gentlemen often liked to make you wait for an appointment. They thought it made them look very busy and powerful.

'Monsieur LaMarquette will see you this afternoon at three o'clock, Mademoiselle.' The secretary paused slightly, waiting for her reply. 'Is that possible for you?'

'Yes, indeed,' answered Yasmin. 'Three o'clock then.'

She hung up feeling pleased. That was certainly quick, she thought. Maybe he's not intractable after all.

She looked down at her black corduroy skirt with a black and beige sweater. Nice enough for her own office, she thought, but certainly not what she should wear for a business meeting. She'd have to go home and change her clothes. Elegant, she thought. She should look rich. He'd be more inclined to give her the loan if he thought – Yasmin stopped herself, realizing that she was already rich, and Henri LaMarquette knew it better than anyone.

She went to the town house at lunchtime to change. She pulled a severely tailored black suit out of her closet. She hadn't worn it since last fall when she was in England. Bought at Harrod's, it had been perfect for cocktail parties given by her professor. But this was Paris in the spring, and she hesitated.

No. It would be quite suitable, she decided. It fit her beautifully, and if she wore the cream silk blouse with the long tie at the throat, that would soften the effect a little, but not look too feminine.

Yasmin reviewed her papers and charts, including the proposal from the marketing firm, and put them carefully in the slim brown leather attaché case she carried. After going over the whole presentation one more time in her mind, she put a string of pearls around her neck. She wanted Monsieur LaMarquette to be impressed with her businesslike appearance.

'You look *très elegante*, Mademoiselle,' Françoise crooned as Yasmin picked up her attaché case. 'You are meeting someone important, perhaps?'

There was a sly twinkle in her eye as she said *important*. Yasmin could easily guess where her thoughts were leading. Françoise continually worried about Yasmin's lack of a social life. When she sat down to her solitary dinner each evening, the cheerful woman would pull a long face, then chide her about eating alone at home again.

'Just business, I'm afraid, Françoise.'

'Then you will be home tonight for dinner?'

'Of course,' Yasmin answered. 'Where else?' She double-checked her appearance one last time in the mirror and left, taking a taxi to the bank.

On the way, Yasmin gazed out the window and thought about the upcoming meeting. With any luck at all this could be the beginning of her actual management of the Saint-Clair vineyards. If she sufficiently impressed Monsieur LaMarquette, it would pave the way for dealing with him exclusively. Until now Hassan had been his main contact. Now she would be. Once the plan was successful – as it surely would be – she was on her way.

The taxi left her at the curb in front of an imposing building in the center of the financial district. Yasmin had never been into the bank before. That, too, had been Hassan's domain. She took a deep breath, straightened her spine, and slowly climbed the steps toward the big glass doors enclosed in black iron grillwork. The door was opened for her by a uniformed doorman who ushered her into the large rotunda. The barrel-vaulted ceiling and the marble floors made her heels resound with loud clicks.

She crossed to a large desk in front of a long, green baize door. The gray-haired woman behind the desk looked up at her across the tops of her glasses.

'May I help you, Mademoiselle?'

'I am Yasmin de Saint-Clair. I have an appointment with Monsieur LaMarquette.'

'Of course. I am Madame Claudel. Monsieur LaMarquette is expecting you. Please come this way.'

Madame Claudel got up from behind her desk, and opened the door. There didn't seem to be any furniture in the room. All Yasmin could see was a huge expanse of Chinese carpet, and beyond that, long multipaned windows. The woman waved Yasmin inside. She stepped over the threshold as the door closed quietly behind her.

'I knew I'd see you sooner or later,' came an oddly familiar voice from off to the left. 'What brings a nice girl like you to a place like this, anyway?'

She turned and saw a most unexpected face. The shock of blond hair didn't obscure the broad, high forehead and slanted blue eyes set over wide cheekbones. Yasmin gasped at the sight of Charles LaMarquette sitting behind

352

a huge carved mahogany desk. She'd completely forgotten him.

Perhaps he was just sitting in for his father because he knew she was coming, she thought. 'Actually, I came to see your father on business,' she said.

'Why? You don't want to see me?'

'I didn't say that,' Yasmin stuttered. 'It's just that I have some business to transact with him.'

'*Mon Dieu*, not business again. It keeps rearing its ugly head around this place. *Dégoûtant*. Perhaps I can help you instead?'

'I'm afraid I really should speak to your father. It's something he should handle, since he manages the Saint-Clair holdings.'

'Well, I'm afraid that you have to deal with me, Mademoiselle de Saint-Clair. You see, the old man retired,' Charles said with a smile. 'He retired shortly after I met you in January. Since this is a family bank, and I am his firstborn male issue, I've sort of inherited the position. Handed down from father to son, if you know what I mean. Now I fear I must work for a living. From now on I will handle your affairs.'

Yasmin swallowed. This was most unexpected, and unpleasant. Charles LaMarquette didn't seem to have a serious bone in his body, she thought miserably. He'd probably never pay attention, or even begin to understand what she was planning to propose.

'I didn't mean to upset you,' Charles said, looking worried. 'I used the word *affair* loosely, you understand, so please don't get angry with me. As I recall, you are easily insulted.'

Yasmin had to smile. Looking at him more closely, she realized that Charles LaMarquette was extraordinarily handsome. Tall and slim, his features were strong and distinct. Thick brown lashes fringed his blue eyes, and a lock of silky blond hair fell across his forehead. And that interesting Slavic tilt to his eyes she found intriguing.

Charles probably has always attracted women, she told herself. 'That was why he persisted in his outrageous behavior. It was the behavior of a man who had never known rejection. Since she had rejected him out of hand six months ago, that only meant he was going to try harder. Taking a deep breath, Yasmin tried to turn the conversation back to business.

'I can just as easily present this material to you as to your father,' she said. 'Shall we get started?'

'*Certainement*,' Charles said, leaning back in the large carved chair. Putting his fingers together at the tips, he rested his chin on them. 'What can I do for you?'

Yasmin opened her attaché case and carefully arranged the papers on his desk. She outlined the present status of the Saint-Clair vineyards, went back over their history, then began to talk about her plans for expansion. Each step of the way she handed Charles another set of papers to refer to. Charles did not interrupt her once. When she had gone over every detail, she sat back and waited.

There was a long silence while Charles reexamined the sets of figures she'd set forth in her expansion plan.

'It's an excellent plan, and an impressive one. In fact I think it may be the beginning of some far-reaching innovations in the French wine industry.'

'I'm glad you approve,' Yasmin said, feeling pleased.

'However, I fear we can't help you.'

'Why not?' Her heart sank.

'I took the liberty of going over your accounts when I heard you were coming to see me. Even though the plan is a good one from the point of view of the Saint-Clair vineyards, I must consider what is best for the bank, first and foremost. The Saint-Clair operation is overextended at present, so it would be most unwise for me to authorize a loan of this magnitude at this time.'

'Overextended? I don't understand.'

'It is this way in all agricultural operations. The overextension is not a result of poor planning, it's just the way a vineyard operates. The bank loans you money every year against the crop. At the moment, the crop isn't harvested so its worth is still not yet evaluated. Until the grapes are in and crushed, we cannot consider giving you additional capital. It doesn't mean that your operation is unsound, by any means. It's just our policy to be fairly conservative in these matters. I'm sorry.'

Yasmin stood up. 'Well, I guess that's that for this year,' she said quietly.

'*Mais, non,*' Charles answered quickly. He leaned back, putting his hands behind his head. 'That's that until your grapes are in. Then we'll talk again about the loan. In the meantime, however, would you consent to leave these papers with me? I'd like to study them further. That way when I go before my directors, I can bring up the possibility of an extension for you in the fall.'

'Of course,' Yasmin said. She carefully placed the rest of her papers back on his desk. 'Thank you for your time.'

Suddenly Charles uncoiled himself from behind the desk. 'Would you consider having dinner with me sometime?' he asked quietly.

Yasmin glanced up at his face and caught a glimpse of a very serious man. It occurred to her that the lighthearted playboy she'd met in January was only a facade this man cultivated. Underneath he was very much the hardworking banker who carefully calculated and weighed all the risks. Perhaps he wasn't such an idiot after all. It might even be pleasant. But she didn't want to discuss dinner or anything else with Charles right now. She was too disappointed at being refused a relatively small loan.

'I don't think so,' Yasmin said. 'After all, is that standard banking procedure?'

'You know it isn't,' Charles said. 'It's just that I know I made a bad impression on you the last time we met. I was hoping to correct it.'

'A fast way to correct it would be to give me the loan I want,' Yasmin said, realizing she sounded shrill. 'I'll present the information to *my* board and see whether or not they'll agree to a dinner invitation. It might take until the fall harvest is in, however.'

'You're making this into a joke,' Charles answered.

'I'm sorry. Look, this is a silly conversation. I really must be going. Thank you for your time.'

As she walked dispiritedly in the front door of the town house, Françoise was on the telephone. She waved her hand as Yasmin walked by, saying, 'Of course, Mademoiselle. Mademoiselle Yasmin has just come in the door this very moment. Here she is . . .'

Gloomily Yasmin took the telephone. 'Yes?'

'I'm here!' came Hillary's voice, giggling out of the earpiece. 'Come to the Ritz immediately! I'm starting to get bored already, and besides, I *must* hear everything!'

'I'll be there in half an hour, Hillary,' Yasmin replied, feeling as if a hundred-pound weight had lifted from her shoulders. 'I can't tell you how glad I am to hear your voice! I've had a horrible two weeks, and I need to talk to someone who isn't pessimistic.'

'You're talking to the right lady,' Hillary said archly. 'Make it here in fifteen minutes . . . I'll order the champagne and caviar for starters right now – room 620!'

Yasmin tossed her briefcase on the sofa in the library, then hurried up the stairs, unbuttoning her jacket. She threw on a pair of tweed slacks and a matching sweater and scarf. Then, remembering she was going to the Ritz, she grabbed her sable coat, as she called out, 'Françoise, I won't be home for dinner after all. My best friend is here from America and we have lots to talk about!'

She heard Françoise call faintly, 'Have fun!' as the front door slammed behind her.

Yasmin was in a fever of anticipation as she waited for Hillary to open the door to her room. She wondered if her old friend looked the same, and how she would appear to Hillary.

Then the door flew open, and she saw a glamorous, heavily madeup, gorgeous little blonde. 'Oh, my!' said Yasmin.

'Take off that silly scarf,' said Hillary, looking her up and down critically. 'No, come inside first. No wonder you had a ghastly day.'

'I wasn't wearing this scarf,' Yasmin said as Hillary pulled her into the room and grabbed her in a hug.

'Let me look at you,' Hillary said, standing back. 'Yasmin . . . why is your hair up like that? You should let it hang down. Oh, dear, there I go again, changing everyone, trying to fix them up! You have no idea how much trouble I get into with people.'

'But you're beautiful!' Yasmin said. 'I could probably use some tips.'

'Well, dear, I work at it. But you don't *have* to work at it – that's what your problem is. So, just to be difficult, you work at being plain. Right?'

'You better give me my champagne right now,' Yasmin said, noticing two bottles of champagne set on a silver tray. A small silver bowl full of beluga caviar sat in a dish of ice between them. Hillary obviously meant business. 'Oh, Hillary, it's so good to see you again!'

'Here,' Hillary said, handing her a beautiful round goblet filled with fizzy liquid. 'It's the wrong kind of glass, but what the hell. Drink it fast, and you won't notice. Now please tell me about your father first. What happened?'

'Well,' Yasmin said taking a sip, then dropping her coat on an armchair, 'that's pretty much where this story begins. You see, Hillary, I left out an awful lot of things about myself. The only way I can tell you what's been happening since we last talked is to tell you how it really all began.'

Even though Yasmin had always thought she would never want to tell anyone the truth about herself, she found herself spilling the whole story out to an amazed Hillary. It felt wonderfully cathartic.

'Ye gods, Yasmin,' Hillary finally said. They had gone through both bottles of the champagne, and the caviar dish was empty. 'That's incredible! There's more to you than meets the eye, and you've been busy too. But with dumb things. Do you honestly mean to tell me that you aren't interested in Hassan? He sounds very attractive to me. Maybe he should be my third husband. What do you think?'

'Take him, please!' Yasmin laughed. 'And while you're at it, you can have my annoying banker too.'

'God, you're up to your ears in gorgeous men! And you haven't gotten laid in years! How can you stand it! That's bad for your skin, you know. You also know what they say, don't you? Use it or lose it! Yasmin, you need help! I got here just in time, I can see that!'

'But I don't want to get laid, as you so casually put it,' Yasmin snapped. 'I want to be in love, and I want someone to love me too!'

'Well, you're not going to fall in love if you don't give anyone a chance . . . and if you don't go out with a man once in a while, how are you going to know whether they even speak the language, for Christ's sake? Yasmin, you're very smart and very dumb at the same time.'

'But all they ever want to do is make love.'

'What's wrong with that? If you don't feel like making love, just say so!'

'It's been such a mess, Hillary – my life, I mean.'

'*Your* life! You don't know the meaning of the word *mess*, my dear. My life is a complete disaster, but at least

358

I have fun. Each of my husbands was fun – before I divorced him. But there are other men. Your life is as neat as a pin, and I'd kill myself if I were you, just out of sheer boredom!'

'But, don't you see, I'm not bored – '

'You're so bored, you don't even know that you're bored. Look, I'm going to show you a good time while I'm here, then you'll know a thing or two about fun, so I can trust you to have fun on your own. Jesus! I have to nursemaid a grown woman here.'

'Oh, Hillary.' Yasmin giggled. 'You always made me laugh . . . that's what I loved about you. Thank you for coming back!'

'You can thank me by introducing me to this Arab man. He sounds sexy. What's his name again? Who cares? I'll probably forget it anyway. I always do. That's another trick you must remember, my dear. Never call them by their real names. Call them all "darling." That way you won't make any unfortunate mistakes in the heat of the moment, if you know what I mean. For some reason they always lose their hard-ons when you call them the wrong name in the middle. Aren't they silly?'

'You really want to meet Hassan?' Yasmin said, uncertain.

'I think I'll come to your office tomorrow and meet him,' Hillary said. 'Don't worry. I'll give you a lesson in how to wrap a man around your finger.' She waved a perfectly manicured finger at Yasmin.

'I probably need that lesson.'

'You *definitely* need that lesson. Now look, I have to go to sleep. If I'm going to wrap men – or poison snakes, do we think this Hassan is the poison snake variety? – around my finger, I need my beauty sleep. Do you want to stay here?'

'No. I'll take a taxi home. But thanks anyway. All my work clothes are in *my* closet, not yours.'

359

'Good,' said Hillary, weaving slightly as she walked Yasmin to the door. 'I'll see you tomorrow at one o'clock. We'll have lunch – or breakfast, depending on your point of view. Okay?'

'Perfect,' Yasmin said, giggling.

That night as Yasmin lay in bed, she thought about Hillary and how well she seemed to handle things, and wished she could be that way. Maybe she *will* be able to give me lessons, Yasmin thought. But she doubted that Hillary could handle Hassan! That I'd like to see! she told herself before falling asleep.

But see it, she did. The next day Hillary swept into their office like a small whirlwind dressed in silk, furs, and diamonds. Hassan, at first annoyed at her unexpected presence, soon melted under her barrage of meaningful glances. In the end he took them both out to lunch, then kindly offered to escort Hillary back to her hotel. Hillary accepted, but looked totally bored at the prospect.

As she kissed Yasmin's cheek before getting into the taxi, she hissed into her ear, 'This one is a cakewalk. Looking bored is all part of the act. I'll call you later. Line up the banker, okay? I'm drowning my sorrows in men.'

Yasmin watched the cab pull away from the curb. It was all she could do to keep her expression smooth until it was out of sight. Then she burst out laughing, and walked back to the office. Line up the banker, indeed, she thought. But then she said out loud, 'Why not?'

As she dialed the telephone number of the Credit Française, she smiled wickedly. Madame Claudel put her through very quickly, and it was a stunned Charles LaMarquette who agreed to have dinner with Yasmin and her American friend the next evening.

'I thought I wasn't going to see you again,' he said.

'Well, this is special,' Yasmin said smoothly. 'She's here for a month and doesn't know anyone. And oddly enough, I don't know that many people either. But I think you'll enjoy her. She's an interesting conversationalist.'

'You make her sound like a fat librarian with hairy moles,' Charles said, obviously perplexed with her change of heart. 'But that's all right. As long as you're there, I wouldn't mind if she were a rhinoceros.'

'Don't worry,' Yasmin laughed. 'She's hardly a rhinoceros. See you tomorrow then. Six o'clock. You know the address?'

'Of course,' Charles said, and hung up.

But Yasmin wasn't laughing the next evening at quarter to six when Hillary called her at home to cancel the dinner date.

'Hillary! How can you do this to me? It's too late to call Charles LaMarquette and cancel, so I'll have to go by myself!'

Hillary had chuckled sweetly. 'So what's wrong with that? Are you afraid of him?'

'Don't be ridiculous! I'm just not interested in him, that's all.'

'Go out with him anyway. Maybe he'll introduce you to some of his friends, and you'll like one of them. That's how it's done, silly.'

'But he's my banker, and what's worse, he won't give me the loan I desperately need!'

'Maybe he will, if you handle him right.'

'Did you plan this from the beginning, Hillary?' Yasmin was suddenly suspicious.

'Maybe,' Hillary said. 'Actually it wasn't a plan. It was a fall-back position. I wanted to make sure I had something interesting to do in case your Arab friend was a washout.'

'I take it he wasn't a washout, then?' Yasmin said. She'd noticed with interest that Hassan came to work around noon, which wasn't unusual for him. He often had morning meetings. He didn't say anything to her about Hillary, and she hadn't asked.

361

'Hardly,' Hillary said. Her voice got softer. 'But I'll say one thing – that man isn't marriage material, even for a third husband. But he makes for a great joyride. I decided to see him again tonight, that's why I can't make it. I told him I wasn't sure what my plans were, and I'd call him later. I waited until the last possible moment – just to set his teeth on edge. Sorry I'm calling you so late, but – '

'But nothing,' Yasmin said. 'I'll bet you timed this whole thing.'

'Timing is my forte, lovey.'

'Listen, I'll speak to you tomorrow, and I'll try and have a nice time with Charles. You have a nice time with Hassan.'

'I will, darling. Believe me, I will.' And Hillary hung up, just as the chimes on the front door rang.

Yasmin stepped out into the front hall as Françoise let Charles in. She was surprised, not having remembered him being so tall. And standing there in her hall, Yasmin was struck again by his extraordinary good looks.

He was wearing a beautifully tailored dark brown corduroy jacket over a striped shirt. His trousers clung to his muscled legs, and if she hadn't already known he was a skier, she would have guessed.

'You look lovely,' he said as his eyes traveled over her.

Because she'd thought they were going out with Hillary, she'd dressed with more care than usual. Her dress was a cream-colored light wool with padded shoulders. The tailored neckline dipped low between her breasts, and it was belted tightly around the waist. Unable to decide what to do with her hair, and knowing that Hillary would probably scream about the bun and the glasses, she'd let it hang loose down her back.

'Where's the rhinoceros?' Charles whispered.

'She couldn't make it,' Yasmin said, feeling mildly annoyed at Hillary once again. 'I'm afraid you'll have to make do with just me.'

A broad smile creased Charles's face when he heard the news. '*Perfectement*,' he said. 'Shall we go?'

Much to Yasmin's surprise, she had a very good time with Charles. They wandered around aimlessly until they got thirsty. First they stopped at a small *boîte* on the Left Bank. Sitting in the outdoor café, they drank Pernod until they were lightheaded. Then they wandered along until they found themselves in Gare de Lyon.

'I have an idea,' Charles said suddenly. 'I will introduce you to the most exquisite decor in all of Paris.'

'That sounds lovely.'

'*Bien*. It's called Le Train Bleu.'

And Yasmin thought it was wonderful. A betassled, befringed, bedizened, plushy version of extreme haute Belle Époque decor, the restaurant had flowing lines and fountains of ornaments that reached up to the ceiling before bursting into a bloom of architectural vegetation that delighted the eye. She felt as if they were about to climb aboard a *wagon-lit* as they sat looking down on the great glassed-in station below. There, the arriving and departing trains spewed out passengers and porters and suitcases and boxes. Inside, the chandeliers cast a golden glow over everyone. She almost felt ready to run away that very moment. Charles made her laugh delightedly, and for the first time in a long time, Yasmin felt normal.

Normal and ordinary and everyday. The give and take of their conversation wrapped around them in an amber glow, and she was flirtatious and funny, and as relaxed and happy as she'd been in the days when she and Hillary would sit close together, watching everyone and everything and making their sly comments on life and love and the general scene.

After dinner they climbed to the top of the Eiffel Tower and watched the twinkling lights of Paris below them. Charles put his arm around her to ward off the chill of the night air, but he went no further. And in the taxi back to the town house, he kept her laughing merrily as he described the rise and fall of the Paris telephone system from 1910 to 1971. It seemed like such a peculiar conversational gambit for a first date, that Yasmin was enthralled.

'*Bien sûr,*' Charles said when she mentioned it. 'Women fall like flies when I describe the Paris telephone system to them. It's one of the great all-time, foolproof seduction routines. I'm happy that you liked it.'

But when he took her to the door, he kissed her on the cheek, smiling fondly. 'I had a good time,' he said quietly.

'I did too,' she replied.

'Can we do this again sometime?'

'I'd love to.'

'I'll call you.'

He walked off down the street whistling tunelessly, his hands thrust deep in the pockets of his trousers.

For a moment Yasmin was flooded with regret that he hadn't wanted to come inside with her. But she didn't call him back. She stepped inside the town house wondering why she'd had such a good time with a man who was so different from her. Yet in some ways, she thought, he was very much the same.

I wonder if that means I'm starting to like myself, she thought idly as she climbed the stairs.

22

But even though Yasmin had a pleasant evening with Charles, she didn't see him again for the rest of the month.

She and Hillary took a short trip to Lausanne to see Solange. It was midterm week at Lautremont, and the atmosphere was gloomy. Solange was pleased to see them, since there was little to occupy her, and Yasmin and Hillary had a wonderful time reminiscing about their years at school – the memories came flooding back to them once they were in the familiar old buildings.

When they got back to Paris, Charles was out of the country at a banking conference in Belgium for two weeks, but he left word for Yasmin that he'd like to have dinner with her again on his return. It was just as well, since Yasmin's days and evenings were busy because Hillary's parents came through Paris. She spent a good deal of time with the three of them, watching Hillary twist her father around like a pretzel and run her poor mother ragged.

On their last evening in Paris, Hillary's father and mother planned to take them to a party thrown by a movie producer who was a friend of theirs.

'This is your chance, Yasmin,' Hillary told her over the phone. 'I'll be over in an hour to help you dress.'

'I can get dressed by myself, Hillary,' Yasmin said with a hoot of laughter. 'Or do you have something up your sleeve again?'

'Who me?' Hillary had said, with an exaggerated innocence that worried Yasmin.

'Just give me a hint.'

'I'd prefer it to be a surprise, darling. Don't get all twitchy. You'll see when I get there.'

Yasmin had misgivings as she waited for Hillary that night. 'Allah, give me the strength to resist her if it's too outrageous,' she said softly.

And it was . . . and he didn't.

Hillary came in with a big box under her arm and a rascally look on her face, and Yasmin knew there was very little hope.

'Here's the thing,' Hillary said. 'I think you've wasted enough time with all this banking crap and business garbage. I've decided that you need to be discovered!'

'Discovered doing what, Hillary? Walking naked across the Champs-Elysées?'

'Close, but no cigar. I've decided you need to be a movie star. You'd be great, I tell you. And this is the place to be discovered. This party is going to be crawling with directors and producers.'

'Why me? What about you? You'd make a much better movie star than I'd ever be.'

'I never said I *wasn't* going to be discovered, did I? Now stop grousing and try this on.'

Without taking off her floor-length mink coat, Hillary threw the box on the bed and tore off the cover. Pulling out mounds of tissue paper, she lifted out a shimmering gold metallic dress and held it up for Yasmin to see.

'I got one for myself, too, but it's black. I look great in black because of my skin and hair. This one is for you. Now put it on, and don't wear any underwear, because the seams will show through.'

Hillary had a cat that swallowed the canary look on her face. Yasmin shuddered with dread, thinking about the trouble her friend was about to get her into. But it wasn't until she slid the dress over her head that she had any real picture of how bad it was going to be.

'I can't go out in public in this,' she gasped when she

saw her reflection in the mirror. The dress clung to her, the gleaming gold almost the same color as her skin. A plunging bodice dipped between her breasts and was barely held up by one slender sparkling strap on the left shoulder. The right side was slit up to the hip. Every hollow, dent, and curve was outlined with vivid clarity. She looked naked. She practically was.

'But no one looks at you unless you wear something stunning,' Hillary crowed. 'And believe me, that is stunning on you. And who in God's name told you to do that with your hair?'

With one smooth motion Hillary was at her side, busily pulling the pins that held the knot of hair at the back of Yasmin's neck.

'Forget about my head,' Yasmin said. 'You can practically see my pubic hair!'

'That's what it's supposed to look like. Stop squalling,' Hillary snapped. 'You look better than you've ever looked in your life.' Then she opened her coat, and spinning around, let it fall to the floor. 'Check it out on someone else, lovey. It looks good, doesn't it?'

Yasmin had to admit that it looked fabulous. Hillary was petite, but her figure was beautiful. Her breasts were large, but they sat balanced high on her narrow rib cage, and her waist was high and small. One shapely pale leg thrust out of the long black slit, and her tiny foot was barely shod in a delicate black sandal with a high spiked heel.

'Now look at us together,' she said, linking her arm in Yasmin's and dragging her in front of the mirror.

The two of them stood there, gazing at their reflections, the worried expression on Yasmin's face in direct contrast to the expression on Hillary's face. Hillary was plainly delighted with herself.

I wonder what's wrong with me? Yasmin thought. She wanted to hide all the time, and dressing flamboyantly made her feel so uncomfortable. Hillary didn't seem to mind. If anything, she appeared more than pleased with herself.

'All right,' Yasmin sighed. 'I'll wear it, and I'll see what happens. But if I need rescuing, you'd better – '

'Don't be ridiculous, Yasmin. You're perfectly able to take care of yourself. If you can't, well then, sue me! Besides, I can practically guarantee you that in a dress like that at a party like this, you won't stand out a bit. Every budding starlet in Western Europe will be there – wearing even less, too – hoping to turn a blow job into an acting job.'

They'd gone to the party and were a minor sensation. Even though what Hillary had said was true about the starlets, the two of them were new, and in that circle newness was worth a lot.

The party was held in a huge loft in Montmartre. The air was so blue with smoke, that it was hard to see. Films from hidden projectors were being projected on the ceiling and on three walls of the studio, and loud rock music belted out of five huge speakers. As Hillary's father took glasses of champagne from the waiters circulating with difficulty through the crowds of people, he mumbled something about leaving early.

Yasmin watched the older, elegantly dressed couple fade into the crowd, then turned her attention to what was going on in the room around her. In one corner a group of people seated around a small table were sniffing cocaine. Standing by a long window was an actor she thought she recognized. He was surrounded by pretty girls and looked completely bored. People were passing drinks, passing joints, and in other corners, passing out.

Hillary flitted around like a bumblebee, and so many men asked Yasmin to dance, to talk, to go to Crete for the weekend, to get married, or to go to bed with them, that she was never alone with one of them long enough to have to worry about any of them. In fact it turned out to be easier to deal with a crowd than it had ever been for her to deal with one man, all alone.

'How many screen tests have you been offered so far?' Hillary said to her when they met in the crowded bathroom. 'I've gotten six, so far.' The two women laughed together.

A pretty girl with flaming red hair was collapsed, weeping on a chaise in the corner of the room. Another girl was just sitting there, watching her.

'I'd like to leave soon,' Yasmin said as she combed her hair and repaired her makeup. 'I have to get to the office tomorrow. I'm still trying to work out a way of convincing Hassan to expand.'

'Do what you want, darling,' Hillary said. The words sounded strange because she'd pulled her mouth into an *O* to put on her lipstick. 'By the way, I'm going to Brindisi tomorrow.'

'You didn't tell me,' Yasmin said, surprised.

'I didn't find out until this afternoon,' Hillary said. 'Actually I was having a rather nice time with Hassan, but he's a bit too slick, even for me. I've found a delicious old duke. I think I'd like *him* to be my third husband. I need stability in my life, don't you think?'

Yasmin laughed. 'You're incorrigible. By the way, I was meaning to ask you about Hassan. I figured you would tell me sooner or later, and *he* certainly never says anything.'

'Well, darling,' Hillary said, looking at her with an odd expression. 'He's fantastic in bed, but he seems to be stuck on you.'

'You're wrong, Hillary. That's all over now.'

'You may think it's over, but he apparently doesn't. All he wants to do is fuck and ask me questions about you,' Hillary said, turning her attention back to her hair. 'It's irritating.'

'What kind of questions?' Yasmin was suddenly curious.

'Oh, you know. The usual boring questions. Not that you're boring, love. But I'd really rather talk about myself in bed – not you. It's almost as if there are three of us in there. Kinky, but boring.'

'I wonder why?' Yasmin said, thoughtful. 'Maybe he's just curious.'

'Obsessive would be more like it,' Hillary said, putting her makeup away. 'Anyway he's all yours, darling, whether you want him or not. I'm going to devote my attention to getting a title. The world is full of fucking machines, and I'm already up to my ears in money, so what's left?'

'Send me a postcard, all right?'

'And hopefully a wedding invitation too.'

With one last look at the weeping girl on the chaise, they went back into the din of the main room. Yasmin finally found her coat and waved good-bye to Hillary – who was whispering in the ear of a tall, handsome man with thick blond hair, and didn't see. Yasmin refused two invitations for drinks at 'someplace quiet,' and got a taxi home.

Hillary called her the next afternoon from Orly, then blew out of Yasmin's life as unexpectedly as she'd blown in.

Over the next few months there was no expansion because there was no loan. Yasmin fairly itched to do something big with her vineyard, and continued to search for ways to put the plan into effect. But it was slow, grindingly boring work because it felt as if it was leading no place. She did, however, take the opportunity to arrange the company's assets so that when the time finally came, she could easily shift gears to accommodate whatever operational changes would have to occur.

Charles called her many times during those months, and they went all over Paris together. Yasmin felt carefree whenever she was with him. They went to wonderful restaurants and bistros, as well as the theater and concerts. But they did delightfully different things too. Once they sat in Les Halles at five o'clock in the morning and watched the produce come in from the countryside. Another evening they drank wine and chatted for hours with a canal barge operator.

The summer passed quietly as Yasmin and Charles got to know each other better. What surprised Yasmin most about Charles was that he never asked her to go to bed with him. At first she waited apprehensively for the inevitable question. Whenever their evenings came to an end, she began to get skittish and jumpy, trying to figure out what she wanted to do when the question finally came. But after a while, when it never came, she relaxed in his presence and stopped being as conscious of her every move.

But once she accepted the idea that he probably wasn't going to pounce on her, she began to get restless about that too. What was wrong with her? she wondered. Wasn't she attractive? Or maybe it was something else. Maybe he didn't like girls at all, she thought at one point. But that didn't seem to be the case either. Every now and then she would catch him looking at her with an enigmatic yet hungry expression. Yasmin had seen that expression before and she knew what it meant. But even though they often held hands as they strolled along the streets of Paris, Charles never made a move to touch her in any but the most friendly and brotherly way.

Yasmin began to feel very comfortable with Charles as a friend. Hassan, however, didn't seem comfortable with their relationship.

'You're seeing a lot of our banker,' he said to her one

371

day. His voice was casual enough, but his eyes were hooded.

'Charles is a good friend,' Yasmin answered just as casually. 'We sightsee together, go to museums, nice, pleasant things like that.'

'You're not sleeping with him?' Hassan's expression remained veiled, but the tension knotting his arms was sneaking into his voice as well.

'No. Should I be?' Yasmin felt like teasing him.

'By this time I'd expect it,' Hassan said, his face relaxing a bit. 'But who knows? He's probably a queer. I never would have guessed it, but sometimes it's hard to tell – '

'I don't think so,' Yasmin replied guardedly. 'But maybe he respects me – '

'Respect!' Hassan's voice exploded in derisive laughter. 'Maybe you're right, but who am I to give you advice?'

But still, she noticed that he seemed to keep track of her meetings with Charles, though in a casual and unobtrusive way.

One late afternoon as they were crossing the Champs-Elysées, one of the thousands of Paris taxis almost side-swiped Yasmin as she stepped off the curb. Charles grabbed her, pulling her back out of danger. Caught off guard by the suddenness of his action, Yasmin fell against him and hung limply in his arms. To her surprise, his mouth rested softly against her forehead as his arms tightened around her. She could feel his heart pounding through the thin cotton of his white shirt, and his breath, warm against her skin, was coming in rapid bursts.

Then just as suddenly he let go of her. Startled, Yasmin looked up at him, and the expression on his face caught her short. It was so filled with longing and pain, it was hard to keep her eyes focused on his. Realizing she'd seen the look, he turned his head away from her as if trying to keep her from reading it.

Not knowing what to do, Yasmin said, 'Charles . . .'

With chameleonlike rapidity, he turned back to face her, a broad smile splitting his patrician features.

'I can't take my eyes off you for *un moment*, can I?' he said lightly. He smacked her gently on the bottom, as if she were a child.

Yasmin was unprepared for the lightness after the brief glimpse of the depths of desire in Charles's eyes. Periodically she would think back to that look she'd seen so briefly on his face. But since it was never repeated, after a while she decided it must have been an aberration, or perhaps some memory from the past that had nothing to do with her. But it had been so very strange, she couldn't quite put it out of her mind.

A few days after that incident Hassan came into the office, a very sober expression on his face. After detailing the wide-ranging effects of the current recession in France, he went on to say that in America the opposite was happening. American business was in a mini-boom, and as a result, there was more money around than in recent years.

'The time is ripe, Yasmin,' he said. 'We should put your plan into effect.'

'I'm delighted,' she replied, hope rising like a bubble in her chest. 'Do you mean to tell me the money is available now? Can we liquidate some holdings?'

'That's what we have to discuss. Unfortunately we're in the same cash position we were in this spring. But that doesn't change the fact that the time is ripe. If we don't make our move now, we'll have missed an extraordinary opportunity.'

'I don't understand what you're proposing, though.'

'You should go public,' Hassan said without hesitation. 'If you issue stock, you can raise as much cash as you need.'

Yasmin's heart sank. 'You know I won't do that,

Hassan.' She knew that going public and issuing stock meant losing control over the vineyards and all of the assets. There would have to be a board of directors, and though she would probably be chairman of the board, that wasn't certain. There would be an election of officers and a vote by the stockholders. What if they thought she was too young? she wondered. What if they didn't want the company in the hands of a woman? No. It was too risky. 'Absolutely not,' she said.

Yasmin also realized abruptly that as the months had gone by, her position had altered. Even though Hassan had told her to organize the expansion herself in preparation for taking control, there was no expansion to organize. The end result had been devastating to her. He'd locked her away from the actual running of the company more effectively than if he had locked her out of the office. While she was doing research, he was taking care of the day to day activities. Instead of making herself more of an active member of the firm, she'd been losing track of more and more as time went on.

Up until this moment Yasmin hadn't quite realized what Hassan had achieved. By sticking her with the details of a yet to be realized plan, her duties around the office had gradually turned her position into something resembling a research assistant. And she had allowed it to happen! she thought. Now, if a board of directors were going to vote for a chairman, they would never vote for her. She didn't go to business meetings, make deals, meet clients, or have a working relationship with any of the important people they dealt with. Hassan did all that – to free her so she could work on her expansion. She cursed inaudibly. What an idiot she'd been not to see it!

'I most definitely won't even consider going public, and that's final,' she said, turning her back on him.

'Don't be ridiculous, Yasmin. At this time the amount

of francs that you could raise would be quite large, and you could do a lot with that amount of money.'

'I refuse to give up control of my company.'

'You're being naïve, Yasmin. It's the only way.'

'Then it's not going to happen,' she said firmly. 'If I have to effectively sell the company to make it bigger, then I'd rather stay the way I am and wait. The status quo is ten times better than selling André's vineyard down the river. Another time like this will come, when we will be in a better position to make our move.'

Hassan stood up slowly, a look of exasperation on his face. 'I can't force you, but think about it. Sleep on it. Believe me, you'll regret making a decision like this one in haste, Yasmin.'

He strode to the door, and turned back to face her. Yasmin caught a flash of smoldering resentment on his face. 'If you're as smart as you think you are, you'll take my advice,' he said. 'Anyone would give you the same, even your pansy banker friend, Charles.' Then the door slammed behind him, and Yasmin was left alone.

'Charles,' she said. Her thoughts were being spoken out loud. 'Charles will know what to do . . . and besides, what if what Hassan says is right? Perhaps now is the time.'

Picking up the phone, she quickly dialed the number of the Credit Française.

'I want to see you,' Yasmin said when she was finally put through to Charles.

'Let's have dinner, then. Shall I pick you up at – '

'No, not dinner. This is business. May I come to your office?'

There was a slight pause. '*Certainement*. This afternoon?'

'What time?'

'Let me see.' Yasmin could hear papers rustling. 'Four o'clock would be best.'

'Good, I'll see you at four o'clock.' She was about to hang up when she heard Charles's voice.

'Can you tell me why?'

'Why else would I demand to see my banker?' Yasmin said, deciding that it would sound funny if she refused to explain. 'I want money.'

'*Alors*,' Charles said with a laugh. 'I was hoping you would learn to like me for myself.'

'I do. But I like you for your money too.'

Yasmin hung up and started to prepare for her meeting with Charles. In a way she was sorry they had a relationship outside of business. It would make it harder for her to pressure him, and harder for him to refuse her with grace. Maybe for that very reason he'll feel he has to give me the money, she thought, even if it's against his better judgment – whatever that is.

But he didn't.

Late that afternoon, after presenting her case most convincingly, Charles was still not inclined to finance her expansion of the vineyards.

'Hassan has already discussed the idea of a public offering with me, and I think it's the best way for you to go. I really can't see why you object so violently.'

Yasmin explained how she felt about relinquishing control, but Charles didn't feel that was an issue of any consequence.

'You're being old-fashioned about this, Yasmin. Going public would not only be the best thing for your company at this particular time, but it's also the way of the world. Not only would it give you operating capital at a time when it's crucial, but you would also be making a great step toward going with the times. The era of the family-owned business is fast coming to an end. The only way for you to expand and become big enough to take on the giants is to play the game the way they play it – and that means having money, and lots of it.'

376

'I can do the entire operation with loans, Charles,' Yasmin said coolly. 'There is no reason to use my own money at all. As a matter of fact I think it would be far better business not to use my own assets. I need a loan from you to start the market test. With the results I can then go to American banks – that is, unless you want to handle it for me – for the rest. But the amount of money I'm going to need for the start is relatively small.'

'*Oui*, but Hassan also mentioned that Bertrand is having some problems because of the frost in September. In addition, there is going to be an increase in the cost of this year's pressing, and the number of bottles that are on advance order has dropped significantly from last year. You know that. You've been watching the figures.'

'That's true, but in the past advance ordering has often been light and then caught up later in the year. Once the cold weather sets in, even in the lowest of years, the orders pick up.'

'I wouldn't count on it this year, Yasmin. The economy is terrible. It's affecting everything, especially high-priced stock like your own. Besides, as your banker, I can't sanction more money for expansion at a time when it looks like your debt will increase rather than diminish. It wouldn't be keeping your best interests at heart.'

'Forget my best interests for a second,' Yasmin said, exasperated. Charles's conservative outlook was irritating her. 'Don't you agree that this is the best time for a launch?'

'*Bien sûr*. I agree wholeheartedly.'

'Then I fail to see why you're refusing me the money. You know very well that the line ought to do well in the United States, so it hardly constitutes a gamble on your part.'

'Why should I, or even you for that matter, gamble, however? Why not agree to go public? All your problems will be solved. Furthermore your lawyers agree with both me and Hassan as well. In fact we've set up a meeting with them for tomorrow.'

Yasmin was coldly furious. 'Why would you set up a meeting with the lawyers without considering what I wanted to do? You're both trying to bulldoze me into a decision I have no intention of making. I'm surprised that you, of all people, would do that to me. I won't do it, and that's final!'

Charles stood up and walked around the desk, but Yasmin was already out of her chair. As she stalked to the door, she felt anger stiffening her shoulders against any words he might have.

'You cannot have such a meeting because I won't attend,' she snapped. 'And furthermore, you have no decision-making power without me!' Her voice had become low and dangerous. 'You forget I hold ultimate control in this company, and it's about time all of you understood that.'

'Wait, Yasmin!'

Charles caught up with her and put his hand on her arm. 'We won't force anyone to do anything. The meeting is merely to discuss the ramifications of such a move. You should be there and hear what they have to say, *n'est-ce pas*? After all, your lawyers may very well end up agreeing with you.'

Yasmin stopped for a second. That was, of course, true. 'All right,' she said slowly, turning to face him. 'I'll listen to what they have to say, and I'll also make sure that all of you listen to what I have to say. The fact that you and Hassan have discussed all of this and set up a meeting behind my back leads me to believe that the management of my firm is going on behind my back too. I am beginning to think that I can't trust either of you. But I'll attend the meeting. Afterward, perhaps we should all have a talk about our relative positions.'

'Good,' said Charles, satisfied to have gotten this far. 'Tomorrow afternoon at two-thirty.'

'I'll be there.'

But in the taxi going back to her office, Yasmin didn't feel quite as confident as she'd sounded in Charles's office. She had a very strong intuition that Messieurs Fauquier, Renan, et La Tour were probably in agreement with Hassan and Charles. The odds seemed stacked against her, and she was afraid that the pressure would be too great for her to hold out against them. André would never have allowed the firm to go out of his hands, she thought. His father hadn't allowed that to happen – even in the worst times – and neither had he. Following in his father's footsteps, André had done everything in his power to keep the vineyard in the family. Yasmin had every intention of doing the same thing. But it felt to her as if the doors of a trap were slowly closing.

'What paranoia,' she said out loud, and the cab driver turned his head to look at her out of the corner of his small, piglike eye.

'*Quoi?*' he intoned. His voice sounded like an electric meat grinder.

'*Rien,*' she said briefly. But in her heart, she knew it wasn't nothing. It was a very real fear to her. Unfortunately the financial situation was clear. It was all down in black and white, wasn't it? She could do nothing, and leave things the way they were. But then she'd in all likelihood be up against a debt by the end of the fiscal year. The only answer seemed to rest with a public offering of stock. She wanted desperately to put her plans into effect, and convinced that this was the time to do it, she was drawn toward accepting the decision being pushed on her by all the men in her life.

The taxi pulled up in front of the building on Avenue Montaigne. Yasmin quickly paid and got out. As she walked into the *ascenseur*, wondering what could possibly come of the meeting tomorrow, she was struck with an amazing thought.

'Of course!' she said with a laugh. 'The paintings and the art and the villa in Tangier!'

Delighted, she quickly went into the office and sat at her desk. Her memory of André's collection in the villa was that it had been sound, and even contained some valuable pieces. In today's art market, with the astronomical sums museums and collectors were paying, she could certainly get quite a bit of money if she sold off some of the better ones. It might bring in enough cash to get her started. If not, she could sell the entire villa.

Yasmin recalled Von Rothenburg asking her over six years ago if he could have some of the collection. She'd refused. Now, she realized that for her to sell the pieces without giving him first option would not only be cruel, but would also be flying in the face of their friendship.

Hoping he wasn't off on one of his interminable jaunts, she called and was in luck. Not only was Oskar in Switzerland, he was so excited, he was ready to fly to Tangier the following day.

'Don't be silly,' Yasmin said happily. 'I'll go and make an inventory. You'll be the first to get it, and you can choose whatever you'd like.'

'At an exorbitant price, I assume,' Oskar said, his voice filled with gloom.

'Of course. I'm not doing this for my health, you know.'

'Whoever it was that said the best things in life are free was completely wrong,' Oskar went on miserably. 'He probably knew nothing about the best things in life, and that's why he said it.'

'Now don't go getting all weepy and morose on me,' Yasmin answered, sensing that Oskar had already begun to bargain. 'You'll get everything for a little bit less, because I won't be paying the dealer's fee. Doesn't that make you feel a little bit better?'

'No. I never should have taught you everything I know. The past is always coming back to haunt me. If only I'd just allowed you to answer the phone and left it at that.'

'Poor Oskar,' soothed Yasmin. 'You know, you never did teach me everything you know, anyway. I was meaning to make you do it when I was still working for you, but things were always getting out of hand.'

'I'm not as dumb as I look. Why do you think I always left you with such a mess? Self-protection, that's why. Now when are you going to make this alleged inventory, my dear?' Oskar's voice shifted rapidly out of gloomy and into curious.

'Well, I thought I'd go tomorrow. I can hardly wait. Besides, I'm under tremendous pressure here to make a decision. The sooner I know what's in that villa, the better I'll be able to turn any confrontation to my advantage.'

'Wise move, wise move,' Oskar said gravely. 'Skip nothing, my dear, and I'm especially in the market for ormolu clocks and anything you can find that's a signed He Tianjian. I'd like a few more of his riverscapes.'

'It'll cost you an arm and a leg, Oskar. Are you sure?'

'I'll pay anything you ask, darling.' The hunger was quite vivid in his voice. 'Has no one ever told you that I'm fabulously wealthy?'

'Thank heavens,' Yasmin said. 'I want to raise at least ten million francs.'

'Chicken feed,' Oskar said cheerily. 'Hurry to Tangier, and then hurry home. Actually, why not just call me while you're there. I don't think I can stand the suspense. I've been waiting to get my hands on that collection for years. And no dawdling either. I was planning a trip in two weeks, and we might as well get everything settled before I leave.'

'And before I change my mind, right?'

'Naturally.'

Yasmin booked a morning flight to Tangier, then made another call.

'Charles, I'm glad I caught you in,' she said. 'I've decided to cancel the meeting with the lawyers tomorrow.'

'Why? I thought – ' Charles started to say.

But Yasmin, incensed all over again, cut him off. 'Look Charles, I'm sorry to sound so cold, but I can't presume on our friendship to demand that you give me a loan. You cannot, therefore, presume on our friendship to set up meetings without my prior knowledge or approval. I understand that you and Hassan think of me as a figure-head, not as the real head of my business. However, let me make something clear to you. I've taken a good long time preparing for this, and now I'm ready. I've had enough of being treated like a silly child by you, and by Hassan as well. I intend to manage my fortune, and I intend to do it now.'

'You have every right . . . *Cela va sans dire –* '

'I know that,' Yasmin went on. 'Would you please notify everyone that the meeting is cancelled and that I will reschedule another one in approximately one week. That one will take place after I've had a meeting with my lawyers, on my own.'

'Of course, Yasmin. But please understand, I've never thought of you as a figurehead,' Charles said softly. 'I did not realize you were under that impression.'

'As long as that's clear in everyone's mind from now on, what you, and Hassan, and my lawyers thought in the past is of no consequence,' Yasmin said coolly.

'I suppose you'll tell Hassan in the morning?' Charles said.

'I won't be available for a couple of days. Why don't you call him yourself?' Yasmin replied. 'I'll see you next week.'

She hung up before Charles could ask why she would

be unavailable. She felt good. As soon as she came back from Tangier, she planned to change the structure of the firm. Hassan would no longer be acting director – she would. Surprised at her own boldness, and also surprised at the amount of time it had taken her to move, Yasmin suddenly realized that she was ready – ready to take over, and ready to take on anyone and anything that tried to stand in her way.

But now there was work to do. Before she went home to pack, she wanted to review the books and confirm the projected costs. She also decided to calculate the numbers for the last five years to determine what the percentage of advance orders had been each year by 1 September. That way she might be able to get a better handle on what she could expect this year, recession or no recession.

In fact, she thought as she pulled out the books, she'd go back ten years and see what the advance orders looked like over a long period of time and have an even broader view. A spread sheet showing bookings and orders would have far greater validity if it were based on a ten-year cycle than a five-year cycle. That would encompass André's management of the vineyards as well as Hassan's.

At two o'clock in the morning Yasmin had everything on paper that she needed, and had also begun to get a very strange picture from the books. Having never looked at what was recorded during André's control of the vineyards against Hassan's control it it, she'd never seen how different the sets of figures looked. Now, faced with the two of them together, Yasmin had a nagging feeling that something wasn't right.

But exhaustion was beginning to take its toll too. Leaning back in the chair, she pulled off her glasses and rubbed at her eyes. They itched horribly from the eye-strain she always seemed to get when she looked at columns of numbers for too long. Annoyed with herself, she wished she had an inexhaustible supply of energy on which to draw. There had been many times like this in school when despite her best intentions, her body demanded food and rest at the most exasperating times.

Thinking of school, Yasmin was suddenly reminded of something one of her professors had always harped on. She could almost hear his voice droning on in the huge, paneled lecture room: Look for the patterns, the repetition, the rhythm and flow of the numbers; numbers are like a river – they flow smoothly unless shifted off their course by an obstruction.

The picture that had formed in Yasmin's mind was one of a rushing stream with rocks and embankments that changed the flow of the water, sending it spiraling or rushing off in another direction. The eddies and pools of blackness shifted the river in its course, and in some places, the high embankments prevented any deviation from the direction that nature intended.

Thinking of the figures she'd just examined, she knew instantly that the rhythm was wrong. It was being changed by something; some obstruction was redirecting its course. But it was nothing she could put her finger on. After all, it could simply be a reflection of the two different men and their divergent ways of seeing the vineyard and recording its fluctuations. There was also the difference in their educations. André had been taught how to run his business by his father. Hassan had learned how to deal with any concern, even a vineyard, at Harvard.

Yasmin went back again. But there was no explaining away the oddness of the shifts. It was nothing specific, but there were small discrepancies that couldn't be explained by a difference in accounting methods. Numbers that had shown fairly consistent dips and rises during the time André had managed the vineyards were for no reason running smoothly. Under Hassan's management they ran too consistently. She wondered if it was all in her head, since she was so tired.

It was fast approaching three o'clock, and she hadn't packed, hadn't eaten, and definitely needed some sleep. Wearily, Yasmin realized that even if she were to continue looking and working, she'd accomplish nothing. She decided to take the figures with her to Tangier, where she'd have time to check it after completing the cataloguing.

As she lay in her bed, she wished there were someone she could discuss it with. Ordinarily she would have felt comfortable drawing on Charles's friendship and advice, but now she knew she couldn't use him as a resource. Charles would never do anything to harm her, of that she was fairly certain. It was just that her vision seemed so much more far-reaching than his. Perhaps the natural caution of a banker kept him from seeing the profit she knew she could make.

As in everything, Yasmin finally realized that she had only herself to rely on. In a way, she thought, that wasn't bad. Then she'd only have herself to blame, or more likely, to congratulate. That would feel infinitely better than the momentary relief sharing her worries would bring.

PART SEVEN

Tangier, 1983

23

As the plane landed in Tangier, Yasmin was flooded with a contradictory mix of emotions that was so strong, she almost wished she hadn't come back. The last time she'd been in the airport was seven years ago. On that night she had been in shock – frightened, lonely, and grieving for André. She had also been consumed with guilt for the money she had just taken from the safe. As she'd slunk out of the city, her prospects couldn't have been dimmer. How could she have known what lay ahead? Now she was coming back first class, and had a car waiting for her at the airport gate.

Yasmin had called the villa that morning to inform Salima and Zayd of her impending arrival. Salima had sounded pleased, but Zayd was his usual taciturn self. He'd replied shortly that he would meet her flight, but it was the sound of Salima's voice that started the welter of conflicting emotions. She had not heard Arabic spoken in the familiar dialect since she'd left Tangier.

Oddly enough part of her also wanted very much to go back home. She could almost smell the delicious scent of the majestic cedar and pine trees that surrounded the meadows and small lakes high up in the mountain ranges of the Rif. But there was no time for such a visit, and besides, nothing would be served by it. The only person she would have wanted to see was her mother, and her mother was dead.

In a way, she wanted to see Khadir, too, or at least see the Medina and the Petit Socco where she'd lived for a while. The style of high-walled house that surrounded the inner courtyard with its fountains and carpets was still one that she loved. No matter how poor or rich a

Moroccan family was, they still built their houses around this central courtyard that formed the main living area for the family. Even her family's house in the hills had been designed that way, though by no means so sumptuous. Yasmin still didn't feel quite used to the strings of rooms Europeans considered proper houses. Perhaps just a short drive through the Petit Socco, she thought, and then found that her heart was beating faster.

As she collected herself and walked out of customs, she saw amid the throng of djellabas the unmistakable form of Zayd. He was leaning impassively against the wall, obviously not eager to see her. In fact Zayd made no move to meet her or to take the suitcase or bulging briefcase from her. Ignoring his deliberate slight, Yasmin smiled at him briefly.

'I'd like to go to the villa, Zayd, but would you please drive me through the Medina on the way. I'd like to see how things have changed.'

'The changes aren't worth noticing,' Zayd muttered as he closed the car door after her. Minutes later they were moving slowly in the traffic out of the airport and onto the road that took them into Tangier. Yasmin sat in the back, saying nothing as they rode into the city. Enclosed in her thoughts, she watched the familiar landscape drift noiselessly by the window.

The day was dry, and it looked as if the rains wouldn't come for a while. For that, at least, she was grateful. It seemed strange after the crisp, early fall weather in Paris to be suddenly transported to the balmy weather of the Mediterranean. Then a tugging in her heart made her turn her eyes away from the view. There is no going back, she thought firmly. There is nothing here for me but memories of misery and heartache. She kept her eyes lowered for a while, but as they sped into the city, the noise and the crowds pulled her out of her reverie and made her look around.

Across from the Place de France, a line of modern

hotels lined Tangier Bay. A camel caravan was plodding along the beach, carrying tourists back to their hotels. In the haze that hung over the sky, Yasmin could just make out the tip of Spain, nineteen miles away.

So many influences, Yasmin thought as she watched her people mingling with the expensively dressed Europeans in the Medina. First the Phoenicians in the twelfth century, then the Carthaginians, who'd captured it from the Phoenicians. After that the Romans, the Vandals, the Arabs, the Portuguese, the Spanish, and the British. Then, after the division of Morocco in 1912, France and Spain made Tangier an international city. Then came the invasion of the shady dealers, the spies, and the writers. At least they didn't kill everybody for sport, Yasmin thought. And now the best of all possible worlds. After Tangier's international status was ended in 1956, the spies left and the tourists came. That was good, because every Moroccan knows tourists spend more money than spies do.

Yet despite all the outside influences, Yasmin realized that the Moroccans kept to themselves, kept most of their customs, and saw every new invasion as a bigger and better opportunity to make money. This was evident as she watched a crowd of youngsters standing around a table full of what looked like Americans. Their little hands were extended, and their eyes were huge and solemn as they watched each forkful of food go from plate to mouth. The tourists couldn't hold out long against such pathos, Yasmin thought with a private laugh. Even the littlest Moroccan knew a good opportunity when it presented itself.

But her laugh was cut short as the car slowly made its way down the next street and past Abdul Khadir's compound. It was impossible to see over the high wall, and Yasmin didn't even know if the brothel was still there. For all she knew, Khadir could have gone elsewhere. But she could see the interior almost perfectly in her mind's eye. A sigh of relief shuddered through her as she thought of what her life might have been like had she not been rescued by André. But these thoughts were for the past, not the future. Yasmin knocked on the glass that separated her from Zayd.

'I've seen enough for now,' she said. 'Let's go to the villa.'

The car sped up Old Mountain Road with its plush Hollywood-style residences. As she looked out, she could see the tall pines and the well-kept gardens of the rich. This was where she belonged, she thought with a satisfied smile. Not down there in the Petit Socco.

After driving through the gate and stopping, Zayd got out and opened the door for her. She stepped onto the gravel drive as Salima came out the wide front door. Overcome by her warm familiarity, Yasmin hugged her hard, and after slipping her arm around the older woman's shoulders, they walked into the house.

But being back in the foyer was like a slap in the face. Yasmin slowly allowed her eyes to wander across the black marble floor and up the long, curving staircase. Her eyes lingered on each of the paintings. So full of memories, she thought sadly. She tried not to dwell on the other pictures that flashed through her mind like a parade of tin soldiers. I must be very businesslike, she told herself, and simply decide what is worth the most and make lists. But her eyes continued to take everything in, the little bronzes, the marble statue at the back of the hall. Yes, endless lists. That would keep her from thinking.

'Would you like something to eat?' Salima's voice interrupted her thoughts, bringing her back to the present.

'*Naham*,' answered Yasmin, hardly aware of the fact that she'd said yes in Arabic, slipping easily back into the language without even noticing. 'I think I'll go upstairs for a moment . . . get my bearings, unpack, look through the house.'

'All right. If you need anything, call me. Otherwise I'll bring you something in half an hour,' Salima said as she turned toward the kitchen.

Yasmin slowly climbed the stairs. She went as if drawn by an invisible hand into the room that had been hers, and saw that Salima had made the bed and aired the room. It looked as if she had just left it a few weeks before. Again she felt as if she were caught in a time warp.

She spent the next half hour walking through the house. She opened every drawer and closet; checked every painting, vase, clock, and statue; examined the books, then the linens and the furniture. What a lot of it there is, she thought with a growing sense of satisfaction, realizing there would be little problem raising the cash she needed. Then, hearing a faint bell ring, she went back downstairs.

Feeling a good deal better after she'd eaten, Yasmin spent what was left of the afternoon and the evening cataloguing the paintings. She wanted to keep all of them, but knew that her ultimate goal was more important. There were a few Claude Lorraines, and a Corot which would, by itself, bring her a great deal of money. She also found a beautiful majolica plate that had Oskar Von Rothenburg's name written all over it in invisible ink. She could almost see his expression of cupidity and delight.

The only room she avoided was the study. She couldn't quite erase from her mind the picture of André lying on the floor. Tomorrow, she thought, finally exhausted.

She fell into a leaden sleep and didn't awaken until the sun, pouring in through a crack in the curtains, slanted across her pillow. The brilliance of the light was unexpected, and for a moment she didn't know where she was. But then the smell of the eucalyptus, and the faint sound

393

of waves crashing against the cliffs far below, filtered through, and she remembered.

After a light breakfast of yogurt and figs, always her favorite, Yasmin continued the inventory of what was in the house. It wasn't until late in the afternoon that she stopped, aware of the sound of tires crunching on the gravel of the drive. Wondering who could be coming, she brushed a strand of hair out of her eyes and looked out the window.

With a shock she saw Charles getting out of a car then bend down to pick up his suitcase. She admired his athletic body, narrow in the hips and broad across the shoulders. He still bore the summer tan that looked so striking against the pale blond of his hair. Surprised, Yasmin forgot she was wearing the loose cotton dress that Moroccan women wore around the house. She'd found it in her closet, and it still fit. Her hair was tied in a long scarf because of the dusty work she had to do.

As she ran into the front hall, she caught a glimpse of a street urchin in the mirror and realized with horror that it was herself. But it was too late, Zayd had already opened the door. Charles stood framed against the brilliant light, a broad smile creasing his face at the sight of her.

'What have we here!' he said with a laugh as he walked into the hall. 'It didn't take you long to get into the spirit of the place, did it?'

'What are you doing here? I wasn't expecting – ' Yasmin said, looking down at her dress apologetically. Zayd melted out of the room. 'It's the latest thing in Chechaouene,' she said, plucking nervously at the rough cotton. 'Is anything wrong?'

Charles looked at her with a curious expression, and then put down his bag. His smile had vanished, and now his soft mobile mouth was slightly opened.

'Why are you here?' she asked again when he didn't answer.

'Françoise told me where you'd gone and I couldn't

stay away from you,' he said, but the light tone of his voice was very different from what she saw in his eyes. He quickly covered the space between them and took her in his arms. 'Oddly enough, that happens to be the truth.'

Yasmin searched his face for some hint that he was joking. But there was no trace of humor in this serious person who held her tightly in his arms. Then he slowly lowered his head until his mouth touched hers. As his arms tightened, the exquisite warmth of his lips moving over hers, lingering and exploring her mouth, made her go inexplicably soft.

With a rush of amazement, Yasmin suddenly realized how right it felt. Unable to tear herself away, she kissed him back, opening her mouth to meet his tongue with hers. They stood together, unable to break the tender suction that held them glued together. It was Charles who finally pulled his head back to look at her tenderly.

'It wasn't until you stormed out of my office, and then called me later – so angry – that I realized suddenly I might lose you for good. I couldn't sleep, because I knew that I was letting you slip through my fingers. You're not easy, you know. When I came at you so strong – when we first met – you backed off at one hundred miles an hour. So I tried to slow down. I decided if I didn't push you – and made friends with you first, instead – you would be able to accept the fact that I want you in other ways too.'

'I'm not that difficult,' Yasmin said quietly.

'*Oui*, but you are,' Charles said. He kissed her forehead. 'You misunderstood everything I was saying to you, and I handled you so badly that night I first met you. I knew it would take a long time to make up for that initial mistake.'

'You didn't have to fly to Tangier to tell me this,' Yasmin said. 'You could have waited.'

'I was going to wait,' Charles said, 'but it was impossible. I had to tell you everything . . . how I felt . . . and besides, I didn't want to run the risk that your anger would harden and become permanent. A week is a long, long time when you're in agony, *n'est-ce pas*? Just the thought that I might never see you again drove me insane.'

He kissed her again, and she felt her knees go weak as butter. It flickered through her head that part of her anger at him might have arisen because she didn't know how he felt about her. She'd gotten to like him so much, had gotten so comfortable with him over the summer, that his aloof behavior had come to mean rejection to her. Perhaps she had wanted this, and wanted it more than even she had known. Charles stopped her thoughts with another kiss.

'I guess I should have tried one of those before,' he said softly.

'It met your standards?' Yasmin asked with a slight smile.

'Met, and then went beyond,' he answered. 'Do we have to stand here all day, or can I change my clothes?'

'You can do anything you want, but I think you'll have a hard time walking if you don't let go of me for a minute. I take it you're planning to stay,' she said, looking at the suitcase standing forlornly in the middle of the floor.

'Will you have me?'

'Of course. Why don't I show you to one of the guest rooms. They're not prepared of course, but Salima can take care of that later.'

Reluctantly Charles released her. But he kept one arm around her waist as he bent to pick up his suitcase. Yasmin turned with him, and arm in arm, they climbed upstairs.

'In here,' Yasmin said, smiling at him. She pushed open one of the long carved mahogany doors that opened onto a large room graced at one end with a fireplace and dominated by a huge bed. White sheets had been thrown over everything in the room as protection against dust. The faint, ghostly quality of the light that filtered through the pearl-gray curtains cast a strange glow. The only color in the room came from the radiant Persian carpet on the floor. A mixture of reds, oranges, and purples, its sheen was even more brilliant because there were no colors to compete with it.

In a single motion Charles set down his luggage and turned toward Yasmin. Before she could open her mouth to speak, he picked her up and carried her over to the bed. His eyes, normally a sky blue, had changed color, shifting into a dark glowing violet. Unable to take her eyes off him, Yasmin said nothing as she felt herself being gently placed onto the expanse of white sheet. Charles lowered himself until his body rested only inches above hers, supported on either side by his tanned, muscular arms.

'I hope you don't think I'm being forward, Mademoiselle, but I have always thought that the lady of the house should do her best to make guests feel immediately welcome.'

Not waiting for any answer but the one he saw in her eyes, Charles pressed the length of himself down over her, his mouth once again seeking hers.

The smile Yasmin had begun to feel tugging at the corners of her mouth was immediately obliterated by the insistent pressure of his lips. The soft fullness surrounded her mouth, and she felt dizzy with pleasure, as if it were the only part of her body with any nerve endings. She thought she would float away on a cloud of wonder. Why hadn't she known it would be like this? Why had neither of them known – and for so long too. They had wasted all those hours wandering around Paris, eating and talking, when they could have been kissing like this instead.

Yasmin was again aware of his clean soapy smell, and she began to melt and slowly come apart. Then Charles rolled away from her, leaving her breathless and languid.

His hands flicked open the buttons of her dress one by one. She was wearing nothing beneath the loose garment. Slowly he touched one of her nipples. It crinkled tight and hard in answer to his fingers, and he groaned.

'It's not going to be easy to control myself,' he said, looking searchingly into her eyes, as if to ask whether she minded this sudden, explosive intimacy. One of Yasmin's hands strayed up until it touched his cheek lightly. Stroking the smooth skin of his face, her fingers slid down until she could trace the sculptured edge of his mouth. She smiled briefly before he kissed her again, his tongue tracing a delicate pattern against her lips, then inside her mouth. Flicking the tip of her tongue with his, an insistent, throbbing tremor set itself into motion between her legs.

As he kissed her, he continued to unbutton her dress. Soon there was nothing holding the edges of the soft material together. The dress slid back, exposing her skin to the air and his incredibly knowledgeable hands. As Yasmin ran her fingers lightly through his silky hair, Charles traced patterns of fire on her naked body. Starting first at the pulse in the base of her throat, the sensitive tips of his fingers made their slow exploration down to circle first one nipple, then the other.

Then his mouth pulled away from hers. She gasped as the hot suction began on her distended nipples, sucking them to hard little points. A light sheen of perspiration made her skin glow with tawny light. She arched her back slowly, and his hands responded by gliding down her quivering abdomen to the silken shadow between her legs. By now her impatience made her feel uncontrolled. But Charles seemed to be in no rush.

'I can't believe we wasted so much time,' he said softly as his fingers entwined in her soft pubic hair.

'I was thinking the same thing before,' she answered, her voice throaty and deep. 'I don't want to wait any longer.'

'But this is so delicious,' Charles said. 'The discovery, the newness, is like a drug. I want to make it last forever. I want to learn every inch of you, taste every part of you . . .'

His mouth came back down on hers as his fingers moved in languid circles on the insides of her upper thighs. Every now and then his thumb would brush against the swollen, sensitive flesh hidden there. Finally she couldn't keep back her soft cry, begging him for more. As her knees lifted in agonizing entreaty, Charles's mouth left hers and he moved down and off the bed. Her eyes opened for a split second as the tangled knot of desire inside her coiled into a demanding quiver. He was staring down at her, stroking gently between her legs, opening her fully to his gaze and finally his mouth.

Yasmin's moan began to increase in intensity as she felt him teasingly circle the little button of pleasure hidden there. Then, with jolting electricity, he pushed his fingers deep inside her. The combination of mouth and fingers twisting, molding, sliding, and stroking pushed her beyond comprehension and crystallized the arching, screaming ascent into pleasure and madness. Ravenous, her body spiraled and twisted through racking convulsions of pleasure so intense, it was almost pain. But at the same time she knew she had never felt anything quite like this. It was as if she'd been numb every other time in the past, and now her entire body was totally alive and overwhelmingly sensitive.

Yasmin lay weak and spent as Charles stood up and carefully removed his clothes. As the racking shudders began to subside, she opened her eyes and caught sight of him standing at her feet like a bronze statue. He stood motionless for a while, watching her. Then he slipped his hands under her knees, and bringing her legs wide apart, knelt over her. Resting the diamond hard flesh against hers, he moved it gently in the welcoming slickness. Then

399

slowly, patiently, his eyes dilated with aching anticipation, he pushed deep inside her body.

The feeling of him buried inside the slick warmth was unlike anything Yasmin had experienced before. Instead of being an invasion, it was the galvanic joining with a part of her that had been missing all these years, and the relief, the singing pleasure of being joined once again with this missing part of her, made her cry with joy. Yasmin felt the sliding sensation of him moving with delicious precision was the way she had been made in the first place. Until now she hadn't realized quite how lonely she'd been. Tears slid slowly down her cheeks to mingle with saliva as his mouth claimed hers, joining them in a piercing, synchronized rhythm.

As Charles rocked gently against her and in her, Yasmin felt a knot of overwhelming urgency reform and begin to build in the pit of her stomach. Her body molded itself against him and followed his lead as she locked her legs around his back.

'I love you, Yasmin,' he whispered against her mouth. '*Je t'aime.*' His large, strong hands held her head on either side, and his eyes looked deeply into hers, as if they could see inside her soul and know her every thought and wish. Yasmin was pulled inexorably into the vortex of tenderness and love she saw on his face. Her eyes stayed open, drinking in the wonder of being with him. Then slowly, slowly, she felt her rhythm shift and become more demanding. She moved her hips, opening herself for more and more of him. With hard, demanding pressure, his thrusts became more urgent. Charles's head lifted, and suddenly her pleasure spun and caught sharply as she was dragged into the undulating storm they shared. In the distance she heard his voice hoarsely calling her name, mingling with the keening wail of her cries of pleasure.

For a long time they lay glued together by the juices of their bodies, then the sound of Charles's breathing became more even, and Yasmin felt herself returning to some semblance of control. But she also felt him still buried deep inside her, and wished with every fiber of her being that they would never have to move from that position.

'I hope you don't mind my being so forward.' Charles's voice was muffled by her hair.

'Not at all. The pleasure was all mine, I assure you.'

'*Mais non* . . . I beg to differ. The pleasure was most certainly all mine!'

'Our first argument,' Yasmin said with a soft laugh. Then, as the muscles in her body clenched with laughter, she felt Charles slip out of her. Suddenly she felt so bereft and alone, her bottom lip almost began to quiver. 'And so soon in the relationship.'

'I'll make it up to you, *ma chère*,' Charles said, raising his head to look at her. 'Sooner or later.'

'Sooner would be better.'

'I love the sound of your voice when you come. It's so husky. But what will the neighbors think?'

'It's not the neighbors I'm worried about, it's the servants.'

'I think they'll understand. After all, they weren't born yesterday.'

'By the way, are you hungry?'

'Only for your luscious body, I'm afraid.'

As Charles nuzzled his face back into her neck, Yasmin suddenly had a thought. 'I forgot to ask why you came.'

'I thought I already told you. I couldn't live without you another second.'

'Really?'

'Actually, yes. But I had another excuse just in case. By the way, do you ever read the newspapers?'

'Sometimes.' Yasmin was surprised by the jump. 'Why do you ask?'

'There has been considerable unrest in this area lately.' His voice was suddenly serious. 'The 1981 ceasefire over possession of the Western Sahara is very shaky right now. Didn't you know?'

'No.'

'Well, the Polisario guerrillas are on the move again. The region is rich with phosphate and iron, and everyone wants a piece of the pie, I'm afraid. Not only that, the drought they had a year and a half ago has made the fellahin ready to join any populist movement that promises them food. Things may get explosive. I wanted to make sure you were safe.'

'But aren't those guerrillas always stirring up trouble in one part of the Sahara or another?' Yasmin asked. 'That's been going on for years, ever since 1975, right?'

'*Oui*,' Charles said slowly. ' But I have it on good authority that Muammar el-Qaddafi of Libya is now supporting them. They are feeling their muscles.'

'But what does that have to do with Tangier?' Yasmin said. She was pleased that he worried about her safety, but thought his concern was farfetched. 'That's almost seven hundred miles from here.'

'The frontier . . . *c'est vrai*,' Charles said. 'But the Polisario Front is also supported by Algeria. That's a good deal closer. Besides, aren't you glad I came? Do you want me to leave?'

'Of course not,' Yasmin said, throwing her arms around him. But his expression turned serious again.

'Also I was a little worried about Hassan. He was behaving in a way that I decided was very strange. He was livid when you cancelled the meeting. I could see where he would have been annoyed, but he was so angry, I thought perhaps there was more at stake than I'd realized.'

'He wants me to go public very badly,' Yasmin answered. 'But I thought you supported him in that.'

'I do. But if you decide against it, that's certainly your prerogative.'

Yasmin looked away for a moment, trying to marshal

her thoughts. She'd assumed that Charles knew about her old relationship with Hassan, but perhaps he didn't. What he didn't know was that apparently Hassan hadn't given up. That, more than the plan of going public, was annoying him. By her refusal to do what he wanted, Yasmin was only making it even clearer that she didn't want him, or his advice either.

'I think perhaps I ought to explain about Hassan,' she said slowly standing up. 'I wouldn't want you to find out later and think I was withholding information from you. You see, we'd had an affair when I was first in Paris, right before I went back to school.'

'I knew about that,' Charles answered.

'Hassan thought it would start again when I returned, and he was very angry when I refused. He says he wants to marry me, Charles, but I told him to forget about that. I told him to forget about me altogether except as a business partner.'

'I gather he didn't take it well.'

'No. I guess maybe that's why he was so upset when I cancelled the meeting.'

'*Pourquoi?* I don't see what one has to do with the other.'

'Power. He wants to have power over me. If not physically, then at least as someone who guides my business. I've rejected him, and I'm sure he finds that infuriating.'

Charles chuckled softly. 'I thought we had agreed, sometimes you can be very difficult.'

'Only when I'm right,' Yasmin answered.

'Anyway, *ma petite*, I had this overwhelming urge to come here. To warn you about everything, including how I feel about you.'

'You only started feeling that way after I left Paris?'

Charles got up and slowly began to pick up his clothes. He looked at her for a long time before answering. 'I think it was the argument in my office. I hadn't realized until then how very much it would hurt me to lose you. I felt I was losing you, so I came.'

Yasmin slowly pulled the cotton dress on. 'Did you really mean it when you said you loved me?'

With a beatific smile, Charles put his arms around her. He kissed her gently on the forehead saying, 'With all my heart, I'm afraid. So be careful with it. It breaks easily, and I can't stand pain.'

He kissed her once again, and again Yasmin was caught off guard by the exquisite mobility of his mouth. It was the most delicious thing she'd ever felt. Without thinking she raised her arms and twined them around his neck. As she kissed him, she felt him slowly pressing her back against the wall. Then his hands came down and he carefully lifted her legs up until they were wrapped around his hips. Entranced by his mouth, it was with a shock that she felt the thick hard knob of flesh pressing insistently against her belly. Slowly Charles raised her hips up until his penis was firmly resting against the slick wetness between her legs, then just as slowly, he lowered her onto him, piercing her with what Yasmin felt was diabolical, maddening deliberation. Wrapping her legs tighter, she managed to thrust against him, forcing him inside of her deep and hard.

'*Mon Dieu*, Yasmin. I can't keep away from you,' he said, and with ravenous impatience pinned her against the wall and swept her up in the fierce tide of his passion. Spread wide, she clung to him desperately as he pounded into her yielding body. Within minutes she felt herself lose all pretext of control. His strong arms held her tightly as he groaned with pleasure.

Suddenly he pulled her away from the wall, and without coming out of her, carried her slowly back to the bed. The sensation caused by having him walk as he was embedded inside her amazed Yasmin. Wrapping her legs tightly around his slender hips, she hooked her feet together in the hollow of his back.

404

'You fit me so well,' he murmured as he started to lower them both onto the already rumpled dust sheet on the bed. 'It feels as if you are a part of me.'

'I was just thinking the same thing . . .' Then she lost herself again as his mouth covered hers.

Without moving they lay together, entwined in each other. Deep inside her body she felt him throbbing. But he made no move to bring them both to the peak of sensation. Instead, reveling in the closeness, he held them at bay while he explored her mouth with his.

As the time passed, Yasmin lost all sense of herself as a separate entity. Instead of feeling he was her long lost half, she felt that she had always been whole. Her body lost its memory of their separateness, and when he started to move ever so slowly, it was as if she were moving. As her fingers fluttered across his back, she felt she was touching her own body, not the body of someone else. Every contour and hollow felt as familiar as her own hand.

As their bodies merged into one, as all the nerve endings – so exposed by agonizing sweetness – seemed to join, she felt her mind was joining with his as well. The pleasure intensified, became molten, soldering the two of them into one single quivering body that glowed with fiery pleasure. This must be what it feels like to be a shooting star streaking through the black night, Yasmin thought, briefly, then became a shooting, glowing ball of light that soared through the inky sky inside of herself.

24

They had fallen asleep. When Yasmin opened her eyes again, not realizing how much time had passed, she saw that it was very dark.

'What time is it?' she said, her mind still fuzzy and formless from sleep and pleasure.

'Does it matter?' Charles said, kissing her softly.

'No, but I thought you might be hungry.'

'*C'est vrai*,' he said, then reached down next to the bed and pulled his watch out of the heap of clothes. 'It's eleven. That's late for Salima, *n'est-ce pas*?'

'Yes, but it doesn't matter. I can get us something from the kitchen.'

'Why don't I take you out,' said Charles. 'All those nice supper clubs are just getting going around now.'

'I wonder if I can walk,' Yasmin murmured.

'Lie here for a moment,' Charles said. 'I'll get you a glass of water. That's a bathroom behind that door, *oui*?'

'Yes,' Yasmin said. 'Thank you.'

He extricated himself from the ruined sheets and padded across the floor. She heard water running, then he returned. Holding her in his arms, he watched as she drank the glass right down.

She felt better, but still very languid. When she stood up, her legs quivered slightly. She laughed happily. 'You see, it's too much for me not to be in your arms.'

'That and being hungry, I suspect. I can't seem to find your dress anywhere.'

'It's probably under the bed. I'll find it tomorrow before Salima does the room. What will she think?'

'She'll think your future husband has come to join you in Tangier, of course. Get dressed, and we'll see if food gives you enough strength to face the rest of the night with me.' Charles kissed her again, and she wondered if they'd ever get out of the bedroom. They would starve to death slowly and delightfully, she thought.

Yasmin finally got away and was able to wash and dress. All the beautiful clothes André had bought for her were still hanging in the closet. She looked at the Balenciagas and the Worths and all the dresses they'd found in the boutiques on their trip from Switzerland. They were still hanging in their plastic bags.

She picked out a long black crepe dress from Worth and tried it on. The neckline was cut low, and the wide, gleaming satin midriff band cut high under her bosom then draped across her hips. The satin insert came to a point just at her buttocks, where a small amount of the crepe was gathered, forming a train that brushed the ground as she turned. The dress clung to her revealingly, a bit too revealing, Yasmin thought as she turned in front of the mirror. The lines of her bra and panties showed clearly. I will wear nothing underneath, she decided with a secretive smile. Then twisting the gleaming ropes of her hair up on top of her head, she twined a long string of pearls through the strands of silky black. The pearls slipped in and out of the coils, catching the light softly.

'You look gorgeous,' Charles said as they drove down toward the city. He had turned to look at her in the half light of the setting sun. 'I didn't know you had clothes like that.'

'Watch the road, darling,' Yasmin chided.

'How come I have never seen you dressed like this before?'

'These clothes are from another life,' she said lightly. 'I have so many past lives, I can't keep track anymore.'

'At least you don't change personalities when you change lives.'

'How would you know?' Yasmin said.

But she looked out the window, unable to face Charles,

wondering how much he would accept about her and all her past lives. After the party at Oskar Von Rothenburg's almost a year ago, he had never said another word about the fact that she'd come from Tangier. It was almost as if her life had begun in Lausanne, when André had sent her to school.

She had an awful premonition about being here in Tangier, as if the proximity of the truth would somehow make it come out of the walls, the whole city suddenly begin to whisper that she'd come from a brothel. She was desperately afraid that knowledge would drive Charles away. Or it would drive her away from him instead? she wondered. Either way, she had never been able to deal with people's response to her shocking past.

Even Hillary had been titillated by the thought. She made a comment about what a great sexual fantasy it was. It may have been a great fantasy for someone who didn't live it, but to Yasmin the reality was less exciting. Now, she remained lost in thought as Charles drove them down to the city.

They went to one of the newer supper clubs on Boulevard Pasteur. After the flood of hippies had swarmed through Tangier, the city had become a regular stop on many tours of Spain. On the grand European tour, the twenty minutes by hydrofoil from Algeciras had brought an influx of tourists, and the character of the city had changed to accommodate them. Restaurants and shops that Yasmin didn't remember had opened.

After dinner in a dark, elegant club, when they stood up to dance, she discovered that Charles was a wonderful dancer. They hadn't quite danced at Oskar's party, as she recalled. He'd only wanted to stand in the middle of the room, holding her. Now, however, she let the music carry her in a dreamlike haze.

They returned to their table and Yasmin leaned against Charles as she sipped her Cointreau. The sensation of being alone together – sealed off from the outside world in a shimmering bubble – persisted, and she decided not to question the delicious security she felt.

Then suddenly the bubble broke as a gratingly familiar voice shattered its surface. Yasmin looked up to see Hassan leaning over their table.

'Well, what a surprise,' he said with a nasty smile. Yasmin wondered if he was drunk. 'What have we here? My banker having dinner with my woman . . . and both of them looking as if they'd just tumbled out of bed.'

'Siesta,' Charles said lightly after a short silence. 'Charming custom, *certainement*. Don't you agree?'

'I do,' Hassan said with a sneer. 'But your choice of partners is perhaps unwise. Or didn't Yasmin tell you about us? Sometimes she leaves out the most important bits of information.'

Yasmin was too stunned to speak, but apparently this was between Charles and Hassan.

'*Oui*,' Charles said slowly, 'she did mention it. As a matter of fact we were just discussing you before dinner.' Charles's voice was light, but it didn't match the expression on his face. 'But there's no sense getting bogged down in ancient history, is there?'

'May I join you?' Hassan didn't wait for an answer. He slid into the chair that faced them. 'Ancient history, eh? Is that what she told you? Perhaps her sense of time is mildly distorted. But, of course, it's understandable . . . considering her background.'

Charles smiled, but his soft mouth had become a thin straight line and his eyes narrowed slightly. He raised his glass slowly and took a sip as Hassan continued.

'Didn't you know? She's a prostitute. Used to work right here in the Medina as a matter of fact. That's where André found her. She worked in Abdul Khadir's brothel. Have you ever been there? It's a very nice place, actually. André paid quite a lot for her, too, as I recall.' Then he turned toward Yasmin's pale, shocked face. 'You were thirteen or fourteen then, right, Yasmin?'

Yasmin didn't move. Immobilized, she felt like a bird confronted by a snake. Hassan's obsidian black eyes were bottomless, and she was filled with a nameless horror as she felt herself being sucked into the maelstrom of evil she saw there. Why is he doing this to me? she wondered numbly.

'Of course, that Khadir is a thief, but he's a smart thief. Obviously André wanted her badly, so he paid the price. In any event, as part of his property, she naturally came to me after his death. I was delighted when I finally found her. André had excellent taste.'

'*D'accord*,' Charles said softly. 'I agree.'

A shudder passed through Yasmin. Charles's privileged upbringing would never allow him to see her in the same way again, she thought miserably. He would probably lose whatever interest he'd had in her. He would detest her. He'd only be able to see her as a prostitute, a little whore with upwardly mobile social pretensions. Tears began to well in her eyes, blurring her vision and making the room waver in a surrealistic haze. Or worse, he'd stay around because the whole idea would be so titillating.

She wished she could move, say something, do something to make it all stop. She knew somewhere in the depths of her feelings that she should get angry, make a scene, drive Hassan away. But it was as if she were filled with lead and her jaw wired shut. She could neither move nor speak. Besides, it was already too late. Why bother? The damage was done. She would have told him the whole truth eventually, but when it would be easier for Charles to deal with. Not now, her mind screamed. Not now. But the reality was inescapable, and she couldn't do a thing about it.

Then Charles spoke. 'Fascinating story, wasn't it? As you probably remember, I was living here when all that happened.' Charles took another sip of his drink. He set his glass down carefully on the table. 'My father was in charge of the Tangier branch. Why, I even remember

410

how much Yasmin cost. Seventy-five thousand francs, *oui*? But worth every sou. And André had to pay in Kruggerands, wasn't it? All fascinating, *certainement*, but again, ancient history.'

'It certainly is.' Hassan said engagingly. 'And history *does* have a tendency to repeat itself, doesn't it? Now maybe I should take little Yasmin home, so she won't keep repeating her own history.'

'I wouldn't dream of it,' Charles said with a broad smile. But Yasmin could feel his muscles tensing. 'I was looking forward to taking her home myself.'

'I'm sure you were.' Hassan's voice had suddenly changed from a purr to a hiss. He stood abruptly, shoving the chair back onto the dance floor. His tall body, with its broad shoulders and slim hips, seemed to loom over the table. 'Well, just this once. But return her when you're through. Preferably undamaged.'

'Actually,' Charles said softly, 'I think I'll keep her . . . it looks to me as if she needs protection from slime like you. Now, leave before I get angry.'

Hassan laughed, but there was no humor in it. 'Suit yourself. But you'll be sorry.'

He backed away from them, and weaving slightly, strode away from the table. Yasmin watched miserably as he quickly took the stone steps out of the supper club two at a time and disappeared.

There was a short silence, then Charles said, '*Très intéressant*. I get the feeling that man is jealous. What do you think?'

But Yasmin didn't answer. She put her head down on her folded arms and sobbed quietly. What an awful scene. What a sad ending to such a perfect day.

Charles put his arms around her and slowly raised her chin so she couldn't help but look at his face. 'Are you really upset?' he asked with a tender smile.

'Of course I'm upset,' Yasmin said, nodding. 'I wouldn't, certainly, ask you to keep seeing me under the circumstances. But I did have a lovely time with you. I want you to know that.'

'What are you talking about? That psychopath? Why should anything he just said have anything to do with you and me?'

'Well, he told you about me, and I suppose that's enough to make anyone want to end this relationship. It's a little hard to take.'

'Of course it's hard to take, Yasmin. But not for me – for you. I always knew about it, but you're the one who lived through it. I'm just glad you managed to emerge in one piece.'

Yasmin watched incredulously as Charles waved at the waiter to bring the check.

'*Alors*, why don't we continue talking about this somewhere else? You've had a livelier evening than I'd planned. I'm only sorry that what he said upset you so much.'

'It upsets me that I'm going to lose you.'

'Look, Yasmin, I love you. I've loved you for a long time, now. André confided a great deal in my father. I knew everything about you before I fell in love with you. It didn't particularly bother me then, and it certainly doesn't bother me now.'

'That's very nice of you to say, Charles,' Yasmin said, standing up. 'But you don't have to. I understand.'

'No, you don't. Why do you think I've been so careful around you? Why do you think I didn't try to seduce you back in Paris? Do you think I did that because I didn't like you? Wasn't attracted to you? If so, you're missing the whole picture. I know what you've been through, and I know you think no one will like you for yourself. I decided to grind my teeth and wait for you to fall in love with me. I admit I jumped the gun a little today, but at least you didn't scream and run.'

'So now I love you, but do you love me is the question presently on the floor.'

Charles followed her out of the club. 'Maybe you don't believe me right now, but I'm sure that after twenty or thirty years you will, so I'm not worried. Why should you be worried?'

His face had such a likable, charming look to it, that Yasmin finally had to smile. She wondered whether it looked strange to him to see her laughing while tears were running down her cheeks.

Burying his face in her neck, he bit her lightly, and she clung to him, feeling better. It was almost as if the scene in the club had never taken place.

'Did you really know all about me?' she asked.

'*Bien sûr*. That was one of the reasons I wanted to meet you, I'll admit. But once I met you, I discovered you were completely different from what I'd expected. That put me off for a while. But then I got to know you, and you turned out to be even better than the fantasies. So you see, I win all the way around. I had a delicious sexual fantasy for a while, but when I finally got the chance to validate my fantasies, I found the reality to be even more delightful.'

They kissed again, then got in the car and drove up Old Mountain Road. But Yasmin was not completely relaxed. How had Hassan known she was in Tangier? What was he doing here? Which also raised the question of why Charles had come too. She knew of course, that his explanation was a good one. But still . . . the merging of all the events was nearly unbelievable.

And Hassan. Did he know what she planned to do? Had he somehow figured out that she was prepared to overrule his authority? Or had Charles told him what she said over the telephone before she left?

'Charles, did you tell Hassan I was planning to run the business when I returned?'

'I mentioned that you felt you were ready,' he said, not paying attention to the import of her words. 'Yes. When

413

I called and told him you'd cancelled the meeting, I said you were rescheduling for next week. Why do you ask?'

'Curious. I wonder what brings him here.'

'Well, he does still manage all the mining interests, you know. He's probably on business.'

'I wonder . . .' Yasmin said, her voice trailing off. She also wondered whether there was any connection between the two men. After all, Charles and Hassan both wanted her to go public, and her announcement to Charles the previous day would have been startling to both of them. But before she could question Charles further, the car drove past the big gates of the villa and stopped. Charles opened the door for her, and caught her in his arms in a kiss that drove all thoughts out of her head.

'Come,' he said against her hair. 'I want to let your hair down and run my fingers through it.' He began pulling the pins and the pearls out one by one. He dropped them into his jacket pocket and shook the silken tendrils until they hung down her back to her hips. 'Did I ever tell you how I feel about your hair?' he murmured. '*Mon Dieu*, I could wrap myself up in it, it's so long.'

With his arms aroung her waist and his fingers tangled in the slippery coils, he led her into the house.

In Yasmin's room they fell onto the big bed together. Charles rolled onto his back, pulling Yasmin on top of him. He reached down until he held her hips firmly in his broad hands, then dragged her up onto the bulge between his legs. Tilting his hips slightly, he rocked her gently against him.

'How would you like to talk about the first thing that comes up?'

'Fine with me,' Yasmin whispered softly as she placed her mouth on his, savoring his soft, mobile lips once again. They parted as her tongue slowly, delicately tasted first one corner of his mouth, then the other. He hooked his feet under hers and slowly spread her legs apart, then pulled her even more firmly against him. As he gently

414

rocked her, his hands slipped up and around her mouth, his fingers shaping her lips into a round *O* a moment before his tongue gently went to work. In rhythm with his hips, it darted slowly in and out of her mouth, licking her top lip in a rasping way that felt just like . . . she couldn't believe it. His flickering tongue began to draw circles on her swollen lips, darting, probing, caressing . . .

Oh, Allah, she thought. This feels just like . . . it's what his mouth does to me down there . . .

Combined with the smooth undulating pressure, she felt the tension begin to build and coil and twist through her. Yasmin moaned, and her body picked up on a rhythm of its own that matched his but took it one step further. His tongue continued to paint rivers of sensation on her pursed lips, making her feel as if his mouth were on another part of her body altogether. Then the sensations took over, piercing through her with swordlike swiftness. The tension built until it suddenly released itself in a flood of roaring sound that threatened to engulf her, and then finally did.

Limp, she fell against him as he gently stroked her back through the material of her dress. Then he shifted slightly, moving her to one side. Her head lolled back as she gazed at him with limpid brown eyes filled with love and awe. Slowly he raised her hand to his lips and kissed her palm. She shuddered quietly.

His tongue flickered across the buttery skin, then he took her thumb into his mouth, first the tip, then he slowly slid his lips down until they engulfed it completely, sucking and nibbling at her flesh. She moaned softly as she watched his melting gaze on her face. He slid his hand down and reached into the top of her dress. His hand cupped her breast, then found the hard little nipple. He pinched it between his fingers, then tugged at it gently, each tug sending a shockwave down to the pit of her stomach.

Rolling her onto her back, he lowered his head to the tightly crinkled rosebud and sucked it into his mouth hard. As he sucked, he pulled her dress up over her thighs until his fingers slithered into the throbbing slit between her legs. Parting the flesh, he looked for and found the hard little pearl that impatiently thrust up. He let his finger rasp back and forth across it as she arched her body high to meet his teasing, twinkling, gliding touches.

'Oh, please come inside me,' she whispered, her hands caught in his silken blond hair, pulling his head up to her mouth.

But he didn't. Extricating himself from her grasp, he pulled her dress higher, until her soft belly was exposed to his view. Dipping his tongue into her belly button, he traced a slow path down to her swollen cleft with his mouth. Opening her wide with his fingers, he grasped her swollen flesh between his lips and pulled, sucking at her until she screamed with wild abandon. Hurtling back over the brink between sanity and madness, she swirled off into indescribable pleasure once again.

Just as her shudders began to subside, Charles rolled off her. After quickly unzipping his trousers, he placed his hands under her knees and lifted her legs up until her knees rested close to her chest. He thrust blindly into her quivering body and she moaned with pleasure as he filled her solidly and began to thrust with practiced movements. It was as if he were inside her head, knowing exactly what rhythm and pressure to exert. She felt the pleasure begin to build again, and as Charles began to breathe more raggedly, too, she felt herself peak and then fall over the edge with him.

'*Écoutes*, Yasmin, I have to go back to Paris today, and I'd really rather you came with me,' Charles said the next morning after breakfast.

'I *must* finish this inventory, Charles. It will only take two more days at the most. Then I'll be back.'

'You don't have to do the inventory, you know.' Charles said. 'Under the circumstances, perhaps we can see a way clear to lending you – '

'Under what circumstances?' Yasmin asked, suddenly looking at him. She was shocked. 'You mean now that I've gone to bed with you, the bank – or more exactly the president of the bank – might approve my loan?'

She could hardly believe that Charles meant that. She watched his clear blue eyes carefully and waited for his answer. It was a little slow in coming.

'Well, I meant that since we will be married soon, perhaps the fact that you're overextended won't carry such weight. After all, you'll have not only your own holdings as collateral, you'll have *me* as collateral too,' Charles answered, flashing his charming smile. 'I know that sounds as if . . . but I didn't mean it that way, *vraiment*.'

Yasmin could only look at him, wondering why his remarks bothered her. True, it wouldn't be so strange if she were his wife, but did he really mean that he was going to marry her? And what of the vineyards? Did that mean that he now considered them to be almost *his* property? Was that why the loan would be forthcoming?

Before she could put all her questions into words, Charles took her in his arms. 'I don't want you to stay there alone. I want you to come back with me because I'm worried about you.'

'Why are you worried? Salima and Zayd are here. Nothing will happen to me.'

'I'm worried about Hassan.'

'He was horrible last night, but I thought we decided not to worry about him. He's probably visiting his family and sulking. I'll call you tonight, all right?'

Charles was silent for a moment, a frown creasing his brow. Then he shook his head at her.

'*Ça va*. But don't forget. I'll be waiting to hear from you.'

As they walked together to the car, Charles looked unhappy. 'Now promise me you will call.'

'I promise,' Yasmin said as he got in the car. She leaned her elbows on the window and stuck her head inside to kiss him on the ear. She could see out the other window to where Salima was standing by the side of the house. She had a watering can in her hands and seemed mesmerized by a little cat playing at her feet with the broken blossom from one of the hyacinth bushes. The morning sun slanted crazily across its silky fur.

Yasmin again was struck by how handsome Charles was. The sun glanced through the car window and lit his hair like gold. His perfect profile was almost heartbreaking, she thought, as she watched him lean forward to start the car. He looked so sure of himself, so perfectly aristocratic. He was a man who had always had everything and always would. She wondered whether it had ever occurred to him that she might not marry him? He had waited nine or ten months to take her to bed, but during that time, did he ever think that perhaps she wouldn't want him once he'd declared himself?

She wondered now whether or not she wanted the money for her expansion to come from Charles and his bank, and said, 'You know, I am planning to sell the villa – especially if I don't have the money I need. If the paintings and antiques aren't enough, I still have the real estate.'

'But why sell it?' Charles said, looking at her sharply. 'There is no need.'

'I don't like this villa that much,' Yasmin answered, looking back into the garden. The kitten was rolling around on the ground, trying to grasp its furry tail between its chubby paws. 'I'm not even sure I like Tangier enough to want to come back after this. But I'll see later.'

'We'll talk about all that when you get back to Paris,' Charles said. 'Just hurry and come back. There are other things I want from you too.'

Yasmin felt an extraordinary shudder ripple through her stomach, and she stood up straight. 'You'd better leave, if you're going to,' she said lightly. Events were moving too quickly, and she needed time alone to make sure she felt right about them. 'At this rate neither of us will get any work done.'

Sitting at the library desk a short while later, she wondered why the expansion was so important to her – and that she accomplish it her way. Why she couldn't just sit back and let the vineyard take care of itself and let Hassan run things? That would keep him happy, and she could get involved in something else. Like her relationship with Charles. Why was she so obsessed with building it up and making it something it never was before? Was it because that was what André had wanted to do? But André was dead. Now it was what she wanted to do that mattered, not whatever André had wanted.

She thought about what Hassan had said to her that night so long ago in Geneva. He had talked about obsession then. He had told her that being the object of someone else's obsession had profound effects. No one ever dealt with that part of it, or ever talked about the impact of obsession on the object. They only talked about what it felt like to be obsessed. But in fact Yasmin realized that Hassan had been right. He was in many ways a very sensitive and intelligent man. Then again, no one ever said he wasn't. It was just that he was so . . . so . . . Yasmin couldn't put what she was thinking into words.

Last night he'd been acting like a man who was obsessed. Was he obsessed with her in the same way that André had been? she wondered. And was Hassan right about André? Had André really been obsessed with her? Or was that merely Hassan's projection? There was always that way of explaining his embarrassing speech after dinner.

But Yasmin had a feeling that she wasn't the object of Hassan's obsession. Perhaps she was somehow related to it, but he'd always managed to be so controlled around her. Certainly people who were suffering from obsessions sometimes lost control. She recalled that he'd been controlled when he found her in Oskar's office, controlled when he made love to her the first time and every other time after that, controlled the whole time she'd been in England. Six years was a long time. He'd even been controlled the last time they'd been alone together in the car. Hassan had been interested in her pleasure, but not his own. Yasmin realized that she wasn't dealing with an adolescent, but she had been surprised that he hadn't taken her in the backseat without regard to the chauffeur. Charles would have.

No. Hassan exhibited far too much control around her. He seemed perfectly content to run her affairs and the business of the vineyard . . .

Yasmin stood up so quickly, she knocked over the chair she was sitting in.

The vineyard! Of course. Hassan was definitely obsessed, but not with her. He was obsessed with the vineyard! He wanted it for himself! And he was working to get it every waking minute. Suddenly it was all clear. That was what this was all about. That was what it had been about from the moment he'd found her in Switzerland.

When André died, he died without any other family. He died leaving a massive estate with no one who would logically inherit it all. Except Hassan. This was the life Hassan had grown to love, and need. Not Yasmin. Once the will had been read and it became clear that Yasmin – a little Arab girl from a whorehouse in the Suk – was going to get it all, Hassan took the next best course. He

420

tried to get Yasmin to marry him because by controlling her, he would get control of the vineyards.

For a second she wondered why Hassan had even bothered to look for her in the first place. After, she'd already conveniently disappeared. But, of course, it wasn't up to him. The lawyers, Messieurs Fauquier, Renan, and La Tour, must have been the ones in charge of finding her. Hassan wouldn't have bothered if it had been up to him alone. But when he finally found her, why hadn't he deceived her? After all, Yasmin reasoned, if he wanted it all that badly, he could easily have manipulated the facts. He could have gotten her to sign away the inheritance, and she would not have known what she was doing.

But he couldn't do that, either. He discovered she was surrounded by rich and powerful friends, she told herself. She wasn't just drudging away in a lonely job with no friends to speak of and no one to advise her. No, unfortunately for Hassan, she was not someone who could be bought off. So he had done the next best thing. He'd tried to control her sexually. He'd brought her to Paris and seduced her, showered her with expensive gifts.

Anyone else would probably have succumbed easily during such an onslaught from such a powerful and attractive man. Instead, Yasmin had decided to run off to England and the safety of school. And Hassan had let her go. In his supreme confidence, he had assumed she would come crawling back to him. Things just hadn't worked out that way.

Now Hassan was still as far from his goal as ever – and seeing that Charles was in the picture, he might feel pushed to do something extreme. Yasmin's mind raced along the same track, and she realized that if Hassan couldn't get the vineyards and the title and the money through marriage to her, then he'd have to try another way. Hassan was brilliant, and he was a shark. Whatever way he chose, it would be subtle and clever and it might work. And now he'd have to move fast.

Yasmin sat back down and tried to catch her breath. She looked out the window, almost expecting everything outside to be changed by what she'd just realized. But everything was exactly the same. The day was getting hotter. There was not even the slightest breeze to riffle through the eucalyptus leaves. The mother cat walked elegantly across the driveway with a fat mouse in her jaws. The kitten followed her, bounding and leaping at the shadows.

Maybe that was the reason Hassan didn't want her too closely involved in the business at first. But then he changed his mind, she remembered. He was going to let her handle the expansion all by herself, wasn't he? Or was he? In fact there was no expansion because Hassan said there was no money. But Hassan was the one who suggested going public. That certainly didn't sound like the actions of a man who wanted to get control of the vineyard for himself. Going public was tantamount to giving it away.

Dead end.

But wait. Yasmin had a sudden, awful thought. She ran upstairs and got the books out of her luggage. Carefully opening them up on the desk in the library, she went back over the figures one last time. If what she thought was correct, then she might be able to find some evidence here.

She waved away Salima's offer to make her something to eat. Instead she spent the entire day comparing the figures from the last seven years against those entered during the time André controlled the firm. But this time she did it differently. She didn't look at the bottom line, instead she compared each expenditure against its counterpart and each area of profit against those shown in the later years.

By evening the pattern had become clear to her. At

first it looked just like sloppy accounting, but soon another picture began to form. Hassan had been systematically manipulating the numbers so that what should have been entered as a profit, had not. It was very carefully done. But that, in itself, was surprising. It would be much more understandable if the money were gone. But it wasn't. It was inexplicable.

Then she thought again. Hassan had done it to keep her from finding out that she really did have operating capital. He wanted her to go public for reasons of his own. These books were being kept for Yasmin, and there was probably another set that was correct. Charles might be able to help her reconstruct what was really going on, she thought, her mind flickering back to that night when she'd come to the office late and found Hassan working at her desk. In her innocence she had assumed he was helping her find money for her expansion. In fact he'd been fixing it so she'd think there was none.

Yasmin assumed her suspicions had to be correct, or at least partially correct. But where had the money gone?

Then another thought dawned on her, and its brilliance was breathtaking: Hassan was planning to force her to go public. Then, once the stock was publicly offered, he could buy a controlling interest for himself. What she hadn't seen, and now realized, was that he had been planning to use the company's own money to do it. His plan was one that had two diabolically clever parts. He would buy her business from her, using her own money to do it.

Yasmin had to smile. It certainly was a clever plan. Even in desperation Hassan had managed to come up with something that was almost foolproof.

Stretching wearily, she got up and looked out the window. Oskar was going to be upset when he found out she didn't have to sell the Saint-Clair collection after all. Walking slowly across the room, she felt her toes dig into the delicious silkiness of the Persian rug. She wanted to talk to Charles and tell him what she'd figured out.

Since it was so late, she had no trouble getting a line to Paris.

'*Chérie*! I'm glad you called finally,' Charles said. He sounded distant, but Yasmin wasn't certain if it was the connection or her imagination. 'How's it going, *mon petit chou*?'

'The inventory is done,' Yasmin said. 'But there's something far more important that I've discovered – '

'You have found a Matisse in the closet,' Charles said.

'No, something serious,' Yasmin continued. 'It's about the vineyard accounts. I brought the figures with me. When I was going over them in Paris, I thought I'd discovered discrepancies, and my suspicions were correct. Charles, Hassan has been fixing the books so it appears there are no funds. In fact there are – '

'I doubt that, Yasmin,' Charles said quickly. 'I have my own analysts at the bank who check those books very carefully. We do that with all accounts we handle . . . it's not as simple as you think.'

'Believe me, Charles, I've looked at them, and it's clever. You wouldn't see it with a cursory examination.'

'Ah, Yasmin.' Charles laughed. 'Admit that you're looking for excuses not to go public, *n'est-ce pas*? You can't accuse someone of fraud just because they suggested a perfectly logical course of action to you that you don't wish to follow.' Charles sounded mildly irritated, and his irritation filtered through to Yasmin.

'It isn't as if Hassan was the only one who suggested it,' Yasmin said. 'You agreed with him. I thought you'd be interested in hearing what I've discovered.'

'I am,' Charles said. 'I just think you've made a mistake. That's why I am withholding judgment.'

Hearing the way Charles was talking to her, Yasmin went from irritated to genuinely angry. Made a mistake? Didn't he understand that she wasn't just some little girl who was looking at these books? She saw that he couldn't grasp her background and her education any better than anyone else could. Not only was she an analyst in her own right, the books she was examining were the books of her own firm. And she, not Hassan, was the bank's client.

'I'd be willing to venture that I have enough training to determine what's going on in my own company. More than you do, Charles,' she said.

'Now don't get so upset, *ma chérie*,' Charles said placatingly. 'I'm not calling your judgment into question – '

'The hell you're not!' Yasmin snapped. 'You're talking to me just the way Hassan talks to me. You don't seem inclined to believe that I can function quite well in a business that is my own. You also can't grasp the fact that I'm actually very good at what I do! All you think I'm good for is – '

'But you are good for that, too, *mon ami*,' Charles said. 'Now listen to me for a minute – '

'I think I'd rather not,' Yasmin said, her fury mounting. 'I can think very nicely for myself . . . and by the way, thanks for a lovely evening, but don't think for one minute that that evening buys you anything!'

'But I didn't – '

'Oh, yes, you did,' Yasmin said. 'I don't need your bank, I don't need your loan, and I don't need you either.' And with that, she slammed the phone down on the hook.

She was trembling with anger, and it took a while for the thumping in her chest to subside. Just then the phone rang. She knew it was Charles calling back to apologize, but she didn't want his apologies. He, of all people, should have understood her. But even when faced with her queries, he couldn't wait ten seconds to try and convince her that she was wrong, to try and prove that Hassan was incapable of such treachery. He would rather stick up for Hassan than he would for her. So much for that, she thought bleakly. You're on your own, Yasmin.

The ringing finally stopped.

Yasmin walked slowly to the long French windows and looked out. The cypresses silhouetted against the purple sky again recalled to her the awful night she'd fled Tangier. Some things hadn't changed at all, she thought. Hassan was still out there somewhere, waiting to take away everything that André had wanted to give her. But this time it wasn't going to be so easy for him. This time, he'd fail because she was prepared.

'I see you've been doing your homework,' came a voice from behind her.

Yasmin jumped as if shot.

She spun around to see Hassan leaning indolently against the door. Just like the jungle animal he so resembled, he'd come up on her without making a sound.

'What are you doing in my house?' she said, trying to marshal her reactions. He'd startled her, but that didn't have to put her at a disadvantage.

His black eyes slowly ran from her feet to her face as a predatory smile came over his lips. 'I think it's time we had a serious talk, little desert flower.' he said. Than he gracefully pulled his shoulder away from the doorjamb and started toward her.

25

Hassan moved, catlike, across the carpet to the windows. As he passed her, she thought she caught a faint whiff of alcohol mixed with his scent. He stood with his back to her for a moment, looking out across the moonlit grounds.

'Aren't you going to offer me a brandy?' he asked, his voice harsh and grating. 'It's considered the polite thing to do.'

'Is this a social call, Hassan?' Yasmin answered coolly. Unconsciously she had moved behind a chair, putting a large piece of furniture between herself and his intrusive presence. 'And don't you think you've had enough?'

'That's for me to decide, isn't it?' He whirled around to face her, and her breath caught in her throat. His heavy lidded eyes raked over her, then his facial muscles tightened as he scowled again. 'Don't worry. I don't have the same problem with alcohol you think the rest of our countrymen have . . . or the same problem with anything for that matter. At least not from now on.'

'What's that supposed to mean? You want to discuss your problems? Is that why you came here in the middle of the night?' Yasmin glanced quickly at the grandfather clock standing in the corner of the library. 'It's eleven o'clock, you know.'

'I came to discuss something far more important to both of us.' A slow, cruel smile split his face, and Yasmin's fear increased. 'The brandy, please?' he said.

Yasmin moved cautiously to the cabinet and poured a small amount of the golden liquor into a glass.

'You can do better than that, can't you?' His mouth curved up into a mocking leer, and she felt she had no choice but to fill it.

As she handed him the glass, she looked into his eyes and had the same sensation she'd had in the supper club – of being sucked into a black whirlpool, an evil abyss. She quickly pulled herself together, and the anger she'd felt the night before began to return and build. She was glad, since her anger gave her the strength to confront him, to rid herself of his influence on her life once and for all.

'Hassan, you're right. We have much to talk about. And especially now – '

'Yes, especially now. And how fitting that it should take place in this library. It's where I first saw you. It will be as if no time has passed at all. We'll just start as if the intervening years hadn't happened.'

'No, we won't. Those years *have* happened, and not only that, I know what you've been doing.'

'Of course you do. But that has no bearing on what's about to happen.'

'I'm afraid it does. You've been lying to me, trying to cheat me, Hassan. You want to steal my inheritance, and as far as I'm concerned this relationship – what there was of it – and your tenure as director of the Saint-Clair vineyards is over.'

But Hassan didn't look shocked at all. Yasmin felt a quiver of nervous apprehension course down her back. Was he going to deny it? Why was he wearing that awful smile?

'I know you discovered what I was doing, my dear. I realized it the minute I found that the books were gone. Then when I went to look for you, you were gone too, Charles told me you'd cancelled the meeting with the lawyers, and suddenly he was also gone. It didn't take me long to put it all together. But I'm so glad you chose to come to Tangier at this particular juncture. It helps me more than you know. I'm going to have you and the Saint-Clair vineyards after all, and there's nothing you can do to stop me.'

'You're wrong, Hassan,' Yasmin hissed. 'What you've done is commit fraud. You've been embezzling company money, and that's a crime!'

'I've committed no crime. The money is still there, my dear. I did nothing but prepare an extra set of books for you, and they may very well disappear shortly.'

'What difference does it make if they disappear? You still report to me and my lawyers. If I can't make criminal charges hold against you, I can still fire you.'

'You can't fire me if you're married to me.' Hassan started to chuckle as he took a long sip of his drink, and said, 'This is excellent brandy.'

'But I won't marry you, and there's no way you can force me to.' Yasmin was outraged at his peremptory tone, which made his words even more aggravating.

'Think again, Yasmin. You're here in Morocco, and you're Moroccan.'

'You're a fool, Hassan.'

'You're not listening to me, my little flower. I can abduct you and marry you in the traditional way of our people, then I can keep you indefinitely in my family's house. Why, I even took the precaution of bringing a gun with me. The Polisario guerrillas are moving in the area, and who knows what might happen late at night in those passes.'

Yasmin realized there was some truth to his words. This was Morocco. This was a place where anything could happen, a place where human beings could be bought and sold, where people disappeared, where women were married without their consent, where in the remote regions the law of the sheik was the only law there was. And Hassan was the son of a sheik. That gave him rights and privileges in this country that she didn't have. She had a sudden horrible picture of being kept a prisoner in some dirty-walled palace in the south, in the desert.

'You wouldn't!' she shouted.

'Ah, but I *would*! As a matter of fact it's so dangerous

429

that you might even disappear. Those rebels are quite vicious. I know them well, you see, so I know exactly what dangerous killers they can be – especially when paid well.'

Yasmin could see the fury on his face and the murder in his heart. He was so close to losing everything he'd schemed for, she thought, that he believed he had nothing to lose.

'No one would believe a staged kidnapping or murder like that,' she snapped. 'You'd be caught.'

'Oh, they'd believe it if I were shot trying to rescue you. It would be a terrible tragedy, of course, but at least there'd be someone who could take over the Saint-Clair holdings – once I'd recovered from my injuries, naturally.'

'You would kill me just to be in charge of a vineyard?' Yasmin was incredulous. 'You have money and position here. Why would you want to – '

'Money and position and power here are nothing as far as I'm concerned. Power over what? Goats? Hills and sand?' He spat. 'No, I've always wanted those vineyards. I've always wanted everything that André had, in fact. It represents something to me, something you might even understand. You see, when I was at Harvard, I learned many things. But the most important thing I learned was that no matter how smart I was, no matter how educated – in the eyes of those people, I was nothing but an uncultured barbarian. They never let a chance go by to let me know that they really thought of me as a filthy desert rat, despite my father's wealth, which made me richer than many of them. So I vowed to beat them at their own game.'

'André never felt that way about you.'

'Didn't he? He didn't even realize when he was doing it. Do you know, he never invited me to his precious club to drink gin and tonics with his other friends. Bastards! But it doesn't matter anymore. He's dead, and I'm alive. And I intend to have his vineyards. They'll be huge once

I've put your clever plans into effect. I've meant to thank you for all the research and effort you put in, laying the groundwork. You were so thorough, I probably won't need any more input from you at all.'

'You wouldn't!' Yasmin was outraged.

'Ah, but I would. And if you're nice to me, I might even let you live to see how well your plans have worked. It would be no trouble at all. I could always arrange for your secret return. Of course, I can't vouch for what my friends might do to you while you were in their tender care. But you're a sensuous little thing. You enjoy pleasure and you give pleasure. You could certainly handle it for a few months. It is, after all, what Khadir trained you to do.'

'Hassan, you're sick, do you know that?' Yasmin started to edge toward the door. If she could somehow get near the bell rope, perhaps Zayd would come to her rescue, or even Salima.

'Wouldn't it be easier just to marry me of your own free will, my little flower?' Hassan smiled slowly and began to move toward her. Yasmin's heart sank as she realized he was blocking the door. His forward movement backed her up against one of the leather armchairs. Before she could catch herself, she tripped and fell into it.

'Yes, I think it would be more comfortable if you sat down,' he continued menacingly. Glinting lights flashed in his coal-black eyes as he crouched in front of her. He placed one hand on either side of her on the arms of the chair. Imprisoned, she could only stare back at him.

'Now tell me, little one, why do you give me such a hard time? Why can't you be nicer to me, eh? Ever since I met you, you've bristled every time I come near you. What did I do to make you behave that way? I've searched my mind trying to figure out what it is, but for the life of me, I can't decide where the difficulty lies. I've been nothing but kind and helpful. I've always considered what you want. You don't give me a chance, do you? For a while there in Paris I thought you'd come around, but you backed off again, and I haven't been able to get through to you since. What is it?'

Yasmin stared into his eyes, wondering how to answer. She felt the heat of his body and smelled the male scent of him mixed with cologne and brandy. The combined odors sent her mind reeling for a moment, but with an effort she focused on him and took a deep breath. Perhaps if she could talk to him, put him off somehow, stall for time . . .

'Why can't you understand?' she said. 'I want to get away from my past, not wallow in it, and my past is all wrapped up with you. You're inextricably intertwined with the bad things that have happened to me. Don't you see? You are part of it . . .'

Hassan took one hand off the chair and clasped her small, bare foot. It was almost lost in his broad hand as he caressed her instep lightly with his thumb. She shivered involuntarily as a crawling sensation of disgust crept up her leg. Feeling the reverberations and misinterpreting them, Hassan smiled wickedly.

'You see, you could easily learn to like living with me,' he said softly. 'I understand what you're like. Let me show you and remind you how easy you are for me to please.'

Yasmin opened her mouth to scream, but Hassan moved like lightning. His mouth came down on hers, crushing her lips against her teeth painfully. What emerged was a muffled moan. She had forgotten how powerful he could be. Oh, Allah, she thought desperately, what is happening? Moving quickly and with almost inhuman strength, Hassan pulled her out of the chair, and in doing so, folded her arms behind her back. She was pinned against him as he covered her mouth with his, holding her so tightly with one arm that she couldn't breathe.

With the other arm he reached around into his jacket pocket and pulled out a long rag. Then he lowered himself down to the floor, still holding her. She tried to fight against him, but realized it was impossible. When she was down on the carpet, Hassan swung one of his legs over her and sat on top of her pelvis, never taking his mouth from hers. He pinned her arms under her back and held them there with his knees. Bringing the rag up to her chin, he quickly took his lips away from hers.

She gasped, sucking air into her starved lungs, and tried to scream. But the rag was instantly stuffed into her open mouth, then Hassan wound it behind her neck and knotted it.

Yasmin's eyes were opened wide with fright. The whites rolled at him, but he smiled at her.

'Please don't be so frightened,' he said almost apologetically. 'I said all those things before because I thought I could scare you into coming with me quietly. But unfortunately you are very stubborn. I promise I won't hurt you.'

He sat back and watched her for a few seconds. She thought he was trying to figure out what she was thinking.

'I would take the rag off your mouth if I knew you wouldn't scream, but I think your stubborn streak is even stronger than your intelligent streak. Too bad, because you're going to be uncomfortable for a while. But that's just how it's going to be, I'm afraid. I don't trust you to be quiet. I'm going to take you home with me. That will give us both time to think this thing out.'

He sat there, watching her. Then he touched one finger to the tip of her breast, drawing light circles around her nipple. He watched her expression, but Yasmin only blinked and shuddered. The effects of the alcohol seemed to have disappeared. He seemed to know exactly what he was doing and how to frighten her.

'It isn't just the vineyard I want, you know. You are the most exciting woman I've ever had. Even your friend

Hillary – who is very talented in bed, I might add – is nothing compared to you.'

He caressed her breast lightly through the layered robes she wore, then pushed aside the sheer material and moved his hand up to her throat, tracing her windpipe with his fingertips. His eyes sparked as he smiled at her again.

'After all, who knows? We'll steal some time and perhaps you'll discover in me what I've already discovered in you, but first things first . . .'

Glancing around him to make sure that the house was still quiet, his tone changed from sensuously soft to businesslike. 'First we're going to leave here.'

He stood up, lifting his weight off Yasmin's torso, and she swiftly turned and tried to roll out of his reach. Freeing her arms, she flipped onto her stomach and tried to get up, but her legs were trapped in the twisted fabric of her robes.

'No, no, little one. I think perhaps you aren't convinced of my good intentions yet,' Hassan said soothingly. 'That means I will have to tie you more securely, doesn't it? But I've thought of that too.'

He reached under his jacket and pulled out a coil of fine nylon rope. Yasmin tried desperately to pull the gag off her face and scream at the same time, but Hassan quickly pulled both her arms back behind her and tied her hands together. When the knot was secure, he wrapped it around her waist, flipping her onto her back, then pulled the remaining rope down to her ankles. Those he bound securely while Yasmin twisted violently. She was trying to make it as hard as possible for him.

Her eyes darted around the room, searching for a piece of furniture she could knock over to make some noise. Unfortunately the only thing nearby was the leather armchair, and that was too heavy to move.

'Oh, Yasmin, don't fight me so hard,' he whispered. 'It doesn't have to be this way, you know. We could have

434

everything together. But you are hardheaded. Perhaps that's half your charm – but only in social situations. It's not so charming right at this moment.'

With that he picked her up and carried her easily over to the French windows. He opened one quietly, stepped out onto the terrace, then turned to close it behind him. Yasmin arched hard and tried to kick in a pane of the glass with her bound feet. But feeling her abrupt movement, Hassan quickly moved her out of reach of the glass.

'That wasn't a good idea,' he snarled. 'If you continue to fight this way, I'm going to have to knock you out. I would hate to mark that pretty chin, but it's up to you.'

Yasmin tried to snarl back at him, but it was useless. The gag was too secure, and she started to choke on her own saliva.

Holding her securely, Hassan crossed the lawn. There was a small wooden door next to the iron gates, embedded in the high wall of the garden, hidden behind the cypress trees. Yasmin had never known of its existence. The door itself was arched, and made of heavy, iron-studded wood. Hassan opened it with one hand and slipped through.

As soon as they were out on the road, he looked both ways then trotted across to the edge of the cliff. There was a rockstrewn path running alongside the straight drop to the beach. The moon was high and full, and Yasmin could see the foamy white breakers creaming in to the shore down below.

The muffled pounding sounded ominous, and she wondered what he was going to do with her, where he was going to take her. There was no traffic on Old Mountain Road, no one to see a big man carrying a struggling woman to the edge of the cliff. Whatever chance she thought she had of being saved quickly evaporated, at least for the time being. Yasmin stopped struggling and lay quietly in Hassan's arms.

'That's much better,' he whispered softly. 'You

435

wouldn't want me to drop you right now. It is treacherous here.'

Yasmin kept very still, trying not to upset Hassan's balance. She was uncomfortable, and his arm held her too tightly for normal breathing. Since her mouth was gagged, she had to concentrate all her attention on breathing through her nose, which was pinched with terror.

Walking quickly along the cliff, Hassan carried her for what seemed about five minutes. When he stopped she could see in the moonlight that a Land Rover was parked half hidden in a close stand of cypress trees.

By this time the ropes binding her wrists and ankles had pulled tightly, chafing her skin. Hassan opened the back door of the jeep with one hand and carefully placed her on the floor, lying on her side. He stuffed two duffel bags next to her to keep her from falling. When she instinctively cringed at the touch of his fingers, he chuckled at her reaction. Yasmin fought back her tears, determined to keep him from seeing that she was terrified.

Yasmin heard his shoes crunching in the gravel, then the door slam as he got into the jeep. The engine started and they lurched into motion. Yasmin wondered how Hassan could be so calm while kidnapping her, and couldn't imagine that he believed he'd get away with it. Did he really think no one would look for her? Soon Charles, her lawyers, Oskar, or even Salima or Zayd, would notice her absence. She also wondered where he could be taking her, but didn't have long to wonder. The rocking motion of the jeep soon stopped, and she managed to calm the lurching in her stomach as they skidded to a halt.

Hassan took out the duffel bags while Yasmin tried to get an idea of where they were and if any people were around. As he lifted her out, however, she saw they were in a wide open grassland. The moon was still high and the twinkling stars sparked coldly in the blue-black sky.

There wasn't enough light to see any particular landmarks, but enough of the blue-white moonlight to just make out a small plane standing on what appeared to be an abandoned tarmac. Her heart sank as she realized there was probably nothing but grass and a few shrubs for miles.

A shrill whistle split the air, startling her, and Hassan whistled back. She saw two men get out of the plane and walk toward them. Although she couldn't make out any details, she could see that they were wearing djellabas and white turbans. She suddenly realized that Hassan had not planned her abduction alone, and her fear grew as her meager hopes of escaping dwindled away.

Sensing for the first time how truly helpless she was, Yasmin turned her face to Hassan's chest as the tears rolled down her cheeks. The tears turned to sobs that shuddered through her as he placed her on the floor in the back of the plane then stuffed the duffel bags on either side of her.

There was a rapidfire exchange of Arabic in a dialect she couldn't quite follow. Then the two men, their blue robes looking like patches of emptiness under their faces, climbed into the cockpit. Hassan climbed in after them, and the plane's engine started. They taxied rapidly along the bumpy asphalt, the plane lifted off the ground with a sickening lurch, and they were airborne. It felt to Yasmin as if they were heading straight up. Then the plane veered, leveled off, and after a few bumps, settled into a smooth pattern.

She now doubted that she would ever get an opportunity to escape. A vision of what her life would be like crowded into her head, driving everything else out. The thought of being stuck forever with Hassan in Goulimine, his family's ancestral sheikdom, felt like a death sentence.

Yasmin closed her eyes and hot tears seeped out onto the duffel bag. She didn't care anymore what happened –

as long as it didn't hurt. She felt herself slowly withdrawing into deeper and deeper recesses of her psyche as she pulled herself away from the frightening events taking place. Everything she had previously considered important seemed to fade and then melt into thin air as the plane droned its way to whatever lay ahead.

The trip took a long time. After what seemed an hour and a half, she felt them losing altitude. The sensation made her nauseous, and she wished she could sit up and look out the window. Seconds later the plane bumped down and hopped a few times before they slowed down with alarming rapidity. Yasmin slid against the duffel bags and ended up jammed against the back of the seat where Hassan was sitting. Her arms hurt, and so did her shoulders. She was terribly thirsty, and starting to get hungry as well. The physical discomfort, rather than making her feel passive, however, suddenly made her angry.

She made a choking sound through the gag to get Hassan's attention. She had to get him to take the gag off so she could reason with him. At her strangled cry, Hassan turned around and looked at her thoughtfully. 'Actually,' he said, 'there is no longer any need to keep a gag on you. You can now scream all you like and it won't matter, will it?'

He leaned over and untied the knot that held the gag in place, then pulled the slimy mess out of her mouth. Yasmin tried to spit out the taste, but she had no saliva.

'Is that better?' Hassan asked, his tone so solicitous that it made her shiver.

It took a while for Yasmin to be able to speak. 'Hassan,' she snapped, 'I don't care what you have in mind for me, but if you don't give me something to drink and untie me soon, I'll . . . I'll . . .' But she couldn't think of any threats.

Hassan laughed, apparently figuring out her dilemma.

'I'll get you something to drink in half a second,' he said. 'But I can't untie you yet. Soon.'

A thin pale light was just breaking over the horizon. Yasmin thought it must be about four-thirty in the morning. It was now light enough to get a good look at the other two. As they climbed out of the cockpit Yasmin caught a glimpse of their hard, hawklike, sunbaked faces. These must be the hill men from around Goulimine, she decided. Their blue robes identified them. Known as the Blue Men of Goulimine because the indigo dye from the material rubbed off onto their faces and hands, they were fierce warriors. One of them looked about forty-five, and his beard, which should have been iron gray, was tinged with blue. Hassan got out behind them, and after gesturing toward the steeply rising hills, which were bathed in rosy-pink morning light, he turned his attention back to her.

She was aware of a strong, hot wind blowing hard against the plane. It rocked the light craft with its intensity, and she wasn't cheered by what it portended. Sandstorm, she thought, and the thought made her even thirstier.

'Hurry up,' she yelled, angry and frustrated.

The side of the plane opened and Hassan climbed in with a canteen. It looked like an army canteen, wrapped in olive-green material. He opened it, lifted her to a sitting position, and held it to her mouth. Yasmin drank greedily, then turned her head.

'Now what?' she asked. She felt dirty, aching, and full of venomous bad temper.

'Only a little farther,' Hassan said. 'Then you'll be home.'

'You may be home,' she snapped, 'but my home is in Paris . . . France. Heard of it?'

'Not anymore,' Hassan said with a nasty chuckle. Then he picked her up and carried her through the blowing wind to a jeep parked next to a small hut. The Blue Men

439

were waiting impassively. Yasmin squinted her eyes so she could look around without getting grains of sand in them. There wasn't another soul around. All she saw was sand, with some craggy dun-colored mountains in the distance. She was alone in the middle of a desert with Hassan and his two henchmen.

Hassan dropped her into the back of the jeep and covered her with a djellaba. He climbed in next to her and the jeep took off.

'I trust your ancestral home has internal plumbing,' she snapped. 'Or are you taking me to a tent?'

'Don't worry,' Hassan said, lazily running a finger under her chin. 'It has everything you'll ever need.'

'I doubt it,' Yasmin mumbled. She didn't like the implications of his remark, and she knew she was a long, long way from Tangier. Even if she managed to get out of this place – wherever it was – what then? She didn't relish the thought of wandering around in the Western Sahara, alone and lost. She'd have to think of a way to make Hassan take her back to civilization.

She lay quietly as they bumped along. After a while it seemed they were climbing into the hills, and Yasmin wished she could see where, exactly, she was being taken. But that was impossible. Instead she devoted her attention to thinking of different ways to convince Hassan to let her go. She was sure that if she played him correctly – even if it meant marrying him – that she could eventually get away from him. It just might take some time. She realized that she would have to assume the mild, subservient role of a woman of this country. Otherwise, if her behavior belittled him in front of the other Arab men, she might anger him. She tried to keep calm, knowing that any indication she gave of not being completely passive would merely make him watch her closely.

By the time the jeep shuddered to a stop, she was ready to play the role to the hilt. But her confidence faded when she heard guttural shouts and looked around her as Hassan untied the ropes and helped her out of the back of the jeep.

It really was a walled fortress.

They had stopped in a large, open courtyard surrounded by high walls. The crenelated sandstone walls must have been at least four feet thick, and at each of the corners were high towers. In the towers were more blue-cloaked men wearing white turbans and carrying guns. Heavy bandoliers of bullets were draped across their chests. These fierce hill men of the Western Sahara were known for their bravery and their cunning. It was beautiful out here in the desert, but the sight of the armed men filled her with despair. It was quickly obvious to Yasmin that Hassan's family wasn't just a minor sheikdom.

Yasmin turned her eyes to the buildings inside the walls. Exquisite blue and green mosaic tiles decorated keyhole-arched doorways. Farther inside, she could see an octagonal fountain. Trills of splashing water could be heard spilling into the basin.

Yasmin rubbed her wrists and stamped her feet to get her circulation started.

'Welcome,' Hassan said with a broad smile. 'Let me show you to your rooms.'

26

Hassan led her, limping slightly, through the arched doorways, past the fountain, and into a large room covered with Oriental rugs. Piled one on top of another, the patterns and colors fought with each other for dominance. The morning sun glinting through azimuth windows cast geometric shadows on the whitewashed walls. Low divans lined the walls, and several doorways led off this central room. He took her through one that opened off to the right of the main entranceway and led her down a long hall. No one stopped them.

'In here,' he said as they came to a carved oaken doorway banded with heavy strips of what looked like ancient copper. He led her into a small, spare room with a single high window. The floor was covered with carpets, and multicolored cushions were piled against one wall. She assumed this was the bed, since the only other piece of furniture in the room was a studded leather trunk.

'The bathroom is through there,' he said briefly. 'If you want to change your clothes, there are things in the trunk that will do for now.'

'One size fits all?' Yasmin snapped. 'How many ladies have you abducted here, anyway?'

But she didn't wait for his answer. She walked as quickly as she could on her stiff ankles to the bathroom and opened the door. Inside there was an old-fashioned claw and ball bathtub, with an ancient looking spout carved in the head of a lion. A small commode stood next to it. She slammed the door behind her.

When she came out again, Hassan was still standing in the middle of the room. 'Shall I have some food sent to you?' he asked.

'Yes, please,' Yasmin said. She regarded him carefully before she asked, 'What makes you think that no one will notice my absence?'

'I took the liberty of explaining to Zayd that I was taking you on a trip. Since you are about to become my bride, he thought that was an acceptable thing to do.'

'You told him that?' Yasmin was aghast.

'Yes. Actually, he thought marrying you was a bad idea.' Hassan laughed and tilted his head back to gaze at her from under hooded lids. 'Zayd says you have no morals. He said you'd just spent the night with the blond-haired Frenchman . . . but, of course, I knew that. I told him it was a marriage of convenience. He felt much better about it then.'

'Oh.' Yasmin said disconsolately. She had been hoping that her absence would be noted and a search would go out for her. She'd also hoped that Charles would notice she was gone too. But she'd hung up on him, and refused to answer the phone afterward. He probably thought she was still angry at him, Yasmin realized, and wouldn't start worrying about her for several days.

'Well, I'm going to wash and change,' Yasmin said haughtily. 'If you could have something sent for me to eat, that would be nice. I'm starved.'

'We'll talk a bit when you're ready,' Hassan said. He turned and walked to the door, then stopped and looked at her. 'This doesn't have to be so terrible, you know.'

Yasmin didn't answer. She walked into the bathroom and turned on the tap. Muddy brown water gushed out of the lion's mouth and started to fill the tub.

Indoor plumbing, maybe, she thought glumly. Clean water, however, is another thing altogether.

But soon the water went from brown to beige, and then to almost clear. Yasmin stripped off her filthy clothes, and climbed into the bath, which was tepid, but refreshing after the nightmare events of the last eight hours. It wasn't until she was standing in the middle of the floor that she realized there were no towels.

Annoyed, Yasmin flung open the bathroom door, naked, only to confront Hassan, who was waiting for her with a tray of fruit. A wicked grin spread across his face.

'Much better,' he said softly. 'Much, much better.'

He, too, had changed his clothes, and was wearing a pair of khaki slacks and a white shirt, open at the throat. But he looked tired, and Yasmin could see the dark circles under his eyes. As he watched her, his eyes softened and his mouth grew mobile.

'I thought we were going to talk,' Yasmin said, backing away as Hassan walked toward her. The lazy movement of his muscular body as he crossed the carpet with unconscious silence and grace sent a quiver of apprehension down her spine, and the beads of water drying on her skin made her tremble. 'I'd like to put some clothes on before I eat.'

Hassan blinked, then smiled lazily. He moved back and opened the lid of the trunk. 'Of course. Why rush? I have all the time in the world, don't I?'

He handed her a simple light blue cotton haik that buttoned all the way down the front, and watched her as she slipped it on. She'd managed to button about twelve of the buttons when he took her hand and led her to the cushions.

Yasmin sank down, and reached for the plate of figs on the tray he'd placed on the rug. She popped two of them in her mouth.

'Unfortunately my older brother and his family are in Rabat,' Hassan said as he watched her chew the fruit, swallow, and reach for more. 'He's taken ill. It's most unexpected, and he has gone to see specialists. That means we're alone here for a while. I was hoping to introduce you to him.'

'Sorry to hear it,' she said sarcastically. What did she care about Hassan's brother and his problems? She had problems of her own. Aware of muffled sounds from the outer courtyard, Yasmin said, 'I hardly call it being alone with all those armed guards in the yard. Who are all those men anyway?'

'Tribesmen,' Hassan said. His eyes didn't meet hers. 'They work for my brother.'

'Why the guns?'

'Nothing too important,' Hassan said, shrugging. 'This is a wild country. They haven't had any real need for them, but the guerrillas are on the move. They feel more comfortable with weapons, that's all.'

'Mmm.' Yasmin wasn't totally convinced, but she decided not to press it. She reached for the dish of yogurt and spooned some into her mouth.

'We should talk a little about business,' Hassan said. 'After all, business before pleasure, right?' He reached out, tracing his finger along her cheekbone and down her neck.

Yasmin, alarmed, kept her eyes averted. 'I won't press charges against you, Hassan. You don't have to do this, you know.'

'Please,' Hassan said, cupping her chin with his fingers, gently forcing her to face him. His face hardened slightly. 'Don't presume to tell me how to run my life.'

'Think about what you're doing,' Yasmin said. 'This plan of yours may work for a while, but it can't work forever. I have an appointment with the lawyers next week. They'll be concerned by my absence. Charles will be expecting my return, Françoise as well. And the office. What about Beatrice?'

'I'll tell them we've gotten married,' Hassan said casually.

'Charles won't believe it,' Yasmin answered carefully, forcing herself to speak quietly. There seemed no harm in making her situation with Charles look more concrete than she'd left it after their argument on the telephone. 'He asked me to marry him before he left, and I accepted.

445

It won't take him long to guess that something's wrong. Then – '

'Then, my little desert flower, you will be married to me, and it will be too late,' Hassan said. But his voice was harsh, and he looked uncertain, irritated. 'Your businesses will be mine, your vineyards will be mine . . . and you will be mine as well.'

'I'm not sure that sort of thing counts. I believe there are laws about duress,' Yasmin said. She started to stand up, but Hassan gripped her elbow and pulled her back down on the cushions.

'You forget where you are,' he hissed. 'Here, my word is law, and here, anything can happen, especially to women like you – '

'Don't keep saying that,' Yasmin said, shrinking back against the wall, trying to get away from him. 'I'm not just some girl from a hill tribe. I have money and influence. The longer you forget that, the more trouble you'll be in.'

'Shut up,' Hassan said. 'At this point the net is closing in around me, and I have very little choice. If I let you go, you may decide to press charges against me. I must have time to think out my position. As it stands right now, little fig, this is the best possible deal I can make. This way I have a good chance of getting everything I want. Your whining about the law is of no consequence to me.'

Hassan turned and pulled her against him. He smiled, and in a softer voice said, 'And besides, with this space of time I've provided, perhaps I can convince you to see things my way. After all, you cannot deny that we get on well in some ways, if not all. Perhaps the rest will come with time. But in the meantime . . .'

Hassan let one hand reach up under the haik to touch her naked thigh as he spoke. He stroked her lightly, then proceeded to slowly unbutton her dress.

446

'Why not just relax and let me show you. Let me remind you of how you feel,' he whispered.

'No,' Yasmin said, squirming out of his grip. But she couldn't get away. He held her tightly as he opened the dress.

'It doesn't matter what you'd rather do or not do,' Hassan said. 'There's no place you can go, and no one who will help you here. If you relax, you'll enjoy it more. Remember how you used to enjoy this? Remember how you used to beg me to touch you here . . . and here? I won't hurt you. Perhaps if you would try and see what I want, we could be genuinely happy together.'

As he spoke, he gently caressed her body. She felt as if he were gentling a skittish colt. But his touch didn't calm her. It made her more nervous. His hypnotic eyes held hers locked into their gaze. She knew he was right about not having anyplace to run, and tried to focus on her unformed plan to deceive him into a false sense of security. Perhaps the only way to do that was to stop fighting him, for the moment. Perhaps if he thought she would go along with him, he would realize how senseless his plan really was.

Unable to trust herself to speak, Yasmin tilted her chin up and made herself place her hand lightly on the back of his neck. If he thought she wanted to make love to him, he might take her back to Paris. It was worth a try at least.

'I do love you, Yasmin,' Hassan said as he slipped the dress off her shoulders. When she lay naked before him, he stood up and began to strip off his shirt and trousers. He was upon her in moments, forcing himself inside of her without preliminary.

Yasmin gasped and turned her head away as his body thudded heavily against her. She felt as if she were going to burst apart, and she tried to shift under him, forcing herself to relax so she wouldn't be hurt. But he seemed unaware of her as he plunged into her repeatedly. She

447

thought she heard him saying 'Mine, mine,' in her ear, but she wasn't sure. Then he began to thrust harder and faster. With a groan he lifted her legs up and thrust into her blindly, until with a wild cry he collapsed against her, pressing her down into the pillows.

If that's what he considers a good way to make me fall in love with him, Yasmin thought grimly, he's got it all wrong. His weight was overpowering, and she tried to move her leg.

But Hassan wasn't ready to let her go. 'I've been wanting you for so long, I couldn't wait,' he breathed against her neck finally. 'Now I can take as long as I want . . . and I intend to keep you on the brink of orgasm until you beg me for release.'

Allah, Yasmin thought miserably, what do I do now? But she had no time to speak, because Hassan had placed a plump fig between her lips.

'Lie there and eat fruit, my desert flower,' Hassan said softly. 'I intend to eat the little fig you have hidden here, because from now on it will be all mine . . .'

The fig dropped onto the cushions as Hassan spread her open to him and lazily began to kiss the insides of her thighs. His touch was feather light, like butterflies, and he caressed and tongued every inch of her until, despite herself, she began to respond.

But instead of allowing her to peak, he would stop, holding her firmly in his arms until she calmed down. Then he began again. And again. Despite herself, she finally begged him for release, and when the release finally came, her senses were so overpowered, it was hardly a release at all. And all the while her mind raced from one thing to another, trying desperately to figure out a way to extricate herself from this impossible situation and this horrible, impossible man.

To Yasmin's amazement Hassan didn't leave her room, or her body, until late the next morning. By that time she was emotionally and physically exhausted. She fell into a leaden sleep and didn't wake up until late that night.

The compound was silent. After looking through the leather trunk for something to wear, she finally found a plain cotton underdress, which she covered with a gray and white striped haik. Yasmin slowly opened the door to her room, saw no one, and padded quietly in her bare feet down the hall and back out into the main salon. It was dark and quiet.

'Is anybody awake?' she called out nervously. She didn't want to get shot by one of the men just because she wanted some food.

There was a thud from behind one of the doorways, and Hassan appeared.

'What is it?' he asked sharply. The circles under his eyes seemed deeper, and he looked as if he had aged ten years since she last saw him.

'I'm hungry,' Yasmin said. She wondered what was wrong, why he seemed so anxious. 'You don't have to disturb yourself, though. Just tell me where the kitchen is, and tell those men not to shoot at me.'

She wanted to act nonchalant, to give Hassan the feeling that she had given up any idea of leaving him, that now she trusted him. 'Aren't there any servants here?' she asked.

'No,' Hassan said briefly. 'I'll show you where to go.'

He brushed past her, and she had to hurry to keep up with his long strides. Hassan led her back down the hallway, past her room and through a doorway.

Yasmin found herself in a large room with whitewashed walls and an old fashioned cookstove in one corner. A deep sink was against the other wall, and a row of large cooking pots hung from wrought-iron hooks on the wall. There was a large pot on the stove. Hassan lifted the lid and peered inside.

'Lamb stew,' he said. 'There's enough left for you.'

He reached for a ladle and a bowl and spooned some

of it out for her. As he did, Yasmin again got the distinct impression that something was very, very wrong. She took a taste of the stew. Despite the fact that it was spicier than she would have liked, it was still good.

'You don't really seem prepared for me here,' Yasmin finally said, watching him. 'Do you want me to take over the cooking? I certainly don't mind, and besides, it would give me something to do. It seems sort of like an armed camp here, not a household. Are you sure everything's all right?'

'Don't worry about it,' Hassan said gruffly.

But on some gut level, Yasmin discerned that his gruffness stemmed from worry. If everything was *not* all right – as she suspected – then she might be able to find an opening to get away.

Hassan's lips were compressed in a thin line, and the tension in his body was evident from the way he was standing.

'Are you sure you don't want to talk to me?' Yasmin asked, suddenly solicitous. 'After all, I may be able to help.'

Hassan glanced at her, and she could almost see a calculating look pass across his face before he answered.

'You can't stay here,' he said shortly. 'There's trouble in the hills. My land encompasses some of the phosphate mines, and the bands of guerrillas are making trouble. It's part of the area in question. The Polisarios want access to the mines. They do this periodically, but this time there have been several deaths.'

Yasmin started. Hassan had called it 'my land,' not 'my brother's land.' There was something ominous about that.

'Why can't we go to Rabat with your brother?' she asked slowly.

'I can't,' Hassan said. This time Yasmin saw a gray shadow cross Hassan's face. The set line of his mouth was grim and forbidding. 'My brother is dead.'

'Dead?' Now Yasmin understood. 'When? When did this happen?'

'They called while you were sleeping,' Hassan answered. His voice was hard. 'He had a heart attack and there were complications. Now I must stay and keep the men here. I would take you to Rabat myself, but leaving is out of the question. I just don't know what to do with you. If they make trouble, you will be a detriment.'

Hassan slowly raised his eyes to meet hers. Instead of the clever, cosmopolitan man she'd known in Paris, Yasmin saw another man altogether. This one was barely recognizable. Now the hawklike features and dark brooding eyes looked very Arab to her. The gloss of Paris was gone, replaced by the harsh contours of a proud sheik.

Yasmin's mind raced as she tried to figure out how this totally unexpected turn of events would affect her present predicament and the way Hassan would deal with her. If, for one moment, she'd thought his veneer of civilization would make him accept the fact that she had a right to go back to Paris and to her chosen life, this was no longer an option. The veneer was now gone. It had been shattered by his brother's death.

Thinking back, Yasmin wondered how much of Hassan's desire to drop his heritage and make a place for himself in Paris had to do with the fact that as the second son he had no real place in Morocco. Tradition dictated that his older brother would have all the wealth and all the power, and that Hassan would be relegated to a minor role. But knowing Hassan, Yasmin understood how unacceptable this would be to him. He was too arrogant to accept anything less than total power. Of course he'd gone to Harvard. Of course he'd gone to live in Paris. He'd had no other choice.

Now, however, things were different. Now Hassan was the sheik. It was obvious that his ties to his country had just been immeasurably strengthened. She'd been considering deceiving Hassan into thinking she was ready to stay here, marry him, and hand over everything she owned because she'd been convinced that life in the desert would never suit him. She was certain Hassan would have kept her here only as long as he, himself, could stand it. Now, instead of being able to appeal to his desire to return to Paris and everything he enjoyed, she realized that Hassan could very easily bury himself, and her with him, in this medieval fortress – forever.

Struggling to control her voice and her expression, Yasmin held her arms out to him as if to comfort him. 'I'm so sorry to hear about your brother. I wish there was some way I could help. I wish there was some way I could get to Rabat to be with your family until this is over.'

But Hassan was unreachable. He abruptly backed away from her. 'There is no way.'

'Do you really think there will be trouble?' Yasmin's voice was shaky.

'Who knows what the guerrillas will do? Not only do we have information that they are headed in this direction,' he said, as he watched her carefully, 'but I suspect that your boyfriend is on his way here as well.' Hassan's eyebrows were drawn together in a straight line. 'I had a call from him too.'

Yasmin, desperately trying to control her elation, kept silent.

'He wanted to know if you were here, and I told him you were, and that you were fine,' Hassan said finally. He was watching her carefully, as if somehow he could gauge how she felt about Charles. 'He wasn't talking like someone who was about to marry you, however. He was talking like someone who wanted you to sign some papers.'

Yasmin made a massive effort and kept her expression bland. 'I guess there were some papers the lawyers wanted,' she said calmly.

Hassan smiled at her words, then one eyebrow lifted.

'At any rate I gave him the impression that he'd be welcome here if he decides to make the trip. It occurred to me that if Charles LaMarquette were here and there's trouble, I could trade him as a hostage and keep you. You, little fig, are good for rape, but he, on the other hand, is good for ransom.'

A nasty smile split Hassan's face, and he took Yasmin in his arms. 'I decided you wouldn't mind, little one. After all, since you're now my woman, the fate of that foolish banker will no longer be of concern to you. Correct?'

Yasmin was stunned. When the full power of Hassan's mad intentions became clear to her, it was all she could do to keep from tearing herself out of his arms. But she fought back her desire to lash out at him. If Hassan thought she would go along with his plan to sacrifice Charles, she thought, it might buy her some time. It might also buy her the freedom of movement to save both her and Charles, if that was possible. But she doubted it. After all, Hassan might be able to convince the guerrillas to take Charles in her place, but if they could have both of them – well, all the better.

Yasmin lifted her face to Hassan and forced a smile. 'Very clever,' she whispered. She could barely get her voice to go louder. She was desperately afraid Hassan would see through her, but continued to whisper anyway. 'You were right. I *do* feel as if I am at home. It only took being here to realize it.'

Hassan placed a soft kiss on her upturned mouth. 'You make me very happy. But I'm afraid that I can't show you right now how much. There are many things to be done. And also I should arrange a pleasant welcome for our banker, don't you think?'

Yasmin nodded dumbly. Recalling her trip into this walled fortress, she wondered when Charles would arrive, and how.

'Don't be afraid, my love,' Hassan said, guiding her

through the huge dining area. 'I will show you where to hide, just in case there is trouble. Come with me.'

Hassan led her out to the main courtyard, past the guards, and around to the back of the buildings. There, in the corner of a smaller courtyard, was a low building with a truncated door. He pulled it open and flicked on a flashlight.

'This is the old stairway down to the cisterns,' he said, shining his light on a set of worn stone steps. 'The cisterns were built by the Romans, and when the original buildings here were razed in the eleventh century, the cisterns and steps remained. It was only a question of clearing the rubble. They are fed by underground springs that come from the mountains. That's why we have running water. Most other places in the area have cisterns on the roof to collect what little rainfall there is.'

Hassan started down the steps and Yasmin followed him, resting her hand against the wall in case she slipped.

'You can hide down here. But I doubt that it will become necessary, so don't worry. I just wanted you to know about it.'

They came to the end of the steps and Hassan shined his light up to the ceiling. The cistern was barrel-vaulted and made of ancient bricks. The construction was beautiful. Yasmin was astounded at the architectural genius of the Romans. Buildings that had been constructed in Europe in this century were already falling down, yet these vaults, built thousands of years ago, were still in perfect condition.

'Let's go back,' she said, shivering. She cast one last look around, but the beam of the flashlight was dim in the inky blackness. She didn't particularly like the idea of hiding down here in the pitch dark.

Hassan quickly led her out into the courtyard. She was aware of the men patrolling the catwalks on the walls. The light from the house glinted off the barrels of their guns, and she shivered once again. This was a whole other world from the one she was used to. Life and death were so closely intertwined and so meaningless to those who lived here. It was not how you lived, here in the desert, but how you died.

Yasmin thought of the holy wars. If a man died in battle, he could be assured of going straight to heaven – no matter how evil his life had been. It made for very fierce warriors, and very cruel conditions.

She pulled the haik tight around her and hurried into the house. The warm gleam of the lights glowing off the brilliant reds and blues of the rugs seemed superficially welcoming, as she wondered if she would live through the next twenty-four hours.

Hassan walked with her to the door of her room, then kissed her lightly on the forehead. 'Get some sleep,' he said quietly. 'For all we know, nothing may happen. But if it does, you should be rested.'

Yasmin lay down on the cushions and gazed out her window. The moon was still full, but on the wane. She could see its slightly lopsided shape through the high window. The small lamp in her room cast strange shadows on the walls. More tired than she realized, she fell asleep.

She awoke with a start to the sound of shots. They were sporadic and sounded far away. But Yasmin's head was immediately clear. Not one vestige of sleep lingered as she quickly stood and slipped out into the hall. She heard harsh shouts from the courtyard and decided to look for Hassan, but didn't see him anywhere. Once in the main salon, she slowed down. She could see the top of one wall from inside and could make out figures running.

Suddenly she remembered that Charles was supposed to come. Allah, had he come? Was that him now? Were the men shooting at him, or at the guerrillas, she wondered? Where the hell was Hassan? Then she saw him striding across the courtyard.

'What is it?' she asked, her voice shrill with concern. 'Why are they shooting?'

'We've spotted a band of men in the hills. Here is a gun for you, in case you need it. And remember what I told you about the cisterns.'

Hassan handed her a revolver, and Yasmin was surprised at its weight. 'I don't know how to shoot a gun,' she said in a small voice.

'Just point it and pull the trigger,' he said smoothly, sounding not at all like the man who once seemed so comfortable in expensive Parisian restaurants ordering champagne. 'Now stay out of the way, because if they start shooting, stray bullets will be your worst enemy.' Giving her a push in the direction of her room, Hassan disappeared back into the courtyard.

Yasmin didn't know what to do with herself, but she also didn't want to be alone in her room. Quickly looking around, she decided she'd best explore the house right now. If she knew her way around, she would be at an advantage later on. She just hoped that Charles wouldn't get caught in the middle. At this juncture he would be safer if he never made it to the area.

She followed a corridor that apparently led past the other side of the kitchen. There was a small door at the end of the hall. Yasmin opened it and found herself in what must have been the kitchen midden. The smell alone was proof enough. Past that she could see that the wall was slightly lower than in the rest of the courtyard. She started to turn back into the house when she heard a hiss.

A cat? It was the first thought that went through her mind. But then she was grabbed from behind and flung down on a heap of rotting garbage. Her scream was muffled by a large hand over her mouth, and her struggles crushed under a heavy body.

It wasn't until a few seconds had passed that she became aware of a very familiar, clean soapy scent.

Charles! she thought. But he was still holding his hand over her mouth. She couldn't speak to let him know she recognized him, so she forced her teeth apart and slowly ran her tongue across his palm.

She felt him jolt with amazement. 'Yasmin?' he whispered.

She nodded, and he immediately released her. '*Mon Dieu*, Yasmin,' he gasped. 'What the hell is going on here?'

'There's been trouble in the area, and they are afraid we might be in danger here,' Yasmin said quickly. 'How did you get in the kitchen garbage?'

'It was the only place that wasn't guarded by those thugs up there,' he said. 'I drove up here and almost got killed by some *cochons* hiding in the hills. What kind of a mess are we in, anyhow?'

'Nasty, but not impossible,' Yasmin whispered. 'Listen. I have to get you out of here. Hassan wants to hand you over to the rebels as a hostage. He thinks he can use you to get rid of them, to buy them off.'

'The way you explain it,' Charles said incredulously, 'it sounds as if the only thing worse than being out there is being in here. That does not sound, "not impossible," as you say.'

'Don't worry,' Yasmin hissed. 'I think I can get us out of here. But where is your car? Did you walk?'

'*Non*. I left it in a gully when I heard shots. Thank God you are safe. Has he harmed you in any way?'

'No,' Yasmin said softly. 'Wait here for me, I have to get flashlights and then I'll be back. Thank Allah you are safe too. I'm so glad to see you. I was so afraid you wouldn't come after what I said on the telephone.'

'I was afraid you wouldn't care to see me after what I'd said to you,' Charles said softly. 'Do you forgive me?'

'Of course,' she said, kissing Charles quickly. 'I'll be right back.' She stood and checked the hallway to make sure she was alone, then made her way back into the main salon.

There was no one around, but no flashlights either. Seeing the door to one of the rooms slightly ajar, she peered inside. It seemed to be a study of some kind. A beautifully carved mahogany desk was placed in the center of the room, its gracefully curved legs arching up to hold an expanse of leather-covered wood. Sitting on the baize writing pad were three flashlights and a box of bullets.

Yasmin looked behind her, then dashed across the room and grabbed them all. Stuffing them deep into the pockets of her haik, she wondered if the bullets matched the gun Hassan had given her. But there was no time to check. Hopefully they wouldn't need any of them.

She stopped off in the kitchen and grabbed a handful of figs, adding them to the store in her pocket. Then she slid back out into the kitchen midden. But she didn't see Charles anywhere.

'Charles!' she hissed. 'Come on!'

A shadow materialized at her elbow and made her jump with fright. But it was only Charles.

'Listen,' she said carefully. 'There is a stairway down to an underground cistern. It's fed by springs, and if what Oskar once told me about Roman architecture is correct, they usually built a vaulted tunnel along the entire length of the spring so it wouldn't get cut off by rock slides. Sometimes there is a shelf of stone that follows the spring, but if not, we'll just walk in the water. There's probably an outlet somewhere on the other side of the walls.'

'*Bien sûr*, but how do we get to the stairs?' Charles asked. It was a good question, and Yasmin didn't know the answer. The entrance to the cistern was located in a courtyard crawling with armed men. Suddenly the sound of firing increased sharply, the rat-a-tat-tat of machine guns coming in rapid bursts.

'Quickly,' Yasmin whispered. 'Follow me.'

458

With Charles close on her heels, she hugged the wall of the kitchen and made her way around the back. From their vantage point in the shadow of the house, they could see their destination not twenty feet away. But it was still a large space to cross.

Yasmin looked up on the ramparts. There were at least twenty men up there. But to her delight, she realized they had their backs to the courtyard. Intent on watching what was happening below, not one of them was looking their way.

'Now!' she hissed to Charles, and set off across the courtyard at a run. Twisting her head to the right, keeping her eyes glued to the men on the walls, she was certain they'd make it.

Then a raucous laugh coming from the area of the buildings caught her up short. She whirled around to see Hassan standing silhouetted in the keyhole-arch doorway of the central garden.

'Well, well, well,' came the nasty sound of his voice. 'What have we here?' He was standing with his feet set wide apart, one hand in his pocket, the other hanging carelessly at his side, holding a revolver. 'I see you managed to make it,' he drawled, his gaze directed at Charles, who was right behind her. 'Going someplace?'

Charles stopped abruptly and turned to face Hassan. But before he could speak, Yasmin stepped in front of him.

'Why is there shooting, Hassan?' she asked sharply. She was hoping that if she acted aggressive, he wouldn't understand that she and Charles had been trying to escape.

'The men are having a little fun,' Hassan drawled. 'They think if they shoot into the hills, the guerrillas will run away. It has worked in the past, so it might work now.'

Then he directed his attention to Charles. 'I see you managed to get here,' Hassan said with a deceptively

459

friendly smile. 'But I don't recall seeing you come in through the gates. Where were you?'

'It was a little bit too exciting by your front gates,' Charles replied, an equally disarming smile on his face. 'I thought it was better to come in the back way.'

'I can see that,' Hassan said, gesturing toward the mess on Charles's shirt. 'Would you like to come inside and get cleaned up?'

'*Bien sûr,*' he answered. Yasmin shot him a warning glance, but to no avail. Charles and Hassan walked through the garden, and she followed them into the main salon. Hassan showed him where the bathroom was, then took hold of her arm just above the elbow. 'Yasmin and I will wait for you in my study,' Hassan said quietly.

Without waiting for an answer, Hassan pulled her into the room. His grip on her arm was tight and almost painful. Annoyed, Yasmin shook his hand loose and stalked across the room to look out the window.

Hassan followed her. 'I saw the way you looked at him, you know,' he said softly. He took her shoulders and forced her to turn and face him. 'Don't think you can hide from me. I know you too well.'

'You don't know me at all!' Yasmin snapped. She tried to pull loose again, but he wouldn't let her.

'Tell me, is he really what you want?'

Yasmin didn't want to answer. She didn't want to do or say anything that would jeopardize her position or Charles's life. But apparently the play of her emotions was not hard to read.

'Answer me, Yasmin,' Hassan said. His eyes were dull, flat, emotionless. 'Is he what you want?'

Yasmin could no longer return Hassan's gaze. 'I don't know,' she said, turning away. 'But I do know one thing, Hassan. I know that I'm not sure that you are what I want. I only know that I want my life to be my own.'

'Your life will be your own with me,' he said. 'But I know you don't believe that.'

Yasmin was surprised by his tone of voice and the sudden change in the way he spoke to her. It was almost as if his need for her had lessened and his intense preoccupation with her had dimmed.

She had a flash of insight, and said, 'Now you have what you really wanted all along, don't you? You wanted to be the sheik, am I right? Tell me the truth, Hassan. Isn't this what drove you? Was it really the vineyard and me? It wasn't, was it? You wanted to be the sheik, and you knew that no matter what you did and what you accomplished, your father or your brother would be sheik, and in your eyes, you would be nothing.'

Hassan turned away from her. He seemed about to answer when Charles came back into the study. His face was no longer filthy, but his shirt was in exactly the same condition.

Hassan glanced at him wearily. The sound of sporadic firing continued from outside as he crossed the room and lowered himself into the carved oak chair behind the desk.

'You will have to forgive the welcome,' he said grimly, looking back up at Charles. 'But things here are a bit more complicated than I'd anticipated when I extended the invitation.'

At Hassan's humorless tone, Charles glanced questioningly at Yasmin. '*Vraiment*, I can see that,' he said. 'Perhaps it would be easier if Yasmin and I were to leave.'

Hassan looked from Yasmin to Charles, then back again. 'Perhaps,' he said. 'But there are some things we should discuss first, yes?'

Charles looked puzzled. 'What things?'

'Perhaps Yasmin mentioned it,' Hassan continued as he stood up. 'My brother has just died, and as you couldn't help noticing, I am also having a few problems with the local renegades out there. It had been my original intention to come back home for a while with

Yasmin, introduce her to my family, and see if we could sort out our differences – '

Yasmin was about to speak, but Hassan held up his hand to stop her. 'I think it best, under the circumstances, that she return to France.'

Yasmin was stunned. He was letting her go! He had done such enormous reversals in the last two days, she was having trouble keeping up with him. But before she could think about it anymore, Hassan went on.

'I know there are some difficulties regarding finances with the vineyard, but Yasmin can handle it all without me. I would appreciate it if you would take her back to Paris for me,' he said slowly, watching Yasmin's face as he spoke. It was almost as if he were willing her to keep silent – willing her to let him play the game his way. 'At the moment I am unable to leave Goulimine because of family pressures. I'm sure you understand.'

'*Certainement*.' Charles said quickly, 'but – '

But Hassan had already risen from the chair. Turning, he walked quickly to the door. 'I will arrange a jeep and an escort for you. That should get you out of the area. You can probably find a flight once you're in town.' With that he strode from the room, leaving the two of them alone.

Yasmin stared at Charles, the look in her eyes begging him not to speak just yet. 'I'll get my things,' she said quickly. 'I'll meet you in the courtyard.'

She ran after Hassan. He was just giving one of the men instructions when she caught up with him, so she waited for him to finish.

'Thank you,' she said when they were alone.

Hassan looked at her, then smiled slowly. 'I always told you I wouldn't force you,' he said. 'It's just that I never believed you would reject me . . .'

He tilted her chin up. 'But you are right. Since I now have what I want, what I always wanted, I'm going to

462

give you the opportunity to have what you always wanted. Then, maybe then, you'll come back.'

'Maybe,' Yasmin said with a smile. 'But first I'd like to see if you were really right about my plan for the expansion. After all, just because you think it will work doesn't mean it will, right?'

'It will work,' Hassan said. 'Now go get your things and get out of here. Jalil will be waiting for you.'

Yasmin ran down the corridor, collected her sandals, and made a bundle of her dirty clothes. As she walked back out to the courtyard, she could see Charles sitting in the jeep, waiting for her. At the sight of his aristocratic profile, she stopped for a second. She thought back to all the conversations, all the disagreements, and to their last argument.

It was then that she realized how much her own insecurity had kept her from hearing the meaning of his words. She had always taken such violent exception to his remarks – not because she thought he believed them, but because she herself believed them. She had never really had the total conviction that she could handle herself and her finances without help from a man.

It was she, Yasmin, who needed straightening out, not Charles, she thought. Charles had, from the very first, allowed her room to breathe and to grow. He'd tried not to push her, and he'd always given her whatever help he could when she really needed it. She felt a wave of love for him that made her knees weak.

But she also realized that she owed a debt of gratitude to Hassan as well. In his own hard, difficult, nearly impossible way, he had given her the will to seek out the limits of her own capabilities.

With a sigh she realized that she, too, now had everything she wanted. She also had Charles, who was the man who would finally allow her to be herself.

Allah . . . what a pleasure!